Praise for R. A. Salvatore's *DemonWars* series!

The Demon Spirit

"Absorbing . . . This is one of the finest books yet in Salvatore's prolific career."
—*Publishers Weekly*

"A gripping story . . . some of [his] best work."
—*Booklist*

The Demon Awakens

"Salvatore's best work since the *Dark Elf* series . . . An enthralling epic adventure story, it introduces memorable characters and an intricate scheme of magic the readers won't soon forget. I am anxious for the next."

—TERRY BROOKS

"*The Demon Awakens* is Salvatore doing what he does best. Page-turning action provides the backdrop for engaging characters locked in the eternal struggle of good vs. evil. My favorite since *The Halfling's Gem*."

—MARY KIRCHOFF
Author of the *Defenders of Magic* trilogy

By R. A. Salvatore:

TARZAN: THE EPIC ADVENTURES*

The DemonWars
THE DEMON AWAKENS*
THE DEMON SPIRIT*
THE DEMON APOSTLE*

Forgotten Realms Novels
THE CRYSTAL SHARD
STREAMS OF SILVER
THE HALFLING'S GEM
HOMELAND
EXILE
SOJOURN
THE LEGACY
STARLESS NIGHT
SIEGE OF DARKNESS
PASSAGE TO DAWN

CANTICLE
IN SYLVAN SHADOWS
NIGHT MASKS
THE FALLEN FORTRESS
THE CHAOS CURSE

The Spearwielder's Tales
THE WOODS OUT BACK
THE DRAGON'S DAGGER
DRAGONSLAYER'S RETURN

The Crimson Shadow Trilogy
THE SWORD OF BEDWYR
LUTHIEN'S GAMBLE
THE DRAGON KING

The Chronicles of Ynis Aielle
ECHOES OF THE FOURTH MAGIC*
THE WITCH'S DAUGHTER*

*Published by Del Rey Books

THE
WITCH'S
DAUGHTER

Book Two in
The Chronicles of Ynis Aielle

R. A. Salvatore

A Del Rey® Book
BALLANTINE BOOKS • NEW YORK

A Del Rey® Book
Published by The Ballantine Publishing Group
Copyright © 1991 by R. A. Salvatore

www.randomhouse.com/delrey/

Library of Congress Catalog Card Number: 99-90416

ISBN 0-345-42192-2

Manufactured in the United States of America

First Ballantine Books Edition: September 1999

10   9   8   7   6   5   4

THE WITCH'S
DAUGHTER

Chapter 1

Bastion of Darkness

THE SEA SWELLED and heaved, slamming into the rocky cliffs of the Kored-dul Mountains of western Aielle. Pounding, incessantly pounding, against the gray stone. Again and again the waves rolled in, and each time they were turned away, unable to defeat the strength, the unnatural strength, of the stone.

There was magic here, mighty enchantments, stronger than the stone or the sea. It climbed out of the very earth, rising through the sheer cliffs and up a thousand feet, to the iron fortress of the Black Warlock. Talas-dun, the castle was called, a name that struck terror—and rightly so—into the hearts of all the goodly folk of Ynis Aielle. Few had ever come here; none but a single wizard had ever returned.

Battlement after black battlement circled the massive keep, and iron spires rose into the ever gray sky, the eternal gloom that marked the Kored-dul. No craftsmen built this place, for it was not the labor of skilled hands. Talas-dun was the heart of the Black Warlock, the embodiment of the warlock's evil soul, the fortress wrought of Morgan Thalasi's magic in an age long past.

And after all the centuries, Talas-dun remained impressive,

1

leering down from the jutting tip of a peninsula, three sides to the sheer drop to the ocean and the fourth separated from the rest of the mountain by a wide and deep gorge. A single road wound down the mountainside from the castle's lone gate, forlorn and as barren as death itself. Not a scrub or vine grew here, not a bird circled on the updrafts of these cliff faces, and none of the rodents that were so common to the mountains flitted across the stones.

For this was Talas-dun.

Morgan Thalasi's bastion of darkness.

But if a hero dared now to come close enough, if one of the other wizards of Aielle had come in to inspect the Black Warlock's legendary fortress, he would have been surprised, and at least some of the hopelessness evoked by the sight of this most evil of places might have been washed away. After more than half a millennium, Talas-dun had begun to wear. The evil that bound the monstrous bastion into a singular iron entity could not keep firm to its hold. Cracks lined the iron walls and the stone of the mountain; doors creaked on rusted hinges; a great ballistae stood useless on one tower, its drawstring rotted to breaking. And so it went throughout the structure, from the foundation to the highest tier of the highest tower.

Decay.

Parapets that once thundered under the marching footsteps of a thousand talons, the evil soldiery of the Black Warlock, now sounded only with the murmurs of the sea wind, or with the occasional shuffle of a worn boot. A single shot from a weapon of another age on a battlefield halfway across the world had brought the being that had been Morgan Thalasi to a sudden and disastrous end, and the twenty years since had begun the unmistakable erosion of his legacy, of Talas-dun.

Beyond the closed drawbridge and the open courtyard,

and through the massive doors of the main keep—one hanging loosely on a single bent hinge—the power that had once been Talas-dun lingered on in anguish, caught in a web of confusion that it could not break.

There sat the physical being that had once been Martin Reinheiser, one of the ancient ones who had come from the sea, from a past world, in the dawning of Ynis Aielle's second age. The other three men who had walked beside him then would not have recognized him now. Gaunt and pale, skin stretched beyond its limits over deep-set hollowed cheeks, and eye sockets that more closely resembled the empty holes of a skull, Reinheiser seemed something far different from the man he had once been. Something not human, something not alive.

Eyes twitched and darted, unable to find clear focus, vainly seeking to view two objects at once. One bony hand twitched uncontrollably on the stone arm of the black throne, muscle tearing against muscle until yet another garish blue-red bruise erupted, one of a dozen on this arm alone.

"Stop!" the lipless mouth demanded in a throaty voice.

"Mine!" that same mouth argued, its tone higher pitched. And so it went, hour after hour, year after long year. The being that had been Martin Reinheiser fought against itself, every move, every word, a ferocious struggle that pitted muscle against muscle.

For two wills now inhabited this single body, two powerful wills that would not relinquish control, not for a moment, to the other.

"Mine!" the higher tone argued again, the word stretched into several syllables by the trembling and twisting of the mouth. "I am Martin Reinheiser!"

A grimace of agony crossed over the face as the other will stole the mouth away.

"Get out!" the will of Reinheiser demanded. How many

times had Reinheiser cried out these words, in voice and thought, since that fateful day on the distant battleground of the field called Mountaingate?

It had all been so promising, with the spirt of Morgan Thalasi joining his own, and the warlock's black gemstone, the mark of power growing through the skin of Reinheiser's forehead. What greatness might these two beings accomplish now that they had been joined?

But Thalasi was not interested in exploring the possibilities. He had shrugged off his mortal body, his dominating spirit defeating even the grim clutches of death itself, and had found a new receptacle in the nearest living being, in the body of Martin Reinheiser. And now Thalasi wanted Reinheiser out. The Black Warlock had never intended to share, had planned from the beginning to possess this body wholly. But Thalasi had underestimated the willpower of his host, and the spirit of Reinheiser still stubbornly held on.

"You get out!" Thalasi countered, his customary growling response as soon as he had wrestled control of the mouth. The hand came up from the arm of the stone throne, slapping the face hard.

Of course, they did not need the mouth to communicate. They could read each other's thoughts and emotions—they had no choice but to read each other's thoughts and emotions, fully. But the mouth had become the central battleground of their struggle, a pointed reminder of disadvantage to the opponent of he who controlled it.

The hand came up again, but the other hand shot up to intercept, locking together in wrenching grips. And all the while the opposing wills attacked at the inside, wrestling muscles from each other. More bruises appeared, more sinews ripped away, ravaging the body. The mouth opened and contorted as both sides felt the burning agony.

But even the scream came out only as a gurgle.

* * *

"He's to it again," croaked Burgle, one of the two talons standing guard outside of the Throne Room door. He rubbed a foot against the inside of one leg, scratching the lice that always managed to make a comfortable home of him.

The other guard paused to listen, then smiled wickedly at the groans of agony emanating from beyond the door. "Always at it," he grunted back in the same guttural tone. "That one's lost 'is wits, is me guesses, an' to the ruins of usses all!"

"Blasted wizards," Burgle replied. "Promisin' the world, he does, an' can't find 'is own way outta 'is blasted chair." He eyed his counterpart slyly and grinned. "But Grok'll be fixin' that."

"An' none too soon, fer me thinkin'," agreed the other talon. "Heared he's back in the castle this day. Heared 'e's lookin' fer the boss."

"Ain't hard to find," said Burgle. "Never to be leavin' 'is room!"

Exhausted, the two entities of the Black Warlock found a long enough moment of truce to coordinate the body into a shaky walk from the throne. They stumbled to the wall, grasping a worn tapestry to catch themselves as they neared the lone window in the chamber.

Why? demanded Martin Reinheiser, using internal communication now—no need to renew the fight over control of the mouth. He felt a portion of the body relax, a movement he had come to recognize as a resigned shrug from his counterpart.

Twenty years, Morgan Thalasi replied, again internally. *How long will we battle before the spirit of one of us fades away or is forced out?*

The body will die first, Reinheiser reasoned.

And still we will battle, Thalasi assured him. *Willing the corpse into an undead state so that our struggles will have some material battleground.*

Reinheiser did not doubt it for a minute. Already he could understand that their willpower would live on after death. The body should have long ago died, rarely eating and always tormented, nourished only by the strength of the minds and the hatred that refused to relinquish control.

Yet to harm you is to harm myself, sneered Reinheiser. *But still I—we—fight! And ever we will!* Thalasi could not disagree. He had not foreseen these problems of cohabitation of the body, had not realized the deep sense of violation that could not be resolved, or the uncontrollable battles the two beings were forced to wage. Instincts too primal to be realized guided their struggle, instincts too base for rational thinking to defeat.

Thus they were a doomed thing.

They stumbled and fell, and then crawled back to the stone throne of Talas-dun, knowing that the war was about to begin anew.

But even as the telltale trembling began, as pain became general throughout the limbs and torso, the door to the Throne Room burst open, an interruption that neither of the beings could ignore.

Together the ravaged body's eyes snapped at the figure bold enough to enter without permission. A talon walked through, unusually straight-backed and tall for one of its cowering race. The Black Warlock knew this particular creature's name, "Grok," though he hadn't dealt with this talon for many years. Once, though, Grok had been—and might still be—commander of Talas-dun's dwindling talon regiment. The tall talon strode defiantly up to the throne and stood before the Black Warlock.

The warlock's mouth twisted and turned, and the mouth managed to speak out the talon's name.

"Grok."

Grok eyed the pitiful thing for a long moment. It was a smart creature, as talons go, and it understood the weakened state of the fortress, the weakening of the power of its master. Already many of the various talon tribes of the nearby mountains refused to pay their tithes, and soon the entire region might turn openly against Talas-dun. Grok's force could not defeat such a revolution, even with the high walls of the castle surrounding them. Only the sinister reputation of the Black Warlock had thus far held the renegades in check, but the word was spreading quickly. That being, the hateful and merciless leader named Morgan Thalasi, who had once nurtured the race of talons into vast armies, was no more.

And only this pitiful thing that now sat on the throne of Talas-dun remained.

Grok would change things, here and now. Grok would put an end to the reign of the wretched human and claim the throne for the talons. As the new king of Talas-dun, he would go out from the strength of his fortress, bringing the other tribes one by one under his command.

Give me the mouth, Thalasi begged silently to the will of Reinheiser. Sensing the danger of this intrusion and realizing that Thalasi was better suited to handle talons, Reinheiser relinquished control.

"Why have you come?" Thalasi spat, but still the mouth twisted, Reinheiser unconsciously resisting.

An evil smile spread across Grok's face, a grin that promised death. "Ye're done fer," the tall talon said, its voice hissing through pointy yellow teeth. He poked a stubby finger into his chest. "Grok's boss now!" A curved, rusted blade slid out of the sheath on the tall talon's hip.

Rage bubbled within the Black Warlock, arms and legs flailing violently, slamming against the hardness of the throne.

Grok and the two guards watched the spectacle wide-eyed, Grok wondering if the Black Warlock might simply explode or beat himself to death before the talon had the chance.

The Black Warlock's fingers bled and snapped. The mouth opened wide, gurgles and indecipherable grunts coming out with streams of sputtering saliva. The whole body thrashed and slammed in the great chair.

Grok had seen enough. Its amusement turned to disgust— not an easy emotion to evoke in a talon—and it raised its wicked blade for the killing blow.

And in that instant of terror and rage, for the first time in two decades the opposing wills of Morgan Thalasi and Martin Reinheiser found complete accord. The battered muscles moved in harmony, the eyes focused on a single target, and a clear scream of primal rage and magical fury erupted.

Reinheiser felt himself falling, following the spirit of Thalasi down into the foggy realm of magic, that other-dimensional region that the wizards of Ynis Aielle called upon for their strength. Reinheiser sensed the power tingling all about him, flowing in the natural harmony of its dance. He had no idea, though, of how Thalasi would access it.

Then Martin Reinheiser came to understand. Thalasi was the master of the third school of magic, domination. The Black Warlock reached out for the magical energy with his will and pulled it in, broke away its resistance.

Grok hadn't even begun the blow, and the talon would never get the chance. Showers of blood and gore splattered every corner of the wide room, pieces of bone and blasted flesh flew and fell like a wind-driven rain. And the talon's cloak, torn and shredded, flipped up into the air and then descended slowly, flattening to the stone of the floor, quite empty.

" 'E blew up!" Burgle shrieked, barely able to find its voice.

"And what of you?" the Black Warlock roared, his voice still crystal clear and unspeakably powerful in the continuing harmony of rage.

The two guards fled from the room, slamming the door and wisely falling back into position at their appointed posts.

"Not a piece bigger'n me little finger," Burgle mumbled. His partner shuddered and nodded, praying that the Black Warlock would be satisfied with the single kill.

We must punish the others, the spirit of Thalasi mused. *And leave no doubt about who is in command.* He started to rise from the chair.

But the trembling had returned.

"Why do you resist?" Thalasi demanded in a shaky voice.

I do not! Reinheiser silently countered. *The traitorous guards must be punished!*

Still, the battered body could not find the strength to rise, as muscle worked against muscle. Both wills strained in their common desire, but the focus of crystalline rage, that singular moment of terror when the big talon had raised its blade, had dulled. Their subconscious unity was no more, whatever their conscious desires. After several torturous minutes, the form slumped back helplessly in the throne, the two surrendering their hopes to go out and punish the guards.

The pained eyes darted discordantly, taking in the mess of the room, as both spirits sought to remember that one moment of harmony, that one moment when other emotions too base for petty arguing had washed away the pain.

Do you know what this means? Thalasi pondered.

We have bought some time, reasoned Reinheiser. *News will spread quickly of the fate of Grok. Others will not be so quick to try for the throne.*

"I destroyed him," Thalasi sneered through the twisting mouth.

"Not you, fool," Reinheiser verbally countered, and Thalasi felt him try to turn the corners of the mouth up in a wry smile and quickly counterattacked. *I have found your secret to the darker magics,* Reinheiser went on, silently. *I, too, heard the ringing of the universal powers. I went with you, Thalasi, into that secret realm, understood your journey as clearly as if I had made it all by myself. It was Martin Reinheiser who sent the unruly talon to its horrid grave!*

"Never!" Thalasi hissed, but the words lacked conviction. Even at the height of his power, Morgan Thalasi had never been able to accomplish such complete destruction as the explosion of Grok. The energy that had ripped the unfortunate talon to tiny pieces had flowed through the broken limbs of the battered body of the Black Warlock pure and powerful.

Too powerful.

I know that I was part of the execution, Thalasi thought, surrendering the taxing control of the mouth, a calmness sweeping over him. He had felt the power surge, familiar from the days before he had joined with Reinheiser. But although he had been part of the being that issued the explosive blast, he had been only one part.

And yet, somehow, not a part at all, as if the result of the combination of the two spirits, joined by the threat of the talon, had been a completely new being, something greater than both of them.

Yet I know and admit that it was beyond me, Thalasi continued, asking as much as explaining.

What, then? Reinheiser prompted, equally uncertain.

Unity, Thalasi answered him. *Did you feel it? Of course you felt it, and you know the truth. It was neither Reinheiser nor Thalasi that sundered the flesh of Grok.*

Both, Reinheiser completed the thought.

They did not have to consciously communicate to know that they continued to entertain similar thoughts and emotions. How good that moment of power had felt! Like freedom. The promise of strength beyond anything either of them would have believed possible hovered about them, a dangling carrot.

If they could only reach out and grab it!

Snap the fingers of the left hand, Thalasi begged Reinheiser. *Join me in this action.*

Reinheiser willed the hand to move. It rose up in front of the face, trembling through every inch of the ascent. Both spirits ignored the pain, focused solely on the task at hand. Thumb and middle finger moved tentatively, their tips resting together.

They crossed and twisted as the arm bulged in discordant pain. Desperately trying to retrieve that moment of ecstasy, the two wills frantically pulled at the fingers, ordering them to their task. Muscles knotted and tore, a new bruise erupted in the wrist. Still the spirits fought on to accomplish this simplest of tasks. But more stubborn than their willpower was the impossibility of harmony. Despite all their efforts, the fingers trembled uselessly.

The mouth opened again in a silent scream of frustration.

"Blew 'im to little bits, 'e did!" Burgle said to the gathered crowd. "I seen it, I tell ye! Never hopin' to see it again, neither!"

"Bah, yer words is spit, is all," said another, a large, burly talon that had served as one of Grok's lieutenants and had been expecting a position of authority once Grok took care of the feeble human.

"Burgle's tellin' ye right!" cried yet another. "I seen the room. Bits an' blood liken a wars was foughted."

"Proves nothin'!" yelled the lieutenant.

"Then where's Grok?" Burgle retorted. He turned toward the tower to accentuate his next point. "An' why's the Thalasi still sittin' at home?"

A dozen misshapen talon heads followed Burgle's gaze to regard the high black wall of Talas-dun.

There would be no more threats to the Black Warlock this day or any day soon.

No use, Reinheiser thought at length. *Too many actions are involved in every motion. We cannot hope to synchronize our thought patterns so completely.*

Are we doomed, then? replied Thalasi. *Doomed in this living hell?*

So it would seem.

"No!" This time Thalasi's reply came out audibly, as his frustration momentarily wrenched the mouth to his sole possession. Reinheiser recovered quickly, before Thalasi could utter any more words without obstruction.

Get out! Thalasi's will demanded. The muscles of the torn body heaved to action again, took up their fight.

Reinheiser's reply caught Thalasi completely out of sorts. Always before, Reinheiser had met the challenge with equal vigor, demanding that Thalasi get out and return the corporeal body to its rightful owner. This time, though, Reinheiser issued no challenges or demands.

Are we to endure the agony of our battle again? Reinheiser asked calmly.

The will of Thalasi relented, and the body slumped back to the stone chair. *It felt so good,* he lamented.

The power, added Reinheiser. *Never have I felt such power!*

But how? Thalasi wondered.

Defense, answered Reinheiser. *The critical moment, it would seem, incited emotions too powerful for the discord of our wills. The critical moment brought us harmony.*

Harmony, Thalasi mused. *Yes, and how wonderful it was.* A moment later he sent the word back to Reinheiser once again, this time as a question. *Harmony?*

Reinheiser did not understand, though he sensed from Thalasi's growing excitement that an idea had suddenly occurred to his counterpart.

Harmony, Thalasi thought again, more insistently. *Music. What do you mean?*

Thalasi wasn't sure if he was grasping at straws, if in his desperation false hopes were floating through his mind. *Music, harmony.*

Still Reinheiser did not understand.

There is a place in the loft of the central tower, Thalasi explained. *A place where emotion overrides conscious thought. Help me, I beg you, to get our broken body there.*

Reinheiser shut his thoughts off from Thalasi for a long moment, considering the possibilities of his counterpart's vague hints. Was this just another one of Morgan Thalasi's devious tricks? Was there a weapon up in this loft, a magic unknown to him, Reinheiser, that Thalasi could use to drive his will from his own body, to fully possess the mortal form they both now inhabited?

Help me! Thalasi pleaded. *We must attain harmony; I must feel that surge of power again.*

The lure was simply too great, and the alternative too grim, for Reinheiser to decline. Slowly, painfully, the body rose from the throne and stumbled to the door.

Dozens of yellow talon eyes fixed upon the crawling progress of the Black Warlock, wondering how one so obviously feeble could exude such unspeakable power. But if they needed any reminders to keep them in line as the dual being that was the new Black Warlock inched his pitiful way across the stone floor of Talas-dun, all they had to do was glance through the open doors of the Throne Room.

To the gory puddle that had once been Grok.

Chapter 2

The Dance of Rhiannon

FAR FROM THE gloom of Kored-dul, winter's last sunset sparkled across the sylvan boughs of magical Avalon. The forest teemed with life, shaking off the sleepy mantle of the snowy months in a burst of joyful vitality. Songbirds heralded the end of the day, and the animals of the night stirred in their quiet dens.

A chill wind blew down from the Crystal Mountains, a reminder of the season past, but its bite was not so sharp. Spring had come early to the wood this year.

Near the eastern borders of the great forest, in a wide field protected from the north winds by walls of towering evergreens, a young woman watched the darkening sky breathlessly for the first starlight. And when it twinkled into view, she smiled in contentment and broke into her carefree dance, the dance of Rhiannon.

"Be knowing that me eyes are better for seeing such a sight," said Bellerian, the venerable Ranger Lord. He stood off to the side of the field, under the boughs of a wide pine.

The wizard Ardaz, gray-haired and with a bristling beard, sniffled and wiped the wetness from his eyes, drawing an exchange of smiles between Bellerian and the third person

15

in the group, a woman of beauty beyond the realm of mortals. "Me brother's a sentimental sort," Brielle explained to the Ranger Lord.

"Twenty!" Ardaz cried. "Just a day, I know it was just a day ago that I held the little babe in my arms. Look at her now! A woman! I do dare say!"

"Twenty years might not seem as much to the likes o' a wizard and witch," Brielle replied. "Suren the time has brought me girl to womanhood, but it has not touched us at all."

"Yer fortunes," Bellerian grumbled lightheartedly, stretching a creak out of his aging back. "Me wish it be that the turnin' clock'd leave me bones alone."

"Just a baby," Ardaz went on, too caught up in his nostalgia to hear the words of his companions.

Brielle winked at Bellerian and moved out to join her daughter. The Ranger Lord started to follow, but Ardaz, understanding what would come next, held him back.

And then the mother, the witch of the wood, joined her daughter in dancing. Their graceful movements, heightened by the mysterious flow of gossamer gowns—white for Brielle, black for Rhiannon—caught the essence of the forest night and translated its beauty into an art that the eyes of those less knowledgeable in the ways of the sylvan world could understand. For watching Brielle and Rhiannon was to watch the dance of the earth in all its glory, an ancient dance, older than the race of man. The dance of life itself.

They twirled and crossed, rising up high into the air and floating to gentle landings that did not even bend the blades of newly sprouting grass under their bare feet. So alike they seemed, in spirit and body, but if Brielle, with her shining golden locks and sparkling green eyes, was the light of day, then Rhiannon was the mystery of night. Black hair rolled across her shoulders as she spun, soft as the moonlight and impossibly thick. But even if it fell across the porcelain features of her fair face, it could not dim the light in her eyes, the palest blue but with a depth that belied the lightness of color.

Bellerian and Ardaz could only watch silently, entranced as the witch and her daughter continued their dance. The hugest and clumsiest of dragons could have crashed through the forest to stand right behind them and they would not have sensed its presence.

And then, after a long while that seemed too short for the onlookers, Brielle leaped in a twirl and froze in her landing, arms wide and eyes unblinking. Rhiannon spun a full circuit around her, coming to a stop in a similar posture, facing her mother and staring into Brielle's green eyes, staring into her soul.

Inches apart stood mother and daughter, finding the truest serenity in their bond.

"If my life now found its end, I would surely die a contented soul," came a voice from the side when the mystical moment began to wane, and out from the boughs walked Arien Silverleaf, the King of the Elves, with a brown-skinned man at his side. They crossed the field to join the witch and her daughter.

"My greetings to you, Mistress of Avalon," the noble elf greeted Brielle. "Blessed are we to be invited to the beauty of your realm." He bowed low and sincerely.

Ardaz and Bellerian walked out to join the gathering. "Splendid," cried the gray-bearded wizard. "Then we are all here. Oh, we are, we are indeed! I do so enjoy a party! I do, I do! What fun would life be without them, after all?"

"And glad I am that ye could come to celebrate me daughter's birthday," said Brielle. She paused and smiled when she took note of Billy Shank, the man at Arien's side, his mouth frozen in a silent whistle, his eyes wide and glazed as he looked upon Rhiannon, the legacy of his dearest friend, for the first time in almost two decades.

Brielle brushed her hand across her daughter's forehead, pushing back the thick mane. Rhiannon kept her eyes to the ground—not an impolite posture, but rather, an embarrassed one. So at home among the creatures of the forest, the young woman was not accustomed to human visitors.

"This is Billy Shank," Brielle said to her. "The others ye know. He was a friend o' yer father's, a friend dear and true."

Rhiannon peeked out of the corner of her eye at Ardaz, her uncle Rudy, and found courage in his assuring smile. Then she looked at Billy, and found only friendship reflecting back at her from his dark eyes. He was passing middle age and a bit round in the belly now, with flecks of silver in his black hair. But the wrinkles that creased the edges of his mouth and eyes all turned up to smile at her, and even Rhiannon's profound shyness could not dispute such sincere friendship.

"Me thanks to ye," the daughter of the witch whispered. "To ye all, for coming to me party." Her voice grew louder as she spoke, gaining confidence in the knowledge that she was among only friends.

Ardaz bounded over to her and kissed her noisily on the cheek. "And our thanks to you, dear girl!" he cried.

"For what?"

The wizard's laugh erupted and then ended suddenly. "Why, for everything! And for nothing at all, I do dare say!" He lifted her in his arms and spun her around.

And thus the party began.

Arien, Ardaz, and Bellerian had come to the magical forest in great anticipation this night. They had joined in such celebrations before and knew that they would not be disappointed, could never be disappointed, by an evening spent with the fair ladies of Avalon. But for Billy Shank the night was especially wonderful. He had been to Avalon on several occasions, but this was the first time he truly appreciated the sweetness of the enchanted forest, the primordial magic that marked this place above all others in the world.

An oaken table was brought to the field, and a feast of cakes and fruit, and of water as crystalline as the stars on a clear and moonless night and bringing a tingling chill that invigorated the body yet somehow warmed the soul, was set before them. But if the meal was wondrous, the manner in which it was served stole Billy's breath altogether.

Birds flew down from the trees, clutching golden plates and chalices in their claws; a great buck emerged from the trees, jugs of drink swinging with its strides from the many points of its majestic antlers; and a huge bear brought the dinner tray.

Laughter erupted from all assembled at the sight of Billy's shocked expression when the bear set a place before him and then squatted down beside him for its own feast. Only a moment later a gigantic owl swooped down from the trees and landed on Billy's shoulder. It cocked its head, stared, only an inch from Billy's wide eyes, and hooted out, "Who?"

And the merriment erupted again, Billy joining in this time. Brielle slapped her daughter playfully on the shoulder. "Ye told the bird to do that," she scolded.

Rhiannon bit her lip and turned away, sobbing with laughter.

Ardaz heard the comment. He continued to laugh, but secretly pondered the implications of his sister's words. Rhiannon told the bird? Was she, then, blessed like her mother?

By the time the meal was finished, Billy and the bear had become great friends—though the bear kept sticking its paw into the honey on Billy's plate—to the continued merriment of them all. Rhiannon, more comfortable with each passing second, grabbed the hand of Arien. "Dance with me," she begged, a plea the elf-king had no intention of ignoring.

And they danced and sang, all of them, and the animals and the forest itself joined in their song. They called to the stars and were answered; they whispered to an unseen loon and heard its long, mournful cry in response.

And when the night had passed its midpoint, a bright light, colored as a rainbow, appeared in the middle of the field, near the table. Ardaz and the others looked at Brielle, but the witch had no answers for them.

The light spun and swirled and took on a vaguely humanoid shape. Then it was gone, and where it had been stood a white-bearded man, his face wizened with age, his old bent body bedecked in a flowing white robe and the pointed cap of a mage.

"Istaahl!" Brielle and Ardaz cried in unison.

"I see that I am late," the White Mage of Pallendara, the great human settlement far to the south, said with a bow. "My many apologies."

"But ye said ye could not be attendin'," Brielle replied.

"Yes, for it is the celebration of the equinox in Pallendara, you know." He winked at the others. "But mortal men simply do not know how to throw a proper party. Most of them are already snoring comfortably in their beds.

"Or in someone else's bed," he whispered and winked as if he had revealed some great secret.

Rhiannon blushed and looked away, and Ardaz snickered in amusement.

"But the night is only half through," Brielle said, casting him a stern glance that reminded him to keep his bawdy remarks to himself in the presence of her innocent daughter.

"Yes, well," stammered Istaahl. "Their merrymaking nears its end; I will not be missed."

"And how are your old bones?" Ardaz asked the newcomer. "Mine will creak and groan in the morning, I do dare say!"

"Truly you are old beyond your centuries, Silver Mage," Istaahl teased. "But I have the vigor of springtime yet in my step."

"And truly you wag your tongue, White One. That you do, that you do," Ardaz countered. "Idle boasts from idle bodies, I always say." He jumped up from his seat, a magically enhanced leap that sent him soaring into the air, only to land softly on the other side of the oaken table. "My feet might fly on moonbeams, White One, while yours plod through the mud."

"Rudy," Brielle teased her brother, using his original name, the name from the other world before he became Ardaz. "Are me ears hearin' a challenge?"

"Then back to the dance!" demanded Ardaz and Istaahl, the two oldest of friends, together.

The celebration took on a new depth for Rhiannon with the arrival of Istaahl. He was the wizard of the court of King Benador in Pallendara, the greatest city in all the world, set on the southern shores of Ynis Aielle, and whenever he happened by the forest of Avalon, he filled Rhiannon's ears with tales of the world beyond, with tales of the rolling plains of Calva and the ways of the good King Benador and his people. The young woman danced with the White Mage often, prompting him continually for songs of the wide world.

Brielle watched her daughter with growing concern.

"You protect her too closely," Ardaz whispered into his sister's ear, seeing her scowl. "She is a young woman now, and wants to learn of things beyond the borders of your domain.

"Blessed as it may be," he added quickly, seeing Brielle's glare.

"Never I do!" Brielle countered. "I let ye all in whenever ye might want to be in. Ye're all me guests right now!"

"All?" chuckled Ardaz, glancing around at the five others who made up the celebration. "Where are the rest of Arien's people, the half-thousand merry elves of Illuma Vale barely two miles from your front door?"

"Too much trouble for a simple party," Brielle replied. "I'd've not bothered them so."

"Bothered them?" Ardaz's laughter mocked the witch. "They would have jumped, dear sister, at any invitation the fair Brielle might have extended to them. You know it, too. Yes you do, yes you do! And the rangers! Bellerian's rangers. Walking the boughs of Avalon, back and again, back and again, back and again . . ." He got lost in the web of his own words for just a moment, then snapped his fingers as he got his train of thought back on its rails. "Just looking for a peek at you, they are, or your enchanting little girl! No no, Jenny, it's not for the bother you keep them away. It's for Rhiannon. Or more for yourself, I do dare say!"

Brielle looked up at her brother. She knew that he was concerned under his laughing facade. He had called her Jenny, her ancient name, and one Ardaz usually reserved for grave moments. "Ye think I'm holding her too close?"

"I dare say I do indeed."

As if on cue, Rhiannon whirled over to them then. "Me heart's found the gift!" she said to Brielle. "Ye promised me ye'd grant it if it was within yer power."

Brielle nodded, suspicious.

"I'm wanting to go to the southland," Rhiannon explained, and she glanced over at Istaahl. "To Pallendara and to the Four Bridges, and to all the world in between."

Brielle snapped a cold glare over Ardaz. "Ye knew," she hissed.

The wizard managed to cast a wink at Rhiannon before he looked away.

"And are ye going back with the White Mage, then?" Brielle asked, her attention back on Rhiannon, and her tone unmistakably disapproving.

"Oh, no, me mum," Rhiannon answered, trying to keep her cheer in the face of Brielle's simmering anger. "Too quick that way. I'd be missin' all the sights!"

"Then who?" demanded the witch. "The world's not so safe, me girl. I'll not have ye wanderin'—"

"Belexus and Andovar," Rhiannon blurted before Brielle could finish. "Off to the south they're going, in a fortnight they be meaning to leave. I know ye could get Bellerian to make them take me along. Please, me mum."

"And have ye been talking to the ranger lads?" Brielle asked slyly. "Do ye know the hearts of Bellerian's son and Andovar?"

"Oh, no," Rhiannon replied. "Never would I do such a thing against yer asking! I know ye want me keepin' clear o' travelers in the wood."

"Then how do ye know they're meaning to go?" Brielle was no longer angry, or accusatory, believing her daughter implicitly.

"Me friends heared them talking in the wood," Rhiannon explained. " 'Twas the birds that told me."

Ardaz caught Brielle's attention with a glance of curiosity. So it was true, the Silver Mage mused. Rhiannon's power was indeed beginning to bud.

"Please, me mum. Suren I'd love to be goin' with them."

Brielle took a long moment to study her daughter.

Rhiannon was a young woman now, and no longer her little girl. Still, the witch feared the possibilities of letting her run off on her own. Rhiannon had lived the entirety of her young life in Avalon, and she would not be prepared to handle the harsh world outside of the forest's protected boughs.

"Would ye not rather be going to the east, to the far lands?" Brielle asked on a sudden thought. Rhiannon seemed not to understand, but Ardaz opened his eyes wide and stared at his sister in disbelief. "Yer uncle Rudy'll be going out there. Would ye not enjoy his company on a long road?"

When Brielle looked over to Ardaz for support, he was shaking his head emphatically.

"Ye said ye were going," Brielle protested. "To study some ruins yer pet found. Ye said it yerself!"

"And so I am. Yes indeed I am!" Ardaz retorted. "But not with her along, oh no no no!" He winked slyly at Rhiannon again to let her know that he wasn't saying these things as an insult to her character. "Why would a young thing like her want to travel beside an old buffoon like me? I dare say, I would not doom my little Rhi to such a fate as that."

Brielle's eyes shot darts at her brother.

"Please, me mum," Rhiannon said again. "Truly I want to be going, and ye said ye would grant me wish. Would ye talk to Bellerian for me, then?"

Helplessly outnumbered, Brielle gave a resigned shrug. "I will talk to the Ranger Lord," she replied.

"Me thanks!" Rhiannon cried, and she threw her arms around her mother's neck. Brielle accepted the embrace for a few moments, then put Rhiannon back at arm's length.

"I said I'd be talking to the man," she explained. "No more than that did yer ears hear me promise. Now get ye back to the dancing; we'll be talking on the morrow."

Knowing that she had at last broken her mother's stubborn resolve, the young woman leaped back across the field, her graceful step springing even higher on the cool grass.

"Let her go," Ardaz said when Rhiannon was back to her play.

"So young," Brielle replied softly.

"By our counting," Ardaz countered, his tone suddenly quite serious. He looked into the green sparkle of his sister's eyes, held her with the intensity of his own gaze. "Her power is budding, so it would seem," he said. "But we do not know which she will follow, mother or father."

"What do you mean?" Brielle asked, a bit frightened by her normally cheerful brother's grim tone.

"Has she the gift of long years, as do we?" Ardaz asked bluntly. "You do not know, nor do I. Perhaps Rhiannon will live through the centuries, and then twenty years will not seem so long. But perhaps . . ." He let the thought hang, knowing that he had lighted a thousand contemplations in his sister's mind.

And truly Brielle was dazed by the words. She hadn't even given that notion much consideration, assuming that her daughter would live by her side through the dawn and wane of centuries to come. But Ardaz was right, Brielle had to admit; she had no way of knowing.

"Let her go," Ardaz said again. "The life is hers to live."

Brielle nodded but could not reply past the lump that had suddenly welled in her throat.

Much later, but still before the approaching dawn had pinkened the eastern sky, Billy Shank and Bellerian slumped down on a mossy bed at the edge of the field. The two wizards trotted by them, shaking their heads in good-hearted sarcasm, and returned to their merrymaking.

"Mortal men," Istaahl muttered to Ardaz.

"So now we might die happy," Bellerian said to Billy. "To have looked upon these precious and rare sights."

"Now I understand Del's love of this place," Billy replied, referring to the friend he had lost twenty years before, the friend who had loved Brielle and given the witch her daughter. "Truly it is a magical land."

"And rarer still is the gathering we joined this night," Bellerian explained. "Suren there be magic in the air."

Billy regarded the five still at play on the field. The fair witch and her brother Ardaz, Istaahl from faraway Pallendara, and Arien Silverleaf, the Eldar of the elves, who had become Billy's closest friend over the past twenty years. But most of all Billy found his eye lingering on Rhiannon, Brielle's daughter, Del's daughter, so innocent and beautiful.

Looking down from the heavens, his lost friend would have been proud indeed.

"Ardaz of Illuma, Istaahl of Pallendara, and Brielle of Avalon," Bellerian continued, speaking the words solemnly, as if to remind himself of the gravity of the assembly.

"And the Eldar of Illuma," Billy added. "If King Benador had come, then all the leaders of the world would be here."

Bellerian nodded. "But the good young king of Calva and even yer own friend o' the elves pale by the side of th'other three. Look at them, Billy Shank, and know yerself to be a blessed soul. The powers of all the world they be; any one o' them could defeat an army, could lay ruin to all the world or shine the light of hope upon it. They check themselves, and a blessing that be, for the bounds o' their powers'd steal yer breath away and never give it back."

Billy knew well enough the truth of Bellerian's observations. He had seen Ardaz in battle once before, and if the Black Warlock had not appeared on the field to counter the magic of the Silver Mage, Ardaz would surely have destroyed the entire army of Pallendara all by himself.

Bellerian shook his head, as if he couldn't believe his own words. "The powers o' the gods given to man," he mumbled. "The three wizards of Ynis Aielle all come together."

Twenty years is a long time in the life of a mortal man, but if Bellerian, the knowledgeable Ranger Lord, had taken a moment to consider his words, he would have remembered that Ynis Aielle boasted of four wizards, not three.

Too many, in the last two decades of peace, had allowed themselves to forget the lurking specter of Morgan Thalasi.

An organ? Reinheiser balked, considering the massive pipes that climbed high into the chamber. *You dragged me all the way up here to view an organ?*

You can play, of course, Thalasi countered, a rhetorical thought, for Thalasi knew Reinheiser's every memory and knew that his counterpart was an accomplished musician.

I created this instrument in my first days here, he explained to Reinheiser. *My only companion for centuries other than the wretched talons, and I care not for their company.*

Reinheiser began to understand. *You want us to join in the song,* he realized. *Every movement so precise and so practiced.*

Here we might find our harmony, Thalasi replied. *It only occurred to me after the encounter with the usurping talon, after I had felt the ecstasy of our joining.*

It will not work, Reinheiser reasoned, and Thalasi felt the sincere disappointment in his thoughts. *There remain too many subtle variations.*

Perhaps, argued Thalasi. *But with the instrument as an audible guide, the futility of our battles will become evident at every misstep. Only when the song flows in harmony will our minds be flowing in harmony.*

Reinheiser remained unconvinced, but Thalasi did not have to remind him of their other options. He followed Thalasi's lead in bringing the body to sit down.

And then they played.

* * *

For an unbroken stretch of many days, notes rang out from the central tower of Talas-dun. Rhythmless and off-key, the sound grated in the marrow of the talons of the fortress, and they slumped down and tried to hide their ears whenever they had to cross too close to the place. Whispers spread among the ranks—but only whispers, for none had yet found the courage even to go in and mop up the remains of Grok—that the Black Warlock had gone mad.

But the helpless talons could only sit and wait, and endure the torture of the monstrous music.

Quite the opposite of the talons' suspicions, the spirits of Thalasi and Reinheiser were preserving their sanity up in that tower room. Ever so gradually, the notes of their playing began to take on the semblance of music. For the first time, the two separate identities found a way to truly anticipate the actions of each other.

In merely a week Reinheiser admitted the value of Thalasi's plan. In two they found their way through an entire melody without a single error. And still they played, following the music, falling within the music.

It consumed them wholly and broke down the defenses that had kept them apart for so long, as each laid bare his desires to the other. The music was the cause, the harmony their only goal.

And they reached for it and clutched at it. Together.

Talons gathered outside the central tower, basking in the powerful notes of the Black Warlock's song. The dim-witted beasts could not understand the depth of what their dark master had accomplished, but they knew from the confident roar of the massive pipes that the man who finally emerged from the central tower of Talas-dun would bear little resemblance to the wretched being that had crawled and scratched his way up there.

Fingers glided across the keys in complete confidence,

never a bar was missed, and the sheer power that flowed through those once battered digits sent the huge instrument spiraling to new heights of musical majesty.

"Are you there?" the being called out in a strange dual-toned voice.

"Of course I am!" he answered himself.

It was time to go.

The Black Warlock stretched his legs and strode confidently out of the room to the tower balcony. He knew that his talons would be nearby, listening, waiting for some word, any word, of the fate of their master. And here he was, returned to them, whole again and powerful. More powerful.

"And I am Thalasi, not Reinheiser," the Black Warlock muttered, testing out the depth of his newfound tranquillity with a proclamation that before would surely have brought resistance from the spirit of Martin Reinheiser.

"Of course," the being agreed with himself. The logic was inescapable. "Morgan Thalasi. A name that strikes dread into every heart of Ynis Aielle." The Black Warlock found no internal rage at the declaration, though the will of Martin Reinheiser remained an equal part of his makeup. Morgan Thalasi was the obvious choice for the name, both for keeping the talons in line and striking terror into the hearts of foes.

The part of the Black Warlock that remained Martin Reinheiser understood the value of this and accepted the conclusion without argument. All that mattered was the harmony.

And the power that harmony would bring.

He walked out onto the tower balcony. The day was remarkably clear for Kored-dul, and the Black Warlock could see for many miles from the high vantage point.

"Go out!" he cried to the talons assembling at the base of the structure. Their whispers faded away to a hush at the simple utterance of those two words. They sensed the change in the Black Warlock, sensed the hushed power of the being, and they wanted to hear the commands of their true master, the one possessed of the powers of a god that most of them knew only from the tales their fathers and grandfathers had told them.

"Go out to the dark holes and valleys," Thalasi roared. "Find your kin! Tell them that Morgan Thalasi has returned to lead them all! Tell them that Morgan Thalasi is hungry!

"Tell them that Morgan Thalasi claims this world!"

The proclamation resounded off every stone in Koreddul, found its way to every talon ear. The call to arms and to glory. And they came, every one, willingly, hungrily.

The Black Warlock had returned.

Chapter 3

Gatherings

"YE'VE CHOSEN YER steeds and the road?" Bellerian asked.

"Ayuh," replied Belexus, seeming the very image of his venerable father. Gray flecks peppered his unkempt black locks, but his huge corded muscles still held the hardness of youthful strength. "Across the bridges to the west and Corning, then back to great Pallendara afore we ride for home."

Bellerian remembered the roads well, though he had not traveled them, except for a brief trek to the great city, in nearly half a century. He had once been a nobleman of great repute in the court of Pallendara, but then an unlawful king had stolen the throne and sent all of Calva into tumult. Bellerian had escaped to the borders of Avalon, taking many of the children of his fellow nobles—children who would become the proud warriors known as the Rangers of Avalon—with him.

Bitter years, those decades of Ungden's rule had been, though Brielle and Ardaz had offered a good life to Bellerian and his troupe. Always the Ranger Lord turned his eyes southward to the rolling plains, where the scourge of Ungden the Usurper exacted a heavy toll on the land and people alike. The reign of terror lasted for three full decades,

31

ending in the bloody Battle of Mountaingate, when the ancient ones came to Ynis Aielle. With Ungden's forces defeated and the Usurper himself slain, Benador, the heir of the rightful king, sat on Pallendara's throne, and after twenty years of the goodly man's rule, the scars of Ungden were few and fading.

But Bellerian could not bring himself to return to Pallendara, the place of his early life. Avalon was his home now, but still, his son's mention of traveling across Calva tugged at Bellerian's heartstrings, and he found his eyes turning once again to the rolling fields south of the enchanted forest.

"Prepare a third horse," Bellerian instructed his son.

Belexus looked at Andovar, his most trusted friend, standing beside him. Andovar wasn't as formidable as the son of Bellerian, but he stood tall and straight, with the piercing eyes and firm chin that marked the proud rangers.

"Will ye be riding?" Andovar asked hopefully. "Suren we'd be blessed to have the likes o' Bellerian beside us."

"Me thanks for yer kind words," Bellerian replied. "But 'tis not for meself that ye'll be needing the third mount. Ye'll have a guest for the trip, one ye'll come to welcome beyond the company of an old man."

"Who, then?" asked Belexus, intrigued by his father's wry smile.

"A favor has been asked of us—of yerself—from one deserving our service," Bellerian began slowly, searching for the right method of springing such amazing news on the two men. "The daughter of this deservin' friend desires to see the world."

Sour looks passed between Belexus and Andovar, the old Ranger Lord noted. These two were not an ungrateful lot, he understood, and they would certainly heed his wishes, but they had fancied a journey of excitement and exploration through the coming months and were not thrilled at the prospects of carrying along an inexperienced child.

"Ye know we'll take the lass," Belexus remarked. "But—"

"But?" Bellerian cut in. "Ye'll take her, indeed! And gladly!" They hid their disappointment well, but Bellerian could sense that they still did not understand the true meaning of his words.

"Would it bring ye a smile if I told ye that 'twas the Emerald Witch, Brielle herself, doing the asking?"

Belexus snapped his eyes up on his father; Andovar swooned and nearly stumbled to the ground.

"The Lady," Andovar breathed. He had spent the bulk of his life walking her domain, hoping for a tiny glimpse of the fair witch or, in more recent years, her enchanting daughter. But Avalon was a wide forest, and Brielle and Rhiannon kept few friends.

"Ye're asking that we take Rhiannon along with us?" Belexus gasped, both afraid and hoping that his father would confirm the fact.

"That I be," chuckled Bellerian. "I'm asking, as Brielle herself asked o' me. Are ye willing?"

"We are!" Andovar roared before Belexus could open his mouth.

Both Belexus and his father could not contain their laughter. Andovar looked away, embarrassed, but soon joined in their mirth.

"A great responsibility follows ye, then," Bellerian said, his voice suddenly grave. "Rhiannon's a woman now—aye, what a woman, indeed—but unknowin' of the ways of the world."

"The witch's daughter will be safe beside us," Belexus assured his father.

Bellerian did not doubt it for a moment. "Ye are the finest warriors in all the world, and yer honor is above question.

But ye might find other trials ridin' the road beside the likes o' Rhiannon. Her spirit is no more bridled than her mother's, and she's not versed in the ways of the men outside her wood."

"Fear not for Rhiannon," Andovar replied. "Fear for any fool that might try her honor!" Instinctively, Andovar's hand fell to his sword hilt.

Bellerian smiled, but did not reply. Andovar spoke the truth, and it was that very truth that concerned the Ranger Lord. He knew the love that Andovar had for Avalon and its mysterious mentors, and suspected that the ranger would take on the entire garrison of Pallendara if any of them brought the slightest harm to Rhiannon. But Bellerian was satisfied. He looked at Belexus and winked, knowing that his level-headed son would keep the reins tight on his overly exuberant companion.

"Let her run, but keep her safe," Bellerian instructed both of them.

"How many?" Thalasi demanded in that peculiar dual-toned voice that only added to the terror he exuded.

"Lots an' lots!" Burgle replied with a strained smile, obviously hoping the answer would suffice. The creature couldn't count past ten, after all, and the ranks of the talons gathering around Talas-dun numbered more than a thousand times Burgle's mathematical limit. From every corner of Kored-dul they came, heeding the summons of their master.

"You have done well," Thalasi said. "I will forget your unfortunate intrusion." The Black Warlock led Burgle's gaze over to the wall of the Throne Room, to the dried crimson stain.

Burgle slouched low and tried to appear very small, wanting only to be dismissed.

"Indeed," Thalasi went on, "your service has more than

amended the foolishness of Grok. And I always reward such devoted service."

Burgle stayed low and trembled. Thalasi had recently given a similar speech to the other guard who had been in attendance on that fateful day. And only a moment later, when a smile lit the talon guard's face, the Black Warlock had pulled the talon's heart right out of its chest.

"You shall be a commander of the legions," Thalasi decreed. "Captain Burgle. And let any who disobey your commands answer to me!"

Burgle straightened, eyes wide, hardly believing its unexpected fortune.

"Go now," Thalasi instructed. "Gather the leaders of the tribes. Tell them that we ride to war on the waning of the summer's highest moon."

For the rest of the day the Black Warlock studied his talon army from the window of the Throne Room. Thousands of the creatures milled about the mountainside beyond Talasdun's high black walls, separated by definitive borders into tribal clusters, each bearing the disgusting standards—a severed hand, a bloodied eyeball, and others of similar sort—of their respective chieftains. Thalasi knew that their devotion was wrought solely of fear; a leader of a talon tribe was its undisputed ruler, until another warrior of the tribe summoned the courage to challenge it and defeat it. Once Thalasi brought those revered leaders under his thumb, the rest of the rabble would fall into line.

Weapons clanged as skirmishes broke out among the rival tribes. "Such hateful things," Thalasi remarked, seeing his troops at play. He would do nothing to temper the anger; a few dead soldiers were a small price to pay for the level of bloodlust the battles maintained in the talons.

Thalasi's eyes wandered out beyond the encampments, beyond the dark mountains, viewing the rolling fields of

Calva. A different angle than the eyes that looked south from Avalon.

But the same destination.

Belexus and Andovar led the horses to a small glade on the southern edge of the enchanted forest, the appointed spot for the meeting that both of them, especially Andovar, so eagerly awaited.

Bellerian was already there when they arrived, the wizard Ardaz, holding the bridle of a fine roan stallion, at his side.

"We have bringed the third horse, as ye requested," Belexus said to his father, not understanding the presence of the roan.

"So ye have," replied Bellerian. "But the fourth'll be needed. Ye're to have company on the first leg o' yer journey."

"Yerself?" Belexus asked, aiming the question at the Silver Mage.

"With your permission, of course. I would not intrude, heavens no," Ardaz replied, bowing low. "I have some business—so very important, you know—far to the east. A farmer's tale of some ruins, an unknown village or something or other. Could be important, you know, I do dare say!"

Always patient, the three rangers did their best to show interest in the wizard's rambling story, however confusing.

"But my course goes south, only a bit," Ardaz explained. He winked and dropped his voice to a secretive whisper. "Want to keep the old bones in the civilized world as long as I can, you know. No need for hard ground when the bed of a Calvan inn is nearby."

A great squawk erupted from the trees, and two birds glided down to the group. The larger, a raven, landed plop on Ardaz's shoulder and immediately transformed into the more familiar form of his black cat, Desdemona.

But Belexus and Andovar hardly noticed the magical polymorph, entranced by the more dramatic transformation of the second bird, a white dove. The bird landed on the ground before them and puffed into a cloud of white smoke that swayed about, forming into a shapely column.

And Brielle stepped from the column.

Andovar had to consciously remember to breathe. He had seen the witch a few times, though only from afar, and was not the least bit disappointed at the closer view. Quite the opposite; the beauty of Brielle could withstand any inspection.

"Me Lady," Belexus stammered, and he fell to one knee.

Brielle's expression, somewhat embarrassed, showed that she was indeed touched by the great ranger's respect. She looked over at Andovar and he dropped similarly, though he still could not find words to address the witch.

Brielle bade them both rise. She had seen them before, of course; the witch saw everything that moved through her forest. And she had known before her formal meeting with Bellerian that the two rangers would take fine care of her daughter. Still, her mothering instincts of that special little girl would not so easily let go.

"Ye'll take care o' me girl?" she asked, more to measure the desire of Belexus and Andovar in having Rhiannon along than to question their ability. The two would not disobey the requests of Bellerian, and would surely take Rhiannon if the Ranger Lord asked them to, but Brielle did not want to impose. "And bring her back to me at the summer's wane?"

"We shall indeed," Belexus assured her. "And honored we are that ye'd trust us with such a task."

The Emerald Witch glanced to Bellerian. "They do ye proud, Ranger Lord," she said. Then to Belexus and

Andovar, she added, "And know that never I doubted ye, either of ye. But do ye truly want me girl along?"

Now Andovar piped in, unable to control his excitement. "As we want the warming of spring," he cried suddenly and eagerly. "I beg of ye fairest Lady, let the lass come. We'll watch her and protect her, do no' be doubtin', and suren the joy o' Rhiannon'll brighten our days."

"Enough said, I do believe," Ardaz chuckled from the side. "Are you appeased, dear sister?"

"And how long will ye be riding with them?" Brielle asked him.

Ardaz fumbled his fingers over his beard; he hadn't really considered his exact course. "To the northern villages . . . er, it would seem . . . perhaps as far as Torthenberry," he replied. "A few days, one would expect, though I must get to those ruins. A farmer's tale, you know. Could be important, indeed it—"

"Yes, me brother," Brielle stopped him, "so ye've said many times." Indeed, Ardaz had talked of little other than his coming exploration since the farmer's tale had reached his ears last midwinter. He had delayed going to investigate only because he refused to miss the celebration of Rhiannon's twentieth birthday.

Brielle looked again at the eager faces of the rangers and gave a resigned shrug. "Come on, then," she called to the thick boughs beyond the glade.

The branches rustled and the raven-haired daughter of the fair witch, outfitted for the road, stepped shyly out into the open.

"Here are yer new companions," Brielle said to her. "Ye know their names." She turned back to Belexus and Andovar, standing in a stupor equal to their shock upon first seeing the elder witch of Avalon. For Rhiannon, stepping into the glade, was obviously possessed of that same unearthly beauty, that same wild spirit, so far beyond the experiences of the two men, or of any mortal men.

"Me daughter," Brielle told them, though she saw right away that Rhiannon needed no introduction.

"Me greetings, fair lass," said Belexus. "Glad we are that ye might be joining us."

"And glad I am to be going," replied Rhiannon. She looked over at the three waiting horses. "Are we to ride, then? Never have I . . . I mean—"

"Pallendara's a long walk," said Andovar, drawing a smile from the young woman. "She's yers." He indicated a black and white mare, small and sleek.

Rhiannon walked up to pat the horse on the flank and whisper something soothing into the beast's ear. The horse relaxed visibly, and then Rhiannon, to the amazement of the rangers, undid the mare's girth and started to slide the saddle from her back.

"Won't be needing it," the young woman assured them, and as soon as the saddle fell free, she slid easily onto the horse's back.

Belexus looked to Brielle for answers, not wanting to start an argument about the wisdom of riding bareback over such distances.

"She won't be needing it," Brielle echoed. "She's the horse's assurances that it won't be letting her fall."

Belexus and Andovar exchanged shrugs. Given the company assembled to see them off, how could they begin to argue?

The four riders broke out of the southern edge of Avalon later that afternoon and crossed the ford to the Illume-lune River before nightfall, setting a camp on the flat top of a huge, wide stone.

"Yer place," Andovar remarked to Ardaz while the wizard

cooked the meal. "The Justice Stone." The ranger turned to Rhiannon and Belexus. "Here it was that Ardaz saved the elves, the Night Dancers of Lochsilinilume, in the dawning of their race."

"He took them to this place under the guise of execution," Belexus explained. "But only a trick, he played, and then the Night Dancers were hidden away."

"I have heard the tales," Rhiannon replied. "Ye saved them all, did ye, Uncle Rudy?"

"Shhhh," Ardaz sputtered, but too late.

"Uncle Rudy?" Belexus and Andovar chimed together, putting a deep blush into the wizard's cheeks.

"Rudy's his real name," Rhiannon went on, enjoying the game. "Rudy Glendower. And me mum's his sister, Jennifer Glendower."

"Names from another time," Ardaz said dismissively. "Before the dawning of our world." His eyes glazed over in distant memories. So very distant, a time across the span of twelve centuries.

"So Ardaz ye be," Belexus agreed, bowing to the wizard. "The Silver Mage of Lochsilinilume." He turned back to Rhiannon. "Owing are the elves, and us all, to the likes of yer uncle."

"And sacred is this place," Andovar added, "to all the elves, and to all the goodly folk of Aielle."

"Dark days, brrr!" the wizard shuddered, remembering that grim trip to the Justice Stone, but he shook the evil thoughts away and grinned anew. "But no need of such wicked memories," he proclaimed. "All turned out for the best, I do dare say. It always does, you know, always does."

"And the road is clear before us," Belexus was quick to add.

They ate a tasty meal—wizard enhanced—and better still for the fine tales they exchanged. Then they stretched out and watched the twinkle of the stars appear against the blackening canopy of the Aiellian sky.

Rhiannon fell asleep a short time later, pleased by the new friends she had made that day and thinking that adventures far from home might not be such a bad thing after all.

They made North Ridge, the northernmost of the Calvan farming villages, two leisurely days later. Spring was in full bloom now, and the sun and gentle southern breezes graced the little troupe. They meandered along their course, in no hurry at all to arrive at any particular destination, and determined to enjoy the sights along the road as they went.

"Problem with humans," Ardaz was quick to say. "So busy rushing to get from place to place that they forget about the lands in between."

"Humans?" Belexus replied. "What are ye then, a talon? And what are we three, by yer reckoning?"

"Oh, I did not mean . . ." Ardaz bumbled. "I mean . . . I am a wizard, after all, and have lived long enough—too long, some would say, but I don't listen. Where was I? Oh yes, I have lived long enough to throw away some of the faults."

"And what're ye saying of us, then?" Rhiannon balked in feigned anger. She managed to slip a wink at the two rangers.

"Well, I mean you three . . ." Again Ardaz found his tongue twisting in his mouth. "You're rangers, and different from most, I do dare say. You walk in Avalon and have learned the truth of pleasures that others might miss. And you"—he grabbed a handful of Rhiannon's raven hair and gave a playful tug—"you've grown under the shadow of that most marvelous, most simply marvelous, forest! The daughter of Brielle would not miss a wildflower beside the road because her eyes were looking farther down it! No no no! We all know better, that we do. We know to enjoy what we might when we might."

True enough. It was exactly these lands "in between" that came to thrill Rhiannon and the rangers. They became great friends on the empty road, particularly Andovar and the young woman, the ranger trading tales to Rhiannon in exchange for the secrets she knew about the ways of the plants and animals they passed. Ardaz, too, grew especially interested when Rhiannon shared those bits of her understanding of nature, knowledge too vast for her young years. She was indeed the daughter of the Emerald Witch, though the wizard suspected that she might claim a similar title for herself in the near future.

And Andovar was interested in everything Rhiannon did, in every graceful move, in every wood she spoke, and in every one of the countless careless laughs that came so naturally from her.

"It seems that I might be protecting the lass from me own companion," Belexus remarked to Ardaz one sunset as Andovar and Rhiannon walked off toward a high ridge together, hand in hand.

"Protecting?" laughed Ardaz. "Oh, no no no!" The wizard watched as Andovar draped an arm comfortably across the young woman's shoulders, and she willingly snuggled up to him.

"Well, maybe watching," the wizard conceded.

The next day, they passed another of the common villages, little more than a cluster of farmhouses surrounded by a low wall. Belexus kept them close to the great River Ne'er Ending, thinking it was wise to travel the less populated western fields first before springing the grandeur of mighty Pallendara on his newest traveling companion. Ardaz readily agreed with the course, as did Andovar, knowing that the smaller villages would be less imposing to Rhiannon until she became more familiar with the ways of the settlements.

"Donnings Down," Ardaz said, recognizing the next town they crossed through. "And after Donnings Down is Torthenberry."

"Where ye leave us?" Belexus asked, obviously disappointed. The wizard's tales had been the best of the lot, and few could steal the tedium from a long road as well as Ardaz.

"I meant to go there, I think I did," Ardaz replied. "But too long we've wandered. Too, too long, I do dare say. Why, May is blooming upon us. No, I have to go now, straightaway."

"What could be so important in the empty east?" Andovar asked, obviously as unhappy about the parting as the others.

"The east?" Ardaz echoed, not seeming to understand.

Rhiannon smiled at his expression, recognizing the fairly common glazed look in the wizard's eye.

"Ye're going to the east, so ye said," Andovar tried to explain.

"Who said?" the wizard demanded.

"Ye did yerself," said Andovar. "To some ruins. The meat of a farmer's tale."

"I did?" Ardaz's face crinkled in confusion. "Of course I did not! Oh, why do you try to confuse me, you nasty boy? But why would I want to go there, if it is so empty, after all? Or are you just trying to get rid of me?"

"No, never that," laughed Andovar, familiar enough with the wizard's forgetfulness to let the issue drop. "Ride along with us, then, for as long as ye wish."

"Well, how can I do that?" Ardaz demanded. He looked

at Belexus in sincere concern. "The boy's bitten," he said with a sly nod at Rhiannon.

"But enough," the wizard said, rising straight in his saddle and pulling out a long oaken staff. "I've business in the east, of course—and no tricks by you!" he added quickly before the flustered Andovar could put his thoughts in. Ardaz mumbled some arcane chants into his horse's ear, and the beast perked up, snorting anxiously to be off at a gallop.

"Good-bye and farewell!" Ardaz said to the three. "A busy summer sits before me." He stopped and snapped his fingers as if he suddenly remembered something, then reached under his robes.

"Grrr," came a muffled reply to his intrusion.

"Oh, silly puss," Ardaz huffed, rubbing the newest of many scratches on his hand. He reached back into his robe more forcefully and pulled Desdemona from her catnapping slumbers. "Go now!" he demanded, and to the astonishment of his companions, he threw the cat high into the air.

Desdemona shrieked in protest, but her cry was transformed into the excited caw of a raven as the cat shifted into her avian state and flew off ahead of the wizard.

"Got to light a fire under them sometimes," the wizard explained to the others.

"She likes her sleep," Rhiannon agreed.

"But she likes the adventures more," Ardaz replied. "You just have to remind her of that sometimes."

High overhead, Desdemona squawked out a complaint at the wizard's delay.

"Well, good-bye again," Ardaz said to them. "And have a fine summer. I will return to the north before winter. Or maybe I won't. One can never tell about such things. But I will return, I do dare say."

"With new tales to tell?" Rhiannon asked hopefully.

The wizard put his arms out wide. "One never knows

when one might walk into a tale," he said, and he kicked his horse off into a blinding run that seemed impossibly swift.

In the springtime sunshine on the peaceful Calvan plain, none of the group, or the wizard himself, could have guessed how prophetic those final words would prove to be.

Chapter 4

The Western Fields

THEIR ROAD TOOK no definitive course, meandering east
away from the river, then north or south to whatever community they could find, only to return eventually to the riverbank. Gradually they moved farther south, but spring was
still in the air and they had no need to hurry. At Rhiannon's
request, they spent an entire week in one village, just talking
to the farm folk and learning their ways. With her knowledge of nature, Rhiannon had more than a few bits of good
advice for them.

And then they went on to the next town, and the next after
that, truly an easy-paced holiday. Belexus approved of the
comfortable pace; he saw Rhiannon reveling in the many
meetings and budding friendships, and he saw something
deeper, something wonderful, growing between the witch's
daughter and his ranger friend.

Surely Andovar cared not where they were or where they
were going. All that came to matter to him was that Rhiannon was by his side, sharing his adventures and widening
his smiles.

And Rhiannon, Belexus was observant enough to know,
felt the same way.

* * *

They rolled down from the rocks of the Kored-dul like the black clouds of a thunderstorm. Ten thousand strong and hungry for blood came the army of Morgan Thalasi. The master himself led the march, borne in a pillowy litter by four of his largest talon soldiers.

Rain greeted the army as it came down from the mountains onto the dreary beaches of the western shore of Aielle. Unbothered, the single-minded force trudged onward. They would leave the beaches soon enough and turn inland, where their feast awaited.

The master had promised.

But as the group prepared to camp that first night down from their rocky homes, they were met by something more tangible than a gloomy weather front. Facing them, fanning out to encircle the front half of the vast camp, loomed a second army of talons, larger than the force that had accompanied Morgan Thalasi.

Rhiannon continued to become more and more comfortable with each village the threesome crossed, and now she was fully at ease with the strangers they met on their way. The little troupe had been out of Avalon for the better of two months, riding that meandering, though generally southern, course along the edge of the great shining river. As summer came in, though, their excursions to the east grew less frequent, for Belexus had some definite goals in mind for this journey—and he had promised Brielle that he would return Rhiannon to Avalon soon after the summer's wane. So he set the pace a bit quicker and kept the course straight along the line of the River Ne'er Ending.

Fully pleased in her dealings with other people, even in large numbers, Rhiannon wanted to press right on to Pallendara, the greatest city in all the world. But Belexus held fast to his plan that Pallendara would serve as their final stopover as the season turned to autumn before they turned back toward home. The ranger wanted to cross over the famous Four Bridges and view the western fields, lands he had never journeyed to before.

The green fields of the season's crop waved in warm breezes over the tilled soil of the wide Calvan farms. Herds of cattle and sheep grazed lazily, for not even the onset of summer could shake the beasts from their perpetual lethargy. Farmers and shepherds greeted the northerners at every stop with friendly smiles and invitations to dinner.

The region had known peace for many years, no monsters threatened the borders, and strangers were a welcome sight. Indeed, the small company could have dined as guests of one farmer or another for every night since they had crossed into the more populated farmlands. But they politely declined more often than they accepted. Their friendship was newly formed, fresh and exciting, and ultimately private. While they enjoyed the company and stories of the Calvans, they enjoyed each other and each other's stories—a supply still far from exhausted—all the more.

"We'll be finding more of the same across the water," Belexus explained to Rhiannon. "The towns're bigger near the Four Bridges, and scattering out wide far, far to the west."

"And how far to the west will ye be taking me?"

"Corning," the ranger explained. "Fair-sized and the second city of Calva."

"Seven thousand strong," Andovar added. "But o' the same flavor as the smaller towns. We'll make the bridges this very morn, and Corning in two days."

"How much farther could we go?" Rhiannon asked. "The land's seeming so wide."

"Another week of hard riding'd bring us to the westernmost borders of Calva," Belexus replied. "Hardy towns of hardy folk. To go beyond them'd be folly."

Rhiannon seemed not to understand.

"The dark lands," the ranger continued. "Home to talons and lizards and beasts darker still. Not for the wise."

His grave tone passed beyond the young woman. Growing up among the flowers of Avalon, Rhiannon could not understand such evil notions as talons.

Not yet.

"We'll be wandering about Corning for a week or more," said Belexus, and he cast a wry glance at the innocent witch's daughter. "And then ye'll be seeing Pallendara."

"Caer Tuatha," Rhiannon said, using the elven name for the great city. "Istaahl and Uncle Ardaz have told me such grand tales of the place. Suren she'll be a fine sight if only half their spoutings run to truth."

"More liken that Pallendara will outweigh the most wonderful o' their tales," said Andovar. He had been to the white city only twice since his childhood, but the image had stuck in his head vividly. Pallendara was the only true city of Ynis Aielle, a place of towers and markets, and minstrels—a thousand minstrels! It rested at the tip of a narrow harbor, and the sails of a hundred boats rose up along the sea wall like the bare, jutting tops of a wintry forest.

"But first to Corning," Belexus reminded them, not wanting their visit to still another splendid place lessened by thoughts of what was yet to come. And as the small troupe passed the crest of a hill, off in the distance, shrouded by the morning mist that rose off the river, stood the unmistakable shapes of the Four Bridges of Calva, structures that had spanned the great river for centuries, before the elves or even the talons had walked the land.

They kicked up their horses with the bridges in sight,

galloping the mounts down from the rise and across the last expanse in a wild rush.

Belexus and Andovar, as skilled as any horsemen in all the world, would never have believed it, but Rhiannon, whispering compliments into her sleek mare's ear, got there first.

A short distance to the south lay the fairly large community of Rivertown, but Rhiannon hardly noticed the place. Before her loomed the Four Bridges, ancient and legendary, arcing pathways of solid stone. The young woman could sense the magic that had created these structures, could feel the song of wizardry humming still in their mighty stones. They were all of the same size and design, and four carts could ride abreast across any of them without nearing the solid stone banisters.

And these railings were perhaps the most special of all. Bas reliefs lined every inch of them, scenes depicting the birth of the new race of man, cradled in the arms of the angelic Colonnae, and images of the rise of Pallendara.

Belexus and Andovar had never before crossed the bridges and were no less enchanted than Rhiannon when they caught up to the young woman.

"They've more tales to tell than Ardaz himself," Belexus proclaimed. "So long they've stood."

"Ayuh," Andovar agreed. " 'Twas here that the Black Warlock first fell." He led Rhiannon down to the southernmost structure. A shining black plaque had been cut into the stone at the entrance to the bridge, commemorating the exact spot where Ardaz, Istaahl, and Rhiannon's mother had teamed together to defeat the Black Warlock in an age long past.

"Three thousand died," Andovar said solemnly. "But not in vain. The talon army was crushed and Morgan Th—" He paused, reconsidering the wisdom of speaking that vile name aloud. "The Black Warlock was thrown down."

"Not to rise again until the time of Ungden the Usurper," Belexus added.

"Me mum has oft told me o' the Battle of Mountaingate," said Rhiannon. "When Thalasi was again thrown down."

"And 'twas yer father that did the throwin'," chuckled Andovar. "A finer man I've never seen!"

Rhiannon smiled and let her gaze drift out into the mist of the river. She had never known her father, and his passing had put an edge of sadness forever on the eyes of her mother. But the joy of Brielle's memories of her times with Jeff DelGiudice, that special man from the other world, outweighed the sorrow, and Rhiannon knew that her mother did not lament for his loss as often as she smiled at memories of her times with him.

"Here now," called a voice from the south. The three turned to see a portly man running toward them, a helmet flopping wildly on his head as he tried futilely to buckle the thing.

"Greetings," Belexus said when the man reached them.

"And mine," the man huffed, trying to catch his breath. "First morning in ten years I overslept. Figures, how it figures, that you'd be picking this day to arrive at our bridges."

"Your—"

"Gatsby's the name," the man interrupted. "Gatsby of Rivertown. Not 'our' bridges, of course—none can be claiming them—but we like to consider ourselves guardians of the place."

"And ye're the gatekeeper?" Rhiannon asked.

The man had to wait a long moment before responding, caught up suddenly in the overwhelming beauty of the raven-haired woman. "No," he stammered, hardly able to withstand the disarming stare of Rhiannon's bluest blue eyes. "Not really. More of a guide, you might say. There is so very much to tell of this place! We keep it all safe—sort of our mission, you might say. Safe, but not secret." He pulled a huge book and a quill and ink set out of his backpack, and fumbled through a hundred pages until at last he found an empty one.

"And who might you be?"

"I am Belexus, son of Bellerian," the ranger replied.

Gatsby's eyes popped up from the page at the mention of the Ranger Lord, a name he obviously recognized.

"Rangers?" he chirped. "Rangers of Avalon." He made a warding sign and mumbled a silent prayer, drawing a laugh from all three. The rangers were spoken of often throughout Calva, even as far south as Rivertown, but they were a mysterious group of mighty warriors, and superstitious farmers were quick to fear that which they could not fully understand.

"That we be!" said Andovar, dropping from his horse into a low bow. "And I am Andovar."

"Nobility!" the flustered man replied. "And the lass?"

"Rhiannon of Avalon," she replied. "Pleased we are to look upon yer mighty bridges, and upon the likes of Gatsby of Rivertown."

Her kind words flustered the plump little man even more, and he fumbled with his helmet, trying to get the thing on properly. "If only we had known," he wailed. "We would have prepared a celebration. It is not often that we see the likes of rangers and children of Avalon"—the last words held an obvious hint of suspicion—"in Rivertown. My apologies that we were not properly prepared."

"None be needed," Belexus assured him. "We are simple travelers and no more, come to see the western fields."

"Not many would agree with your estimation of yourselves," said Gatsby. "But if you insist. Let me offer you a tour, then, as is the custom and the pleasure of the citizens of Rivertown."

"Accepted," Belexus replied, and they let Gatsby lead on. Many hours would pass before the hooves of their horses found the open road again, for their guide's knowledge of the history of the Four Bridges proved immense indeed. He recounted the Battle of the Four Bridges in vivid detail—which Rhiannon did not seem to enjoy, though she could not turn away—and told them of the seasonal caravans from Corning and the other western towns, on their way to market their crops and other goods in Pallendara, ten days' ride to the east.

"Rivertown's all a-bustle when the caravans come through!" Gatsby exclaimed. He pointed to a huge unplanted field just north and east of the settlement. "A thousand wagons put up there, the last rest on the road to Pallendara."

The four of them standing in the sunshine that fine summer morning could not know it, but when next the wagons rolled through, they would find no rest.

Thalasi walked out to the front of his charges, flanked by Burgle and his other commanders, to consider the new development. This army, like his own, was comprised entirely of talons, smaller and more lizardlike than their mountain kin, but unmistakably of the same seed. And unmistakably gathered for war.

Most rode swift lizards, saddled and armored, and all carried crude but undoubtedly wicked weapons.

Five large creatures, the chieftains of the group, walked out from the ranks to face the Black Warlock.

Thalasi then noted the distinct separations in this new army's ranks; they were separate tribes, and had not joined often, if ever. Yet they came to greet him.

He smiled at the extent of his power. His call had carried far, he believed, for he had not expected the talons of

Mysmal Swamp, out from the shadows of Kored-dul and his continued influence, to be so easily assembled.

How powerful he had become!

But then the largest of the opposing leaders spoke and destroyed the Black Warlock's delusions of grandeur.

"Man!" it grunted in open rage, less familiar with words than its mountain-bred counterparts.

Thalasi understood its confusion and threw his hood back to reveal the glittering black gemstone that marked his identity. Still, these creatures apparently did not recognize that evil mark, for a large group of them immediately took up the chant that had served as the liturgy of their entire existence.

"Men die!"

"Do you know who I am?" the Black Warlock roared, and the sheer strength of his dual voice drove the five leaders back a step. But mighty, too, was the ominous chant, growing stronger as more and more of the creatures joined in. Behind Thalasi, his army started in with their own growls and protests. The situation grew grave, the Black Warlock now knew. Mountain talons and swamp talons had never been the best of friends.

"I am Thalasi!" the Black Warrior declared in a magically enhanced roar, his booming voice silencing the cries on both sides. "The master is come!"

The five opposing leaders looked at each other for support. They knew the name, though their legends spoke of "Talagi," not Thalasi. But in any case, that is all the Black Warlock had ever been to these particular creatures: a legend.

"You are man," the largest spat. Unlike their mountain kin, whose solitary existence in the Kored-dul range kept them far from contact with other races, these talons were quite familiar with humans. They constantly skirmished with the westernmost villages of the Calvan kingdom, stealing supplies or simply for the sheer pleasure of killing men.

Taking heart from their leader's undeniable proclamation, the army of swamp talons took up their chant again and rattled their weapons against their shields. Thalasi's army responded in kind, and the whole of the field teetered on the brink of battle.

The Black Warlock realized that he had to act quickly but carefully. He hesitated in using his magical power. In addition to scaring off these potential new recruits, a show of wizardly force, reaching into that magical realm that he shared with his counterparts might ring out across the plains like a beacon to his mightiest enemies, the two wizards and the witch. Thalasi was out of the protection of the Kored-dul Mountains now, and could sense the presence of the other magic users. For his plans of conquest to have any chance of succeeding, he had to make certain that the others did not learn of his return before the western fields were overrun.

Still the Black Warlock had to act or lose everything here and now. The opposing forces were equal enough to guarantee that little would remain of either—too little to carry him to glory.

The five swamp talon leaders shouted commands to their forces; a line of lizard-riding cavalry formed to lead the charge. Thalasi's army roared to similar life, their loyalty to the Black Warlock, wrought of abject terror, standing strong against the specter of the swamp talon army.

Thalasi silenced them all in the blink of an eye.

"I am Thalasi!" he roared in his godlike voice. A pillar of fire engulfed the Black Warlock, blazing yet not consuming his mortal form. Stunned talons on both sides fell back from the spectacle.

Thalasi reached a hand out of the fiery pillar, and a line of flame sprouted from each finger to gobble up the five opposing leaders. They, too, found themselves enshrouded by pillars of blazing white fires, yet they, too, lived on.

Thalasi addressed the largest, the one who had so openly opposed him. "Who is your master?" he demanded.

"Men die!" the stubborn creature growled. The fire devoured it.

"Who is your master?" Thalasi demanded of the other four, witnesses to the folly of their peer's defiance.

They gave themselves over to him wholeheartedly.

Thalasi released them from the fiery pillars and swept his fisted hand in a wide arc. Again the flame leaped out from him, this time reaching out behind the swamp talon army, building a deadly barrier behind them to discourage those who had started to flee. When the herding was completed, Thalasi shut down the magic, hoping that he had not revealed himself to his distant enemies.

"I am Thalasi!" he said yet again. "Follow me, join in my war! Taste the blood of Calvans!"

The rivalry of swamp talons and mountain talons had spanned centuries, grown since the first defeat of Morgan Thalasi on the Four Bridges. But none dared resist the specter of power that loomed before them now, and none wanted to resist the promises of man-flesh.

Thalasi walked across the encampment that night, a new and more complete attack plan formulating in his mind. He had doubled the size of his army this day, and had more to work with now; no need to keep his entire force together as a single entity. He could send them out across the fields to the north and through the Baerendel Mountains in the south, engulfing the entire region in a ring of hungry talons and cutting off any chance of escape.

He looked out over the countless campfires and smiled.

In the morning he met with all of his commanders and laid his plans out to them. Five thousand riders, swamp talons on the swifter, sleeker lizards of the lowlands, would spur to the north, sweeping out the few villages that lined the borders of the desolated wasteland of Brogg, then cut back to the road between the town of Corning and the Four Bridges.

A second group, only a few hundred smaller in number and without the lizard mounts, would cross the Baerendels, not pausing for any battles in the slow terrain, but to get beyond Corning before the main attack force arrived at the city. These flanking riders would slaughter the first, unorganized groups that would surely flee, and then hinder any other retreating forces, giving the northern cavalry the time it would need to get into position.

The whole of the force started out that same day, around the northern rim of the great Mysmal Swamp and down the straight southeastern run that would take them unerringly to the city of Corning.

And through a dozen helpless communities in between.

Chapter 5

Bryan of Corning

MERIWINDLE EASED THE gleaming sword halfway out from its jeweled sheath, remembering the land, his homeland, where it had been forged. The weapon's slender design and graceful hilt marked it as elvish, and of course it was, and so was Meriwindle, though he had not walked the ways of Illuma Vale, that magical mountain valley called Lochsilinilume, in half again more than a dozen years. Not such a long time in the ageless lifespan of an elf.

Still, thoughts of mortality now led Meriwindle's gaze out through the window of his small cottage to the solitary marker in the backyard: the gravestone of his wife.

He would return this year, in the autumn, he vowed, to visit those many friends he had left behind in the elven city. Ever the wanderer, Meriwindle had been the first out of Illuma Vale after the Battle of Mountaingate, when Benador, the new King of Calva, had opened his doors to the elves. What sights the adventurous elf had seen in those days!

But none more beautiful than his sweet Deneen.

She had caught the nimble elf in her gaze, and held his wandering feet firmly in place. Love took them both by proverbial storm, overwhelming them and refuting their denials.

Both of them feared the inevitable joining—not all of the prejudices the two races, human and elf, held for each other had been washed away by the carnage of the battle. Such a mixed marriage would invite whispers, even open hostility. And as Meriwindle and Deneen were the first couple to actually attempt such a union, none knew what to expect from any offspring they might bring into the world.

But emotions greater than fear kept Meriwindle and Deneen together and brought them to marriage.

The whispers did come, but less than the couple had expected, and it did not take long for the northern elf to carve out a place for himself and his soon-to-be-growing family among the kindly farmer folk of Corning.

And then Bryan had come into their lives, had brought to the small cottage on the western edge of town more joy than the couple would ever have believed possible. That baby smile, Bryan's whole face lighting up at the sight of mother or father, surely washed away any of the fears either of them had ever felt. If any believed that the union of the two races was against some unspoken laws of nature, one sight of Bryan would surely change their stubborn minds.

But then Deneen had gone away, taken in the pain of her second birthing, with the tiny girl who would never see the world beyond the womb.

"Are you all right?" came a voice that shook Meriwindle from his memories. He turned to find Bryan, now a fine young lad of fifteen years, standing in the doorway to the little kitchen.

"Yes, yes." Meriwindle brushed away his son's concern, and sniffed away a final thought of Deneen and the unnamed baby girl.

Bryan took a moment to consider his father's position in front of the window, and the view such a seat gave to him, and he understood. "Thinking of Mother?"

"Always," Meriwindle replied, and Bryan did not doubt that his father spoke the truth. A sadness touched the corners of the elf's gray eyes, a sadness that would endure through the centuries.

"Are you still planning to go?" Meriwindle asked, needing to change the subject.

"Yes," Bryan replied, but he quickly added, "unless you would like me to stay. I can change my plans. The others would understand."

He would do that for me, Meriwindle thought, and without regret. What a fine young man his son was growing into! "No," he said to Bryan. "I gave you my word, and you certainly did more than your fair share of the spring planting. But all of the work is done now, and summer nears its high point. As we agreed, you may go."

Bryan's face lit up. He would indeed have remained beside his father without complaint if he believed that Meriwindle needed him. But he was thrilled to be going. He and his friends had been planning this expedition for the whole winter.

"But . . ." Meriwindle said, stealing a bit of the smile. The elf paused for a long, teasing moment. "You must take this." He spun and tossed sword and scabbard to Bryan.

Bryan's eyes popped wide at the gift. So long he had admired the crafted blade hanging over the mantel in the sitting room. His father had trained him in the use of a sword—all fathers taught their children in this land, so close to the wilds of the Baerendel Mountains—but never had this blade been used in those practice sessions. It was a family heirloom, a magical blade from the elven valley, the sword Meriwindle had wielded during the Battle of Mountaingate, when he had fought beside Arien Silverleaf himself.

Bryan slid the slender blade out to feel the perfection of

its balance and to witness the soft glow of blue light that held the magic of the fine edge.

"The Baerendels are a wild place," Meriwindle explained. "It is best to be prepared."

"I fear I might break it," said Bryan, so obviously over-whelmed, his hands trembling.

"I have trained you myself," Meriwindle reminded the lad. "And your talents exceed any I have ever seen of your age and experience. Few understand the dance of the blade as well as you, my son. And that sword is elven make, hard-ened by the magical fires of the Silver Mage and far stronger than its slender size would lead you to believe. No, you'll not break it, nor will you break the armor and shield."

"Armor and shield?" Bryan could hardly speak the words.

"Of course," answered his father. "If you wish to act the part of an elven warrior, then you must look the part of an elven warrior."

Bryan mocked a quick inspection of himself. "But I am not true elven," he said skeptically. "Half my blood is human."

"So it is," muttered Meriwindle, but the disappointment in his tone was feigned, and Bryan knew it. If Bryan was an example of the offspring of elf and human joined, then more would be wise to consider the formula. He was possessed of the best of both worlds, slender and handsome as an elven lad, yet with the hardened muscles and strength more com-mon to the humans.

"You decline the gifts, then?"

"Oh no!" Bryan cried, hoping his father would not rescind his offer. "Truly I will wear them as best I may. Truly—"

Meriwindle stopped him with an outstretched hand. "No need to plead your case, my son," he assured the boy. He walked over and put his hands on Bryan's hardened shoul-ders. "Never has a father been more proud of his child," he said, moisture rimming his large eyes. "You have all my faith. You will wear the outfit more finely than ever I could."

Bryan responded in the only way he possibly could. He gave his father a hug.

Meriwindle answered the excited knock on his door with a mixture of pride and sadness. He recognized the unique pattern to the knock—that of Bryan's best friend—and he knew what that meant.

"Good morning, sir," greeted the diminutive lad at the head of a column of twelve, every one of them outfitted for the road.

"Welcome, Lennard," Meriwindle replied. "Do come in." He called out to Bryan, who was getting ready in another room, while the adventuring party, boys and girls of Bryan's age, marched into the sitting room.

"Are you all gathered and prepared?" Meriwindle asked them.

"All except for Bryan and Jolsen Smithyson," replied Lennard. He drew out a narrow blade, a foil, for Meriwindle's inspection.

"Fine weapon," the elf commented politely, though he had reservations about the wisdom of carrying such a blade into the wilds of the mountains. In trained hands, the whipping speed of a foil could be a great advantage against an armed opponent, poking through defenses before one's enemy ever brought his heavier blade to bear. But the dangers the troupe would likely encounter up in the Baerendels, bears and boars and giant lizards, would better be fought with a heavier blade such as a broadsword or an ax.

No matter, Meriwindle reminded himself. All of the youngsters carried bows and knew how to use them, and Bryan would certainly be prepared to handle anything that came his way.

"Bah, you should have brought the spear," remarked Siana, one of the girls. "That little blade will snap the first time you strike something bigger than you."

Meriwindle tried to hide his agreeing smile. He liked Siana perhaps best of all, and was pleased that she was wise enough to see the logic.

"Never it will!" Lennard shouted back. "In and out." He accentuated his point by snapping off a quick back-and-forth stab with the foil. "Before anyone—or anything—even knows what hits him."

"A bear will know soon enough when it looks down and sees half the silly thing broken off and sticking out the front of its hide," Siana replied without missing a beat. The others, Meriwindle included, shared a laugh at Lennard's expense, but the diminutive lad just shrugged and joined in.

"Should have known better than to match wits with Siana," the defeated Lennard reminded himself under his breath.

"Let the day begin!" came Bryan's call as he entered the room. Meriwindle tried to hide his satisfaction as a general gasp rolled through the group, stealing their laughter. And when the elf turned and looked upon his son, he, too, caught his breath.

The elven sword hung easily on Bryan's hip, hidden by the jeweled scabbard, but from the rest of Bryan's outfit the others could well imagine the sword's incredible workmanship. Bryan wore the chain-mail armor common to the elven folk, yet rarely seen outside of Illuma Vale, a fine mesh of interlocking links so perfectly crafted—and so perfectly fitting Meriwindle's son—that it bent and formed to the contours of Bryan's body like a second skin. The shield was of a shining silvery metal, inlaid with the quarter-moon crescent of Lochsilinilume. A wide-brimmed hat cunningly inlaid with strips of protective metal, high but supple leather boots, and a thick forest-green cloak completed the trimmings over Bryan's normal clothing.

"Are you going somewhere?" Lennard remarked, an awe-inspired smile spreading over his face.

"Just to market," replied Bryan, and he swept off the hat, dipping into a gentleman's bow.

"The Baerendels are not a game," Meriwindle put in sternly. He didn't want to dispel the fun, but neither did he want the troupe moving out from the safety of the town with an improper attitude. "You will find danger up there, do not doubt. Many animals wander the course of those uncharted mountains, and talons have been spotted there on more than one occasion."

"We can take care of ourselves," one of the girls that Meriwindle did not recognize assured him.

Meriwindle regarded the group for a long moment. They were the children of farmers and craftsmen, more accustomed to wielding a hammer or hoe than a weapon. But they were a smart lot, and grown straight and tall under the brilliant sunshine of western Calvan fields.

They all waited now, breathless and anxious, for the judgment of the most famous warrior in all of Corning, perhaps in all of the lands west of the great River Ne'er Ending.

"So you can," Meriwindle told the girl sincerely. "I do not doubt that for a moment. If I did, I would not allow my son to accompany you." The group relaxed visibly, a smile finding its way onto every face. If Meriwindle, the elven warrior who had fought in the Battle of Mountaingate, had faith in them, they could not fail.

"To the road, then!" cried Lennard. "To Jolsen's and then to the Baerendels!"

They filed out of the small cottage with a heightened spring in their step. Bryan lagged behind for some final words with his father.

"Do you really believe that we can take care of ourselves?" he had to ask.

"If I did not, I would surely not let you go," Meriwindle replied.

"We will return within the span of two months," Bryan assured him. "In time for the autumn harvest."

"Of course," said Meriwindle. "And after that . . ." he began tentatively.

Bryan cocked his head, realizing from the suddenly grim tone that his father had something important to tell him.

"I had thought to do some traveling myself," Meriwindle explained. "After the crop is in and safely off to market."

"Pallendara?" Bryan asked excitedly. "We will go with the wagons?"

"A road longer," replied Meriwindle.

The hesitant look on Bryan's face showed that he suspected but did not dare to speak the true meaning of his father's words.

"I had thought to be returning to Lochsilinilume," Meriwindle said plainly. "I desire to walk again through the land of my birth."

Bryan fell back a step, not knowing how to take the news. "But, could I?" he stammered, hopeful and afraid all at once. He would like nothing better than to see the enchanted valley, but he wasn't certain how long his father planned to be gone. Certainly they could not leave the farm unattended. "Would I . . . I mean, there's the farm to consider. Would you want—"

"I most certainly would!" Meriwindle replied with a hearty laugh. He dropped an arm over Bryan's shoulder and shook him. "The farm will be here when—if—we choose to return. But you must come with me. What fun would an old elf find along the road if his most trusted companion was not riding by his side?

"Besides," he continued, giving Bryan another playful shake, "the armor and the blade belong to you now. It is your duty, in return for the gifts, to protect your aging father on his long journey."

Bryan straightened at his father's honest respect, smiling from ear to ear. "They'll be picking a leader before we get out of town," he said, looking back over his shoulder at the open door. "I believe that they meant to choose me when we planned this journey. Now, bearing the sword and armor, it is very likely that I will be selected."

"Then accept," Meriwindle was quick to reply. "But remember always that a true leader speaks less than he listens."

"Come on, Bryan!" came an anonymous call from outside.

"To Jolsen's!" the rest of the anxious troupe piped in on cue.

"I have to go."

Meriwindle gave his son a final hug, then put him out at arm's length to look him over. "You certainly do," he said. For some time Meriwindle had feared the inevitability of this moment, but now, looking at Bryan, the elf found his fears washed away on a tide of sincere admiration.

No more was Bryan his little boy.

Chapter 6

The Black Tide

THE STURDY FOLK of Windywillow Village, the western-most settlement in the Calvan kingdom, were not unused to skirmishes against talons. Tribes of the wretched things lived all about them, in the great forest that gave their village its name, and to the west, in the marshlands of Mysmal Swamp. Plundering talons constantly searched out the homes of the village seeking easy takings.

Mostly, though, what the talons got for their troubles was a general thinning of their raiding ranks. Windywillow Village had become a veritable fortress over the years, with tunnels connecting many of the cottages, and trenches and devious traps lining the perimeter of the entire settlement. And the people here, just over a hundred in number, including the few women, were practiced and fearless fighters.

But when the sun rose through a dreary gray mist on this particular summer morning, Windywillow Village saw the approach of doom.

"Big tribe," one of the villagers remarked over the shouts of alarm at the coming cloud of dust.

"Biggest I e'er seen," another man agreed. "Well, we'll give 'em a taste o' steel an' set 'em runnin' the right way."

But the villager was not so sure. Before long the very ground beneath his feet began to vibrate under the stamp of the approaching army, and the throaty song of the talons carried along on the morning breeze.

"Damn big tribe," he said, considering, for the first time in his fifteen years in Windywillow Village, the option of retreat. But he shook the notion away and clapped his great ax across his shoulder. "Just means there'll be more to hit," he grumbled, moving to his position in the first line of defense.

Less than fifteen minutes later, when the leading cavalry of Thalasi's army burst into view, rushing over the horizon, followed by rank after rank of filthy talon soldiers, the villager thought of retreat again.

But swamp lizards are swift beasts, nearly as swift as a horse even bearing a rider. For the villager, and for all of Windywillow Village, it was already far too late, and had been too late since the first sightings of the dust cloud.

The villagers fought savagely even when their hopes of victory and survival had flown.

Twenty thousand talon soldiers stamped the village flat. Within half an hour not a man, woman, or child remained alive.

From his comfortable chair in his litter, the Black Warlock surveyed the devastation. An evil smirk became a laugh of joy. How easy this all would be! Thalasi's only regret was that he could not take part in the slaughter, that he could not reveal himself. Not yet. The longer the Black Warlock was able to keep the news of his return from spreading throughout the land, the longer his talon army would be unhindered by the countering magics of his wizard adversaries.

He looked to the east, and his laughter continued. Another plume of smoke had already started its lazy climb into the late morning sky; another village had ceased to exist.

They would crush a third that same day, and two more the

next. Thalasi clenched his bony fist in victory. Every kill kept the ranks of his rabble army at peace with each other; every kill spurred the wicked talons on in their relentless hunt for more human blood. With the eager pace they had set this day, and with only minor towns standing in their path, they would make Corning within a week, and the Four Bridges just a day or two after that. Pallendara would never be able to muster its peace-softened troops and get them to the banks of the great river, the only defensible spot in all the southland, in time.

Then the King of Calva would learn of the true power behind the talon uprising. And then the King of Calva would know terror.

Later that night, Thalasi's tireless litter bearers brought him up to the main force of the army, encamped on the flattened ruins of the third sacked village. The Black Warlock's glee only heightened when he learned that a large contingent of the troops, not satisfied with their kills this day, had pressed on into the night to assault the fourth village in line.

Four thousand bloodthirsty talons thundered up to the wall of the small town of Doogenville, smashing the wood and stone with more fury than the defenders at the barricade could hope to repel. The townspeople threw boiling oil, sticks and stones, whatever they could find, at the enraged beasts, to no avail.

The brave men of Doogenville, outnumbered forty to one, knew that they could not hope to win against such a throng, but it was not for their own lives that they fought. To the east of the town, running down the road, went the elderly, the womenfolk, and the children, the only refugees of the first day of the Black Warlock's campaign, the only witnesses to the coming darkness.

And the only hope for the people of the remaining villages.

The mass of the talon army hit the fifth village the next day on schedule but found no resistance, and no sport, at all awaiting them.

The refugees of Doogenville had arrived first.

Enraged by the lack of prey, the talons broke ranks and rushed onward, determined to hunt down the fleeing humans. And when the reports filtering down the line finally reached the Black Warlock, he began to realize his first tactical error.

It would not matter, Thalasi reminded himself. His lizard-riding cavalry would cut off any chance for the people of the western fields to get across the river. Still, Thalasi was wise enough to understand that he had a problem: the rabble that made up his army was beginning to disintegrate, going off on their own without command or direction.

He quickly assembled his captains to repair the damage.

"You fail me!" he roared at them.

The captains grumbled under their breath, but none dared to openly oppose the Black Warlock.

"Regroup the troops!" Thalasi snapped at them. "Send swift riders to halt those in the front until the rest of the force can catch up to them.

"And spur the back ranks on more quickly. The humans are taking flight now; we must beat them to Corning."

"Walking soldiers tired," one of the swamp talon commanders complained. "Cannot run as swift as lizards."

"Then encourage them," Thalasi sneered. The big talon didn't understand. "Whip them! Drive them on! I assure you that the fate they face"—he clenched a fist in the air suddenly, and the complaining talon leader rose off the ground as though a powerful invisible hand had grabbed its throat—

"the fate you face will be infinitely more painful than the lash of a whip."

Thalasi had made his point.

The army regrouped in full just beyond the limits of the empty fifth village, the spot Thalasi had originally planned as their second encampment. But the Black Warlock had to make up for lost time now, and he would hear nothing of rest. Now riding his litter at the head of the army, he drove his forces through the night, overtaking many of the fleeing refugees. Still more of the retreating folk had made it to the sixth village in line, but those who stopped there for but short rest were caught and slaughtered. Like the five villages west of it, the sixth village was literally flattened.

The talons would find little rest until the western fields were secured. Risking the use of minor spells, Thalasi sent magical messages to his northern cavalry and southern mountain brigade, urging them on to greater speeds. The timetables had been turned up now. Thalasi wanted Corning in three days.

Belexus, Andovar, and Rhiannon tarried at Rivertown and the Four Bridges longer than they had planned, but it was a vacation, after all, and the trio refused to be rushed, however slow their progress thus far had been. They finally set out toward Corning on the morning after the sixth Calvan village, unknown to them, had been sacked. They trotted their rested steeds easily down the western road, in no hurry, and saw their destination just after dawn two days later.

A column of black smoke rose in the west, and the large town, second only to Pallendara in the whole of Aielle, seemed all a-bustle. Guards nervously stalked the high wall that surrounded the town, always pointing back to the west, while inside rose cries of distress and calls of alarm.

Recognizing the uncharacteristic tumult—though none of

them had actually seen Corning before—the three northerners galloped down the last expanse of field and up to the city's eastern gate.

"Halt and be known!" a guard demanded, and a dozen bows pointed down from the high wall at the trio.

"I am Belexus of Avalon," the ranger called out. "Come to see yer fair city on holiday. But me eyes be tellin' me that I might find no leisure here this day."

The guard turned away to confer with another, apparently not recognizing the name. The second had a better understanding of the world beyond Corning and the western fields.

"Avalon?" he called down to Belexus. "Rangers?"

"Ayuh," Andovar replied. "That we be. And methinks ye might be using our help."

"If you are as fine with your blades as your reputation speaks," the second guard said, "then indeed we might." The gates swung open and the three were led in.

The sights within Corning were far from what they had anticipated when they began their journey from Avalon. Peace had reigned in this town for fifty or more years, and even way back then, the only battles had been hit-and-run attacks by groups of rogue talons. With the growth of population since the rightful king had regained the throne, and the founding of many more outlying communities to the north and the west, Corning had become too sheltered for rogue bands of talons to even attempt an attack.

Now, though, it appeared that the peace was no more. Lines of pitiful refugees streamed in through the western gate carrying no more possessions than the clothes on their backs. And beyond that gate, out on the western plain, pillars of black smoke belched into the blue sky, and cries of terror cut above the general rumbling of wagons and horses.

Belexus and Andovar rushed across to the western gate,

while Rhiannon dropped from her mount to aid a child running about frantically in search of his mother.

"Talons." Andovar spoke the obvious.

"It is indeed," came a reply from the side. The rangers turned to see a plump man, very official-looking, rushing toward them, an elf at his side.

"Our greetings, rangers," the plump man said. "You have arrived not a moment too soon! I am Tuloos, Mayor of Corning, and this is—"

"Meriwindle," Belexus said.

"Well met, son of Bellerian," replied the elf. "And to you, Andovar."

"And to yerself," said Andovar. "Hoping, we were, to be finding the likes o' yerself on our holiday in yer town."

Meriwindle cast an ominous glance down the western road. "Not such a holiday by what my eyes are telling me."

"Many talons?" asked Andovar.

"A great force!" answered the mayor. "Perhaps as many as four thousand by the estimate of those fleeing Doogenville."

Belexus and Andovar exchanged looks of concern. Talons had never been known to organize into such large bands against the civilized lands, other than the one time Thalasi had led them in the Battle of the Four Bridges.

"But they've had their fun," Tuloos went on, tucking his thumbs under his belt. "They will find a garrison awaiting them at Caer Minerva, and beyond that, though I hardly believe it to be necessary, we will muster the gathered strength of all the western fields right here within Corning's high wall."

"And now we have two rangers to help us organize the defense," Meriwindle added. "Glad I am to have the likes of Belexus and Andovar standing beside me in defense of my home."

"Yer words are kind," said Belexus. "But me hopes are that we'll need not be raising those blades."

"We should out for Caer Minerva," Andovar suggested, looking forlornly down to the west at the continuing stream of pitiful refugees.

Rhiannon caught up to them then, walking through the huddled and confused crowd.

"By me eyes," she declared. "Ne'er have I seen such sufferin'."

"And ye'll find more when we see the wounded," Belexus assured her. He turned to Meriwindle and the mayor, their eyes wide at the sight of Rhiannon, to introduce the young woman. But before he could even begin, Rhiannon stepped out of and to the side of the western gate. Belexus shrugged an apology and led the others out after her.

Rhiannon moved to the empty grass beyond the confusion of the road. She paused for a long moment, looking to the west, then fell to the ground, putting her ear to the grass.

"We have no time—" the mayor began.

Belexus cut him off, believing that Rhiannon's actions, however confusing they might appear, were somehow important.

"But talons approach!" the mayor demanded, and he turned back to the gates. "Four thousand, perhaps."

"More than that," Rhiannon assured him, lifting her head from the grass.

"What?" barked Tuloos. "How could you know?" Rhiannon shrugged, not really understanding the answer. Something had compelled her to this spot, as though the ground itself had called out to her. And when she put her ear close to hear its words, it had told her the truth of the size of the approaching army.

"You could not know, of course," the mayor went on.

"Come, Meriwindle," he said, a bit perturbed. "We have many preparations—"

"Five times that number," Rhiannon said, more to Belexus and Andovar than to the mayor. "And from a long wood beyond the mountains, more're coming to join the force."

"That would be Windy Willows," Meriwindle put in, amazed and not yet knowing whether to believe the young woman or not. He turned to Belexus. "But how could she—"

"She could not!" the mayor insisted.

"Methinks she could," Andovar replied. "How, Rhiannon?" he asked softly. "How do ye be knowing these things?"

Rhiannon shrugged again and looked back at the spot on the field, hardly believing the answer herself.

" 'Tis the grass that told me," she said honestly.

"We have no time for such foolish words," the mayor spouted.

Meriwindle looked helplessly to the rangers. "It does seem incredible."

"Do ye know who she is?" Andovar asked the elf.

Meriwindle shook his head.

"Have ye heard, then, of fair Brielle?" Andovar went on.

Meriwindle's eyes popped open wide. He had lived most of his long life in Illuma Vale, and of course he knew of Brielle of Avalon. "The Emerald Witch," he breathed. "Rhiannon is the daughter of the Emerald Witch?"

"That she is," said Andovar. "And me heart's for heeding to her claims."

"As is mine," Belexus added. "Twenty thousand. Can Corning hold back such a number?"

Mayor Tuloos had also heard of the Emerald Witch, but in Corning, Brielle was only a fireside tale and hardly taken seriously. "What nonsense is this?" he demanded. "The count

is four thousand, no matter what the grass has to say to her."
Rhiannon dipped her head at the bite of his sarcasm, but
Meriwindle rushed to her defense.

"Believe the woman," he told the mayor.

"Meriwindle!" Tuloos cried. "Certainly you have more
sense—"

"Believe her," Meriwindle said grimly. "If the grass
talked to Rhiannon, then be assured that it spoke truthfully."

As if in confirmation, a new pillar of smoke rose up into
the western sky only a few miles down the road.

Caer Minerva was burning.

Thoroughly flustered, Tuloos slumped down from his
haughty stance. "Twenty thousand?" he asked Rhiannon,
his sarcasm gone. But Rhiannon didn't hear him; she had
dropped back to a second call from the grass.

"A lot of talons," the mayor conceded. "But we've all the
men of the western fields at our disposal and our walls are
sturdy enough. I suppose—"

"No!" Rhiannon cried, springing to her feet, her eyes riv-
eted on the growing smoke cloud over Caer Minerva. "Do
not fight with them!" she pleaded, and when she turned back
to the four men, they saw that her face was ashen. "Run
away. Run away as swift as ye may!"

"What is it?" Belexus asked before Meriwindle and
Andovar could get the words out of their mouths.

"I do no' know," Rhiannon answered with a shudder. "But
we cannot hope to stop them. A corruption leads them—
never have I felt such strength!"

Belexus and Andovar exchanged grim looks, then turned
to Meriwindle, who shared their knowing concern.

"He is back," the elf said with as much calmness as he
could muster. Meriwindle had witnessed the evil of Morgan
Thalasi twenty years before, at the Battle of Mountaingate.

Even now the memory, the terror of the appearance of the Black Warlock, remained vivid in his mind.

Mayor Tuloos, never having witnessed the scourge of the Black Warlock, did not understand, nor did Rhiannon, who knew only that something terribly evil was leading the talon army. But over the years, Tuloos had come to trust Meriwindle as one of his closest advisers, and he could not deny the look of sheer horror on the elf's fair face.

"If they are in Caer Minerva, how long do we have?" Belexus asked grimly.

Mayor Tuloos fidgeted for a moment, trying to remember the obvious answer. "Five hours, perhaps," he said. "If the city is fully beaten." He looked again at Meriwindle for an answer to his growing problem.

"We must run," the elf replied to the mayor's helpless expression.

Tuloos turned back to the rangers. "I am hesitant to leave my home," he explained. "Corning is the pride of the western fields. She was built and designed for the very purpose of fending off such a raid."

"Not such a raid," Belexus replied. "If the Black Warlock has indeed risen again, yer height o' yer walls'll not be stopping him."

Tuloos looked from person to person, rubbing his face, trying vainly to find an answer to the dilemma. "Help me, then," he begged the others. "Get the weak off and running, as swift as they may. But I will remain in Corning with a garrison. More will come down the western road, fleeing the destruction of Caer Minerva. I will not leave them stranded and alone in the fields."

"And know in yer heart that we will stand beside ye," Andovar assured the man.

* * *

Rhiannon moved up and down the eastern road, keeping the refugees in organized retreat and whispering words of encouragement to man and horse alike.

Andovar watched her from the town gate, his love for her doubling.

"She does well," Belexus noted, moving up to join his friend.

"No fear in her," Andovar replied. "And her words're keeping the whole in stride."

"Quite a lass," said Belexus.

Andovar put a steely gaze on him. "Do ye fancy her, then?"

Andovar hid his feelings well, but Belexus understood the tinge of jealousy that edged his words. "No, me friend," he laughed, "not as ye do."

Andovar turned back to the road, embarrassed but unable to refute Belexus' observation.

" 'Tis her mother that holds me heart," Belexus admitted, and he clapped his friend on the shoulder. Their chatting was interrupted a moment later, though, when Rhiannon suddenly bolted with her horse away from the line of fleeing citizens, riding hard to the north. She dropped from her mount and to the ground.

"Trouble," Belexus realized, and he and Andovar jumped down from the wall to their horses and rode out after the woman.

"What do ye hear?" Andovar cried when he caught up to her. The woman was standing now, beside her horse, looking toward the empty northland.

Rhiannon turned to her friends, then led their gaze down the eastern road. "They'll not make the river," she explained gravely. "Another force rides to the north. Swift they run, getting ahead o' the fleein' folk."

"They'll cut the way," Andovar agreed, again not doubting the woman.

"How many?" Belexus asked.

"As many as the mayor thought to be the whole o' the force," Rhiannon answered grimly.

Belexus called upon all of his many years of training then, searching for some solution to the devious trap they had stepped into. They could not hope to defeat the approaching army, especially if the Black Warlock was indeed at its head, yet they could not spare enough fighters to destroy the force circling around from the north.

"Ye must ride!" he said to Andovar. "Swift as only Andovar can ride!"

Andovar understood, but was not thrilled at leaving Belexus, or Rhiannon, behind.

"To the bridges and Rivertown," Belexus went on. "Send the cry to every town from here to Pallendara!"

"I'm not for leaving," Andovar replied. "There's a fight coming, ye know that. Me sword'll help."

"If ye fail on yer ride, then yer sword and all other swords'll be to no avail," Belexus told him. "And all the folk running from Corning this day are suren to be killed. The kingdom must be roused! Only the might of Pallendara can turn the darkness aside."

Andovar could not deny the truth of the words. He rushed back to his horse, then turned to regard Rhiannon. "I'm not for leaving ye, me fairest lady," he said. "Ride beside me."

"Ye've yer duty," Rhiannon replied, moving over to him. "And I've me own. They'll be needing me eyes."

Andovar kissed her then, knowing that if he never saw her again, he would die a broken man. But he was a Ranger of Avalon, a disciplined warrior, and his duty was clear. He nodded his accord at Belexus and sprang into his saddle.

Rhiannon whispered into the horse's ear and chanted some arcane verses, stroking the steed's muscular flanks.

"What're ye doing?" Belexus asked her.

She shrugged in reply. "I do no' rightly know," she answered honestly. "But me thinkin's that it might help."

True were her suspicions, for when Andovar kicked his mount to action a moment later, it sped off swifter than any living horse could possibly run.

Chapter 7

Flight

THEY THUNDERED OUT of Corning's eastern gate, a thousand grim-faced riders—nearly half the town's garrison—with the ranger Belexus at their lead.

"They must keep the road clear if the fleeing people are to have any chance of getting across the river," Meriwindle remarked to Mayor Tuloos as they watched the cavalry roll away.

"They will," Tuloos growled. "We must believe in that." He turned and led Meriwindle back across the town. They had their own business to attend.

Belexus spotted the lone rider, coming hard from the south, speeding like the wind, on a course to intercept his group. He gave over the lead position to the next in line and veered his mount away.

"Yer place is not here," he said to the lone rider when she reined in beside him.

"But it is," Rhiannon answered. "Those on the road know well enough the path o' their flight; they'll not be needing me."

Belexus studied the young woman. She carried no weapon, and none would have rested comfortably in her soft hands.

81

But there was something about Rhiannon, some growing power, that the ranger had a feeling might prove critical to the events of this day.

"How can ye help?" he asked.

"I'm no' for knowing,"' Rhiannon answered honestly. For all of the powers she had exhibited that day, the witch's daughter understood them no better than the amazed witnesses. "But if ye fail in yer mission," Rhiannon went on, "those fleeing'll not make the river, whether I'm guidin' them or not. Me place is here."

Belexus' first instinct was to send her back; he had promised his father he would watch out for the witch's daughter. But looking at Rhiannon now, sitting so resolute and grim on her black and white horse, Belexus sensed that she did not need his protection. Indeed, it seemed that her presence would bolster his chances against the talon force.

"Come then, and be quick," he said to her. She nudged her mount up beside his and bent low to whisper her magical encouragement into his horse's ear. Then they were off, gaining on their comrades with each powerful stride.

A tear rimmed Mayor Tuloos' eye as he looked back over his city, deserted except for the remaining garrison and the line of refugees, being guided from the west gate out through the east. But the stout mayor shook the moment of weakness away and turned back to his post on the western gate, reassuring each poor refugee in turn.

"The day will be won!" he told one man. "And fear not, the King of Calva will lend you aid to rebuild your home!" The man nodded and managed a weak smile.

They are all so tired, Tuloos noted. How can they possibly run all the way to the river? He patted the man on the back, hurrying him along.

"Another group!" the lookout called. "And talons at their backs."

Tuloos rushed up to the parapets to stand beside Meriwindle. A few hundred yards down the road came a band of stragglers, mostly women and children, running for their lives. Behind them, and gaining quickly, charged a band of bloodthirsty talons, weapons clanging.

The few able men among the refugees turned to slow the monsters, brandishing pitchforks, wood axes, even clubs.

"They'll not make it," Meriwindle said with a grimace. Even as he spoke, the talons trampled down the meager resistance and bore down on the women and children.

"Mayor!" Meriwindle pleaded, grabbing the man by the collar.

No provisions had been made to split the garrison, and Tuloos had only thirteen hundred men remaining to guard his town. He could ill afford to lose any on the road outside the gates. But, like Meriwindle beside him, the kindly mayor could not ignore the terrified screams.

"Go to them!" he cried.

"To the road!" Meriwindle screamed, leaping down from his perch and rushing to his readied horse. He burst through the gate, sweeping up dozens of volunteers, most riding but others simply running. The noble elf did not look to see who was following; he cared not if he found himself facing the talons alone. In that moment of rage, all that mattered to Meriwindle was halting the talon charge.

But the elf was not alone—far from it—and the soldiers who rode with him were spurred by anger equally great, and they matched the frantic pace. As one they breathed a sigh of relief when they passed the refugees and put themselves between the helpless people and the talons.

One giant of a man, wielding a huge mallet and astride a

monstrous horse, rushed past Meriwindle, slowing the lead talons by the mere spectacle of his appearance.

"Jolsen!" Meriwindle called after the smith, but there was no panic in the elf's voice. Jolsen had lost his wife and all of his family except for the boy, Jolsen, in a talon raid a dozen years before. The huge man had moved to Corning shortly thereafter, and had promised that one day he would avenge those murders.

Though they understood that the main force of Thalasi's army was far behind them, the talons had known only easy victories these last few days and came in with all confidence.

A single sweep of the huge smith's mallet felled two of them, and Jolsen, his sinewy muscles bulging, reversed the stroke easily, back and forth, chopping and swatting.

Meriwindle used the confusion to his best advantage. "Charge on!" he cheered his riders, and the sheer weight of their mounted rush crushed through the first ranks of the enemy. Swords rang out above the screams, and many a soldier, talon and human, died in the first seconds of battle.

And an exhausted Jolsen, smiling in the knowledge that he had indeed avenged the deaths of his kin, went down under a flurry of talon blows. Even as the darkness of death closed over his eyes, the great smith managed one final swing, blasting yet another talon from life.

From the wall, Tuloos watched helplessly.

"There!" Rhiannon cried out.

Belexus followed her pointing finger to the north, but nothing was yet visible to the eyes of the ranger on the open plain. He trusted Rhiannon's instincts, though, and he swerved the cavalry line to follow Rhiannon's lead. Sure enough, only a minute later the talon cavalry came into view, swinging down around to the south for a straight rush at the road.

Belexus knew at once that he was outnumbered by at least five to one, but at that moment, with the memory of the pitiful line of desolate people making their way to the river so vivid in his mind, the odds didn't seem to matter. The ranger understood his objective. He wouldn't engage the talons fully; he couldn't risk complete defeat. He would meet their lead riders from the side, turn them back to the east, and force them to parallel the road all the way to the river.

Where, Belexus could only hope, reinforcements from the eastern towns would be waiting.

Rhiannon, unarmed, broke off to the side and let the soldiers pass her by. She slowed her horse and tried to tune her senses in to the land around her, hoping that the earth would once again speak to her and give her the power to aid in the cause.

The forces came together in a brutal rush, the heavier horses gaining initial advantage over the smaller swamp lizards. Belexus drove hard into the talon ranks, every sweep of his mighty sword dropping a talon to the ground.

But the advantage was soon gone, for the sheer numbers of the enemy slowed the charge to a near standstill. "East!" Belexus cried, knowing that his brigade could not hope to survive a pitched battle, and he started them on their wild run, talons pacing right beside them and the battle moving on in full flight.

Rhiannon easily kept close to the thrashing throng, trailing the fighters by barely a hundred yards. The ranger's plan seemed to be working, she noted hopefully. The talon line, intent on the ranger's troops, followed the flow to the east. And in the continuing battle, where riders of both groups were more intent on merely staying in their saddles than inflicting blows on the enemy, few were slain. Belexus, so skilled with horse and sword, got his share of talons, though, and more than once Rhiannon grimaced as she watched a soldier go down, only to be swallowed up by a sea of the vile monsters.

But then the trailing edge of the talon line, in a rare display of insight, apparently began to understand the ploy. Remembering the commands of their warlock leader—that the road was their primary goal—more than half the force cut back behind the riders, once again aiming for the south.

Only Rhiannon stood to stop them.

Meriwindle could not guess how much of the blood that covered his body was his own. He was still in the saddle, one of the few who could make that claim. But three talons had fallen for every soldier, and, more importantly, the charge had been halted, and the elf looked back now at Corning to see the last of the refugees being ushered through the gates.

But any smile that might have crossed Meriwindle's face was short-lived, for in the other direction, down the western road, now came the main force of Thalasi's army.

"To the town!" Meriwindle cried, and those soldiers who could manage to break away turned back for home. Meriwindle scooped up two of the men, their horses torn apart from under them, and carried them along on the retreat.

"By the Colonnae," Mayor Tuloos muttered from his spot on the wall, for beyond the fighting, all the western field had gone dark, a writhing mass of wretched talons. The boom of their drums and their battle cry rumbled out ominously, drowning all other sounds.

"Men die!"

Tuloos watched a spur of the talon force break to the north, another to the south, and knew at once that his town would be surrounded in a matter of minutes. He could break out now with his garrison, back through the eastern gate and down the road. But then the refugees would have no chance of survival, and the talon army would continue its run unhindered after the remainder of the helpless fleeing people.

"Secure the gates!" Tuloos roared with all the strength he could muster. "To arms!"

A moment later Meriwindle was back by his side. As soon as the elf looked around at the spurs of the talon force, he understood the wisdom of the mayor's decision to close the town. A continuing flow out the eastern gate would only fall easy prey to the circling talons. Still, looking at the overwhelming mass of the Black Warlock's force, Meriwindle had to wonder what hope the walls offered.

Tuloos shared those feelings, the elf knew. The mayor leaned heavily on the wall, watching the events unfolding around him. "We will stop them," he said to Meriwindle.

"We must," the elf replied.

"And reinforcements will arrive!" the mayor went on, mustering courage despite his doubts to the truth of his words. "Andovar will return with the army of Pallendara at his back!"

"Indeed!" said Meriwindle, and his face brightened. He clapped the mayor on the shoulder and turned back to the field, taking care to keep his true feelings of their doom from showing on his delicate elven features.

The talon army rolled on, not even slowing at the sight of Corning's high walls.

"Arm every man, woman, and child," Tuloos instructed.

Meriwindle understood; talons took no prisoners.

She never even thought of fleeing. Her duty was to the helpless souls on the road to the south, and to the valiant ranger and his troops battling the odds so bravely.

And as the talon cavalry approached, Rhiannon felt again that strange sense of power flowing up from the earth itself and gathering within her. "Go back!" she demanded in a voice so suddenly powerful that it caught the attention of

Belexus, far off and moving away. He managed to look back over his shoulder to see the young woman standing so resolute against the flowing tide.

Belexus didn't care that his plan had apparently failed; he didn't care for anything beyond the figure of Rhiannon and the charge of talon cavalry that would gobble her up long before he could get to her side.

But as Belexus would now learn, and as the daughter of the witch herself would now learn, Rhiannon was far from helpless.

Power surged through her body and flowed down into her mount. She tugged on the beast's mane, rearing it up. And when it slammed its hooves back to the ground, there came a flash as bright as a bolt of lightning and an explosion that rocked the plain for miles around. In front of the lead talons the earth split wide, gobbling up those whose beasts could not stop their rush. The rest of the talon force swung abruptly to the east to join their kin, fleeing the power bared before them.

But Rhiannon spurred her steed to the east and chased after them. Each stride of the enchanted horse continued the thunderous rumbling, and the crack in the earth, too, took up the pursuit.

Hope came back to the ranger in the form of awe and even fear. Most vividly of all, Belexus saw Rhiannon's determined ride. She kept just behind the lead of the talon line, using the split in the ground to prevent the monsters from turning south.

Then Belexus realized that Rhiannon meant to carry the split all the way past his force.

"To the south!" he cried to his men, cleaving another talon down the middle. He charged back and forth, herding the soldiers out of the approaching gully.

Talons, also recognizing the danger, pursued the Corning force, carrying the fight to the other side of the coming divide.

But then, suddenly, the battle came to a standstill, a hacking mob of confusion. Rhiannon kept her charge straight in, knowing that if she veered to the south, she would take her chasm with her and strand Belexus and the others in the midst of the entire talon force.

Belexus saw her intent and tried to get beside her, but the press was too great, and the ranger could only watch in horror as a group of talons formed a line in her path to intercept.

"Fly!" Rhiannon whispered to her horse, and the horse leaped high into the air, soared higher than a horse could possibly leap, clearing the stunned talons beyond even the reach of their weapons.

And the ensuing thunder when the black and white steed's hooves crashed back down to the ground rolled the plain like waves in an ocean. Lizard and horse, talon and human, tumbled to the ground, stunned and blinded by an upheaval of dust and clumps of earth.

But Rhiannon, her face streaked with sweat and grime, her black mane matted to her neck and shoulders, emerged from that cloud, charging along her route. And to Belexus, watching her courageous ride, she seemed no less beautiful.

They crashed into the walls, clawing and hacking with wild abandon, ignoring the hail of arrows or the burning death of boiling oil. Possessed with the fury of Morgan Thalasi, the talons knew no fear.

Meriwindle charged about the parapets, spurring his soldiers on. And when a few of the wretched talons managed to gain a foothold over a wall, they inevitably found the noble elf in their faces, slashing away with his sword.

And so it continued for half an hour, the talons blindly

fighting to appease their master and their own hunger for man-flesh. And the proud people of Corning fighting back for their lives, and for the lives of those who had fled for the river.

Tuloos knocked one talon from the wall, only to find two others taking its place. The mayor stumbled backward and fell, and the hulking forms towered over him. He cried out, thinking that the moment of his death was upon him.

But then a sword flicked above him, once and then again, and both talons dropped. Meriwindle pulled Tuloos back to his feet.

The elf was a garish sight indeed, and Tuloos could not understand how Meriwindle was even standing with his life-blood flowing from so many grievous wounds.

"We are holding them!" Meriwindle cried, and all fear flew from Tuloos at the sheer determination in Meriwindle's voice. Here was the elf who had stood beside Arien Silverleaf on the field of Mountaingate, the warrior who had survived the centuries in the jagged shadows of the Great Crystal Mountains.

Tuloos looked around at the carnage that was Corning, the rubble and the dead and dying. But more so, the mayor let his gaze drift out over the eastern gate, down the road to the river.

The empty road to the river.

He knew that the sacrifices made this day in Corning had bought those helpless, fleeing Calvans some precious time. If only he and his men could hold out a little longer.

If only . . .

The talon army calmed suddenly and backed away from the walls, those before the western gate parting wide to reveal a gaunt and robed figure.

"Angfagdul," Meriwindle muttered grimly, using the enchantish name for the Black Warlock. He had seen the likes of Morgan Thalasi before.

"Surrender your town!" the Black Warlock demanded in a voice dripping with a power not of this earth. "Surrender now and I will let you live!"

Mayor Tuloos understood that doom had come, knew that all hope was gone. But he knew, too, the lie that he now faced. The Black Warlock would keep no prisoners other than slaves to draw his carts until they dropped dead in their tracks from hunger and exhaustion. All around him, his weary men leaned on their weapons, their will for this fight fading with the last remnants of hope. To a man, they looked to Tuloos for guidance.

"I'll not make it easy for him," the mayor whispered to Meriwindle.

"Send him a message," Meriwindle replied, and he handed Tuloos a bow.

Smiling, the mayor notched an arrow and took a bead on the Black Warlock. Realizing that he could not hope to take out an enemy so powerful with such a simple attack, he veered his aim away from Thalasi and let the arrow fly. It thudded into the chest of the talon nearest Thalasi, and the beast dropped dead to the ground.

From every wall, from the courtyard below, the remaining people of Corning sent a final cheer into the air.

Thalasi trembled in rage. He hadn't wanted to use his power—not yet. But such arrogance could not go unpunished, and his army could not afford to get bogged down at the gates of this city. He threw his arms up into the air and fell into that magical plane, gathering, demanding power.

Then Thalasi hurled his collected force at the battered town.

The western gates exploded into a million burning splinters. Now it was the talons' turn to hoot and cheer, as they poured through the wide breach.

Meriwindle leaped down from his perch to meet them head-on.

Thus did Meriwindle die.

And thus did the town of Corning die.

In the frenzy of a few moments, the remaining talons on the south side of Rhiannon's gorge were cut down, and Belexus led the charge in pursuit of the young woman. She had slowed, pacing herself to keep even with the weary lizard-riding talons across the chasm.

Still, when Belexus caught up to her, he was alarmed to look upon her pale and drained face, for her magical efforts had indeed exacted a heavy toll.

"Go," Rhiannon told him. "I will keep this group from the road."

Across the splitting earth, only two dozen yards away, more than a thousand talons rushed along, spitting curses at the wicked sorceress that kept them from their prey and from their goal in the south.

"Ye mean to cut the earth all the way to the river?" Belexus called to Rhiannon. "A day o' riding and more that'll be."

Rhiannon knew the grim truth of his words. Already she felt her power beginning to wane. "Follow me, then!" she cried, formulating a desperate plan. "All of ye!" The cavalry fell in stride behind Belexus and Rhiannon as she picked up the pace again, easily outdistancing the talons across the way. And when she had gained enough ground ahead of the leaders of the invading army, she cut sharply to the north, turning the break of the chasm with her.

The change in direction, the breaking of momentum, sapped the last of the young woman's strength. Holding on as tightly as she could, she spurred her mount back around to the west, encircling the terrified talons.

Belexus and the others understood her motives. Though few of the talons were surprised enough to tumble into the new angle of the gorge, the whole of their force had been suddenly stopped and thrown into disarray. Belexus charged ahead of Rhiannon, leading his soldiers head-on into the confused ranks.

Exhausted beyond its mortal limits, the black and white mare stumbled and went down. Rhiannon, barely able to remain conscious, crawled over to the poor beast and wept, caught in a tumult of confusion and revulsion. What awful power had she aroused? It had fully possessed her in a fury that she could not begin to comprehend, much less control. Was it her destiny, then, to rain destruction upon the earth, and upon the beasts of the earth, innocent and evil alike? She stroked the trembling flanks of the horse and spoke softly into its ear as it passed from life.

And then Rhiannon, fainting from exhaustion, knew no more.

Belexus did not miss the fall of his friend, and the sight of it spurred him on to new heights of rage, stole the weariness from his muscular arms. He tore into the talon ranks, hacking down two creatures at a time.

And then a new sight came over the battlefield, a sight that inflicted equal heights of rage in Belexus' soldiers. Rising over the western plain came yet another pillar of black smoke.

Corning was burning.

They drove the talons into the gorge and trampled those who could not get out of their path. The hunter became the hunted as the talon forces were split in half, and many of the creatures broke from the back ranks to flee into the empty northland.

For a full hour they fought, men and talons with nothing

left to lose. Again and again Belexus chopped down a foe, only to find another ready to take its place. But whenever weariness began to slow the ranger's fell blade, he only had to look back beyond the edge of the fighting to the still forms of Rhiannon and her horse.

And for the men of Corning there remained the constant reminder of the billowing cloud on the western horizon. One soldier went down under the pull of three talons, and when he fell, five of the beasts leaped upon him for the kill. But it was the soldier that finally climbed out of that tangle, mortally wounded a dozen times but refusing to stop fighting, refusing to lie down and die, until the talon force had been beaten back.

How many talons died and how many managed to flee to the north in that savage battle would never be tallied, but of Belexus' force of one thousand, only two hundred remained, and the ranger was convinced that five talons had died for every man.

Chapter 8

Baerendel Nightmare

"CORNING IS BURNING!" Lennard cried.

Bryan and the others rushed over the final rise on the mountain spur, excited but not too concerned. A hearth out of control, perhaps, and nothing that the townsfolk couldn't handle.

But as the group, one by one, crested the lip of the stone, their excitement washed away on a wave of dread, for the rising column was too great for any hearth fire.

Bryan scanned the plain to the east of the town, searching for some explanation. Another cloud, this one of dust, rose in the north, as if a long line of horses, wagons, and boots stirred the dirt of a road.

The awful truth became clear to all of them then, and Bryan spoke the word aloud. "War."

"We must get home!" Lennard cried when he had found his breath, but then another call rang out.

"Talons!" shouted Tinothy, the one member of the band who had not yet seen the smoke from Corning. "Talons in the mountains." The boy, at fourteen years the youngest of the band, caught up to them, eyes widening as he beheld the disaster of his homeland.

95

"Where?" Bryan pressed him.

The cloud of smoke held Tinothy entranced.

Bryan pulled him roughly aside. "Where?" he demanded again. "You have to tell me where."

Tinothy pointed absently around the side of the mountain toward a wide valley. "Down there and moving south," he explained, his voice a monotone, purely expressionless.

"How many?"

"Dozens. Hundreds, maybe."

Bryan looked again at the crawling line of fleeing people along the road, beginning to understand.

"Forget the talons," said Lennard. "We have to get home." Several others echoed the young man's sentiments, but Bryan realized a different need.

"No," he said quietly. "There is nothing we can do for Corning. We know not if the town is still standing, and we are two full days' march away."

"Then what are we to do?" demanded Siana, one of the three girls in the band. "We cannot just sit here and watch as our people are destroyed."

Bryan had no intention of doing anything of the kind. "Talons in the mountains," he said grimly. "Do you understand their purpose?"

"They shan't catch us!" Siana retorted, as if the notion that any talons could find them in this wild land of mountains and valleys was purely absurd.

"Moving south," Bryan growled at her, at all of them. "Toward Doerning's Walk." He pointed down to the road, the others began to catch on. Doerning's Walk was the swiftest route out of the northeastern tip of the Baerendels, an intercepting course for the main road of the western fields.

"Too many for us," Siana remarked, the anger gone from her voice now.

"You mean to stop them?" Lennard balked.

"Not stop them," Bryan replied. "We are but a few." The grim light in his eyes when he looked around at his friends inspired their courage and determination. "But we can slow them down."

"What do you plan?" asked Siana.

"We can get to Doerning's Walk before them," Bryan replied. "There are narrow trails where a few people and a few cunningly placed traps can bottle up a larger force for a long time."

"That is our duty," Jolsen Smithyson piped in. He looked back to the smoke cloud, knowing that if talons had indeed attacked the city, his father would have stood resolutely against them. He could not know, however, that his father was already dead.

"You are best with the bow," Bryan said to Lennard. "Go with Tinothy and flank this talon band. A few well-placed arrows should turn them from their course, or at the least slow them. You must buy us some time so we can prepare the party near Doerning's Walk."

Andovar thundered past the leading edge of the refugee line, his cries and determination lending them some hope. "Ride!" they cheered after him, guessing that he was the herald who would alert all of Calva. "The King will come!" others shouted, punching determined fists into the sky, knowing that to be their only hope.

When the sky before the ranger darkened, and that behind him turned crimson with the setting of the sun, he did not stop. His horse, spurred by the magical urging of the witch's daughter, continued its tireless pounding pace, and no weariness came over Andovar's grim visage.

He crossed the great river and through the streets of Rivertown, crying, "Talons! Talons! Gather your arms and courage!"

The brave folk of the town, already more than a little suspicious at the sight of the clouds of smoke on the western horizon, rushed from their homes, shops, and taverns to heed the call of the ranger. A fresh horse was offered, but Andovar, trusting in the magic of Rhiannon, declined.

And then he was off again, to the few towns along his course, and beyond, to Pallendara and the only hope.

Lennard wiped the sweat from his fingers, then replaced them on the bowstring. A hundred yards below him marched the talon force, clearly visible along an open trail.

"How many?" an obviously frightened Tinothy dared to whisper.

"Let fly a few," Lennard replied. "It will take them many minutes to get up that slope. Are you ready?"

On a nod from Tinothy, the bowstrings twanged.

Lennard, an amazing archer, had his fifth shot in the air before the first ever struck. He had gauged the distance correctly, but still it was more luck than skill that three of his five hit their mark, dropping talons to the ground. Tinothy was less successful, but still managed to get one.

The talon ranks split apart in confusion as the wretched creatures dove for cover, not even able to discern the direction of the hidden attackers.

A smile erupted on Lennard's face. "Take that, dogs!" he cried as loudly as he dared. But when he turned his widespread grin upon Tinothy, he saw that his young friend wasn't sharing his elation.

For the tip of a cruel spear prodded through the front of Tinothy's chest.

They hadn't figured on scouts.

Bryan peeked under the long, flat stone. "Deeply washed out," he reported. "If we dig it out more, it will not support their weight on this end." Heeding the command of the half-elf who had become their leader, Siana and three others set about the task.

All along this narrow stretch of trail, with rocky drops on either side, the majority of the group went to work, setting trip wires and deadfalls, and loosening stones along the edges. Thirty yards ahead, in a thick copse of trees, Jolsen Smithyson led the work on camouflaged barricades and trip holes.

"Will this be the last?" Siana asked.

"The last big one," Bryan replied. "Take as much time as you can; this one, above all the others, has to work if we are to have any chance of slowing the talons."

"And how much time is that?" Siana asked grimly.

Bryan shrugged. "I'm going out to scout for Lennard and Tinothy," he explained. "And for our guests."

Tinothy dropped facedown, and an ugly talon leaped astride the dead boy and tore its barbed spear from his back, twisting the weapon as it came out, reveling in the gore.

Solely on instinct, Lennard snapped his foil out and poked the vicious creature. The tip of the slender blade slipped in through the talon's makeshift armor, but the weight of the creature as it fearlessly bore in bent the foil over and snapped it in half. Lennard fell back, barely dodging the first jab of the crimson-stained spear.

Again Lennard's luck prevailed, for as he stumbled, the eager talon overbalanced and came crashing down on top of him. The remaining half of Lennard's foil, pinned point out between Lennard and the falling monster, did not bend so easily.

The talon thrashed wildly for a moment, bruising Lennard about the face with heavy blows. The young warrior thought his life was surely at its end, but then the thrashing stopped and the talon, quite dead, lay still. Lennard took a long moment to find his breath, then gingerly rolled the thing off him. His foil, still impaled deep in the talon's chest, went over with it.

He knew Tinothy was dead, but he cradled his friend gently, not knowing whether to try to carry the body back with him or find a place for it here. The decision was stolen from him, though, as the sound of approaching talons reminded him that he was far from out of danger. He scooped up Tinothy's sword and quiver and scrambled off over the rocks.

Flopping footsteps and angry grunts followed him every step. Stumbling, blinded by tears of remorse and fear, Lennard ran on, down the back paths toward Doerning's Walk, toward his friends. If he could only get to them!

Most of the sounds receded, but Lennard's sense of dread followed him vividly. He splashed into a mountain stream and cut around a huge boulder, looking back over his shoulder for the expected pursuit.

And in his haste, slammed blindly into the chest of a waiting talon.

Lennard bounced back against the stone, glancing up just in time to see doom, in the form of a talon sword, descending upon his head.

He screamed and closed his eyes, and hardly heard the clang as the blade met an intercepting shield and was deflected harmlessly aside.

And then Bryan was between Lennard and his attacker, slashing his elven sword in a quick cut across and then back. The talon dropped its weapon, choosing instead in the last fleeting moments of its life to clutch its spilling guts. Without so much as a grunt, it slipped to its knees in the cold stream.

Bryan spun and threw Lennard to the ground, out of the way of a thrusting spear. Lennard came up spitting water and watching in horrified amazement as Bryan and the newest attacker squared off.

Bryan's father had schooled him well in the crude attack methods of these beasts. Savagery replaced finesse in talon fighters, and the trick to defeating them was to turn their own aggressiveness against them.

Bryan's chance came in the very first seconds of battle, as the fire-eyed talon dove at him recklessly, spear leading the way.

Bryan launched a backhand parry with his sword, dipping the spear to the ground. The talon, unable to break its momentum—and not wanting to, anyway—lurched forward, where Bryan's shield connected heavily with its face. The monster staggered backward and Bryan threw his shield out wide, following quickly with a perfectly angled slice of his blade, lopping the creature's head from its shoulders.

"By the Colonnae," gasped Lennard. "Bryan?"

But the young half-elf had no time to consider the events. "Where is Tinothy?" he asked.

"Dead," Lennard muttered.

Bryan hardly flinched at the news. "Quickly," he instructed, grabbing Lennard by the elbow. "We have only minutes to get back to the walk."

"Hold your shots," Bryan whispered as the trudging column of talons approached. Behind the wooden barricades, the friends twitched nervously, eager to let loose the first shots and be on with it. But Bryan wanted the monsters to spring the first trap or two before he set his friends into action.

The talons came on, more wary than before, but hardly expecting to find the ground beneath their feet laced with cunning traps. The leading rank stepped out across a long, flat rock.

Bryan and his friends pulled back on their bowstrings. They could only hope the rock would tumble as planned.

As the front talons crossed to the front edge—the section that had been dug out—the stone rolled and pivoted, dipping the leading talons into a crevice and sending those behind them into a slide down the now sloping trail. Several of the creatures had the life crushed out of them as the stone settled down at its new angle.

Bryan's arrow went first, knocking deep into the chest of one of the unfortunate beasts splayed across the stone facing. Hoots and howls erupted as the talons recognized the ambush for what it was and came charging over the raised tip of the stone. Arrow after arrow soared in, most finding their mark.

But talons, for all of their other weaknesses, were not cowardly creatures, and they came on fearlessly, leaping down from the stone and rushing toward the copse. A trip wire sent one slamming down; loosened rocks gave way on the edge of the trail, spilling several others on a bouncing ride down the steep descent on the side of Doerning's Walk.

And more arrows thudded home.

"Run!" cried Lennard when the leading edge of the charge neared the copse. Bryan held his position, not so quick to give up such easy kills.

But then one of the group, Damon, standing right beside the half-elf, caught a spear in the chest, and the talon followed its shot closely, springing atop the barricade.

Bryan wheeled and fired, point-blank, blowing the thing back. He realized, though, that the position was lost. Five others of the group had already fled, following Lennard's lead, but the remaining six waited bravely, looking to Bryan for direction. In his rage, Bryan would have stayed on until the talon tide buried him, willingly giving up his own life in exchange for the talons he would surely slay.

But he could not be responsible for the deaths of more of his friends. Like Tinothy, and now Damon.

He fired a final shot and broke back from the wall, slinging his bow and drawing his gleaming sword. "Go! Go!" he cried to the others.

Connie, a girl with shining blue eyes and an innocent smile, lost her head to a talon sword.

And then they were running, one group to the west behind Lennard, and Bryan wisely taking the others to the east. The enraged talons forgot all about their mission and took off in hot pursuit, hungry for the blood of the young ambushers.

Siana led the way, with Bryan taking up the rear guard. Several talons got close to them in their wild flight, but each time, Bryan, possessed of a fury beyond anything he could ever have imagined, cut them down with vicious chops and perfect maneuvers. A short while later the five turned around a rocky outcropping and, confident that no pursuit was close behind, stopped to catch their breath.

Lennard and the others had less luck.

Though they had started with more ground between them and the talons, the group had no organization to their flight. They split apart around boulders or crevices, and lost time trying to find each other. Directionless, and with no clear destination in mind, they soon heard the flopping stamp of talon feet all about them.

An agonized scream told Lennard that their number was down to five. He stopped and looked about, searching for some way he could help. A talon spear found his leg.

Lennard dropped heavily to the ground, clutching his wound. Then the talon was above him, its sword up for the kill.

A heavy rock smashed the ugly creature's head apart.

Blackness, from pain and fear, swirled over Lennard, and he hardly noticed when he was lifted from the ground in the strong arms of Jolsen Smithyson and borne away.

"Come on," Bryan prodded after the others had regained their breath. They gathered their belongings, thinking Bryan to be leading them farther away. But to their astonishment, the half-elf started back around the outcropping toward the talons.

"Where are you going?" Siana demanded.

Bryan cast them all a look over his shoulder. "The talons are scattered," he explained. "We can find small groups of them to hit."

"You are crazy!" the girl retorted. "We cannot go back there!"

"We have no choice!" Bryan shot back.

"Think of Connie, and Damon!" said another.

"Think of the line of people we saw on the road," Bryan countered. "Our people, helpless unless we can keep the talons tied up in the mountains." His visage softened then as he looked upon the sorrow-filled, weary faces. Perhaps he was pushing the others too hard.

"You go and find a safer spot to rest," he conceded quietly. "I'll go after the talons. I can move faster alone anyway."

But when Bryan started away, he heard the sound of the other four following at his back.

They played hit-and-run with bands of talons for the remainder of that day, striking from a distance with their bows, or rising from cover suddenly in front of a talon group and cutting the monsters down before they even knew they were being attacked.

Bryan and his friends knew the odds, and realized that sooner or later they would get themselves into a situation where they would find no escape. But whenever fear threatened to take the fight out of them, they remembered the cloud of dust from the refugees on the road and the cloud of smoke over Corning, and remembered their duty.

Disaster struck near sunset. The group surprised a band of four talons and quickly dispatched them. But another, larger band was close by, and got into the fight before the young warriors could escape. Bryan and his friends won out, but when the last talon fell at Bryan's feet, he looked around to find that he and Siana were the only two left alive.

Their spirits fell with the fall of day, and they walked slowly away, seeking a safe haven. Siana leaned on Bryan for support, but the tears ran as freely down the cheeks of the half-elf as on her own.

All told, they had killed more than four dozen talons that day and wounded several score more. More important, they had halted the march. It would take the scattered bands of talons the rest of the night to get back together, and the people on the road would get through.

But to Bryan and Siana, the victory brought little consolation.

"At least seven," Bryan noted grimly. "Tinothy first, then Damon and Connie on the walk, and—"

Siana held up her hand to stop him, for she needed no recounting. She had witnessed six of the seven deaths Bryan spoke of. "Do you think Lennard and the others got away?" she asked him hopefully.

"Lennard is a smart one," Bryan replied. "And they had a better lead." But if his words held conviction, it was feigned. Despair flowed over him fully that dark night. In a single day he had witnessed the burning of his city and, later, the deaths of seven of his closest friends.

Siana sensed his turmoil and put her own aside. She moved to him and snuggled close, lending him some of her strength. "We did a fine job," she reminded him. "They won't be getting back to their march anytime soon, and more than a few talons died this day. Our traps worked pretty well, I would say!"

Bryan looked down at her smiling face and was comforted. He kissed her then, and hugged her close.

But when the exhausted young warriors drifted into the solitude of slumber, the black despair came rushing back at them in their dreams, vivid recollections of the horrors they had witnessed that day.

Chapter 9

To the Bridges

BELEXUS AWOKE JUST before dawn. As the light grew around him, so too did the scene of carnage. He and the remaining cavalry contingent had camped just beyond the stench of the battlefield, too weary to continue that day and wanting to watch for any return of the talon forces that had fled.

But the night had been quiet, except for the occasional cry from the south.

From the road.

Movement from one figure caught Belexus' eye, the one he had been most concerned about. Rhiannon walked slowly across the field, head down, toward the legacy of her display of power. Belexus forced himself to his feet and rushed after her. He felt his spirits sag when he moved next to her. So frail she seemed, only a hollowed shell of the confident and carefree woman he had escorted along the road these past couple of months.

When dawn fully broke just a moment later, the two friends saw the enormity of Rhiannon's accomplishments. She had cut a gorge nearly a half mile long and fully twenty feet across, and deep beyond sight. More than three hundred talons had fallen to their deaths along the chasm, most in the final battle when Rhiannon had bottled them up. No guilt for those talon dead brought a tear to Rhiannon's eye this morning, but when she looked upon her handiwork, she did indeed cry. She had scarred the land, had loosed a terrible strength that was beyond her control or comprehension. The power had consumed her and forced itself through her, leaving profound questions hanging unanswered. Questions of her very identity.

"Suren ye saved our lives," Belexus remarked to her, seeing the moistness rolling across her fair face. "And more important, ye kept the beasts running to the north. Ye kept them away from the road."

Rhiannon only shrugged helplessly, finding no words that could slip past the lump that had welled in her throat.

Belexus felt her pain as he studied the deep torment on her face. He understood that Rhiannon's distress was far too deep for simple words to dispel. He looked to the south, where the dusty trail of rushing refugees continued to line the horizon, and to where a larger, more ominous cloud swelled in the early light.

"Come," he said. "We must away to the south in all speed. The talon army is in pursuit."

They were all tired, and most were wounded, but not one of the brave cavalrymen issued a word of complaint when the command came to break camp and ride with all their speed. They knew their duty, and knew, too, the suffering their kinfolk along the road would endure if they could not slow the talon rush.

Rhiannon cast a final glance at the destruction, at the black and white gelding the power—she—had destroyed. She accepted Belexus' hand and rode in front of the ranger, needing his support just to hold her seat.

* * *

There had been no rest for Andovar that night, and no more stops along his road. Like the wind itself, the enchanted steed flew across the southern fields, merely a blur to onlookers. The horse did not tire; it gained momentum with each mighty stride, and Andovar, grim-faced, spurred it on, refusing to let any weariness defeat his mission.

The road connecting Corning and Pallendara was normally a week of hard riding. Andovar and his horse, flying under the power of the young witch, found the great city soon after the dawn of the second day.

"Talons to the west!" he cried, not even slowing as he soared through the open gates. The Pallendara city guard swarmed all around him to his call, and only minutes later the ranger found himself in audience with King Benador.

"My greetings, Andovar," the young King said to him happily. Benador knew Andovar, and all of the rangers, as brothers. It was they who had sheltered him and taught him the duties of his proper station when the pretender Ungden had reigned in Pallendara, and it was they who helped him regain his rightful title.

Despite the familiarity, the ranger, as always, was amazed when he looked upon the young King of Calva. Benador had passed the age of fifty, only a few years younger than Andovar, but the wizards of Aielle had seemingly put Benador's aging process into a state of stasis. Nurtured under the enchantments of Ardaz during the reign of Ungden, and even more so under the magical influences of his own magician, Istaahl, since he had taken the throne, King Benador was possessed of the vitality and appearance of a man in his early twenties. His curly light brown locks danced and flopped about his neck and shoulders, and his eyes twinkled as a child's.

But Andovar knew the truth of Benador's experience and

wisdom. He did not let the King's boyish charm dissuade him from the grim duty at hand.

"It has been a long time," Benador said warmly.

"Longer still, we both would wish, when I tell ye o' me purpose," Andovar said grimly. As he recounted the disaster of the western fields, Istaahl entered to join the discussion.

"You have heard enough of Andovar's grim words?" Benador asked.

Istaahl nodded. "And the invaders are led by Morgan Thalasi," he replied.

Benador's eyes went wide.

"That was our guess," Andovar agreed. "Though we've not proof of it."

"We wizards work with different intent, yet we call upon the same universal powers," Istaahl explained. "I have sensed magical disturbances from the west throughout the day yesterday and all the night. I had meant to confer with Brielle this morning to further investigate, fearing the very truth you bring to us, gallant ranger." Suddenly realizing the timetable involved, the wizard cast a curious glance Andovar's way. "How did you get here so quickly, all the way from Corning?" he asked.

" 'Twas the witch's daughter," Andovar replied. "Put a spell on me horse an' quickened the pace. Suren all the world was a blur to me eyes.

"And 'twas Rhiannon who warned us of the comin' o' the Black Warlock," Andovar went on. "Suren the lass deserves the thanks of all Calva, of all the world."

Istaahl paused to consider this revelation. Brielle had suspected that Rhiannon had some power about her, and now there could be little doubt.

"We must be off at once," King Benador decreed. "With all of the force we can muster. We will meet the talons at the great river and hold them there until the strength of all of

Calva can be gathered and brought to bear." He looked at Istaahl for further suggestions.

"You have no choice," the White Mage replied to the inquiring gaze. "But I will not join you, not yet. I must contact the other wizards. Together we can hold back the Black Warlock."

"While we destroy his rabble," Benador said with a determined grimace. He clapped Andovar on the shoulder. "You have had no rest," he said. "But if you plan to ride beside me to the Four Bridges, as I hope, you will find little idle time in the next few days!"

Two hours later, to the cheers of those who would remain behind, the Warders of the White Walls, the elite guard of Pallendara, charged out of the city's gates, King Benador and Andovar at their lead.

From his tower window high above the city wall, Istaahl watched them go. Five hundred strong and superbly trained and outfitted, they would cut down the talons ten for every man. But no smile crossed the White Mage's face as he watched the onrush of the proud army. He knew that even they would find only disaster if he and his wizard peers could not hold back the strength of Morgan Thalasi, strength that could sweep all the soldiers in the world away in the course of a single day.

The flight of the refugees had actually gained momentum during the dark hours of that wicked night. The two hamlets between Corning and the river, alerted by the ride of Andovar and by the thickening smoke on the western horizon, met the line with wagons and carts and a fresh garrison to form a rear guard.

But swift, too, came the forerunners of Thalasi's army, and in numbers sufficient to bury any impromptu defensive attempts. Thus, when Belexus and his remaining cavalry found the trailing end of the fleeing refugees near midday, they saw as well the leading edge of the talons, dangerously close and gaining with every stride.

"More fightin's before me, and ye've not the strength to help this time," Belexus explained as he set Rhiannon into one of the wagons. Rhiannon, so weak and exhausted, would have tried to dissuade him, but beside her in the wagon she saw a young boy, barely ten, gravely wounded and needing attention.

Belexus would not have heard her complaints in any event. As soon as the wagon began to roll away, he called his troops together to lay out the battle plans. They would not meet the talon line head-on, nor would they dig in and fight a pitched battle. Instead they would follow the wagons in flight. Let the overeager talons come at them in clusters, with no proper formation, only to find a coiled snake when at last they caught up with the group.

But for all of the wisdom of the ranger's plan, and for all of the determined grunts and shouts of the brave cavalrymen, Belexus had cause to worry. The Four Bridges were fully five miles away, and considering the rate of the approaching army, the ranger wondered if the last groups of refugees would even get halfway there before they were overtaken.

"Present torch!" the sergeant cried out.

Ten men, the front line of Rivertown's defense, snapped to attention and brought their arms out wide, bearing a torch in each hand.

"Present grenades!" the sergeant ordered.

The second line, one hundred strong and including Gatsby, the record keeper, performed a similar movement. But instead of torches, each member of this group held two flasks of highly flammable oil, stoppered with oil-soaked rags.

The sergeant leaped into his saddle and rushed off ahead, seeking a better view of the drama unfolding before him. The last groups of refugees were coming on fast now; Thalasi's army was right on their heels, hurling spears with devastating effect. But the brave men of the Rivertown regiment known as the Firethrowers had already put more than a mile between themselves and the Four Bridges.

The flight was a dead run. Wagons crossed by the Rivertown regiment, bouncing and tossing wildly. In back of the last group, Belexus' line of cavalry had fully engaged the front talon ranks, fighting a retreating action but trying to hold the monsters long enough for the helpless refugees to get to the bridges.

They wouldn't have had a chance if it weren't for the Rivertown Firethrowers.

"Light torches!" the sergeant cried, nervous beads of sweat now evident on his brow and on the faces of all of his men. He watched as two men made their way up and down the line of torchbearers, igniting the items. Behind them the grenadiers shifted anxiously. The sergeant had to hold them until the last moment, to time their strike perfectly to allow all of the fleeing people to get behind them.

As he came up on the Rivertown line, Belexus recognized the intent of the defensive line. The ranger held his troops for a moment longer, then ordered them into full flight. They pounded away from the leading talons and crossed through the Rivertown line just as the sergeant put his men into action.

In one fluid motion the grenadiers of Rivertown swept into small lines and rushed through the line of torchbearers, lighting their flasks as they passed. The charging talons were barely fifteen feet away when the first flaming grenade crashed in, but in mere seconds two hundred burning flasks of oil erupted in the faces of the horrified monsters. A wild rush of fire scattered and decimated their center ranks, and the screams of burning talons replaced battle cries.

Proud tears streaked the sergeant's face as he watched his troops perform their practiced maneuver to perfection. He understood what their bravery would cost them, for though they had broken the center of the talon line, talons to the north and south had continued their sweep beyond the ranks of the Rivertown Firethrowers and were now turning in toward the road, cutting off any chance of escape.

Belexus wanted to turn his troops back around and rush to the rescue of the brave men of Rivertown. Such an act would steal the meaning from their sacrifice, though, for they had gone onto the field that day knowing their duty and accepting their fate. And with Belexus' cavalry continuing their rearguard action, they had bought enough time for the helpless refugees to get to the bridges.

The Rivertown Firethrowers drew their swords and put a song on their lips as the black walls of talons closed around them. They had done their duty.

Not a man of them survived the next ten minutes.

The remaining garrison of Rivertown, along with the forces of several neighboring villages and those refugees still fit to fight, had already organized a hasty defense of the bridges. Lines of archers showered the talons closest in pursuit, and skilled horsemen rode out to catch the wagons and put them in proper lines for getting across the bridges safely and quickly.

Belexus took his troops in full stride straight across the

central two bridges, then spun them about to survey the battle and determine where they would best fit in.

The talons did not slow when they reached the massive, arching structures. They crashed onto each bridge, flailing away wildly and crying out for the deaths of the human defenders.

But the men and women of Calva, fighting for their homes and the lives of their kin, met the monsters with equal savagery. And whenever the talon press threatened to break through to the other side of one of the bridges, Belexus and his troops met them and drove them back.

The Black Warlock, following in the middle ranks of his army, snickered with wicked satisfaction at each mutilated human corpse he passed. The sight of the carnage inflicted by the Rivertown Firethrowers stole that evil smile, but only for a moment, for farther up the line came the shouts that the army had finally reached the Four Bridges. Thalasi spurred his litter bearers on when he heard the ring of weapons and the cries as the forces engaged. By the time he came upon the scene at the bridges, it had become obvious that his talon soldiers would not break through. The bulk of the talon army was still miles behind, plodding down the road on weary feet, and while these leading groups of his force alone outnumbered the enemy across the way, the defenders were better organized and firmly entrenched in defensible positions.

Thalasi considered calling back his charges, holding them until the rest of his dark force could catch up. But then a more devious alternative came to mind. Why should he hold back any longer? A simple flex of his magical muscles here and the bridge would be won. With his talons spilling into the eastern Calvan fields, he could not be stopped, not by the army of Pallendara or by the feeble wizards that would stand to oppose him.

The Black Warlock clutched at the air around him, gathering in his power. He slipped into the magical plane, bending the powers to his vile call. They resisted, as they always resisted the likes of the perverted warlock. But as always, Thalasi's sheer will pulled them in to his desires. In mere seconds he felt the tingle of explosive magic surging within him, greater and greater as he spoke the first runes of his spell.

But then he heard the music.

It wafted down on the northern breezes, as sweet and pure as a clear-running brook. But to the ears of the Black Warlock the perfect notes rang out as discordant, fighting back against the guttural strains of his own magical intonations, blocking the notes he needed to launch his strike. His hollowed eyes widened in rage as he came to understand.

And from the south came another call, a soft but insistent moaning leading the edge of a breeze from the sea. Just as Thalasi began to counter the effects of Brielle's disruption, the cry of Istaahl sounded in his ears.

Thorny vines sprouted up out of the earth to entangle Thalasi's legs, pulling at him. He was on the defensive now, fighting with all his strength just to ward off the sudden and unexpected attacks of the wizard and the witch.

And all the while his talons died by the score on the Four Bridges.

The talons finally broke off the encounter when the sun dipped below the rim of the western horizon.

"We have won the day," Belexus remarked to another soldier, one of the cavalrymen who had ridden beside him in the northern encounter. All four of the bridges had been secured, a thousand talons and more lay dead, and, for all that

Belexus could tell, the Black Warlock had not even entered the contest.

But there was no proclamation of victory in the ranger's observation. Belexus remembered vividly the heavy cost of their "victory." All of the western fields had been lost to the enemy. Even now, in the waning light, the ranger could see the swell of monsters across the river as more and more of Thalasi's minions marched down the western road to flock into the encampment.

"Twenty thousand?" the other soldier pondered. "Thirty? My heart fails at such a sight."

"They will come on again tomorrow, if not this very night," a third soldier standing nearby replied. "And again after that if we hold them back."

"Then we will have to hold them tomorrow, and again after that," Belexus declared. He threw a calming wink at the two men, then trotted his mount away to let them consider his words.

"I would give us not a chance of holding them, even in the next of the engagements," the first of the two remarked, his eyes following the unshakable movements of the departing ranger. "Were it not for the likes of that one at our lead!"

The other soldier agreed with the observation, but when he looked back at the darkness gathering across the river, he could not help but shudder.

Across the river, Thalasi stalked up and down the talon ranks, enraged and concerned as his plans continued their downward spiral. He had wanted to get across the river quickly and without heavy losses, but the stubborn Calvans, and his own blunders, had foiled that notion.

He watched now as more defenses were set in place on and around the bridges. He knew as he viewed the scene that other eyes were also watching, the eyes of a witch in a distant wood and the eyes of a wizard in a white tower. For three hours they had held his magical intentions at bay, countering his every move.

And the third of his powerful enemies, the wizard Ardaz, had not yet even entered the battle.

Chapter 10

Bryan's Choice

"THOUSANDS OF THEM," Siana cried in dismay, looking out over the fields to the west and north. From her high mountain vantage point, the young girl could see dots of light—campfires—stretching off to the horizon.

"Talons," Bryan observed. "They have heard the tides of war and are coming to join the main force down by the river."

"What can we do?" Siana whispered hopelessly. "What can anyone do?"

"We must warn the people," Bryan replied in an even tone. "Come, we can get to the river this very night." They started off at once, down the mountain trails they knew so well. They passed by several talon camps without incident, though Bryan would have dearly loved to stop and pay a visit upon the evil things.

For now, though, he had his mind focused on the mission at hand. Someone had to get across the river and warn the defenders at the Four Bridges of the true size of the gathering talon force. Skirmishes with roving bands seemed unimportant next to delivering the warning.

But a few hours later, plodding along the eastern foothills

of the Baerendels with the great river in sight, Bryan and Siana came upon an encampment they could not ignore. From inside a small cave, its entrance hastily blocked by piled stones and brush, the two heard groans of pain.

Bryan recognized the voice before he even entered; Lennard had been his closest friend for all of his life.

"Bryan!" Jolsen Smithyson cried when he saw his friends. The large lad dropped his sword to the floor and gave Bryan and Siana a great bear hug.

Bryan pushed by him, more concerned with the garish wound showing on Lennard's leg. Jolsen had broken the shaft off the spear and had tried his best to get the tip out and clean the wound, but the talon's strike had been vicious indeed, twining tendons and shattering bone. Lennard lay on a fleeting edge of consciousness, more delirious than awake.

"Can you carry him?" Bryan asked Jolsen.

"I fear to move him," Jolsen replied. "Or leave him. I meant to go back out along the trails to see if I could find any of our friends—"

"Forget the others," Bryan snapped coldly, startling both Jolsen and Siana. "We have to get Lennard across the river."

"The others might be out there," Siana reminded Bryan. "Wounded like Lennard, and lying all alone in the cold of the night."

Bryan felt the pain as intensely as Siana and Jolsen, but he understood his place in this predicament. "We go to the river," he said. "Jolsen will carry Lennard."

Jolsen and Siana exchanged concerned looks. "What if we refuse?" Siana dared to ask.

"Then I go alone," Bryan was quick to answer. "And you will remain here to watch Lennard die, and probably to find a similar fate for yourselves at the hands of the foul talons."

"You do not offer us much of a choice," Jolsen remarked, his voice holding an uncharacteristically angry edge.

"There is none to offer," Bryan replied in the same tone. "We have not the time—the troops camped across the river have not the time—to waste. If any of our friends are alive out there—and I know that none of those who fled Doerning's Walk in the group beside me remain alive—they will simply have to fend for themselves." He led their glances to Lennard.

"How long do you think he might live out here in this filth?" he asked earnestly. "We have to get him across the river."

Jolsen's eyes narrowed, but he did not refute the half-elf's observations. The big lad was fairly certain that all of the others who had fled from Doerning's Walk were indeed dead, but he could not shake the terrible notion that one of them might be out in the night, huddled in a hole, trembling with fright.

They cleared the mountains about an hour later and picked their way cautiously across the short expanse of open field. The bulk of the gathering talon army remained miles to the north by the bridges, but some of the scum had made camps even this far south. The four got safely to the river, though, and moved north along the bank in search of a way to get across.

Dozens of cottages lined the great river this close to River-town, many having docks and small boats. Bryan and his friends came upon such a place only a short while later. Talons now inhabited the main cottage, but the human cries inside told the friends that the original inhabitants had not escaped in time.

"Two guards on the wharves," Bryan remarked from his concealment behind some shrubs.

"What about inside the house?" Jolsen asked, unable to block out the wails.

"If we work it correctly, we can get the guards too quickly and quietly for any others to join in," Bryan explained.

"But we cannot leave!" Siana hissed as loudly as she dared.

Bryan gave her an icy glare. "We'll get the guards and ready the boat," he instructed her coldly. "Do as you are told."

Siana wanted to respond but could not find the words. Her expression of horror spoke for her, though, and Bryan realized that he might have been a bit too rough.

"We have to make certain that we will fulfill our mission," he explained. "And we have to save Lennard. Once we've got the docks secured, we can attend to the people in the house."

That promise appeased Siana and Jolsen, for neither wanted to go against Bryan. Not out here, not with other people's lives hanging on their every decision. They followed Bryan's lead to a closer position to the docks, drawing their bows as they went.

"Wait till I am close," Bryan whispered. "Your shots will lead me in; I'll make certain that the job is done. Then get Lennard to the boat and wait with him there." And before either of his friends could question him again about the plan for the talons inside the house, Bryan disappeared into the darkness.

The two arrows whistled off together, both finding their marks but only Siana's killing a talon. Before the remaining creature could cry out to its friends, though, Bryan was upon it, his sword's fine edge turning the talon's intended shout into a quiet gurgle.

Jolsen scooped up Lennard and followed Siana down to the docks, where Bryan had untied two boats.

"The house?" Siana questioned.

"Trust me," replied Bryan. "Get in one of the boats and

hold a position a few feet from the docks." All their eyes turned abruptly back to the cottage at the sound of yet another cry of pain.

"If I do not return," Bryan went on, "get across the river and warn the soldiers of the approaching talon forces."

Jolsen complied, setting Lennard down softly and taking up the oars. Siana, though, appeared doubtful.

"I am coming with you," she insisted, fitting another arrow to her bow.

"Not this time," said Bryan. He flicked his sword out, severing the eager girl's bowstring. "Do not make me cut anything else," he threatened, his sword still dancing out in front of him and an angry glower flashing in his elven-bright eyes. "Get in the boat."

Stunned, Siana backed away and slipped into the boat without taking her eyes off Bryan. And then he was gone again into the gloom.

"Don't yous fight me!" the talon roared, as much in amusement as in anger. The young girl on the bed kicked out again, only to have her foot clawed viciously by the wretched thing. She tried to cry out, but had no more screams left to give. Sobbing, she lay very still on the bed and waited for the inevitable.

"Better!" croaked the talon, giving the smooth leg a final twist. "Now yous gets to see me weapon," the beast proclaimed, unhitching its belt.

It wasn't what the talon had intended, but an instant later the tip of a sword exploded through its backbone and out the front of its chest. The talon slumped to the floor. Bryan took its place.

The terrified girl started to shriek, and Bryan did not try to stop her; the other talons in the house would expect such a noise. The half-elf put his sword away, slowly easing the girl into a gentle hug. He waited patiently for many long moments as the last of her sobs died away, then offered a hopeful smile to her tear-streaked face.

"Come," he whispered. "I will get you away from these beasts and across the river." The girl snuffled away the pain and slipped off the bed to follow, pausing only to give the dying talon a kick in the face for good measure.

"Who else?" Bryan asked her.

"My mother and brother," she replied. "Downstairs, in the room beside the kitchen."

"Go out the window and to the docks," Bryan instructed her. He pointed to the open window—the window he had come in through—on the closest end of the hall. "Friends are waiting." He started to go the other way, but the girl grabbed him by the arm and turned him about.

"Please," she whispered. "You must get them out of here. And if you cannot . . ." She paused, stuck on the words, then steadied herself and continued. "Do not leave them at the mercy of the talons, I beg of you. If you cannot get them out, take their lives quickly and painlessly." Her voice died away and she had to grab at her mouth to stifle a rising sob.

Bryan wiped a tear from her cheek. "On my life," he promised, "I will get them out." He sent her off then, and waited until she had slipped safely out of the window.

Then the young half-elf moved down the dim hallway toward the staircase. He paused at one door, hearing loud snoring. Not wanting to leave any enemies at his back, along the route he might need for escape, he slipped in and deftly cut the throats of the two talons sleeping within.

Then to the stairs. Below him, in the glow of a blazing hearth, he saw three talons milling about a sitting room. On a sofa sat a middle-aged woman, beaten almost to unconsciousness and staring blankly ahead at an empty wall.

"Herry up!" one of the talons croaked. To emphasize its

words, it strolled over and slapped the woman across the back of the head.

A young boy darted through a door off to the side, bearing a tray of food and drink and being hurried by the thongs of a fourth talon's whip.

There might have been more of the monsters about, but in his simmering rage Bryan didn't care. He took two running steps down the stairway and leaped out into the center of the room. He landed in a roll and came up between two of the beasts, cutting them down before they realized he was there.

A third, the one behind the boy, reacted quickly, though, snapping its whip out around Bryan's ankles and tripping him up. Stumbling away toward the far wall, Bryan turned about just in time to see the approach of the fourth talon's spear. He tried to get his shield in its course but could not deflect the spear far enough to the side. The crude weapon slipped through, thudding into his chest.

Bryan curled reflexively, catching the shaft between his arms. He thought his life to be at its end, but was amazed to realize that the nasty weapon had not dug in.

His armor, his magical elven armor, had stopped the point.

Bryan fell back against the wall, taking the spear with him. He groaned and swooned, playing upon the over-zealous talon's hunger for the kill. Thinking its spear had completed the job, the stupid thing strode right in to retrieve the weapon. It reached out to grasp the spear shaft, then stopped in confusion as the weapon fell suddenly to the ground. The talon's puzzled expression only heightened when it realized, beyond its belief, that no blood stained the spear tip.

The ugly brute looked back at Bryan for an explanation, and got a sword between its ribs in reply. Bryan yanked his blade back out, and as the talon dropped to its knees, he savagely brought it back in, lopping off the monster's head.

The fourth talon shrieked in horror and bolted for the kitchen door. In a single movement Bryan slipped his arm out of his shield straps and hurled the shield across the room. His aim proved perfect, the shield clipping the talon on the side of the leg with enough force to send the thing sprawling headlong on the floor.

Before it could regain its feet, Bryan was upon it, slashing and hacking away until the mess of blood and gore beneath him hardly resembled a talon.

When the second boat, bearing the mother and her two children, floated out to join the first, Siana and Jolsen looked curiously back to the shadowed figure on the docks.

"Come on, Bryan!" Siana insisted.

But Bryan had made his decision. How many more families remained on this side of the river, hiding from talons or already captured?

"You know what to tell them," he replied to Siana. "Farewell, and pray that we might meet again."

"I do not wish to leave you," Jolsen Smithyson said stubbornly, and he pulled his boat around, back toward the docks.

But Bryan was gone.

Chapter 11

Give and Take

THE CRY OF battle, the ring of weapon against weapon, shattered Rhiannon's slumber before the first light of dawn. She had slept among the refugees, in an encampment on the field normally reserved for trading caravans just outside Rivertown. Looking back at the bridges, Rhiannon could see the unfolding events. On again came the talon horde, ferociously charging across the expanse of the Four Bridges. Caltrops, crossed spikes, and wires slowed them, though, and then the valiant defenders, Belexus at their lead, sprang upon them.

Rhiannon felt a tingle of power growing within her once more, prickling her skin, stealing her breath. Tremendous power, might beyond anything the warriors could imagine, and she felt as if she could shatter the talon army with a thought.

But the witch's daughter was more terrified of that unknown strength than of the talons—she could not rid herself of the image of the field she had battered and cracked, or the sight of her poor horse dying—and she cried out in dismay and pushed the urges away.

* * *

The magic-wielder on the western side of the bridges held no such reservations. The Black Warlock sank within the magical plane, once more grabbing at all the power his fragile mortal form could endure. He gathered the energy and then threw it into the sky in the form of two blackened thunderclouds that sped away from him with preternatural fury, the roiling dark shapes barely containing their explosive power.

The first of the violent storms broke over Avalon in the north; the other released its fury upon the tower of the White Mage in Pallendara. Hardly seeming cognizant of the battle unfolding before him, the Black Warlock stood behind the thick ranks of his talons, his arms outstretched to the skies, his mind drawing power from the plane of wizards.

Morgan Thalasi's grimace revealed his intent and determination; he would feed the power of his storms until he could draw no more, until sheer exhaustion laid him low.

Lightning crackled into Brielle's forest, sundering trees and lighting wind-whipped fires, a furious, relentless barrage.

But nature was the Emerald Witch's domain. Brielle was nature's guardian, while Thalasi was no more than a crafty thief. As swift as thought, Brielle countered the Black Warlock's storm with cloudbursts and opposing winds of her own.

This time, though, the Black Warlock was not caught by surprise by the magics of the witch. This time Brielle would have to fight with all of her strength just to save her homeland.

Istaahl found himself in similar straits. One bolt thundered through his magical wardings and cracked a line across the side of his tower. The White Mage called upon his own domain of power to counter, summoning a mighty wind from the sea to blow the black clouds of Thalasi away. But Thalasi fought back, resisting all of Istaahl's considerable gusts.

"Not this time!" the curious dual voice of the Black Warlock roared. Thalasi clenched his bony fists and grasped the magic even harder, pulling the universal powers to his will, perverting them to their very limits for the sake of his battle.

They would come to his call, or he would tear them into chaos for their resistance.

Most of the traps on the bridges were expended now, their barbs and spikes covered to ineffectiveness by the sheer number of talon corpses. But the talons, their numbers swelled throughout the night, pushed on right over their fallen kin, driving the defenders steadily backward.

Then, inevitably, they breached the southernmost bridge, and eager talons swarmed onto the eastern fields.

The Black Warlock howled in glee at the sight, but did not dare to relinquish his assaults on his more powerful enemies and join in the conquest.

Again came Belexus and the battle-weary cavalry of Corning, blowing their horns and urging on their steeds. The ranger led a brutal charge down the second bridge, trampling and hacking his way until the press of horse and steel got him and his soldiers to the western banks. The talons fell back readily, willing to let the horsemen onto the open field where they could be assaulted from every side.

But Belexus had other plans. As soon as he and his men came off the second bridge, they swung to the south and back onto the bridge that had been lost, coming up behind the pressing talons and splitting them off from their rear support.

Half of the cavalry unit secured the bridge, while Belexus and the other riders cleared the remaining portion of the bridge and came all the way back onto the eastern fields, trapping those talons who had crossed within a noose of defenders.

The Black Warlock watched his victory unraveling before him. "No!" he cried, seeing yet another of his unskilled army's attacks foiled. Thalasi could stand the sight of defeat no longer. He released the fury of his storms in several quick, vicious strokes against the wood and the tower, then pulled himself from the magical battle with his rival wizards and rushed to squash the defenders on the bridges.

Desperate bolts of power roared out of Istaahl's tower to counter the sudden rush of Thalasi's storm. Istaahl heard the thunder again and again as lightning crackled into his home. Somehow the walls of the White Tower withstood the blasts, and the storm burned itself away in only moments.

In Avalon, the witch's conjured storm, so pure in its call to the magical forces, had been gradually winning through, and as soon as Thalasi turned his attention from his battle with Brielle, she blew his dark clouds to harmless bits of scattered energies.

A line of fire shot out from the Black Warlock's finger, incinerating a dozen men and their mounts on the southernmost bridge. Spurred by the appearance of the godlike leader, the talons roared in again.

Thalasi, running even closer to the fray, pointed his hand again for another strike.

But a vine rushed out of the earth and caught his feet, tripping him facedown. And a crack opened in the ground behind him, like an earthen mouth hungry for his flesh. Thalasi clawed at the ground, but the vine's insistent tug dragged him backward.

* * *

Belexus did not see Thalasi fall. He rushed back out onto the bridge to shore up the wavering line of cavalry. Right past his comrades he charged, diving fearlessly into the talon ranks.

His troops watched in horror, thinking their leader slain. But it was Belexus who emerged from the jumbled pile of flesh, still secure in his saddle and scattering talons with each mighty swing of his sword. The ranger's blood ran from a dozen wounds, but his fury would admit no pain. And the talons, thinking him some immortal demon who had risen up against them, fell back and fled altogether.

"Damn you, Brielle!" Thalasi spat, too concerned with his own predicament to even consider the disastrous events on the bridge. He uttered a quick spell to counter, thrusting one of his arms straight down into the ground up to the shoulder, an impromptu anchor.

But then the wind of Istaahl, gathered from the might of the sea, slammed the Black Warlock in the face, nearly tearing that anchoring limb from its socket.

A primal scream of tremendous power erupted from Thalasi's thin-lipped mouth, splitting Istaahl's wind apart. The Black Warlock spun about, one of the fingernails on his free hand growing out to the length of a scythe. One swipe of that unnatural blade severed Brielle's vines cleanly, and a second scream of rage from Thalasi shook her earthen maw apart into a formless sandy pit.

Thalasi staggered to his feet, thoroughly drained. In Avalon, Brielle slumped against a tree, and in Pallendara, Istaahl the White fell to his knees. Never had any of the three witnessed such a singular display of power.

For all of them, the battle this day was ended.

* * *

Without the guidance, or even the visible specter, of their warlock leader, the talons could not sustain any offensive thrusts. They battled back and forth with the defenders for several long hours, but never found another foothold on the other side of the river.

And through it all loomed Belexus, fearless and strong. Talons fled at the mere sight of the ranger—at least those talons who had some measure of wisdom.

For others there was only the doom of a mighty sword.

"They'll win the day," came a soft voice behind Rhiannon. She turned to see the young boy she had attended to on the wagons the day before.

"Suren they will." Rhiannon smiled at him.

"My arm's all better," the lad said, and he thrust the limb out for Rhiannon's inspection.

She grasped the arm gently and turned it to see the wound. It hadn't been too serious, just a small gash and a deep bruise that had looked far worse than it truly was. Rhiannon had done what she could, applying a clean strip of cloth to the cut and gently massaging the bruise, more to give the distressed boy some comfort than for any medicinal purposes.

But when she removed the cloth now, her breath was stolen away. In trembling surprise Rhiannon turned the arm and looked all about for some sign of the injury.

The arm was healed; not a mark remained.

Rhiannon could only guess that some of the power had flowed through her on that wagon ride, too subtle perhaps for her to even sense it. The implications now overwhelmed her. Could that same force that had sundered the earth, had torn the ground apart with such appalling fury, be used for healing?

Every day, it seemed, the world got more intriguing, and more terrifying.

The fighting ended before sunset, the talons fleeing from the death corridors that were the Four Bridges, and the defenders retrieving their wounded and dead, and trying to replace some of the wrecked defensive barricades.

For one of the principals, though, the battle had apparently ended forever.

"You should come," a grim-faced soldier said to Rhiannon as the first stars twinkled in the sky.

Rhiannon knew at once his sad tale.

"The ranger took many hits this day," the soldier explained. "His blood stains the stones of every bridge; alas, not much is left within him. We fear he will not live the night."

When the Black Warlock surveyed the scene on both sides of the bridges, he was not unhappy. He had lost many talons this day, many more than the defenders lost men, and Brielle and Istaahl had showed themselves to be more powerful foes than he had anticipated. But still more talons flocked to the encampment that night, and many of them brought news that more and more tribes had heard of the battle and were rushing to join in the glorious campaign against the humans. And while Thalasi's army continued to swell, the ranks of the defenders could only dwindle.

He understood that sheer weight of numbers would get him across the great river the next day, or if not, most assuredly the day after that. Istaahl had learned of the return of Morgan Thalasi during the first battle on the bridges, Thalasi assumed, unaware of the ride of Andovar. So the King in Pallendara had been warned. But had the White Mage or King Benador really fathomed the weight of the assault?

Even if they had, the army of Pallendara would still be at least a day too late.

Once the talon army gained a foothold on the other side of the wide river, they would stamp the ground flat all the way to Pallendara.

Her face ashen, Rhiannon followed without a word as the soldier led her to the camp up by the bridges and to the small tent that held the fallen warrior.

How weak mighty Belexus seemed to her now, his face hollowed and his muscular arms lying slack by his side. He was breathing but could not answer, could not even hear, when Rhiannon knelt beside him and whispered some words of comfort into his ear. The soldier's estimate had been accurate; the young woman knew at once that Belexus would not live through the night.

Rhiannon sat there in silent sadness for many minutes, and then her sorrow began to transform. She felt the power growing within her, and at first pushed it away, instinctively fearing it. But the image of Belexus lying near death frightened her even more, and when her subconscious let the power in again, she fought against her revulsion and fear to accept it.

"Leave us," she instructed the two soldiers in the tent. They looked at each other, owing their respect to the ranger who had led them, not wanting his passing to be without proper witnesses. Rhiannon insisted again, her voice stern and powerful, and they could not ignore her pleas.

When the soldiers were gone, the witch's daughter leaned over her fallen friend, sensitive fingers touching his wounds, drawing the pain out of them. Rhiannon flinched as the ranger's pain became her own, burning, burning beyond anything she had ever imagined. She held on stubbornly, knowing that she was drawing the wounds away from Belexus, determined that he would survive even if the cost proved to be her own life.

Rhiannon wasn't certain how much she and her magics would really be able to help, but after many minutes— minutes that seemed like agonized hours—Belexus appeared to be resting more comfortably, and the burn of drawing the injuries had lessened dramatically. Some color had returned to the ranger's face and his breathing now came deep and steady.

Rhiannon would have liked to stay with him, but she knew that many others had suffered grievous wounds this day. She left the tent, sending one of the soldiers back in to watch over Belexus and bidding the other to take her to those most seriously injured.

All through the night, the power of the earth flowed through the witch's daughter, each attempt at healing sapping her own strength. Soon, even walking became a difficult task, requiring more strength than the young woman had left to give.

But Rhiannon ignored the concern of the soldier guiding her, and would not relent, and those left in her wake seemed the better for her visit to their bedside.

The talons came on again before the next light of dawn, their numbers greater than at the start of the previous day. The beasts understood that they had worn the defenders down; their master had promised them that this would be the day of victory.

In the first moments of battle it seemed as if Thalasi's predictions would swiftly prove accurate. Disheartened and weary, the defenders gave ground step by step. Within fifteen minutes the defense of two of the bridges had nearly collapsed.

But then the ranger came out of his tent. Though still

weak, the fire in his pale eyes simmered no less intensely. Belexus rushed to his mount and moved out to the back ranks of his comrades. His mere presence inspired the men and stole some of the heart out of the talons, and the ensuing rally of the defenders pushed the monsters back on every bridge. Without even lifting his sword, Belexus had turned the tide of the battle.

The Black Warlock, confident that the swell of numbers during the night would push his talons through, paid little heed to the give-and-take assaults on the bridges. He was weaker this day, drained from the magical expenditures of his previous battles against Brielle and Istaahl. But the witch and wizard were equally exhausted, he recognized, and though the storms over Avalon and the white tower in Pallendara were less powerful this day, so too were the defenses fighting against them.

There would be no sudden, vicious assault forthcoming from Thalasi; his method of attack held consistent and persistent, designed only to keep Brielle and Istaahl from throwing any offensive magic against the talons. And Thalasi knew that he had to conserve some of his own strength. For some reason he could not understand, the third of his enemies, that most hated wizard Ardaz, had not yet made an appearance, personally or from afar, on the battlefield.

Rhiannon continued to grow weaker that day, though she tried to keep her eyes averted from the action on the bridges. The lines of wounded only lengthened when rumors of the young woman's magical healing powers spread throughout the refugee camp, and Rhiannon, no matter how much the magical acts sapped her vitality, would not turn anyone away.

Here she felt as though she was giving some positive

value to the horrible power that possessed her being. Whenever a lull in her work brought Rhiannon the sounds and sights of battle, that power threatened to transform into something darker, something the young woman could not tolerate.

She could not forget the scar she had torn across the land, nor the cries of those, however evil, she had sent to their deaths.

The momentum shift in the battle carried the defenders through the morning, and many talons fell to the sword. But fresh talons, hungry for their first taste of battle, kept replacing their fallen comrades, while the defenders had to continually shrug away their weariness and fight on.

Belexus came to the same conclusion as the Black Warlock: the bridges would fall. He sought out the general of the Rivertown garrison, a leader wise enough to recognize the inevitable.

"Ye should set the wagons off again," the ranger explained.

The general had feared that advice, though he knew it was honest. "How much strength will our soldiers find when the rest of the people have fled?" he asked.

"Ayuh, ye're right enough in that," replied Belexus. "But how much life will the others find when the defenders are no more?"

Within an hour the field beside Rivertown was nearly deserted, and the long line of refugees, even longer now with the addition of the Rivertown populace, made its trudging way down the eastern road.

Now the task before the valiant defenders was to buy time for their kinfolk, and when night came on, not a single bridge had fallen. But the number of able defenders rapidly dwindled; Belexus took up his sword again out of necessity, though he was in no condition to partake of battle.

* * *

Watching from one of the few wagons remaining near Rivertown, Rhiannon fought against the destructive urging of her power. She knew that she had to act—the men could not hope to survive for much longer—but her instinctual revulsion of this foreign strength, of its consuming and uncontrollable nature, kept her focus too blurred for any definite action.

Confused and feeling betrayed by her weakness, the witch's daughter could only slump back and watch in helpless frustration as more men died.

Thalasi ended his storms when the sun went down, knowing that Brielle and Istaahl could not hope to strike out across the miles at his force without many hours of rest. The Black Warlock, too, was drained beyond his limits, and didn't even think of using any magics against the defenders of the bridges. He had other tasks to attend. His rabble talons had done well in wearying and depleting the ranks of the humans, though the cost in talon lives had been excessive, but they could not organize well enough to properly complete the attack, to gain a secure foothold on the other side of the river.

Thalasi let the course of the battle continue on the bridges, concentrating instead on assembling a spearheading force of reserves that could wait until the precise moment and simply bash through the weakened human lines.

And the Black Warlock could be patient, so he believed. His only objective now was to get his army across the river, and at this point he didn't see how he could possibly fail.

The battle slowed in the blackness of a moonless night, and Belexus and his charges held on. Every minute, they knew, took the fleeing people a little farther from the talon horde.

The Black Warlock was not concerned. He let the deepest hours slip by, waiting for the brightening of predawn to loose his killing reserves.

And when the moment at last arrived, the talons, spurred by threats of Thalasi, were up to the task. They plowed through the length of the southernmost bridge and swung back to the next, trapping the humans on this second bridge. More and more talons poured onto the eastern field, securing the hold.

The second bridge fell in only minutes.

Tears streaked down the cheeks of the witch's daughter. They would all soon die, even Belexus, and she could not find the strength within herself to help them. The surge of power came again, and she tried to welcome it, tried to use herself as its focusing channel.

But her deepest instincts fought back, holding the power in check.

A thousand defenders remained, but ten times and more that number of talons stood against them in the openness of the field. There could be no retreat; to break ranks and flee would only mean that the defenders would be hunted down individually and slaughtered.

Few would have fled anyway. Watching Belexus, wounded again but refusing to yield, refusing to show any hints of fear, the humans fought and sang.

Without hope.

His plan running of its own accord, the Black Warlock loosed all of the magics the night had restored to him in a renewed attack against the witch's forest and the wizard's tower. Now, with his too-numerous talons leading the way, only his magic-wielding enemies could deny his victory, he believed, and he would give them no opportunity to launch an offensive.

His army was barely minutes from complete victory.

The sound of a hundred horns split the air, the thunder of pounding hooves shook the ground. And above the sudden confusion that startled the men and talons alike came the powerful blast of one note, one so familiar to Belexus.

"Andovar!" he cried. "Fight on, brave warriors, for the army of Pallendara is come!"

Eyes turned to the east and the hearts of the men leaped in hope and pride, while the talons cursed and shrieked in rage.

On came the Warders of the White Walls, led by the Ranger of Avalon and by the King of Calva himself. Five hundred spear tips glistened in the morning light, though the riders seemed little more than ghostly silhouettes with the dawn breaking behind them.

And on the flanks and behind the elite soldiers of Pallendara came groups of volunteers from all of southern Calva, five times greater in number and no less determined than the professional soldiers they followed. Farmers and fishermen who had grabbed up their weapons and ridden in the wake of their beloved King. But it was the practiced regiment of the great city soldiers, who had spent the bulk of their lives in training for just such an occasion, that swiftly turned the tide of battle. The Warders formed a wedge-shaped formation, and King Benador drove them into the talons in a thunderous rush, trampling and scattering the invaders with such brutal efficiency that the bulk of the talon force turned tail and fled back across the river.

Fully engaged with his magical opponents, his powers almost depleted, the Black Warlock could only watch as his army was repelled once again. He would not gain the river this day, and with the kingdom of Calva so fully roused, the cost of breaking through, if ever he could, would be expensive indeed.

"How?" he demanded. He had not believed that the army could possibly arrive for another full day. "It is not possible!" he cried out in such fierce rage that he sent his closest talon commanders and his litter bearers fleeing into the field.

But Thalasi's denials were futile; this day the Black Warlock's bark had little bite. In an hour the bridges were secured once again, and the new army now facing Thalasi, well-trained and led by the King, would not be so easily pushed aside.

Rhiannon watched the victory unfold with sincere relief. Her guilt had been lessened by the charge of the Warders, but she would not soon forget the torment that her welling powers had put her through this morn. Would she ever come to terms with this hideous strength? Or was she a damned thing, always to be torn apart by magics she could neither control nor understand?

They were questions Rhiannon wanted to sit and ponder, but a short time later the witch's daughter had to put her emotions aside once again. One side effect of the battle did indeed concern her directly.

The lines of wounded began anew.

Chapter 12

The Lull

ANDOVAR WATCHED THE large tent patiently as the quiet hours of night drifted by. He wanted to rush inside to the young woman who had stolen his heart, but he understood that the wounded needed Rhiannon more than he. Every so often her shadowy silhouette crossed the side of the tent, hunched and weary.

The ranger did not like to see the spirited lass that way.

When the moans of the injured had become a soft murmur, and the witch's daughter had turned down the lamp inside the tent to a slight glow, the ranger could wait no longer. He moved to the flap of the tent and pushed it aside. Rhiannon had her back to him, barely five feet away, yet so weary was she that she did not even sense his presence. She was bent over a basin, washing the blood and gore from her delicate hands.

She knew it was Andovar as soon as he laid his gentle hand on her shoulder. Rhiannon spun into him, crushing her face into his chest, and all the frustration and sorrow she had suffered these past few days came pouring out in a deluge of tears and quiet sobs.

Andovar fought back the wetness rimming his own eyes,

knowing that he had to be strong for her at this moment. He was a Ranger of Avalon, living on the borderlands of civilization, and had known battle before, had lived it all of his life. But Rhiannon, grown twenty years under the springtime canopy of her mother's enchanted forest, had no experience and no understanding for the horrible sights that fate had so abruptly thrown in her path.

"Ye knew I'd return," he said after a short while. "I'd not leave ye in yer trials."

Rhiannon nodded and stepped back from him. "Never did I doubt ye," she replied. "But never could I guess if ye'd be in time."

"But I am a ranger," Andovar protested with a spirit-lifting chuckle. "Me duty it is to arrive on time. And I'm not for missin' me duty!"

A smile crossed Rhiannon's tired face, a wonderful smile that for an instant washed away all the pain and weariness. She started to say something, but Andovar's lips pressed in against hers.

And for both of them, for that brief moment, everything was all right.

But only for a brief moment.

Rhiannon pulled back suddenly and turned away.

"What is it?" Andovar asked.

Rhiannon still could not look him in the eye. "Many the things I have done," she started to explain. "Terrible things."

Andovar did not understand.

"The earth itself split apart at me call!" Rhiannon confessed. "And I know not how many I killed."

Now Andovar understood. Belexus had told him of the young woman's—the young witch's—actions against the talon cavalry. She had saved the day, but Belexus had observed, correctly it would seem, that the act had disturbed Rhiannon greatly.

Now Rhiannon did look Andovar in the eye, and her expression was one of terror as much as remorse. "I do no' know how I did it; truly I do not. The power grew in me and forced itself through, from the very ground at me feet, it did."

"Ye did as ye had to do," Andovar replied softly. "Ye should feel no guilt for killing an enemy that picked the fight."

The ranger didn't comprehend that killing the talons was but a small part of Rhiannon's trauma. "I'll be takin' no credit for the killing," she said sharply. "For suren 'twas not meself that did the deed. Ye canno' understand, though I know ye mean to try." She paused, searching for the words to express her feelings of being possessed, of being violated, by the terrible power.

"And how many have ye saved this day?" came a voice from the tent flap. The two turned to see Belexus enter. "I number meself among them, for me wounds had me down and dying just a day ago."

Rhiannon shrugged; the good deeds she accomplished seemed almost unimportant compared to the confusion this power, even in the act of healing, brought to her. And compared to her failure in the course of the day's events, when she had pushed the power away and denied its call, when she was too weak and cowardly to use it even to save what remained of the brave defenders of the bridges, any good she had done surely paled.

"Many still draw breath because of the work of Rhiannon," Andovar agreed. "Ye have brought comfort and rest; look around ye for the proof." He led her gaze to the dozens of men sleeping peacefully on the cots of the large tent. "What guilt then should ye feel?"

"But how many would have felt the pain not at all?" Rhiannon cried. She looked at Belexus, and he could not understand the apologetic expression etched into her delicate features. "I could've crushed them, every one, when they came on us this morn! I felt it growing in me, and stronger than the fury when I tore up the western field."

No anger crossed the faces of the rangers, only sincere pity.

"But I pushed it out!" Rhiannon hissed, a new wave of tears rolling down her cheeks. "I threw it away, though me own cowardice sent men to their deaths!"

Andovar pulled her close and hugged her with all his strength. "No," he said.

Belexus agreed. "Ye did as ye could, lass. And more than any other, it was. Ye owe yerself no guilt, and no apologies do ye owe to any others, though me guess's that many owe ye their thanks."

"And the day was won," Andovar reminded her.

Rhiannon buried her face in the folds of Andovar's cloak and did not reply. Belexus left them with a nod to his friend, and Andovar put his head on Rhiannon's and held her as her sobs soon transformed into the steady rhythm of merciful sleep.

And still he held her, slipping into a chair and cradling his love until the first light of dawn pinkened the eastern skies.

The Black Warlock did not sleep that night—again—and truly this wretched being no longer required any sleep. The thing that Morgan Thalasi and Martin Reinheiser had joined to become little resembled a living creature now, and each day the absolute evil that bound the two spirits stole more of the remaining resemblance away. But this drawing vileness did not take from the life force of the being. Quite the contrary, the Black Warlock felt himself growing stronger every day as the harmony of the two spirits increased into a singular obsession for power.

But at this moment Thalasi knew only rage. His plans for

a swift and brutal march to the Calvan seat of power had come to an abrupt end, for though his talons still outnumbered the human defenders across the river, the rabble force could not hope to break through the skilled defenses of the more experienced soldiers. Both sides would dig in now, with reinforcements streaming in daily. Thalasi could only guess which army would eventually prove the larger.

And so it was with the battle of magics as well. The Black Warlock knew that he would only get stronger, but he had lost the offensive against his rivals in Avalon and Pallendara. Istaahl and Brielle would confer and seek methods of combining their powers against him.

And what of Ardaz? The Silver Mage of Lochsilinilume had not yet even made an appearance, a situation that the Black Warlock knew would not last much longer.

Above all the other contemplations and possibilities that the Black Warlock faced on this calm night, one inescapable fact hammered at him relentlessly: he had erred greatly. If his talons had been better organized and controlled, the sweep across the western plains would not have sent so thick a line of refugees in flight down the roads to warn the more eastern towns. And even after those initial blunders, if he had better coordinated the assault against the Four Bridges, his army would have broken through and gained a firm foothold on the eastern bank before the forces from Pallendara had joined in the battle.

"I have taken on too much," the Black Warlock lamented aloud. "I have played too many roles in this war." He looked around at the vast talon encampment, tribes separated by clear boundaries, and with a dozen fights breaking out between the anxious, dispirited beasts every minute.

"What choice do I have?" Thalasi asked. "Where among this rabble am I to find a proper general?"

He shook his head in dismay, but while he lamented, a

tiny spark from that part of his spirit that had been Martin Reinheiser sent a chilling memory into the path of his thoughts. In his life before the joining, Reinheiser had known a cunning tactician leader who could change the course of this battle.

Hollis Mitchell.

"A pity I killed that one," the Black Warlock whispered, but even as he remembered that fateful day on the field of Mountaingate when he had shoved Mitchell over the cliff, another notion took root in his craven mind.

How strong was he? he wondered, subconsciously turning his gaze to the north. He was a master of the third school of magic, after all, the discipline predicated on its wielder's desire and belief that he could bend the natural laws to suit his own needs.

"How strong am I?" Thalasi roared loudly, sending several nearby talons squealing and scampering for cover. "Strong enough, perhaps, to tear the spirit of Hollis Mitchell from the realm of the dead and bring him to the battle as my general?"

An evil smile made its way across the Black Warlock's face as he considered the magical energy he would need to teleport himself to Blackamara, the foul fen beneath the field of Mountaingate. How strong was he?

It was time to find out.

Far to the east, beyond the borders of the civilized world, Ardaz put a magical light on the tip of his oaken staff and moved eagerly down the newest of the tunnels he had discovered. "Oh, simply splendid!" the Silver Mage bubbled as he came upon yet another room full of centuries-old artifacts, hand tools, and plates made by the hands of men.

"The world is a bigger place than we know, I do dare say," Ardaz explained to Desdemona, though the cat did not apparently share his excitement and would have preferred to be left to her slumbers. Ardaz had spent more than a week at the catacomb of ruins, and hadn't even come aboveground in the past three days.

And, more important to the drama unfolding halfway across Ynis Aielle in the west, the wizard had not dipped into the magical realm of his strongest powers. For if Ardaz had ventured to that other plane, that realm of universal energies, he would surely have noticed the disturbances in the very fabric of the normally harmonious powers, bends and tears that could only have been brought about by great strains on the natural order.

And only one being in all of Aielle could have done that kind of perverted damage.

If Ardaz had found cause to venture into the magical realm, he would surely have realized that Morgan Thalasi once again walked the land.

From a perch in a high tree on the side of a mountain many miles away, Bryan watched the thousands of campfires burning on the fields on both sides of the river. How serene it all seemed, as if the plain was a still lake mirroring the twinkles of the stars. Swords and spears lay at rest now; the weary armies had settled into their time of exhausted truce.

But for Bryan, the day's work had only begun.

He tensed when he heard the return of the stupid talon, this time leading three of its buddies.

"I tells yous I sees it, I did!" the talon insisted.

"A treasure chest?" snickered another. "Bah, ye're witless, ye are. Who'd'a put a chest o' treasure all the way out 'ere?"

"Mountain man trappers," a third talon reasoned, but the argument soon became a moot point, for the first of the band led them through the little clearing—right under the boughs of Bryan's tree—and to the partially concealed iron-bound chest. It took the considerable strength of all four of the beasts to drag the box out.

"Hey!" one of them cried. "Locked it is!"

"Soon to be unlocked!" declared the largest, and with the thought of piles and piles of gems and jewels lending strength to its arm, the creature brought its heavy sword crashing down on the lock.

Bryan waited patiently as the four talons took turns slamming the lock, hoping the noise wouldn't attract any more of the beasts. He had left the key lying right beside the chest, after all, and the talon who had initially found the chest had pocketed it—and apparently forgotten all about it!

Finally they got through the lock, and the largest of the band grasped the heavy lid and heaved it open. One of the others started to remark on a curious scraping noise, like flint on steel, and another noticed at once the heavy smell of oil.

But none of the warnings registered fast enough for the pitiful beast holding the lid, and when the chest exploded into a ball of fire in its face, it was caught quite by surprise.

As was another when Bryan landed softly behind it and cleaved in its head; and as was a third when the young warrior got his blade away from the second just fast enough to shove it into the gawking talon's open mouth.

It all happened so quickly that the remaining talon, the one with the key in its pocket, having recovered from the blinding burst of flame and caring nothing for the unfortunate trap springer, who now rolled about the ground in a dying frenzy, was still staring blankly into the opened chest as its other two comrades fell dead.

"It's only rocks," the stupid beast grumbled.

"You did not believe that I would use real gold to bait you," Bryan reasoned.

The creature turned to face the half-elf, and more pointedly, to face the half-elf's leveled sword, with one dirty finger hooked over its lower lip.

"You have my key," Bryan explained calmly. "You did not have to break my lock."

"Huh?" the talon replied.

Bryan thought it fitting that "huh" was the last word this particularly stupid talon ever spoke.

Chapter 13

So Many Dead Heroes

"A QUIET MORN," Andovar remarked to Belexus when he came out later that day, leaving Rhiannon sleeping in the tent.

"A bit of a skirmish they've fought across the northern bridge," Belexus replied. "But the talons have not the heart to try to cross again, the men're wise enough to keep the bridge at their backs when e'er they be fightin' their way to the western bank."

"It will slow down now for a bit," Andover agreed. "Both sides're needing to lick their wounds."

"Time for us to go, then?" Belexus asked.

"Me thoughts are the same," replied Andovar. "Let us get back to Avalon. Suren if the word's spread there, yer father will have the others gathered and waitin'."

"And not to doubt the elves as well," said Belexus. "Arien Silverleaf'd not let the moment of need pass without sending some aid to King Benador."

As if on cue to the mention of his name, the two spotted the white charger of the noble King trotting across the field toward them.

"A quiet morning," he said, sharing Andovar's sentiments. He dropped from his saddle to the side of the two rangers.

"Me thoughts to the word." Andovar smiled.

"My people were fortunate indeed to have the likes of Belexus and Andovar traveling the region when the Black Warlock decided to strike," said Benador. "And the likes of the young woman as well, if the tales I've heard about Rhiannon's actions ring true."

"They do," Belexus assured him. "Without the daughter of Brielle, the northern fields would've been lost and the road cut off. More than few o' those folk that got across the bridges would have fallen afore e'er they reached the Four Bridges."

"That I do not doubt," said Benador. "And I have witnessed myself the miracles of her healing hands. How many more would have died of their wounds were it not for the daughter of Brielle?"

"Me own bones'd be for the vultures," replied Belexus. "Suren too many were the cuts I took. The talons had me for dead."

"She has the powers of her mother," said Benador, more than a little intrigued by the possibilities. "It would help our cause to further explore this potential strength of Rhiannon."

Andovar had been listening to it all distantly, his thoughts still locked in the tender moments of the night he had spent cradling the witch's daughter. But now the ranger purposely turned back into the conversation, concerned that his friends might unwittingly add to the pain of that beautiful young woman.

"The lookin' for such strength's for the eyes o' Rhiannon alone," he interrupted.

"What do you mean?" asked the King.

"The lass canno' tolerate the power," Andovar started to explain. Behind them, Rhiannon moved out of the tent. She started out to join the three, but held back, catching a bit of their conversation.

"Ayuh," agreed Belexus. "Rhiannon fears the power, and knows not how to control it."

"But the northern fields—" Benador started to argue.

"Nearly killed the child," Belexus finished. "And she did not purposely call forth the strength."

"A possessing thing it is," Andovar remarked.

Benador shrugged. "Then my hopes are that Rhiannon will find her strength and the knowledge she needs," he said sincerely. "Surely such power is a personal thing, and not for the whims of meddlesome outsiders such as a foolish king."

Rhiannon bit her lip and forced the trembling out of her small frame. Benador spoke the truth, but even if he and the others left the decision concerning the use of the magic to her, she could not dismiss the gravity of their need. Rhiannon did not need the stress of prompting words; the carnage on the fields around her, the horde of evil talons across the river, and the specter of the Black Warlock were surely impetus enough.

Andovar put his hand on Benador's sturdy shoulder. "Foolish?" the ranger said skeptically. "Me eyes think not."

Benador shrugged the compliment aside. "What are your plans?" he asked. "I have the troops, but few skilled and experienced enough to lead them. My army would certainly welcome your command, as I would welcome your advice."

"First we're needing yer own," replied Belexus. "What fighting do ye foresee?"

Benador looked over at the bridges. Another band of talons had crossed the western entrance to the northernmost structure, and once again a cavalry contingent of the Warders of the White Walls had charged out to smash them back to the western bank.

"They'll not get across by the bridges alone," Benador assured the rangers. "We have enough strength—and more flowing in every day—to defend such narrow corridors no matter how large the talon force becomes."

"And what o' the Black Warlock, then?" Andovar asked. "We've seen the likes o' Thalasi on the field before, and he's not to be forgotten."

"And yet he's made but a small appearance," added Belexus. "Me heart fears that he's waiting, holding back, to strike full."

"He has made but a small appearance at this battle," Benador corrected the ranger. "But last night I spoke with Istaahl, my wizard in Pallendara, and learned of the Black Warlock's efforts. Thalasi has summoned storms over Pallendara and over Avalon, has sent his fury across the leagues to battle his most formidable foes."

Andovar and Belexus exchanged concerned looks. Still unnoticed behind them, Rhiannon held her breath.

"Not to fear," Benador assured them. "Brielle and Istaahl found ample strength to fend off the evil necromancer. The wood and my city took only slight damage in Thalasi's assault. And Istaahl has assured me that he and the Emerald Witch can hold the Black Warlock at bay for some time to come. And a bright spot might yet be found in all of this, for we have not yet heard from the Silver Mage. We can only hope that Ardaz makes his appearance soon, though none have yet been able to contact him."

"He is off in the east," Belexus said. "But I've no doubt that the likes o' that one will join in the battle in time to lend his aid. Ever does the Silver Mage arrive when most he is needed."

"So I have been told," chuckled Benador. "It seems, then, that we have a stalemate, for some time at least. Thalasi will not get across, and I have no desire to ride onto the western fields against so great a talon army.

"But a stalemate may not be such a bad state of affairs,"

the King reasoned. "Talons are not an orderly bunch, and have as little love for each other as they have for humans. Summer has passed its midpoint and is soon to wane, and when the first of the chill winds blow down across the open plain from the north, many of the beasts might decide that this warring campaign is not so much fun after all."

"Suren the Black Warlock'll have his troubles keeping that bunch in line," agreed Andovar.

"That is my hope," said Benador. "If the snows of winter find us still fighting a draw at the riverbank, I suspect that the force across the river will break apart for the shelter of their dark holes."

"And what o' yerselves?" asked Belexus. "The cold wind'll put a chill into the bones of yer men, as well."

"But not so much that we will abandon our lands," replied the King. "First lesson of war: severe weather always serves the defenders. And we have ample housing for those displaced, though with the western fields deserted and most of the men of all the kingdom in camp at the bridges, the crops will be meager, I fear."

"But we're to get through it," declared Belexus. "And in a fortnight ye'll have the Rangers of Avalon by yer side, and, unless I miss me guess, a host of elves besides."

Benador gave the rangers a curious look. "You have made your decision, it would seem."

"Ayuh," replied Belexus. "Meself, Andovar, and Rhiannon'll leave ye this day, back for the forest to the north. Suren ye can fight yer back'n'forth battles without the likes of us, and when we return, ye're sure to find another fightin' force beside us."

"Good riding, then," said the King. "Know that every day we'll await your return. And be comforted by my guarantee that Thalasi will not get across the river while you are gone!"

"I'm not for going," came a voice behind them, and they

turned in unison to greet the approach of Rhiannon. She seemed less haggard this day, to the relief of them all, but dark circles still rimmed the bottom of her eyes, contrasting with the light glow of the orbs.

"Yer mother surely fears for ye," Belexus reasoned.

"Me mother knows where I am, not to doubt," Rhiannon replied. "And she'd want me here, that I know." She turned to Andovar, who was obviously not pleased with her announcement.

"I cannot be leavin'," she said to him. "Even small battles bring sufferin', and I've a dozen already who'll be needin' me tendin' for many days to come. I know me place in all of this, and for the time, me place's here."

Andovar could not deny the resolve in the young woman, or the truth of her words, however he felt. But Andovar knew his place as well. The Rangers of Avalon did not assemble often in these times of peace, but when Bellerian called out for them, as surely he would now, their duty did not allow for exceptions.

"Come," Rhiannon bade him, and he took her arm and followed her back into the tent of healing.

"Ye know I must be off," Andovar said when they were under the privacy of the tent folds.

"And I know, too, that ye'll be back," Rhiannon replied, that heart-stealing wisp of a grin turning up the edges of her mouth.

Andovar pulled her close and kissed her softly on the cheek. "That I will," he said. "Keep a safe place for me in yer heart, me sweet Rhiannon."

"Ye've put the place there yerself," she assured him, and with no more to be said, the two stood in a silent embrace until Andovar had to go.

* * *

"Another storm?" Arien Silverleaf asked, exiting the tunnel to stand next to Ryell, his closest friend and adviser, and Sylvia, his daughter.

Ryell shook his head. "Quiet so far," the elf said, his gaze never leaving the forest at the bottom of the mountain trail and across the long and narrow field.

"Brielle has held on," Sylvia put in hopefully.

"But what do the storms foretell?" Arien asked, maintaining a grim view of the situation. "If it is indeed the Black Warlock—"

"Who else could it be?" Ryell quickly put in.

Arien nodded his agreement; he knew enough of the realm of magics to understand that only Morgan Thalasi could empower such destructive forces against Avalon. "Then we cannot believe that his assaults are against Avalon alone."

"So the smoke clouds we have seen in the western sky foretell a darkness indeed," said Sylvia. "Calva is at war."

"We cannot be certain," said Ryell. "There may be other explanations."

Both Arien and Sylvia cast him incredulous looks, and Ryell, for all of his hopes, had little conviction in the notion.

"If Calva is at war, then we should go to their aid," he said. "King Benador is our friend; his ascent to the throne has changed our lives greatly, and all for the better."

"Should we assemble, then, all of us, and ride off to the west and south?" Sylvia asked. "Some scouting would seem prudent before all the valley is roused."

"Our scouting has been done for us," Arien explained. He pointed down to the dark boughs of Avalon. "Brielle has all the answers we need. Back to Lochsilinilume, then. We will call out the whole of the valley. If Calva is indeed at war, then the elves will take their place beside the soldiers of the kingdom!"

Sheltered in a nest of sheer mountain walls, Lochsilinilume,

Illuma Vale, was as magical and secure a place as anywhere in Aielle. This was the land of telvensils, glittering silver trees, and the unending song of the elves, sweet and sad all at once. But as delicate as these folk appeared, and as much as they abhorred violence, they came together with the precision of a professional army when the call of Arien Silverleaf went out.

And then they came down from the Crystal Mountains on proud horses adorned in jingling bells, five hundred strong, their grim faces belying the almost childlike joy that forever rimmed their eyes.

Benador rode with Belexus and Andovar down to the eastern bank of the great river. On the opposite bank, a hundred yards away, they could see the squat forms of talons milling about, and every so often an arrow rose up into the air on an arcing trail toward their side. But talons were not skilled at making either bows or arrows, and the vast majority of the shots fell with hardly a splash into the water.

The archers on the Calvan side, bending great bows of yew, had better luck, and every so often, just to keep the talons honest, they sent a whistling volley across the river. Grim faces lit with laughter as the distant talons scurried this way and that to get out of harm's way.

"A pity," Benador observed, "that heroes come to light only in times of great pain. And a few have been made this day." He pointedly let his gaze fall alternately on each of the two rangers.

"More than a few, by me seein'," Belexus replied. "Eight hundred died on the northern fields, stopping the charge o' the mounted talons, and a thousand and more fell with Corning, giving their own lives that the fleeing folk'd put more ground between themselves and the invaders."

"Meriwindle and Mayor Tuloos," Andovar agreed. "And a thousand more whose names I do not know."

"I'll not argue the point," said Benador. "But still, some rise above the efforts of the crowd to make known their names. Belexus at the defense of the bridges and Andovar for his tireless ride will surely find their names scribed on the parchments of the bards."

"Me thanks for yer praise," Belexus replied. "But others'll be putting their names on the same parchments."

"Not to doubt," laughed the King. "Already we have heard tales of valor echoing from across the river, carried under the cover of night by stragglers. One group came in just this morn, farther to the south. Mere children—warriors of necessity. They crossed to warn us of the continued gathering of the army of our enemies. And with them they brought a woman and her two young children who had been captives of the talons, and were alive now only because of the heroic efforts of yet another lad who remains across the way."

"How many do ye still put across on the talon side?" asked Andovar.

"Not to know," replied Benador. "They drift in every night, and logic tells me that dozens of others will not survive to cross for every one that does. For all of those who do manage to make it across to safety inevitably have tales dark and bold to tell of their desperate escape from the occupied land, tales of friends who appeared to aid in their cause, or of strangers who rescued them from the very clutches of talon scum."

He took a wide survey of his own forces, then across the way to the wide, flat plain of the western fields.

"So many heroes will emerge from this," the King said, his voice plainly edged in sorrow.

"Too many," Belexus agreed sadly. He remembered Meriwindle, the noble elf he had met briefly in Corning, centuries old but with centuries yet before him in his long-lived life.

Except for the intrusion by the Black Warlock.

"And how many will be needed?" Belexus asked, speaking as much to the mourn of the wind as to his companions. "What toll o' death and terror will appease the likes o' Morgan Thalasi? Or does the foul wizard never plan to take his beasts back to their dark holes; will we have to fight them every inch?" Belexus looked back at his friends.

"Too many heroes," he whispered. "Too many dead heroes."

Chapter 14

Showdown

BRIELLE DRIFTED THROUGH the afternoon mist of Avalon, floating like a ghost in her woodland domain. Bone weary from her battles against the storms of the Black Warlock, the fair witch knew that many days would probably pass before she was allowed any true rest. For she and Istaahl, and Ardaz whenever he returned, were the only known guardians in all the world against the workings of Morgan Thalasi. Ever vigilant they had to be, for without their countering enchantments, the Black Warlock could sweep down great numbers of Calvan soldiers with ease.

They had been lucky so far, for the valor of Andovar and his heroic ride and the good sense of her own daughter had foretold the coming of Thalasi early on in the conflict. And only the appearance of the Black Warlock himself even tied Brielle to the war. Without that link, the earth-staining perversion that was the Black Warlock, Brielle would have found little powers at her disposal in the battle at the Four Bridges. Hers was a magic of the earth, a sentinel's role of guarding her secluded domain against any uninvited intrusion; and beyond her domain, the borders of Avalon, the

Emerald Witch would have had little influence or purpose fighting in a war between men and talons.

Now, however, Brielle found herself wholeheartedly in the middle of it, the earth providing her with all of the power she could contain in her efforts against the unnatural perversion that was Morgan Thalasi.

She moved to a small clearing, and to the hollowed stump of a tree in its midst, its bole filled with water from the last rain. Reflections from a dozen stars dotted the still black surface, but with a simple chant and a wave of her hand, Brielle dismissed them and brought up the image of Istaahl's room in their stead.

The White Mage of Pallendara accepted the intrusion readily; he had been sitting before his crystal ball awaiting Brielle's call.

"You have held out against the insinuations of Thalasi," Istaahl said to her. "His attacks against my tower were lesser yesterday, and have come not at all since. I feared that he had sent the whole of his wrath against you."

"Nay, his attacks against me wood came weaker, too," Brielle replied. "And not a rumble this day. It seems that the dark one has his limitations."

"And a good thing he does," said Istaahl, straining to show a smile. "I have not worked so hard in many, many years. I do not know how I would have fared if Thalasi had come on again with the same fury as his first attack.

"But I do not trust his show of weakening," Istaahl went on. "I fear that the Black Warlock may recover quickly, and that only the magic I have set in my tower walls will hold the strength to keep him back. In my heart, my place is on the battlefield beside my king, yet I fear to leave the White Tower lest neither it nor myself could stand alone against the Black Warlock."

Brielle, with her daughter somewhere down on the ravaged plain, understood Istaahl's torment, for she, too, wished but feared to leave her domain. Again risen from an apparent grave, this new embodiment of Thalasi was too much of an unknown factor; Brielle couldn't risk separation from the forest that gave her strength. "Have ye noticed something strange in his attacks?" she asked. "Shifts in the power and the like?"

"I have," Istaahl was quick to agree. "As if his attacks were guided alternately by different hands."

"Mighten be a waver as he shifts his concentration back from yer tower to me wood," Brielle reasoned logically. But she suspected something different—though she had no idea of what. "Suren a dark day on the world when that one came out o' his hole."

"And a dark way ahead," Istaahl added. "The Black Warlock will not be one so easily put back into his hole. Have you located Ardaz yet?"

"Nay, that one's off on a hunt and not to be looking back this way for many weeks. I've spies about, and suren he's soon to feel the rumble o' the magic war."

"Still," said Istaahl, "the sooner the Silver Mage returns, the better off we all shall be. Thalasi holds us even, though he has not, at least to my knowledge, flexed his magical muscles in many years. I fear that he may gain a bit of an edge with practice."

"Not to worry," Brielle replied. "Ever has me brother been the last to arrive, but ne'er once has he been too late for the game.

"I'm for going now to me rest," Brielle went on. "The onset o' the night might bring a new trick or two from the dark one, and already the sun's sittin' low in the west."

"Agreed," said Istaahl. "And if an attack does come to you with renewed fury, call on me for aid. I am weary, but I'll fight for beautiful Avalon to the last of my breath!"

"Me thanks," said Brielle. "But fear not. Morgan Thalasi'll have to be showin' much more than he has thus far to truly bring harm to me wood."

Istaahl, of course, knew the truth of the witch's words. If the Black Warlock managed to conquer all of Calva, and all of the world surrounding Avalon, the enchanted forest would still stand untainted. And the effort Thalasi would need to conquer that last shining island would be tenfold his exertions in bringing the rest of the world under his dark fold. For in her domain, in the forest that was the extension of the purity of her magic, Brielle was the mightiest of the four wizards.

"Farewell, then," the White Mage said as his image faded from Brielle's divining pool. "And fight well."

"And to yerself," Brielle replied, and then she moved away from the small clearing, seeking a hillock that would show her the sunset beyond the western plains.

Rhiannon labored all through the afternoon tending to those freshly wounded in the day's skirmishes and those still healing from the days before. With each soothing charm the young witch grew more at ease with the magical energy flowing through her body. Its course ran smooth and straight, hardly disrupting the normal rhythms of Rhiannon's own life force.

But whenever Rhiannon's thoughts turned dark, to the gorge she had carved into the plain or to the bloody battles on the bridges, the magic fluctuated and burned, threatening to overwhelm her in a pit of possession so very deep that she doubted she could ever climb out.

Around her there remained enough blatant, brutal suffering for Rhiannon to ignore those dark urges, though, and concentrate on her healing.

* * *

More than a hundred miles to the north, Brielle sent her perceptions into the untainted soil of Avalon and sensed the subtle vibrations of her daughter's work. She feared for Rhiannon, though she trusted implicitly in the young woman's good sense and resourcefulness.

Brielle hoped that only she, so attuned to the emanations of Rhiannon, could feel the budding power in the young witch; certainly Thalasi would be quick to strike if he learned that yet another magic-user was growing to power against him.

The vibrations from Rhiannon's magic rang stronger to Brielle this day, clearer and purer, and the Emerald Witch was pleased that Rhiannon would soon come into her full strength. But the elder witch knew, too, the pain that inevitably accompanied the acquisition of such power. She wanted to fly out right then to the south and scoop Rhiannon up in her protective arms, but she had to trust her daughter, now a young woman and no more a girl. If Rhiannon wanted, or needed, to come home, she would. And if she did not return to Avalon, Brielle had to assume that some more important duty kept her away.

Then a wicked jolt rocked Brielle back on her heels, a discordant twanging in the song of the earth that brutally reminded her of her own duties. Only Morgan Thalasi could disrupt the earth song so wickedly, and either the Black Warlock's power had grown exponentially during the course of the day . . .

. . . or he was very close.

"Come out, come out, wherever you are!" the Black Warlock hissed, a taunt from a child's game of another world. He stood now, confident and arrogant, on the western border of Avalon. Seeing no answer to his call forthcoming, he sent another searing line of fire into the thick boughs, and the flames leaped higher into the evening sky.

"Oh, do come out and play, Brielle!" he shouted, his tone a mocking whine. "I do so hate to play all by myse—"

A blast of wind exploded out of the forest, smothering the Black Warlock's flames in the blink of an eye and slamming into Thalasi's skinny frame with the force of a hurricane. His cloak whipped out behind him, the folds in his shirt and pants buffeted and tore. But the Black Warlock only smiled and casually held his ground.

And then Brielle appeared on the edge of her domain, surrealistically limned by the first twinklings of the evening's starlight. Even Thalasi had to pause and gape in the face of the stark power of the Emerald Witch, so beautiful and terrible all at once.

"Get ye gone!" Brielle commanded, and Thalasi almost obeyed in spite of himself.

"Pitiful," he snorted instead, masking his initial awe. "I have come to visit; is this how you welcome guests?"

The curious dual tone of the Black Warlock's voice surprised Brielle. "Ye gave up yer right to be calling yerself me guest many centuries ago, Morgan Thalasi," she retorted. She looked curiously at her enemy, wearing the body of Martin Reinheiser. "If that's who ye truly be. And now ye come to me, wrapped in a new coil but smellin' no less foul."

"Morgan Thalasi," the Black Warlock echoed, dipping into a low bow. "That is indeed who we be."

"Then ye've possessed yer lackey," Brielle laughed. "And have ye let Martin Reinheiser remain within, or have ye kicked him out?"

Sudden rage sent a tremble through the Black Warlock's face, as Brielle had suspected: the two spirits were not as completely aligned as Thalasi would have hoped.

"Reinheiser is in here," the Black Warlock began, "and he is not. There is only we, two together in one."

"Two smells for a single stench," the witch mocked.

"Impudent!" Thalasi roared, his bony hands clenching his sides. He composed himself quickly, though, knowing that a calm attitude would be necessary in dealing with Brielle so very near her domain.

"Why have ye come out?" Brielle asked him earnestly. "What do ye hope to be gaining? Suren ye'll kill thousands o' men and talons alike, to yer pleasure. But suren ye'll be driven back as e'er before."

"Not this time," Thalasi countered, his voice a hiss, his eyes angry dots of simmering fire. "I . . . we are stronger now, Jennifer Glendower. The time has come for Morgan Thalasi to claim the world that is rightfully his."

"Never it is!" Brielle snapped back, equally enraged. "Twice before ye've made the claim; twice before ye've been sent slinking back under yer rock."

"Third time is the charm," Thalasi purred. "This time I will get that which I deserve."

"Ye've long ago been given more than ye deserve," Brielle countered. "Blessings o' the Colonnae upon ye, but did ye put them to rightful use? No, not a one such as yerself! Ye turn the powers for whatever's pleasin' yer whims and with not a care for those around ye."

Rage bubbled inside the hollowed sockets of Thalasi's black eyes. Again his bony hands shook and clenched.

"If ye truly are to get what ye deserve, Morgan Thalasi," Brielle continued, undaunted by the growing volcano that was her enemy, "then me thinking's that ye should be feeling terror."

"You puny . . ." Thalasi stammered, barely able to spit out the words. "You are nothing more than a sentry, a guardian for powers you cannot begin to understand. You dare to taunt me? Look upon me, Jennifer Glendower. Look upon the godlike being that is the Black Warlock!"

Brielle's answer, an overripened apple, splatted into Thalasi's face.

His roar bent the mightiest oaks and sent Brielle's golden hair standing out straight behind her. She squinted through the blast to see the Black Warlock polymorph, bending and stretching his form to gigantic proportions.

A dragon.

His inhale sent the trees back over the other way, and the return blast of his breath came out in an explosion of searing fire.

But Brielle was ready for such an obvious attack. She threw her hands out in front of her and called upon the element of water. A geyser erupted from her fingertips, meeting the dragon breath halfway between the combatants in a snarling hiss of harmless steam. Still Thalasi breathed his fire, and still Brielle's water gushed forth to beat it back.

Even dragons run out of breath.

He was Thalasi again, in human form, soaking wet and with wisps of steam trailing out of his nose and mouth. "You have survived only the first round," he promised, and he clapped his hands together, sending a shower of sparks flying into the night air about him.

Feeling the sudden collection of his power, Brielle burst into her own somatic gestures, waving her arms in a circular motion in front of her.

Thalasi's lightning bolt thundered in, but Brielle's conjured mirror blocked its path and sent it back toward its caster.

As soon as he loosed the bolt, Thalasi had set up a defensive pattern of his own, and the lightning bolt found yet another enchanted mirror blocking its path. It ricocheted back and forth between the two magic users, seeming no more than a singular cracking light until its energy dissipated in a shower of harmless sparks.

Blind anger launched Thalasi's next attack; if he had taken

the time to think, he never would have used this particular method. A black vine lined with rows of cruel thorns dripping poison rocketed out of the ground and rolled out menacingly toward Brielle.

The witch laughed and snapped her fingers in response to the spell. "Ye mean to use me own earth against me?" she asked incredulously. The vine still came on, but Brielle accepted it.

For soft flowers now bloomed where the thorns had been, and the stem's sickly color now showed bright in vibrant green. It encircled the witch, a triumphant wreath.

And now it was Brielle's turn to attack. She lifted her hands into the air, and the grass around the Black Warlock responded by growing to the height of the man, each blade reaching in to entwine him with razorlike edges.

"Damn you!" Thalasi roared, and a ring of fire started around his feet and swept out in a wide arc, destroying Brielle's grass.

Brielle struck again even before her enemy's fires had completed their work. She pointed a single finger at the ground under Thalasi's feet and spoke a word of doom. The hard ground became mud, and the Black Warlock dropped in and disappeared from sight.

Brielle replaced her finger with a clenched fist, and the ground returned to its previous solid state. Then the witch waited cautiously. She may have humiliated the Black Warlock, but she did not believe for a minute that her simple trick had destroyed him.

A rumble under her feet confirmed her belief.

The ground exploded into man-sized divots, and Thalasi, a dragon once again, roared up into the air. His fiery breath came on, its fury tenfold. But again Brielle met it with a thick and unrelenting spray of water.

And so it went, back and forth for many minutes, each

magic-user assuming various forms or manipulating the environment to strike out, and the other inevitably countering with appropriate and cunning defensive actions.

And then they were both in their human forms again, facing each other and gasping too hard for breath even to shout out further insults. Thalasi slammed his bony hands together, and the lightning crackled and built.

Brielle put up her mirror in time, and Thalasi created his before the bolt came thundering back. But this time neither would let the charge dissipate. It was time, they both understood, to finally determine who was stronger. Brielle added a second bolt to the dizzying volley, Thalasi a third. Back and forth the lightning crackled, every circuit exacting a toll upon each of the defensive shields.

Brielle stood resolute, drawing on Avalon for further power. Thalasi, though, so far from Talas-dun, his bastion of strength, eventually began to weaken. The witch recognized the waver in his defensive field, and she added yet another blast on the very next rebound.

The darkness of the night was stolen away in the instant of the explosion; the ground rumbled as far away as the talon and human encampments across the Four Bridges, and up in the Crystal Mountains, where the elves were preparing their march. And when the smoke cleared, the Black Warlock sat on his butt, many feet back from where he had begun the encounter, his clothes burned and smoldering.

"You have not seen the last of me!" he cried in defiance. He slammed his fists on the ground, sending two cracks in the earth rushing out toward the Emerald Witch. Brielle easily halted the charge of the gorge, but when she looked back after casting her countering spell, the Black Warlock was gone. She spotted him high in the distance, in dragon form again, flying far away off to the north.

Brielle turned her attention back to her forest, and to the

blackened, savaged oak tree that had absorbed the brunt of
the Black Warlock's initial assault on the wood. The witch
stroked the charred bark tenderly, hearing the painful mourn
of the great tree's death throes. For centuries it had stood,
one of the cornerstones of Avalon, one of the very first trees
nurtured by the magics of Brielle. It had performed its task
to perfection, pulling in the wrath of the Black Warlock, accepting the assault of flames with its wide branches so that
other, younger trees might escape the devastation.

And the oak had paid with its life.

Brielle remained with the tree until it cracked apart,
sending a renewed shower of sparks flying into the air, and
toppled with a heavy crash onto the open field beyond the
forest's thick borders.

The witch had won her confrontation with Thalasi, but the
effort had cost her dearly, in strength and in the scars that
would linger for many years on this edge of the forest. And
the battle had unsettled Brielle as well, for she knew, and no
doubt Thalasi knew, too, that if they had met in combat anywhere other than Avalon, the very heart of Brielle's powers,
the outcome would surely have been different.

The only weakness the witch had detected in the Black
Warlock was the subtle discord between the two spirits in-
habiting the single being. But this gave Brielle no cause
for hope; what remained of the individual spirits of Martin Reinheiser and Morgan Thalasi seemed diminutive and
was likely fading away quickly. The bond between the spirits
would only strengthen, Brielle supposed, and when the joining of the two was truly completed, the resulting being would
be even more formidable.

She must take care not to turn her back on that one for
even an instant.

Especially over the next few hours. For Thalasi had gone
north, not back to his talons in the south. Brielle could guess

his destination easily enough. Beyond the northern ridge of Avalon, in a box canyon, loomed the foulness of Blackamara, a tangled, evil swamp. Thalasi would find solace in that pit of perversion as surely as Brielle gathered her strength in Avalon. And within the dark gloom of Blackamara, the Black Warlock would be virtually untouchable while he recuperated.

Brielle slumped heavily against an unharmed elm, asking the earth to give her still more power this dark night. She needed to rest, but she knew that she could not. Thalasi lurked but a few short miles away, and her forest had to be defended by magical wards in case the Black Warlock decided to pay another visit on his way back to the southland.

With a last look to the dead oak, Brielle gritted her teeth and started off along Avalon's borders, determined that Morgan Thalasi would not catch her or her forest unawares ever again.

Chapter 15

The Staff of Death

STILL ENCASED IN the body of a dragon, the Black Warlock slammed through the thick canopy of Blackamara, tearing vines and splintering limbs, and swooped down to the swamp's muddy ground in a furious rush.

"Never again!" he roared, and the sound of his dragon voice echoed off the high cliff walls surrounding the swamp, shook the trees in Avalon to the south, and sent an alert running through the encampment of the elves who had gathered on the field of Mountaingate.

Then Thalasi walked as a man again, startled by his own outburst. He did not know how much strength Brielle had left to her, but he didn't think it prudent to so blatantly announce his whereabouts. He stalked through the dark, twisting boughs, taking no heed of the snakes and poisonous spiders and darker things that roamed the gloom of the Blackamara night.

New trees did not grow in this swamp, and the fetid water rarely shifted. Little had changed in the twenty years since the Black Warlock had walked through here, and after a few minutes he began to recognize some of the paths. He followed their winding course up to the base of the high eastern wall, and then south a short distance. Bones of hundreds of victims, man and horse, who had fallen over the cliff during the infamous Battle of Mountaingate, littered the region, but the Black Warlock knew exactly where to look, and soon he had found the open grave of an old companion.

"Ah, Captain Mitchell," he whispered, bending low to consider the skull and jumble of bones, relieved to find them fairly intact. Thalasi wanted to go after the spirit right then, to relieve his embarrassment over the defeat he had suffered by bringing forth the commander who would lead his army to victory. But little remained of the Black Warlock's power; Brielle had taken everything he had to throw at her. He could not hope to cast such a powerful enchantment in his present state, and he realized that if he truly wished to regain his strength, the sun would rise and ride across to the western sky before he again opened his eyes.

"A curse upon that witch," he spat, wondering how his talon army would fare throughout the next day without his guidance and protection. Would Brielle recover faster than he? And what of Istaahl; would the White Mage sense his absence and use the advantage to strike out against the wizardless army?

He shook the thoughts from his head. Even if the talons were scattered by the forces—magical and otherwise—of his enemies, the cost would be worth the gain. Thalasi knew now that he could not possibly hope to break through to the eastern fields without a trusted general guiding the movements of the army. "And you," Thalasi growled, holding the skull up before his dark eyes, "shall be that general."

And then he was off, back toward the very heart of Blackamara, which was manifested in the form of a gigantic black willow tree. He knew the place well, for this embodiment of perversion Morgan Thalasi himself had planted centuries before.

He arrived shortly after dawn, seeing the monstrosity in all its evil splendor. The willow loomed a hundred feet in height, its trunk three times the girth of a fat man, and was supported by a root system so vast that its underground tendrils reached out to the perimeters of the swamp. Naught but evil could fester above those black roots, transforming, perverting, the pureness and health of the earth into a foul and wicked thing. All around beyond the boundaries of Blackamara the land was a tribute to the majesty and beauty of nature——the northern fringes of Avalon were only a mile or so to the south—but within the borders of the swamp, on the ground tainted by the roots of Thalasi's black tree, the power of the earth had become something sinister indeed.

Brielle and Ardaz had joined forces and attacked the place once, many centuries before. They had sent their magic crashing down upon the swamp, splintering hundreds of trees and tearing the spoiled ground asunder. But the black willow had survived, too entrenched to be displaced even by so powerful an attack, and the swamp had only grown up again, thicker and more evil than before.

Thalasi viewed the tree now and was comforted. He found a nook in the massive trunk and curled up to sleep, using the skull of Hollis Mitchell as his pillow.

All through the day, the black willow sent its power flowing into the weary body of its creator, and when Thalasi awoke, the sun low in the western sky, he felt stronger than he had the previous day, even before he had tangled with the Emerald Witch.

He stroked the tree gently, his child, then climbed onto the lowest branches. "Awake, heart of Blackamara," he called softly. "The master is come; the master needs your help."

The tree rustled quietly though no breeze blew through its widespread branches. Thalasi's evil smile widened. He spoke again to the willow, louder, using the arcane tongue of the wizards. Enchantish, it was called, and when employed by the other wizards of Ynis Aielle, its many multisyllabic words and tight phrases normally rolled out in a melodic chant speaking to the harmony of the universe. But from the mouth of the Black Warlock, enchantish sounded an evil and harsh language indeed, the croak of demons and ghouls, the discord that offended the purity of the natural world.

But no less powerful came the twanging chanting of Morgan Thalasi. He was a master of the third school of magic, a school that did not ask but rather demanded cooperation from the powers of the universe. Each cracking syllable sent a thrilled shudder through the trunk of the black tree.

He chanted for over an hour, running through a ritual he had devised many years before but had never needed to attempt. Certainly any encounter with the realm of the dead would not be without risk.

The willow answered the Black Warlock's call with the fall of a broken branch, about five feet long and three or four inches in diameter. Thalasi scooped the gift up in his hands, sensing the power the tree had put into it.

"Serpent!" the Black Warlock commanded, and the dark wood became a venomous viper writhing across Thalasi's skinny wrists and forearms. The serpent head wriggled to within an inch of the Black Warlock's face, and he blew into it gently, soothing the enchanted beast.

He knew what he must do now, though any conscious thought of the act surely sent a shiver running through his spine. Yet this being that he had become was much more than mortal man, he knew, so he tilted his head to the side, offering his bared neck to the serpentine gift of the black willow.

The snake coiled and struck, sinking its venom-dripping fangs deep into Thalasi's neck. But the snake had not bitten in any attempt to inject its killing poison—and the poison would have had little effect on the likes of the Black War-lock anyway. Instead the snake's vampiric fangs drew out the lifeblood of Thalasi, sent the potent fluids of the Black Warlock into the thing that would become his magical staff. As Thalasi felt his strength draining away, his knees buckled under him, but still he held the serpent close, giving it every ounce of power he could spare.

He would regain his strength in time, but that which he gave to the staff would be eternal.

And when it was over, sometime later, the snake became a broken branch again, though now its surface shone with ebony smoothness and its length verily vibrated with evil power. Holding, cradling, the wicked thing, Thalasi recovered his strength quickly. They were joined, blood in blood, he and his staff, his extension of perversion.

The Staff of Death.

"Greetings, my lost friend," Thalasi said to Mitchell's skull. He tapped the object with his staff, and a red light appeared in each of the empty sockets.

"Good," murmured the Black Warlock. "You have heard my call. How do you find the realm of the dead, Hollis Mitchell?"

"That is not for the ears of the living," came a distant re-ply, as much empathic as audible.

"Of course," said Thalasi. "Perhaps we can talk more when you have arrived."

"Arrived?" The voice reflected concern. "Leave the dead in their sleep, Martin Reinheiser. Especially ones who owe you a wicked debt. I have not forgotten your treachery; eter-nity itself will not erase my anger!"

"Reinheiser?" chuckled the Black Warlock. "But that is only part of the being you will face. Sleep again, Hollis Mitchell," he said, and he tapped the top of the skull once more, extinguishing the red dots of light. "And know that when you awaken to walk in the world of the living, you will be the slave of Morgan Thalasi."

Thalasi dropped the skull into a deep pocket of his robe and clenched his staff tightly. He conjured an image of Mitchell's grave below the cliff face, every detail coming into clearer and clearer focus as he deepened his concentration. And then the Black Warlock stepped through his thoughts, walked a mental bridge back to the remaining pile of Mitchell's bones.

Carefully, Thalasi lifted the bones free of the muck that had begun to envelop them and reassembled the skeleton. He knew that what he was about to attempt was a powerful enchantment indeed; it would test him to his very limits, and even the slightest error could prove catastrophic. But arrogance had ever been the calling card of Morgan Thalasi and of Martin Reinheiser, and even the specter of embodied death could not dissuade the Black Warlock in his quest.

When the skeleton was complete, Thalasi walked a slow circuit around it, his staff tracing out the circumference on the soft ground. The staff glowed with an eager black light; this was the primary purpose of its creation.

"Hollis Timothy Mitchell," Thalasi called softly. *"Benak raffin si."*

Another circuit, another summons. And again.

The ground around the skeleton bubbled, and a thin wisp of black smoke rose up and wove in and out of the bones. Thalasi controlled his excitement and continued the ritual. He didn't know exactly what to expect, but he sensed that the spirit of the dead captain was near, very near.

"Benak raffin si," he whispered again.

"You dare to disturb the dead?" thundered an unearthly voice. The Black Warlock wheeled to face the skeletal sickle-wielding figure that every man since the earliest days of the race had come to recognize as the embodiment of the netherworld.

"Mitchell?" Thalasi squeaked, his heart failing at the sight.

"Hardly," replied the specter. "You know who I am, Morgan Thalasi Martin Reinheiser. I purposely assumed the form that you would surely recognize."

After the initial shock had worn away, Thalasi found himself more curious than afraid. He stooped over a bit, trying to catch a peek under the low cowl of the specter's hood. "Charon?" he asked, now more curious than afraid.

"Charon, Orcus, Arawn—my names are many," replied the specter.

"As are your powers, by every reputation, attached to any of the names," said Thalasi. "So Death himself—itself— has answered my call," he mused. "Truly I have outdone myself."

"Fool," retorted the specter. "Truly you have overstepped the bounds of mortals. You are strong, Black Warlock, but I am blacker still!" The specter uplifted its arms, its bony fingers reaching out toward Thalasi. "Death has indeed answered your call, warlock—your own death!"

Thalasi swung at the bony hands with his staff. The specter caught it in midswing, but the contact between the embodiment of Death and the perverted staff was not what either of the combatants had expected. Black shocks of electricity engulfed both of them, cutting and tearing, draining at their vital forces with a chilling eagerness.

"What have you done?" the embodiment of Death demanded.

"I have beaten even you, inevitable victor!" laughed Thalasi. The lightning crackles wounded the Black Warlock deeply, but he knew already that in wielding the ultimate perversion that was the staff he had created, he was the stronger. He and Death were linked; he could feel the specter's horror and pain.

"Fool!" Death cried again, but it was Thalasi's response that carried the most conviction.

"Death will not take me," he growled. "I am no longer a part of the world you rule. And I can hurt you." To emphasize his point, the Black Warlock clenched the staff tighter, sending a wicked blue-black bolt coursing through the corporeal form of his nemesis.

"But I ask only a small thing of you," Thalasi continued, not even trying to mask his sarcastic snicker. "Grant me my wish and I shall let you return to your dark realm."

The specter's eyes shot lines of killing red energy at the Black Warlock, but Thalasi accepted the pain of the blast and returned it twofold with another crackle of his staff.

"I want Mitchell."

"Mitchell is mine," Death replied. "Fairly won and fairly taken."

"I gave him to you; I shall take him back."

"I will have you—"

"You will have nothing!" Thalasi boomed. "I will hold you here, and those that enter your realm will find no one to greet them. Lost souls forever lost!"

The specter's grasp of the staff weakened at the wicked truth of the Black Warlock's words. Death could not be so engaged with one resistant mortal—if Thalasi was indeed mortal. With a flash that knocked the Black Warlock to the ground, the specter was gone.

Thalasi glanced around nervously. Despite his boasting, he was not so certain of the wisdom of making such a powerful enemy. A moment later another being did rise above him as he sat on the ground, but to the relief of Thalasi, it was not the return of the embodiment of Death.

"Greetings, old friend," smiled Thalasi, holding his staff

out in front defensively until he could fathom the intentions of the one he now faced: the wraith of Hollis Mitchell.

"Greetings," Mitchell replied, his voice grating and broken.

Thalasi rose slowly, taking full measure of the wraith. It looked vaguely like Mitchell, the bloated corpse of the captain, at least, though its form wavered and shifted between two opposing planes of existence. Thalasi had taken the essence of Hollis Mitchell from the realm of the dead, but a part of the wraith existed there still, a fact that would only heighten the being's power.

Thalasi almost laughed out loud. "What will my talons think when they look upon the likes of you," he asked, "with a bloated face colored in the grayness of death, and eyes that are no more than simmering red flames?"

"If I am horrid, and truly I am, then only Martin Reinheiser can take the credit," the wraith answered.

"Oh, truly you are," agreed the Black Warlock. "And truly you are angry."

"I face now the being who murdered me," Mitchell replied. "Should I be otherwise?"

"Indeed you should," Thalasi replied immediately.

The wraith cocked its head to the side, a curiously human gesture from so unnatural a thing.

"Ever did Hollis Mitchell crave power," Thalasi explained after he took a moment to consider the somewhat disturbing movements of the wraith. "I have given you that. Power beyond your belief!"

"An undead thing," remarked Mitchell. "Yes, I am powerful," it admitted, taking a quick measure of itself, "but at what cost?"

"What price should we set upon the throne of all the world?" Thalasi laughed. Suddenly Mitchell seemed more curious than angry.

"Yes, the world!" Thalasi said again to the wraith's blank, simmering stare. "Did you think that I would battle with the likes of Charon simply to torment you? Do not be a fool, old friend. I would not have called you back to my side without due cause."

"What cause?" All traces of anger had slipped from the wraith's voice. Mitchell understood the power of the wizard standing before him; he knew that this being was somehow much more than the hollowed shell of his old companion, Martin Reinheiser.

"Do you know who I am?" Thalasi asked.

"I knew you as Reinheiser."

"And still I am and yet I am not!" the Black Warlock proclaimed, his weirdly dual-pitched voice lending credence to his words. "Within me remains he who was Martin Reinheiser, and he who was Morgan Thalasi. You see the result of the joining, a power beyond your comprehension. A power mighty enough to wrest you from the arms of Death itself.

"You will forget my treachery, Hollis Mitchell," Thalasi promised. "Beside me, you will come to rule the world." He moved to the side, to the skeleton of a horse.

"Witness my power," he said, and he touched his staff to the white bones. He would not summon the spirit of the beast; he did not need it and was in no mood for another contest against the embodiment of Death. But where the bones had been, now stood the animated body of a horse, coal-black with dull eyes. Thalasi added a few enhancements to his handiwork and created a saddle and bridle, handing the reins to Mitchell.

"Its run is swifter than any natural beast," the Black Warlock proudly explained. "Its breath is fire! Water and air will neither slow nor turn your ride! Truly a fitting steed for the commander of my talon army."

Mitchell took the reins eagerly, taking full measure of the enchanted mount. The horse's eyes glowed like embers, and sparks shot out every time it lifted and dropped one of its hooves to the ground. Physically the stallion appeared gaunt and frail, but Mitchell understood the power within its frame. Magical, unearthly power.

The stallion dropped to its knees at Mitchell's mere thought, to allow its master to mount easily. The wraith did so, and turned back to the Black Warlock, but Thalasi was off on another chore. He returned to Mitchell's side a moment later, bearing yet another gift for his general.

"Your weapon," he explained, handing it to Mitchell. It was the leg bone of a horse, capped with a human skull, a garish mace that glowed blue-black.

Mitchell's twisted smile widened when he took it.

"What shield will stop your blow?" Thalasi asked him.

"None!" the wraith roared.

"Wrong!" Thalasi retorted. "You are mighty, wraith of Mitchell, and you will rule all of the world. All of the world except for me." Thalasi pointed his staff at the wraith and uttered a simple rune.

The form of Mitchell wavered and faded. For a second the hellish stallion seemed a broken pile of waste again, and the mighty mace appeared as simple bone. But Thalasi's lesson was a quick one, and in the blink of an eye the stallion, mace, and wraith were restored to their previous strength.

"Know always who is the master," Thalasi remarked. "If ever you forget, I shall—"

"You promised me rulership," Mitchell interrupted.

"And so you shall have it," said Thalasi, a smile widening on his thin lips. "Once the wretched people of this world are conquered, my purpose will be fulfilled."

"And what is your purpose, Black Warlock?"

"Power!" Thalasi growled. "I care not for the petty

responsibilities of such a pitiful command. When I am finished with this place, I will find another. And another after that."

"Will there be no end?" Again Mitchell seemed amused.

"Never!" Thalasi sneered, white drool on his lips. "That is the joy of infinity and eternity; there will always be something more for the taking, and always the time to steal it.

"I am back to the field now; too long have my talons waited for my return. You will ride south—be wary of Avalon's cursed borders—and keep the great river to your left-hand side. With the tireless energy of your mount, you will rejoin me in three short days." He held his black staff out in front of him and launched himself into a dizzying twirl. And then he was gone, walking through his thoughts to the talon encampment beside the Four Bridges.

Mitchell took his mace up and spurred his stallion on, gliding easily through the tangle of Blackamara. He slowed as he approached one huge boulder, smacking the thing with all his strength. When the smoke and crackling power diminished, the horrid wraith chuckled at his handiwork, for the rock had split and cracked under the blow of the skull-headed mace.

Perhaps he would indeed find this second journey through the realm of the living enjoyable.

Chapter 16

Tales of Valor

"HE'LL LOSE IT for sure," the excited girl cried. "We came to you as soon as we heard of your miracle-working, but too late for his leg."

Rhiannon moved beside the feverish young lad to examine the wound. The talon spear had dug very deep, severing muscles and tendons, even snapping the bone. And now infection had set in: the limb was purplish and green and pus oozed from the edges of the bandages.

"A wicked cut," Rhiannon remarked. She put her hand on the lad's sweaty head. He was beyond sensibility, lost in a feverish delirium. "What is his name?" Rhiannon asked the girl.

"Lennard," Siana replied.

Rhiannon moved close to the lad's face. "Lennard," she called softly.

Lennard stirred slightly, but could not respond.

"Will he live?" Siana asked.

Rhiannon tossed her a comforting smile. "The wound is bad and the sickness has set in," she explained. "But we might be findin' a way to fight back against it. Ye should be leavin'."

"I wish to—" Siana started to say, but her large friend, Jolsen Smithyson, standing behind her, put his huge hands on her shoulders and urged her toward the door.

"It will be better if we go," he said.

"Save him, won't you please?" Siana begged, resisting Jolsen's gentle tug. "We have lost so much, and with Bryan still across the river . . ."

Rhiannon did not miss the reference to Bryan, a name that she and everyone else in the encampment had been hearing quite a lot lately. Rhiannon decided that she would have to speak with Siana later on about this mysterious hero.

But for now, she reminded herself, taking another look at the ugly wound, she had another matter to attend.

She waited until Jolsen had escorted Siana from the tent, then let the magic well inside her. She waited until her body throbbed with the power; she would need all the strength she could muster against so wicked an infection as now ate away at Lennard's leg.

And then the young witch pulled away Lennard's bandages and attacked the wound with fury. Her hands burned as soon as they came into contact with the rotting skin, but Rhiannon grimaced away the pain and held her ground. Behind the closed lids of her eyes, she could envision the battle in imaginary embodiments: a grotesque lump of disease, with sickly stumps of arms reaching out to smother her, and she slapped back with hands that glowed of the earth's power, a hiss of ugly smoke bursting from the bulbous fiend's form with each strike. They went back and forth in their struggles for many minutes. The monster lump almost smothered her in its wretched hug on several occasions. But each time the resilient witch beat the thing back, and gradually it began to shrink and lose its form.

Rhiannon did not know how much time had passed, minutes or hours, when she again opened her eyes. She was lying across the waist of the young man. She was incredibly weary and her hands hurt still, but she knew that those ills would eventually pass. And to her heartfelt relief, Rhiannon saw that Lennard's misery would also pass. He rested comfortably now, all hints of his fever gone and a look of genuine peace etched on his young face. The wound was still wicked, but the infection had been fully beaten and it seemed that the leg would heal cleanly.

With great effort Rhiannon pulled herself up to her feet. She wanted nothing more at that moment than to fall down on a cot and sleep.

But another battle had been fought that afternoon across the Four Bridges, small but vicious, and more groups of pitiful refugees had no doubt found their way across the river. Rhiannon knew without even looking beyond the tent flap that the line of wounded had been renewed.

After a short, impromptu nap curled up on the floor beside the bed of her last patient, Rhiannon emerged into the brightening morning sun of the next day. Siana and Jolsen were just outside her tent, waiting anxiously but patiently for her.

"How is he?" Siana was quick to ask.

"Comfortable," Rhiannon replied with a smile. "Suren 'twas a wicked disease that put its claws into him, but me thinks he's fought the thing away. He's a brave lad, and not to be giving up."

"And he had a bit of help," Siana said, her eyes rimmed with tears and her hand resting easily on Rhiannon's arm.

"A bit, perhaps," Rhiannon admitted.

"Can we go to him?" asked Jolsen.

"Ye can, though I'm not for knowing if he'll hear yer words." Jolsen started off toward the tent flap, but Rhiannon motioned for Siana to stay behind.

"I will join you in a moment," the young girl said to Jolsen.

"Ye spoke a name that I'm wanting to hear more about," Rhiannon explained after Jolsen had disappeared into the tent.

Siana did not understand.

"Bryan," Rhiannon explained. "Do ye know o' the lad?"

"Indeed I do," replied Siana. "We were companions, all of us." Her eyes dropped and her voice came out barely as a whisper. "Along with ten others who did not escape when the talons came. I, too, would now lie dead in the Baerendels if not for Bryan."

"Why did he not cross with the rest of ye?"

Siana's gaze instinctively went to the dark form of the distant mountain range.

"He felt there was more that needed to be done," she replied. "Many others have spoken of his deeds in helping them across the river since the night we came in; it would seem that he was right."

"He must be a brave lad," Rhiannon remarked, watching the young girl's distant gaze. Siana's eyes sparkled at the compliment, as surely as if Rhiannon had aimed it at her.

"Oh, he is," she said. "His father is—was—an elven warrior. He fought at the Battle of Mountaingate beside Arien Silverleaf himself. It seems that he passed a measure of his valor to his son."

"Bryan's an elf?" Rhiannon asked, startled. She did not think that many elves lived in the southland, so far from Illuma Vale.

"Half-elf," Siana explained. "His father married a human woman, but she died when Bryan was very young. Bryan and his father stayed on in Corning."

"Meriwindle!" Rhiannon exclaimed, putting the pieces together as she recalled the valiant elf she had met when she and the rangers ventured into the town.

"You know him?"

" 'Twas in Corning we met," said Rhiannon, "on the very morn—" She held the rest of her thought to herself, not wanting to evoke any more unpleasant memories in the battle-weary girl.

"I believe that he died bravely," Siana remarked, steeling her jaw.

"Me guess'd be the same," Rhiannon assured her, and she let a few moments of silence slip by, seeing Siana deep in private thoughts, her gaze distant, to the west.

"How long do ye think he'll be staying out there?" the young witch asked when Siana finally looked back at her.

"Until he has done his work," Siana said grimly. She still held her jaw firm. "Or until the talons finally catch him." She looked at Rhiannon squarely, her hands unconsciously clenching her sides.

"But know this," she continued in the same determined tone. "Bryan will do more than his share in the war."

"He has already," Rhiannon was quick to put in.

"And a hundred talons and more will wish he had crossed the river with the rest of us!"

Rhiannon dropped a hand on Siana's shoulder to steady the young girl. "Go to yer friend," she said, glancing over at the tent flap. "Suren he'll be looking for yer face when again he finds the strength to open his eyes."

The tension eased out of Siana's expression. "Thank you," she said to Rhiannon. "For everything."

And then she was gone, and Rhiannon was left alone in that empty spot on the field, gazing across the river, wondering how many more brave deeds this newfound hero would perform before a talon sword found his heart.

* * *

The cloaked body of the talon rose slowly in the tree. High above it, his feet planted firmly on thick branches and his back against the trunk, Bryan pulled and tugged on the rope, looping it farther over a branch every time he gained an inch of slack. It took the half-elf nearly a half hour to get the dead talon into place, but he knew that the decoy would be worth the trouble if he was discovered.

Then, on the lower branches, Bryan spent another half hour setting the heavy crossbow into place and checking the tension on the trip line. He suspected that none of these precautions would be necessary, but he had survived this long by keeping all of his options open. In the wilds that had formerly been western Calva, carelessness would surely bring his doom.

Back in his high perch, Bryan looked out to the west beyond the copse to the shadow of an outcropping of rocks and a small cluster of houses. Talons now occupied the little settlement, Bryan knew, for every now and then one of the filthy things peeked its head over the wall surrounding the houses. On the field outside the wall, a dozen or so talon corpses lay stretched out in the morning sun, carrion for the vultures. The frontiersmen hadn't fled from this settlement, not all of them anyway, and they had apparently taken their share of invaders before they were overrun.

Bryan shuddered as he thought of the grim fate those people must have met when their defenses finally collapsed. Talons were not a merciful bunch.

"But they shall be avenged," the half-elf vowed to the empty wind, and he looked to the east. Talons were not overly fond of daylight, he knew, and when the shadows of the outcropping slipped away as the sun rose higher in the sky, the activity along the settlement wall diminished. Bryan crept in along the rocks, making a complete circuit of the place, and

saw only one guard, cowl pulled low and leaning heavily—
probably asleep, Bryan thought—against a wooden beam.

The young warrior drew back on his bowstring, taking
deadly aim. Bryan held the shot and reconsidered. Still the
talon did not move; perhaps he could get in closer for a less
risky strike.

He slipped up to the base of the wall, just a few feet to the
side of the guard. The wall was fully ten feet high, but the
nimble half-elf had little trouble scaling it enough to poke
his head over.

No activity.

Bryan stepped over onto the parapet; still the guard did
not move. Bryan knew for certain that the thing was snooz-
ing now. He inched his way in, dagger in hand.

The talon would never again open its bulbous eyes.

There were only six houses inside the wall, and a couple
of smaller storage sheds. Like so many similar settlements
on the eastern end of the Baerendels, this cluster of houses
had no name, at least none that Bryan knew of. The people
here were trappers mostly, traveling down to Corning or Rivertown twice a year to trade their skins for the supplies they
would need. They probably had had no idea of the extent of
the talon invasion when this one small force attacked and
conquered their town.

Bryan moved along the parapet and down a ladder near
one of the houses, a small one-story building. The place had
no windows, but one of its doors was cracked open enough
for Bryan to get a glimpse inside.

"Nothins to eat," he heard. "Nothins, nothins, nothins!
What's these peoples do fer food, then?"

At the door now, Bryan scanned the room: a pantry, with
a large talon going from cupboard to cupboard, knocking
over sacks and boxes and issuing a steady stream of curses
to no one in particular.

When Bryan was certain that the thing was talking to itself, he slipped in, scooping an apple from a shelf just inside the door as he went.

"Nothins!" the big talon bitched again.

"How about this?" Bryan asked.

The startled talon spun about to see Bryan, a clever smile on his face, holding out the piece of fruit.

"Here," Bryan offered to the thing's dumbfounded look, and he tossed the apple up into the air. And when the stupid talon instinctively cocked its head to follow the apple's flight, Bryan drove his sword tip through the front of its exposed neck.

The next room was empty, but snores from the third put Bryan back into a cautious crouch. From the thunderous sounds and the ensuing complaints, he knew there were several of the monsters within. Prudence demanded that he retreat.

But Bryan's elven sword, glowing an angry blue, told him otherwise. He managed to stifle his chuckle for the moment it took him to spring across the empty room and barrel through the door.

Two of the five talons in the room were awake, and Bryan honestly felt that the horrified looks on their faces alone had been worth the risk.

He quieted one of the snoring talons with a sidelong chop of his sword, then got his shield up just in time to deflect a thrown chair from one of the standing beasts. The other talon bolted for the room's second door, but Bryan had anticipated such a move. He flipped his sword up into the air, catching it with his shield hand, while in the same easy motion his free hand grabbed a dagger off his belt and launched it at the fleeing talon. It thudded into the monster's back, hilt deep, knocking the talon off balance.

The talon accepted the blow with a grudging smile; one

dagger wouldn't stop its flight for reinforcements. But the creature's grim elation proved short-lived, for Bryan's thoughts followed the same line of reasoning. Even as the first dagger thudded into the talon's back, two more were on their deadly way.

The second dagger dropped the talon to its knees, the third sprawled it out facedown; it slammed the door open on its rapid descent and lay still halfway through.

"Damn!" Bryan spat. He had hoped to get the thing before it reached the door. He couldn't worry about his failure now, though, for the talon that had thrown the chair was on him, sword drawn, and the other two in the room were quickly coming out of their slumbers.

Bryan smacked away a lunge with his shield, then spun for the door at his back. He reversed his grip on his sword, though, and stopped suddenly, launching the deadly weapon with a lightning backhand out behind him.

It slipped deep into the talon's chest as the creature took its very first step of pursuit, blowing its breath out in a whoosh. Bryan spun about and tore out the blade, finishing the gasping talon with an overhand chop.

Another was up, though, and frantically trying to find its weapon. But Bryan came upon it in a hacking fury, first taking off the arms it threw up to block his slicing blows, then driving deeper into the heart of the thing, smashing it down into the blackness of death.

The remaining talon charged from across the room, battle-ax up over its head. A sudden twisting leap brought Bryan crashing into the thing before it could react, and the half-elf's shining shield flattened its face with enough force to drive its nose way out over its cheek.

The talon reeled backward, blood pouring from its shattered nose, and tried to find its wits.

Bryan followed sword first, easily finding enough holes in the staggered thing's defensive posture to finish it off quickly.

"They are fighting in the house!" the young boy whispered excitedly to his mother.

"Shhh!" the woman scolded, clutching her younger child tighter to her bosom. But the woman, too, had heard the sharp ring of metal and could not deny the truth of her son's observations.

Satisfied that the house was cleared, Bryan moved back into the pantry, replacing the daggers on his belt. He should move on, he knew, back to the wall and over, but he could not ignore the rumbling in his stomach. How many days had he gone without a decent meal?

So the half-elf gathered some food and had a seat, crossing his muddy boots comfortably up on the room's small table.

The sound of talons approaching the door only a moment later told him of his folly.

Two of the beasts burst into the pantry, stopping short to regard the young half-elf, still sitting calmly at the table, peeling an apple with a knife. "Ghost fighter!" one of them roared, and it rose up on its toes.

"Want some?" Bryan offered casually, smiling at the well-earned nickname the talons had given him. Too enraged to be confused, the monster charged.

Bryan flicked the knife into its eye.

The other talon came on and met a skidding table before it got halfway to its intended prey. Struggling to hold its balance, the creature finally recovered and threw the table aside. Growling and sputtering a hundred threats and curses, it stalked in more cautiously.

Bryan stood behind the chair now, sword in hand. He

hooked his boot under the cross-leg and waited patiently for the creature to come close enough.

The talon moved at him defensively, expecting to catch a flying chair at any moment.

"Come on, then," Bryan prompted.

When the talon was only a few feet away, Bryan jerked his leg. The talon hunched immediately, throwing its arms into a cross over its chest.

But the chair never came. Bryan stopped his leg jerk as quickly as he had started it, instead leaping out over the chair toward the talon and driving his sword in a swiftly descending arc. The talon, its hands down at its chest in anticipation of the flying chair, caught the sword squarely on the top of its ugly head.

"They never know when I'm kidding," Bryan remarked, stepping over the thing to finish off the other, still squirming on the floor with the dagger buried in its eye.

For all his outward calm, Bryan knew that the time had come for him to leave. This last fight, particularly the groans of the one-eyed talon on the floor, had caused enough ruckus to stir the rest of the compound. Bryan slipped to the door and peeked out, but then, hearing a scrape behind him, he whirled back, dagger poised to throw.

Instead of another talon, however, the young warrior's eyes met those of a frightened woman, peeking out from the trapdoor of a root cellar, cleverly concealed under a bench along the side wall of the pantry.

"I told ye, Ma," came a young boy's voice from below her.

Bryan looked back at the compound, where talons were now running about.

"Get back down!" he whispered to the woman. "I will be back for you. I promise."

The woman hesitated, not wanting to retreat again into the

dark and dirty hole. "Me and the boy and me daughter been in there the better part of a week—" she began to explain, but Bryan gave her no choice in the matter. He rushed over and gently pushed down the trapdoor, promising again that he would soon return to get her and her children to safety. And when the door was closed tightly, he then slid a heavy box over it to further disguise it from talon eyes.

The woman hid her disappointment well from her anxious son. "Sit quiet," she instructed him. "That one will come back for us, I know."

Bryan slipped his bow off his shoulder as he went up the ladder.

"On the wall!" cried one of the talons, spotting him. "The ghost fighter!" A whole group of the monsters rushed across the compound toward the marauding half-elf, but they quickly changed their minds, and their direction, when the first of Bryan's arrows whistled in.

Bryan got another few good shots off, killing two other talons before the lines of defense and retaliation began to organize around him. As the first spear came out from behind a barricade, he hopped over the wall, dropping lightly to the ground, and rushed off for the protection of the rocky outcropping.

The wooden gates burst open and a score of talons charged out, one of them dropping with an arrow in its throat. Bryan sprinted off into the open, but never too far ahead to dissuade his pursuers. Normally he would have taken that last shot offered and slipped away along the cover of the mountainside, but the appearance of a woman and her children had changed the purpose of this encounter.

Bryan sprinted across the open ground ahead of the talons, sending an arrow whizzing off wildly over his shoulder every so often. One of the talons got out ahead of its comrades, gaining on the half-elf.

"Too close," Bryan noted, measuring the distance to the trees. He notched another arrow to his bowstring and let the talon come on a bit more.

Just as the thing heaved its spear, Bryan spun about and fired.

Bryan's aim proved the better. The talon dropped to the ground.

But on sudden impulse the young warrior flinched to the side, putting himself dangerously in line with the flying spear, one hand reaching for a dagger on his belt. With perfect timing he spun just as the spear connected, feigning a solid hit while taking only a glancing blow.

Bryan stumbled backward and started off again for the trees, purposely leaning to the side, lurching and stumbling, and, secretly, cutting a small line into his forearm.

"Gurgrol's got 'im!" he heard one of the pursuing talons cry in glee, apparently unconcerned that Gurgrol had paid for the effort dearly.

Then Bryan disappeared into the thick copse, heading straight for his trap tree and taking care to leave a noticeable, splotchy blood trail. When he reached the massive elm, he smeared a red stain on its trunk, then wrapped his cloak around his superficial wound and rushed off farther into the mass of tangled underbrush.

Spurred by the apparent hit, the talons crashed into the copse soon after Bryan, tearing apart the shrubs as they went. The blood trail showed clearly, and it led them straight to the elm.

"There 'e is!" shouted one of the talons, spotting the cloaked body straddling the high branches. Spears and arrows went up into the tree, coming closer to their throwers in their descent than they ever got to the high figure. Then one talon got a small rock and whipped it up, bouncing it off a branch right next to the figure.

"Bah, 'e's prob'ly dead already," the talon spat, noting that the figure didn't move.

"If only you knew," Bryan whispered under his breath from a vantage point a short distance away.

The talon leaped into the lowest branches, a knife in its teeth, and began making its way up. Bryan waited anxiously as it stepped on one particular branch—chosen because any talon climbing the tree would have to step on that particular branch to get up any higher.

The branch bent under the talon's weight, pulling tight a hidden string. The beast heard a click off to the side, but didn't discern it as the release of a crossbow.

To the amazement of the talons on the ground, their comrade slumped to the side and came crashing down, quite dead.

"Ghost fighter," one of them muttered, and they all backed away a cautious step.

"Burn 'im!" another cried, and immediately a chorus of assenting cheers rose up. Several of the talons scrambled around in search of kindling.

Bryan knew it was time to leave, but he paused when he was a safe distance from the copse to watch the flames leap high into the air and to listen to the victorious hoots of the talons.

"They never know when I'm kidding," Bryan remarked again, and he went off to find some rest. He would be busy that night.

Again, a lone guard on the compound wall found a dagger in its chest.

The night was more than half through, but the talon party continued undaunted. They danced and sang their guttural songs all around the cluster of houses, paying little heed to the cloaked figure on the wall.

Bryan managed to get back into the house by the ladder, and he found, to his relief, the pantry empty of talons. He heard some shuffling in the next room, but couldn't wait to find out if the talons meant to come out or not. Moving to the trapdoor, he lifted it gently, calling to the woman in a quiet whisper to calm any startled outbursts.

"Come quickly," Bryan prompted, pulling the young boy out of the hole and then taking the infant girl from her mother.

"Did—" the boy blurted before Bryan could stop him. Bryan verily tossed the baby back to her mother, drawing his sword and throwing himself beside the door to the next room. But the talons were engaged in their own games and apparently took no note of the noise.

When he was certain that all was clear, Bryan led the family out of the house and up to the wall, pulling the ladder up behind them and dropping it over the other side. He could kill a score of talons this night, he knew, so engrossed were they in their celebration over the death of the "ghost fighter." But one look at the mother and her two children flushed any such thoughts out of the young warrior's mind. He had only one purpose this night.

"We have to get to the river."

They were in a boat—one of Bryan's hidden and growing stash—a couple of hours later, Bryan rowing the three across to the safety of the eastern bank.

"Why were they at such a party?" the mother asked, the first words she had spoken to Bryan since they left the compound.

"They thought they had killed me."

"You must be mighty indeed to inspire such joy," the woman remarked.

"They make me more than I am," Bryan replied humbly. "And I only use their fear to my advantage."

"You have been doing this a long time?" the young boy asked.

"It seems like years," Bryan replied, and the woman noticed for the first time how weary the young hero appeared.

"And is it over now?" she asked. "They think you are dead; why not let it be so?"

Bryan had to take a long moment to find an answer.

How much longer could he hope to evade the talons?

Why not continue on with this family and join up with the Calvan army in the north at the Four Bridges? Certainly he could use the rest and the company of humans.

But how many more families now crouched in dark holes, waiting without hope?

"I must go back," he said at length.

The woman did not question him further. She had seen too much death and suffering in the past few days to be concerned with the antics of one young warrior.

"Is there anything I can do to repay you?" she offered.

"I have some friends on the other side," Bryan replied. "Somewhere near Rivertown, I would guess. A young girl named Siana, and two boys my own age, Jolsen Smithyson and Lennard—" The name caught in his throat as he wondered suddenly if Lennard had survived his wicked wound.

"Of Corning," he continued when he got past the dark thought. "Find them for me. Tell them that Bryan hopes they fare as well as he."

The woman nodded. "And when, should I tell them, will Bryan return?"

The flash of Bryan's smile caught her off guard. She knew beyond doubt the grim truth behind Bryan's optimistic facade, and she could guess from that resigned smile that Bryan knew it, too.

"Soon."

Then the half-elf was alone in the boat again, rowing off silently toward the western bank, toward the army of evil talons.

So very alone.

Chapter 17

In the Dead of Night

THE MOON CAME up in the cloudless eastern sky, stealing the twinkle from the stars in its glowing path. So serene and peaceful seemed that nighttime canopy, so unlike the events on the land below.

The wraith of Hollis Mitchell spurred the hellish stallion around the western perimeter of Avalon. Mitchell had passed through this wood in his former life, an encounter that still brought a scowl to the evil spirit. And now, even more hateful of places of beauty and life, the wraith looked upon Brielle's forest with open hatred.

Mitchell turned his mount in and rushed up to one of the bordering trees. "For you, stupid witch!" he growled, and he slammed his bone mace at the tree. The weapon crashed in, its evil magic scorching and tearing the trunk.

But Avalon fought back.

Blue sparks encompassed the mace and its undead wielder. Mitchell resisted their power for a few moments, but was then thrown from the back of his mount. He pulled himself up from the ground, stunned.

And then Brielle stood in the shadows of her trees.

"Horrid thing!" she cried at him.

"And you, witch," Mitchell sneered back.

"Be gone from me wood," Brielle went on, rising suddenly tall and terrible. The Mistress of the First Magic, above anyone else in Aielle, recognized the true nature of the wraith, understood its very existence as a crime against the order of nature. "Ye have no place here, no place in all the world!"

"Oh, but I do!" Mitchell shot back. "A place that will only grow larger and stronger. A place that will one day include your trees."

Seething fires burned in Brielle's green eyes; the emerald on her forehead, her wizard's mark, glowered at the sight of the perversion that was the wraith of Hollis Mitchell. But for all of the strength and determination of her anger, an involuntary shudder shivered through the fair witch's spine; Thalasi's power must be great indeed for him to take a spirit from the netherworld!

"Be gone!" she commanded again, and even as Mitchell's face began to twist into a mocking smile, a light as bright as the noontime sun filled the air around him.

"Damned witch!" Mitchell cried, flashing pain burning him.

"It is yerself who is damned," Brielle replied. "Horrid thing, undead thing. By what right do ye walk the world?" She wanted to strike out fully at the wraith, test its strength there and then, and if possible send it back to the realm wherein it belonged. But Brielle had not yet recovered from her most recent encounter with the Black Warlock, and from her subsequent efforts to ward her wood against any further attacks.

Mitchell swung back into his saddle, having no difficulty in directing his stallion away.

"I will be back, witch," he cried over his shoulder as he sped off toward the south. "And next time you will find it harder to get rid of me!"

Brielle shut down the glowing sphere of her enchanted

light and watched the wraith depart. She feared that his words might hold more than a little of the truth.

"By me eyes, she's a beautiful night," Andovar remarked, looking out from the low glow of the campfire to the silvery sparkle of the great river.

"Too true," Belexus replied. "Not a night to be thinking o' war."

Andovar turned a wry smile on him. "But I was not," he assured his friend.

"Rhiannon, then," Belexus laughed. He spent a moment recalling the image of the raven-haired woman, and the exciting contrast of her shining blue eyes. "Ayuh," he agreed. " 'Tis a fitting night to be thinking o' that one. And me guess's that ye've been doing yer share of thinking o' that one."

"More than me share," Andovar replied wryly.

"She has ye," Belexus warned, but Andovar did not fear the truth of his friend's words.

"That she does," he admitted openly. "And when the business o' the talons is finished, she'll have me more, if her heart wants me more."

"Might be a time in coming, then," Belexus said. "The talons—and their boss—aren't for leaving so soon. Mighten be that ye should see yer way to the girl without a worry for the war."

"Too much fighting to be done," reasoned Andovar. "I know me duty, and I'll hold to it. I'm not for courtin' the lass just to leave her with a dead husband."

"Better that she had one in the first place," Belexus argued. "Her thoughts be lookin' to Andovar as clearly as Andovar's heart's seeing her. Ye cannot be living in thoughts o' dying, me friend. If ye're for each other, then get to each other, and let the war do what it will."

Andovar nodded his agreement and let his gaze slide

toward the north. They would arrive in Avalon soon after noon of the next day. "What do ye think—" he started, but Belexus had already guessed his friend's next concern.

"The witch'll not go against ye," he cut in with another laugh. "Suren she'll be glad for her daughter's joy, and glad, too, to have such a man as Andovar coming a'courting for Rhiannon."

"While such a man as Andovar's truest friend comes a'courting for Brielle herself?" Andovar had to ask, now holding a sly look in his own eye.

Belexus lay his head back on the folded blanket that served as his pillow. "I've seen her but a few times," he said, his tone suddenly serious. "But suren I've known her all me life." Belexus wasn't certain of his place or his duty concerning his feelings for the witch, or how she would react to those feelings. Was it the fair witch herself or her wondrous workings in Avalon that had steadily stolen his heart away over the past decades?

Whatever the cause, Belexus could not deny the emotions that filled him whenever he walked through the enchanted forest, and even more so on those rare occasions when he caught sight of Brielle dancing in a distant field or rushing among the paths of her domain.

Andovar recognized that he had sparked a bout of contemplation in his friend, and he let the conversation drop at that. He turned back to the shimmer of the lazily moving water, turned back to his thoughts of the last few days, and of the years that might yet come, beside Rhiannon.

"Fate is kind," the wraith hissed when he spotted the campfire across the way and heard the voices, those most hated voices, that came back across the years in a rush of unpleasant memories.

"Belexus and Andovar," he mused, remembering the times

that the two rangers had rushed to the defense of Jeff Del-Giudice, spouting threats against him. How much bite could those threats hold against him now?

The wraith turned the vile steed toward the river and started across.

He dreamed of home, of starry nights in Avalon and sun-bathed hillocks of clover and wildflowers. But the urgency of his friend's call cut into the meandering visions, awakened the alertness that marked Belexus as a prince of the Rangers of Avalon.

"Belexus!" Andovar whispered harshly again. He was still standing by the great river, a few dozen feet from his dozing friend, and staring out across the flowing water at a globe of blackness that had floated out from the opposite bank.

Belexus propped himself up on his elbows, separating the reality of the moment from the haunting memories of the dream. "What do ye see?" he asked, checking that his weapon was comfortably by his side.

"Darker than the night," Andovar replied. "Come, ye must take heed o' this." Even before Belexus could respond, the blackness crossed the midpoint of the river, and its true image came clear to Andovar in the moonlight.

"By the Colonnae!" the ranger gasped.

Belexus scrambled to his feet at the urgency—the sheer fear—in his friend's tone. But swifter still was the flight of Mitchell's black steed, and the wraith rushed across the remaining expanse of the river and fell over the startled ranger.

"What foulness is this?" Andovar cried, hacking futilely at the undead thing with his sword.

Mitchell took the blows without so much as a wince of pain and then brought his deadly mace down at Andovar. The ranger got his shield up to block, but the wicked weapon shattered the thing and the arm that held it, and drove Andovar to the ground. Mitchell dropped from his seat, straddling the man and raising his mace up for a killing blow.

"Now I repay you," the wraith roared in its unearthly, grating voice. Andovar's sword struck again, to no effect. For the first time in his life Andovar's battle skill would not be enough.

The ranger knew he was doomed.

Then came a sudden flurry of blows so powerful and well-aimed that even the magical wraith could not hold his footing. Mitchell gave ground as Belexus came on, the ranger's sword snapping and driving with incredible force and precision.

Again and again the broadsword of Belexus drove in at its target.

But the metal of the weapon could not truly harm this being from the netherworld, and the ranger's advantage was short-lived. Mitchell, not even trying to deflect the blows, came back on the offensive, swinging his skull-headed mace wildly. Belexus felt the power of the thing each time it swooshed by him, and he realized that a single blow could spell his defeat.

He was arguably the finest warrior in all of Aielle, and the strength in his iron-corded arms was unrivaled in all the world. Backavar, the enchantish word for iron-arm, he was called by his admirers. Belexus Backavar, Belexus Iron-arm.

But for all the truth to his nickname, Belexus gave ground now, steadily and helplessly backing from the horror of the wraith of Hollis Mitchell.

Andovar rolled onto his side and struggled to his knees. His shield arm was useless, a dead thing, and he doubted that he would ever be able to raise it again. More than that, though, the wound had numbed his side, penetrated him with a ghastly chill that crept through his limbs. But Andovar found a measure of his strength returning when he looked at Belexus, his truest friend, frantically parrying the wicked blows of Mitchell's mace now and not even attempting to launch his own strikes. Andovar gathered up his sword again and fought away the deathly cold.

"Farewell, ranger," Mitchell laughed. "You have met a foe this day that you cannot hope to defeat." Belexus could not find a reply to the claim when he looked into the dots of fire that served as eyes and the bloated gray skin of the animated corpse.

The mace came around to bear again, and Belexus, knowing that he could not play this defensive game much longer, sent his sword into it with every ounce of strength he could muster.

His sword blade splintered and fell to the ground.

Without hesitation, before Mitchell could cry out in victorious glee, Belexus leaped right onto the wraith, grabbing the mace-wielding arm and throwing his other arm around Mitchell's neck. He twisted and heaved, pulling Mitchell off balance, and for just a split second it seemed that the sheer strength of Belexus would carry him through to victory. But after the initial shock of the move wore off, Belexus realized his folly.

Mitchell's skin was so cold that it burned on contact. The ranger felt the searing pain stealing the strength from his arms, and when Mitchell put his free hand on Belexus' back, the ranger felt its clawing fingers tearing into his very heart. Then Mitchell laughed wickedly and heaved, sending Belexus flying onto his back. He scrambled to his hands and knees, fighting a wave of weakened dizziness.

"Run, me friend!" came a cry. "To Avalon! Suren the witch's the only one who can stop this beast!"

Belexus managed to focus his eyes just in time to see Andovar's sword tip explode out through the front of Mitchell's chest.

Mitchell glanced down to consider the weapon, then laughed again. He wheeled about in wild fury, snapping Andovar's sword at its hilt, and threw his arm around the stunned ranger.

"Run, Belexus!" Andovar pleaded, his voice falling away for lack of breath.

"No!" Belexus cried, willing himself to his feet. But even as he started back to help his friend, Mitchell twisted Andovar about into an awkward position and wrenched with all of his undead strength.

The image of Rhiannon, the love he would never know, came to Andovar one final time. And then it was gone, stolen in the burning explosion of pain.

Belexus watched in horror as Andovar's body bent over backward, and he heard vividly, so very vividly, the cracking of his friend's spine. Then the wraith grasped the broken form by the neck in one dark hand and lifted it high into the air.

"Doom is upon you, foolish mortal!" the wraith roared. "Tonight is the night you die!" Mitchell heaved Andovar back behind him with such force that the body fell lifelessly into the great river.

For all of his need of vengeance, Belexus knew he could do nothing against the wraith. He stumbled away into the night, choked by anger and sorrow and a horror beyond anything he had ever before known.

Mitchell called to his hellish stallion and thundered off in pursuit. The night was not dark, but even had it been moonless, the wraith would have had no trouble locating its fleeing prey. Mitchell was a creature of the night; darkness only added to his strength.

Belexus heard the pounding of the hooves closing on him. He could not possibly get back to his camp and his own horse in time. He could not possibly escape.

A white form soared by him, the force of its windy wake knocking the weakened ranger from his feet. Belexus was not the target of this magnificent creature, however, for its fury was aimed squarely at the charging wraith and his mount.

And with all the strength of Avalon spurring its rush, and with the blessings of Brielle upon it, Calamus the Pegasus, the winged Lord of Horses, met Mitchell in full flight. A crackle like a bolt of lightning splitting a huge tree sounded, and the flash as the witching magic crashed head-on into the dark enchantments of Morgan Thalasi blinded the ranger for several seconds. And when he recovered his vision, Belexus saw Mitchell sprawled out on the ground, scrambling to find his mace. The black horse was similarly dazed, wandering about in circles and shaking its smoky head back and forth.

Calamus, running now, and in a wavering line that revealed that it, too, had not escaped the fury of the collision unharmed, headed for the injured ranger. The Pegasus dropped to its front knees when it reached Belexus, nudging him to his feet, urging him to take his place on its back.

Belexus climbed on and grasped the snowy mane of the winged horse with all of his remaining strength. He managed to hold his place even when the blackness of unconsciousness overtook him, and he never knew the fury of the ensuing chase.

Calamus took to the air, its mighty wings lifting it high and fast back to the north.

But Mitchell and his stallion were quick to follow, soaring up into the night sky on the wings of the Black Warlock's enchantment.

Toward Avalon the great Pegasus flew, taking as much

care as it could not to drop its rider, but holding fast to the straight course.

Spurring his mount, the wraith of Mitchell steadily gained. That wicked smile, the grimace of the wraith, found its way onto his face again and he raised his mace for a strike.

Calamus dove suddenly in a steep descent, but Mitchell reacted quickly and was back on the tail of the winged horse in an instant. Calamus rolled out to the side, narrowly avoiding the swipe of the wraith's mace.

The dark silhouette of Avalon was in sight now in the distance. Too far, perhaps.

The Pegasus rose again into the sky, finding the cover of a cloud to give it time. Mitchell plunged right in behind, flailing away, his evil mace hissing as it tore through the mist.

Back out the other side, Calamus continued to rise, higher and higher. Then, as Mitchell steadily closed in again, the Pegasus leveled out and bent its head low, gathering as much speed as it could. Calamus could only hope that Belexus wouldn't fall; the Pegasus could not take the time now to ensure that the ranger held his seat.

And even as Mitchell raised his mace for the blow that surely would find its mark, Calamus dropped into an almost vertical stoop. Belexus half opened one eye, and his shock at seeing the ground rushing up brought both his eyes open wide. He could only trust in Calamus. He threw both his arms around his steed's muscular neck and held on for his life.

Mitchell roared in rage when he understood the white horse's intent. He could not match the dive of Calamus; and no flying creature, Calamus included, could hope to pull out of such a stoop.

Not without help.

* * *

Brielle watched both Calamus' suicidal plummet to the ground and the pursuit of the wraith, and knew that the brave Pegasus was counting on her. She waved her hand in a wide arc, and the air around her filled with strands of floating, sticky goo. They clung to the trees and to each other, growing into a symmetrical web.

Calamus pivoted and broke the fall as much as possible, but the sudden motion sent Belexus tumbling from its back. Too concerned with its own landing at that moment, the terrified Pegasus didn't even notice. Belexus hit first, Calamus right behind, their weight driving Brielle's web down toward the earth in a rush. But the strength of the Emerald Witch was in the magical strands and they held, as fine a net as the world had ever known.

Brielle wanted to rush to the fallen heroes, but she still had other business to attend. She ran to the edge of her domain where the black horse soon put down, and faced the wraith of Mitchell once again.

"So that one escaped," Mitchell laughed.

His inference that there had been others present when he had attacked unnerved the witch; her daughter was still traveling with the ranger as far as she knew.

"Not so fortunate was Andovar," Mitchell roared. "And I will get that one, too. You cannot always be there to protect him, wicked witch; I will find Belexus again. The next time he will not escape."

Brielle trembled in agonized rage. She was relieved that Mitchell had made no reference to her daughter, but she felt the loss of Andovar, the ranger she had watched grow into manhood, as keenly as if he had been her own child. Her only answer came out in an explosion of unbridled rage, a bolt of mighty white energy that sent Mitchell flying far from his saddle and reduced the evil mount to a mere pile of ashes.

All boasts stolen from the wraith's tongue, he fled with all speed back to the south, painfully aware of his stupidity in challenging the likes of Brielle, and hoping that his dark master would be forgiving.

Sorrowing over the events of the night, the great River Ne'er Ending rolled relentlessly along its southern course, past the farmlands, past the encampments talon and human, unerringly on its trek to find the southern sea.

And in its waters that night, the great river carried the body of Andovar, the ranger who had died to save his friend.

Chapter 18

River Song

THE FIGHTING ACROSS the Four Bridges slowed considerably during the Black Warlock's absence, and even after Thalasi returned to his forces, he held them in check, knowing that they would be much more effective once their new commander arrived to lead them.

Likewise did the stream of refugees making their silent way across the river diminish. The talons recognized that many potential victims were slipping right through their clawed fingers, so they began to patrol on the riverbanks. Few humans remained alive on the western side, and those unfortunate stragglers who did no longer found crossing to safety an easy feat.

And so for Rhiannon the days became longer and more tedious. The refugee encampment beside Rivertown continued to dwindle—the farther from Thalasi's army the helpless people could get, the safer they would be—and the witch's daughter spent her hours staring into the emptiness of the horizon. In some ways she was grateful for the free time and the lull in the action. Without the sound of battle ringing in her ears, the possessing power did not well within her, tearing her apart. And with little healing to be done, she finally had the chance to find the rest she so badly needed.

But free time also gave Rhiannon the opportunity to contemplate the events that had occurred, particularly the destruction she had wreaked on the field against the talon cavalry and against the earth itself.

In truth, the young witch was not yet ready to ponder the implications of such thoughts. Nor could she sort through the unknown feelings that the ranger Andovar had stirred in her. Rhiannon did not yet understand the true depth of her caring for the man, but she had begun to miss him terribly as soon as he and Belexus had ridden out of sight. And whenever the weight of all the world seemed to descend upon her delicate shoulders, she firmed them up and reminded herself that Andovar would soon return to her side. Together, Rhiannon was beginning to believe, she and her ranger could get through anything.

She found some measure of relief, though, in the three new friends, Siana, Jolsen, and Lennard, who had come across with firsthand knowledge of the young half-elven hero. The three were near to Rhiannon's age and could match every tale the witch's daughter could tell them of wondrous Avalon with a story of their own adventures in Corning and in the Baerendel Mountains. Rhiannon listened eagerly as each new—and no doubt exaggerated—story rolled by, but was especially attentive to those adventures concerning Bryan, the lad that had caught the attention and the hearts of all the Calvan people. More than a dozen groups of refugees had given Bryan of Corning full credit for their escape from the talon-occupied lands. As with all heroic tales, the feats of Bryan grew larger and larger with each telling, but even those who recognized the embellishments did not doubt that the young warrior had truly earned his reputation. And with the talons now working hard to shut down the escape routes, the general consensus was that any others finding their way across would only be able to do so because of the efforts of that special young half-elf.

Rhiannon sat beside the great river to watch the sunset one evening, as she did every evening, listening to the song of the flowing water, quiet and strong, and enjoying the splash of colors hanging low in the western sky. Here each night the witch's daughter allowed herself to contemplate those disturbing questions, but gradually, as the days drifted by, she began to find her longing to see Andovar overcoming her fears of magical powers.

How long had the ranger been gone? she wondered. She had lost count of the days; early on, when the line of wounded was still long and her work did not begin or end with the cycles of the sun, one or many might have passed.

"Five," she decided. Andovar had been gone five days. She could be satisfied with that estimate, but the answer to the other, more important question remained elusive. When would Andovar return?

"Rhiannon!" cried Siana, running down toward the lone form sitting beside the river. "Rhiannon!" She rushed up to the young woman and plopped down on the grass, her smile nearly taking in her ears.

"What's excitin' ye so?" Rhiannon replied, trying to calm the girl. "Might it be Lennard? Has the lad found his walking legs?"

"No, not Lennard. Not yet," Siana puffed, fighting to find her breath.

"What then?"

"It is Bryan!" Siana shouted. "He is alive!"

"Has he come across?" Rhiannon gasped, unable to hide the eagerness on her face. She, like so many others, badly wanted to meet the half-elven hero.

"No," replied Siana. "But another family, a woman and her two children, came into the camp just a few minutes ago, looking for me. She brought news of Bryan; 'twas he who saved her and her children."

Rhiannon, though obviously disappointed, was far from surprised. "Suren that one's making a name that will live on through the centuries," she remarked, a twinkle of admiration in her bright eyes.

"He is making a name with the talons, too!" laughed Siana. "They call him the 'ghost fighter' and greatly fear him."

"As well they should," Rhiannon replied. "Me hopes and heart's out to the lad; so much good he has done. Come now, take me to this woman. I'm wishing to hear another tale of Bryan of Corning. Never will I tire of them!"

Later that evening, Rhiannon attended to the young boy and his infant sister, mostly cleaning their scrapes and washing the grime of their ordeal from their bodies and their thoughts, while the woman recounted the exploits of her rescuer.

"He saved me and mine," she kept saying, her eyes rimmed with tears. "I try not to think of what the talons would have done to us if they . . ." She couldn't complete the thought, and Rhiannon did not want her to.

"Rest easy," said the witch's daughter. "Yer children are fine, and the thoughts of their troubles will soon fall far behind. What ye all be needin' now is sleep. She left the tent with Siana close behind. Jolsen stayed on awhile, talking to Lennard.

Siana started off to the north, toward the Calvan encampment, but Rhiannon took her by the arm and steered her toward the riverbank instead. Rhiannon did not like going to the army camp, with its grim reminders of the soldiers' true purpose in being here.

"Let us go and see the river," she said. "Her song'll put us far from this place."

Siana readily agreed and followed Rhiannon down to the water's edge, slumping down in the grass beside her friend. Rhiannon clutched her knees up close to her chest and let the notes of the flowing water fill her ears.

Siana sat in silence, respecting the privacy of Rhiannon's thoughts. And soon Siana, too, fell under the calming spell of the rhythmic roll of the wide river, and time slipped by both of them without notice and without care.

But then suddenly Rhiannon sprang up, her eyes wide in surprise as she stared at the river.

"What is it?" Siana pressed, amazed at her friend's distress. Unlike Rhiannon, so attuned to the voice of the natural world, Siana did not hear the discordant notes of the river's song.

"Not to me knowing," Rhiannon answered, equally perplexed. She had heard the river's lament, clearly and undeniably, just as surely as she had understood the truth of the talon force and their dark leader back when she and the rangers had arrived in Corning. She stepped down to the water and knelt, putting her hands into the flow.

"Is something wrong?" Siana asked, moving down beside her. "What did you see?"

"Hear," Rhiannon corrected, still examining the water.

"Then what did you hear?" Siana asked.

"Sadness," Rhiannon answered, unable to explain, for she did not fully understand it herself. The river had called to her, its normally impassive voice suddenly filled with sorrow.

A moment later, when a horn drifted into the young woman's hands, she came to understand. She jumped to her feet, unblinking, her chest heaving in a fight to find her breath.

"What?" Siana pleaded, trying desperately to help her friend.

Rhiannon gasped and held out the horn. "Andovar's horn," she managed to stammer.

"Your ranger friend?" Siana asked. "But how did it get in the river?"

Rhiannon knew. The river had told her, and now the horn, verily vibrating with the drama of Andovar's final moments of life and with the residual emanations of the unnatural, undead thing that had slain him, painted the horrible picture all too clearly.

"Me friend is dead," Rhiannon replied, hardly believing the words even as she spoke them. "In the river."

"You cannot know that," Siana argued, rushing to hold Rhiannon's trembling form. "Even if this is Andovar's horn—"

"It is his," Rhiannon insisted.

"And a hundred answers could tell why it is now in the river," reasoned Siana. "You cannot assume that he is dead just because—"

Rhiannon stopped her with a look. The young witch put her gaze directly into Siana's eyes, an expression so sorrow-filled that Siana could not remember the remaining words of her argument.

"He is dead," Rhiannon said again. "I wish it were not so, but I cannot . . ." She couldn't find the strength to finish; all the energy just slipped out of her body, out on the tears that now streamed freely down her cheeks.

"May I enter?"

The morning light filtering through the tent flap found the young woman sitting on a small stool, still clutching her legs close to her chest, as she had on the grass beside the river the night before.

Rhiannon hesitated at the unexpected intrusion, then nodded slightly. The King was on his way into her tent anyway.

"Your friend told me of your discovery," Benador explained, and he glanced around the little tent and saw the horn lying on the single table. "Is that it?" he asked.

Again Rhiannon nodded.

Benador went over to inspect the find. "It does appear to be Andovar's," he conceded.

"It was," Rhiannon said, not a hint of doubt in her shaky voice.

"Many years I spent in the company of Andovar, and all the rangers," the King remarked. "When Ungden held the throne, it was they who sheltered me and prepared me for the day when Pallendara would be restored to the rightful line, the day when I would be king."

"Andovar told me the tale on the road south," Rhiannon replied. "In his heart, he was yer friend."

"He is my friend," Benador corrected.

"Was," Rhiannon replied, undaunted, though another line of tears inevitably began making their way down her face.

"Can you be so certain?" Benador asked her.

Rhiannon's look told him that she, at least, sincerely believed in the truth of her words. "It was Andovar's horn," she said, a chill in her voice. "And Andovar was wearing it when he died."

"My lady—" Benador began, still doubting.

"Ye know who I am?" Rhiannon asked before he could continue his disputing logic.

"Your mother is Brielle of Avalon."

"Then ye should know to trust me words," Rhiannon interrupted. "Andovar died in the river. And there he remains, and there he'll e'er remain."

Benador's mouth still hung open, but he found no words to fill it. She was the witch's daughter, a witch herself, if everything that Belexus and Andovar had told him was true. And while Benador was King of all Calva, he was, in the end, just a mortal man, and he could not begin to understand the powers that this young woman possessed, and could not refute her claims.

"I meant to come and visit you sooner," he began, changing the subject. "But my duty has kept me busy in the camp."

"Ye need not apologize, good King," Rhiannon answered. "We owe you our thanks."

"No more than mine is owed to yerself," said Rhiannon, and she looked the man in the eye. "I've helped as much as I might, but 'tis yerself and yer men who hold back the tide of blackness. Without ye, all the world would have fallen to the likes of the Black Warlock and his filthy minions."

Benador accepted the compliment with a smile. "Your own value cannot be underestimated," he said. "You have saved many a life, and have made things easier for many more still. When all of this is ended, Rhiannon, the daughter of the Emerald Witch, will not be left out of the tales."

"Would that the tales could begin," said Rhiannon. "And that the fighting and dying were through."

"True enough," said Benador. "But we have stopped them here, and we will push them back. My army gathers from every corner of Calva, and help will come from the north, from the elves of Illuma and the Rangers of Avalon.

"But Andovar will not be among them," Rhiannon put in.

"Are you so sure?" Benador asked softly but firmly, moving to her side. He put a comforting arm on her shoulder. "Perhaps you are wrong," he offered. "Might it be that Belexus and Andovar fought beside the river and Andovar was only wounded? Even now he might be in the care of your mother, back in Avalon."

Rhiannon shook her head helplessly. "The rangers will

return," she whispered. "But with them they're sure to bring the tidings I've already given ye."

"Then it will be a sad day in Calva," said Benador.

Rhiannon looked out the open tent flap to the Calvan camp, already astir in morning duties, already beginning their daily preparations for battle.

"One of many," the young witch assured him.

Rhiannon spent the better part of that morning in tormented solitude, wandering through the empty streets of Rivertown. Beyond her grief for Andovar, disturbing questions of her responsibilities haunted and nagged at her. No longer could she deny who she was and what her power meant to her allies in the war that the Black Warlock had thrust upon them.

She took comfort in memories of her healing; a hundred men would have died without her aid. But how many more, Rhiannon had to wonder, would have been spared, and would be spared in the coming days, if she fought openly to drive the darkness back from the Calvan fields?

Again Rhiannon found herself down by the riverbank, staring across to the vast talon encampment. She thought of her first view of the region, before the darkness had fallen over the land, with Andovar telling her of all the strange names and legends. She remembered the tingling anticipation she and her friends had felt on their way to holiday in Corning.

And then had come the war. And now Andovar, her dear Andovar, was no more.

Rhiannon had never known such a loss before, had never felt so helpless. She wanted to change the events, to turn things back and somehow, some way, prevent the death of that man who had become so precious to her. She wanted to wake up from it all and discover it was only a nightmare.

She wanted to go back to that fateful morning and ride out to the north with Andovar and Belexus, to shield them and fight beside them when the darkness came.

But she could do nothing. Nothing.

Just sit here and wish impossible wishes.

"And will it happen again?" she asked herself. "Who else will be finding this sorrow? Meself again?" It seemed so inevitable, so unstoppable. Rhiannon could heal the wounds of some, but the swords of the talons and the powers of the Black Warlock could inflict the wounds on so many more.

Too many more.

They had to be stopped, Rhiannon decided. This madness, this war, had to be brought to a swift end. Rhiannon looked to the north, at the bridges and the soldiers. Brave soldiers. So willing to die in defense of their homes. And across the river went her gaze, to the distant peaks of the Baerendel Mountains. Bryan of Corning was out there, and probably many more heroes, risking their lives every day and doing all they could, whatever the cost, to fight back against the evil invaders.

And all the while she sat here waiting for the lucky few wounded who managed to survive long enough to get to her tent.

Still, she could not deny the importance of her role to those few.

Rhiannon closed her eyes and looked into herself. Finding no answers, she lay back on the grass and called out to the earth. It had told her of the coming of Thalasi, had given her the strength to hold off the talon cavalry and to heal mortal wounds. It had told her of the death of Andovar. Now Rhiannon needed more from the earth.

When the sun passed the midpoint of its daily travels, the young witch had her answer.

* * *

"What is troubling you so?" Siana asked when Rhiannon entered the large healing tent a short time later. She was standing beside a cot, its linen freshly stained with the blood of the war's latest victim.

"Weary I be and nothing more," Rhiannon replied. She looked at the soldier on the cot.

"He took an arrow," Siana explained. "They just brought him in. I did what I could: cleaned and dressed the wound." Rhiannon moved in to inspect the girl's work.

"I hope it is correct," Siana said nervously. "I watched you do it before. I just could not let him lie there and suffer."

Rhiannon's smile when she looked back at Siana comforted the girl. "Ye did a fine job," she said. "Yer heart was in the work."

"It is but a minor wound," the soldier said, bending his head over to take a measure of it. "Lucky shot. But no matter, with your help I can be back on the field this very day."

Rhiannon looked at Siana. "Ye'll get him back on the field," she said.

Siana's face twisted in surprise and confusion, as did the soldier's.

"Will you not help me, then, Mistress Rhiannon?" he pleaded. "So many have told of—"

Rhiannon stopped him with an outstretched hand and a comforting smile. "Not to be fearing," she said. "Siana'll fix ye up right away." She turned to the perplexed girl and handed her a single rose, its stem a vibrant green and its petals glowing a soft blue.

Siana's eyes opened wide. "What is this?" she asked blankly, for she recognized immediately that there was much more to the apparent simplicity of this gift; she could feel the energy vibrating within the enchanted flower.

"A gift," Rhiannon explained. "From the earth to meself, and from me to yerself. Take it and use it. Ye may find that it brings ye the strength to do more than clean and dress the wounds."

Siana took the rose in her trembling hands, then moved, compelled, to the side of the soldier. She needed no instruction; the magic of the flower showed her the way. She pressed her hand against the hole in the man's shoulder and felt the sting of his pain fly out from his body and up her arm. Siana, ever brave, grimaced through the frightening moment, holding strong to her purpose. And then the pain was gone, to her and to the man.

Wide-eyed, the man started to rise, but Rhiannon held him down. "Get yer rest," she said. "Ye'll find the time for fightin' soon enough."

Siana looked at Rhiannon, confused again and now more than a little afraid. Behind her, Jolsen and Lennard, on his first day up from his bed, had come over and now looked on in equal awe.

"How?" Siana asked. "I am no witch."

"You are now," Lennard remarked, but there was no sarcasm in his voice, just admiration.

"The flower gives ye the power to heal," Rhiannon explained. "But ye must stay strong, Siana, and accept the pain from the wounds. This was a slight one, but others'll take the breath right from ye. Hold to yer purpose and trust in yerself. Ye'll get through it."

"You speak as if you will not be around to guide her," said Lennard. "Are you leaving us?"

"I've other duties that need attending," Rhiannon explained. She stroked a comforting hand across Siana's cheek. "Do no' be feared, me girl," she said. "Ye've the strength to use the gift."

Rhiannon walked from the tent then, leaving the three of them staring blankly at each other.

* * *

The night was crisp and unusually chilly for high summer. Rhiannon fumbled through her packs, searching for the gown, gossamer and silk, that she had packed when she set out from Avalon. She paused when she found it, wondering what compulsion had told her to seek the dress. Certainly her tougher leggings would be better fitted to the road she had chosen.

All at once, Rhiannon understood the compulsion. If she was to accept who she was, to allow that frightening power its place within her being, she must look the part.

And then she was out under the stars, floating across the dark fields as if in a dream. A group of soldiers saw her, a ghostly apparition limned in the soft light of the heavens. They stood silent and unblinking, unable to find the words to describe the vision.

Rhiannon moved to the river. She hadn't even considered how she would cross, for she had no boat. But the River Ne'er Ending was a natural barrier, and nothing of nature would stand against the daughter of the Emerald Witch. Without even realizing the act, Rhiannon merely drifted over the great river, the rolling water not even wetting the trailing edge of her gown.

Across the western fields she went, unconsciously using simple magics to make herself invisible to the eyes of talons. She traveled on throughout the night, toward the black silhouettes of the Baerendels.

The playground of Bryan of Corning.

Chapter 19

Council in Avalon

THE RANGER WANDERED through dark, troubled dreams, alone and directionless in a sunless land. For the second time in a week he was close to death, but this time the horrid wounds inflicted by the wraith of Hollis Mitchell were much more insidious, sending the chill of death straight for his heart.

But this time, too, the witch tending to Belexus was more experienced and knowledgeable of such ills, and he was in Avalon, the purest land in all the world. Brielle worked over him tirelessly, pausing only on those occasions when the Black Warlock launched another of his storms against her domain. Those first few hours after Calamus had snatched the ranger from Mitchell's undead clutches had been the most critical. The witch had stayed with Belexus until long after the dawn tinted the eastern sky. Cold were the cruel claws of the wraith, but warmer still was the gentle touch of the Emerald Witch. She insinuated herself into the heart and soul of the mighty warrior, lent him the breath of her own life in his struggles. And when Brielle saw into Belexus' most private thoughts—and into emotions that concerned her and her wood—she was moved. Healing the man became her obsession; one so noble and true as Belexus must not be allowed to die.

And Brielle could not ignore the ranger's feelings for her, feelings he had kept to himself for so long.

" 'Tis good ye have waked," she said to him after several torturous days had slipped by.

That first sight for the ranger, of Brielle leaning over him, smile and eyes so bright and joyful and her golden mane of hair rolling down off her shoulder and brushing his chest, was as great a medicine as any man could ever know. It took Belexus a few moments to recover enough to speak the words he had to say.

"Twice have I been viewin' the land o' the dead," he whispered softly, bringing one hand up to stroke Brielle's beautiful hair. "And twice has a mistress of Avalon pulled me back to the world o' the living. Ye'll never know me gratitude, fair Lady. Ye'll never know—"

"Me daughter," Brielle interrupted, intrigued by the ranger's reference to a previous healing.

"She is well," Belexus replied.

"And she has found her power?" Brielle asked hopefully.

"Many were the feats of Rhiannon in the first days of the war—" Belexus started to explain, but Brielle put a finger to his lips to stop him.

"Our minds have been as one," she said. "Me thoughts saw into yer own, and I'm knowin' all that's befallen ye."

"Then ye know o' yer daughter's troubles?"

"Ayuh, that I do, and I expected as much," replied Brielle. "There's troublins in the growth of such power, me friend; nothing comes without its cost."

"She is strong," Belexus assured her. "Rhiannon'll find her way through."

" 'Tis me hope," Brielle replied. "Me wish is to be beside

her on this dark day, but I canno' leave me wood. And Rhiannon, I know now, canno' come to join me."

"Trust in her," said Belexus.

Brielle nodded and managed to return his smile. "Rest easy," she said. "A council's to begin this night and ye're to attend."

Belexus slumped back, more than willing to oblige. But then another memory came over him, with such violence that he bolted upright. Brielle knew his next question before he had even asked it. "Andovar?"

Brielle shook her head, finding no words suitable to break the news. She knew of the bond between the two rangers, best of friends since their childhood days, always counting on the other in times of trouble—and the other always being there.

"I will avenge his death," Belexus decreed. "Mitchell will not go unpunished."

"Hardly the Mitchell ye once knew," Brielle put in. "An undead thing, a wraith from the netherworld and beyond yer power is me fear."

But Brielle could not deny the determination on the ranger's face when he looked at her, an expression so grim that she took an involuntary step back.

"I will find a way," Belexus promised.

"We will find a way," Brielle corrected. "The passing of Andovar hurts me as it hurts yerself. I'll not let Mitchell take another so dear to me."

She looked away as she spoke these last words, and her voice softened to become barely audible. Embarrassment? Belexus wondered, and then some of the other implications of Brielle's melding with him, this joining of their thoughts and souls, brought him his own measure of embarrassment.

"Ye be needin' rest," Brielle said to him again, easing him down onto the soft grass and pulling a warm blanket up over his chest. She bent low and kissed him on the forehead, then pulled back from him.

"Glad I am that ye found yer way back, Belexus," was all she said as she turned and moved off into her forest.

Sad on sweet voices, the song of the elves drifted through the boughs of Avalon, a fitting complement to the magic of the trees.

Brielle found Belexus standing near a grove of pines, quiet and enchanted by the distant harmony. She watched awhile from afar, letting the ranger enjoy the peaceful song. The witch wished that she could leave him to his enjoyment all the night through, or go and join him, but the business of war would not allow for such breaks.

"Come," Brielle bade him. "We're to be goin' to council this night."

Belexus' eyes stared into the dark wood, toward the elven singing. "They fit in yer wood," he said. "Th'elven song seems a friend to yer trees. A kinship."

Brielle nodded her accord. "Joyful and sad," she said. "A harmony of balance. Suren me wood rings true to the children o' the moon."

"Then they are wise indeed," Belexus replied with a smile, his gaze drifting to the fair witch.

Brielle met his stare for a long moment, accepting his compliment and affection. "Come," she said again, and she led him off down a forest path.

The notes of the song carried them along, and soon they saw the glow of a large fire in the midst of a wide glade. The host of Illuma encircled it, five hundred strong, joined by the Rangers of Avalon. As Belexus and Brielle approached, the words of the song became clearer, and though the elves sang in enchantish, the wizards' ancient tongue that Ardaz had taught them, Belexus soon understood the meaning.

They sang to Andovar.

Belexus' father, Bellerian, and Arien Silverleaf, the Eldar of Illuma, met the witch and the ranger on the edge of the glade.

"By the Colonnae," said Bellerian when he saw his son. "Never would I have believed ye could heal so quickly. When last I saw ye just three days hence, ye seemed on the door o' death. And though the witch told me ye'd recover, me hopes . . ." He let the grim thought fade away unspoken.

Belexus ran a hand through Brielle's golden locks. " 'Twas Brielle that gived me life," he said.

" 'Twas yer own strength," replied the witch. "A lesser man'd not have made it to me wood."

"Surely it was the both of you," Arien Silverleaf said. "And such strength we shall need often in these dark times. And wisdom. The song to Andovar will run through many more verses, for long were the feats of that ranger. Let us enjoy its completion, then find our place of council."

"Is there word o' Ardaz?" Bellerian asked.

Brielle shook her head. "Billy Shank set off on Calamus this morn in search o' me brother," she explained. "But I fear that he is at the far end of the world and will not return to us for many days."

"But he will return to us in time," Arien assured them. "None have come to know the value of Ardaz more than the elves of Illuma, and ever will we trust in him to arrive when the hour is darkest."

"So he will," Brielle agreed, and then they fell silent to hear the continuing song. The elves had known Andovar only briefly, but their melody captured the spirit of the slain ranger so completely that Belexus found himself walking in dreams beside his lost friend.

It went on for more than an hour, and then the four of

them moved to a more private meadow for their council, joined by Sylvia, Arien's daughter, and by Ryell, the elf-lord's closest adviser.

"We have heard the tidings of war," Arien began. "And though they ring out far to the south, in the kingdom of man, their cry to the ears of Illuma is not diminished. We have come to know King Benador and his people as friends these last twenty years, and we will not forsake them in their dark hour."

"Still, we fear to leave our homes," Ryell added. "If the talons are on the march, might they not strike north as well? What protection would Illuma Vale find if our people are all away in the southland?"

"Yer fears are known to me," said Brielle, a bit uncomfortable with the gathering. Such politics were not usually the way of the Emerald Witch, but with Morgan Thalasi at the head of this invasion, these were not usual times. "We will address them before the council is ended. But first we should be hearing the words o' Belexus, for he alone among us has fought in the southland."

Then Belexus recounted his tale, from the rout in the western fields to the mad rush back to the river to the defense of the Four Bridges. All but Brielle blanched when he spoke of the Black Warlock, denial clear upon their faces. But Brielle dashed their hopes that the ranger might be mistaken in his guess.

"With me own eyes I have seen the specter of Thalasi," she assured them. "In the body of Martin Reinheiser, and even more powerful than last we knew."

"But Reinheiser is dead," Ryell argued. "He fell over the cliff to Blackamara. And Angfagdul"—he used Thalasi's enchantish name—"was slain on the field of Mountaingate."

"A wizard is not so easily slain," Brielle reminded them

all. "The Black Warlock has returned. I have battled with him meself."

"Then the talons have a powerful leader," Arien lamented, knowing beyond those flickering hopes that their cause was even more desperate now.

"Two leaders," Brielle corrected. "Another of the ancient ones walks Aielle." As soon as the others took the time to consider Brielle's words, they understood who she was referring to. There had been only four ancient ones, and now two—Billy Shank, off on his quest to find the wizard Ardaz, and Martin Reinheiser, the embodiment of the Black Warlock—were accounted for. If Jeff DelGiudice had somehow returned to Aielle, he most surely would have fought on their side. That left only one.

"Mitchell," growled Bellerian. "Suren that one's a scourge on the world."

"And more so now," Belexus added. "No man is he, but a spirit o' the netherworld, an undead thing of great power. 'Twas he who killed Andovar, and nearly meself."

The words hung in the air like the weight of doom, bowing heads in dismay.

"But we are not lost!" cried Sylvia, Arien's fiery daughter. "Never before in all the world have the men of Calva and the elves of Illuma joined together against an enemy. And three wizards fight on our side."

"Truth in yer words," Bellerian piped in. "The Black Warlock has found himself some mighty foes indeed. He'll not be likin' the reception we'll be givin' to him when he tries again to cross the bridges."

"But can we go there?" asked Ryell, ever the pragmatic one. "What force does Angfagdul hold in reserve in the Crystal Mountains, ready to fall upon the northern fields when the elves and the rangers have gone to the south?"

"Not to fear," said Brielle. She stood and walked to the

center of the group. "Istaahl of Pallendara and meself have fought with Thalasi these many days, and it is our belief that the Black Warlock has erred in his attack. He did not get across the bridges quick enough, afore all the wide world learned of his presence."

"A ruse?" asked Bellerian.

"Nay, too many are with him," Brielle replied. "Thalasi did not figure on the resolve of the Calvans."

"Or on the presence o' yer daughter," Belexus reminded her.

"Me hopes are that the Black Warlock has not yet come to understand the power of Rhiannon," Brielle said grimly. Every minute of every day, the witch feared for her daughter, so exposed right beside the Black Warlock's army. " 'Tis me feeling that Rhiannon'll have more to say in this war.

"But the bridges have been held," the witch continued, "to the rage o' the evil warlock. Thus he has summoned the wraith of Mitchell, and more tricks he'll suren find. But Morgan Thalasi canno' go north, not nearen me domain, or south, where Istaahl holds the sea. He has committed his forces to the bridges, to the heart o' Calva, and if he means to turn his forces aside, he'll find them slowed and cut down by meself and me friend in Pallendara.

"But neither can we leave our domains," she explained. "The Black Warlock is strong indeed, and he does not end his assaults on Avalon and on the Tower of Istaahl. Even as we sit here speakin', the White Mage o' Pallendara fights off another o' Thalasi's attacks." The others, having witnessed many strange storms raging over the western borders of Avalon, understood her reasoning and the seriousness of her words.

"It is only our closeness to our places of power that gives us the strength to keep Morgan Thalasi away, and so are we trapped here," Brielle explained.

"At least until Ardaz returns," Arien remarked. "The Silver Mage might turn the course of battle."

"He might indeed," agreed Bellerian. "But we must fight without that hope. With or without the aid of the Silver Mage, the Black Warlock and his pig-faced army'll be driven back to their holes!"

A determined chorus of agreement sprang up among the fearless assembly. All of them had known adversity in their lives—the elves had lived with it for centuries—and they would not surrender, whatever the odds. And none in the world so enjoyed fighting talons as the grim Rangers of Avalon.

"To the south, then!" cried Ryell. "King Benador is in need!"

"Aye," said Brielle. "Away ye all should go. Winter'll be no friend to the Black Warlock with his rabble army; the stalemate works against him."

"So he has created a new leader to get him across the river," Belexus agreed, painfully aware of the power of the wraith of Hollis Mitchell.

"His hopes are to find the walls o' Pallendara afore the season's change," Brielle reasoned. "Me thoughts say he'll strike out hard afore many more days have passed."

"Then he shall strike out against the army of King Benador, the army of Arien Silverleaf, and the warriors of Lord Bellerian!" Sylvia growled. "And woe is to him!"

"To the south, then!" cried Ryell. "And to the side of King Benador!"

All of them, Sylvia and Ryell included, had their doubts about the certainty with which the rallying words had been spoken. But none of them would speak those doubts aloud.

Now was not the time for the weak of heart.

* * *

Billy Shank watched the gathering dawn. Beside him, the great Pegasus grazed calmly. They had stopped only a couple of hours before, the urgency of their mission overruled by a needed rest. But already Calamus had regained his strength, and when the lord of horses saw Billy approaching, he stamped and agreed that it was time to depart.

Then they were up on the breezes again, climbing high into the morning sky, and all who saw them in their flight, mostly simple farmers of Calva's northern fields, looked upon them in amazement, not understanding the drama of the quest but well aware that this spectacle was merely an extension of the growing conflict along the river.

The world had changed so suddenly.

Billy kept the southeastern line of the Crystal Mountains to his left, cutting a course for the Great Forest, the largest woodland in all Aielle, where he would begin his search for the missing wizard. His only hope, Aielle's only hope, was that Ardaz would spot the Pegasus high up against the sky and reveal himself. The wizard had said only that he would be out beyond the Elgarde River, out in the uncharted wild lands, and Billy knew his chances of finding Ardaz's exact location were slim indeed.

But he had to try. Once again Ardaz had become a critical player in the hope of the world.

Out beyond the Elgarde, beyond the Great Forest, in lands unknown to the Calvans, to the Illumans, even to the wizards of Aielle, Ardaz picked his way among the rubble and tunnels of a deserted town. He had suspected all along that there were others in the world beyond its known borders, races not Calvan, Illuman, or talon, and now he had found his proof.

The wizard danced happily through the ancient ruins, thinking it grand that there was apparently much more to be learned about the world. His eyes did not turn back to the west.

He did not hear the call of Brielle and Istaahl, and could not know that the Black Warlock once again walked Aielle.

They rode out of Avalon with the rise of the next sun, to the blast of horns and the pounding thunder of hooves. On came the elves of Illuma, five hundred strong, their sleek steeds adorned in shining armor and draped in lines of jingling bells. Arien Silverleaf led the way, his silvery armor and shield glistening in the morning light, and his magical sword, Fahwayn, held high above him.

And beside the Eldar of Illuma rode Bellerian, the Ranger Lord, leading his own column of grim-faced, mighty warriors. Though they were but fourscore strong, none who had seen the Rangers of Avalon in battle underestimated their value.

Belexus waited at the edge of the wood as the column passed, the fair witch at his side.

"So grand the preludes seem," Brielle remarked, but there was not a hint of awe in her voice. She understood the end result of such a charge. She had witnessed it before, and she knew that the grime and blood and tears would dull the shine of weapons and armor, and that the mournful cry of a funeral horn outsounded the eager blare of heralding trumpets.

"We go because we must," Belexus replied. "We growl and shout and prance with our steeds because to do else would beat us before we e'er faced our enemy."

"But 'tis a sadness to know where the path will take ye all."

"Ayuh," Belexus agreed. He looked Brielle straight in the eye, his expression a mixture of tenderness and unyielding determination. "But sadder still would the endin' be if we ne'er trod that path. Were that it could be otherwise, me Lady, but the Black Warlock must be stopped and pushed back from the lands of Calva."

"And so he shall!" Brielle replied, her face brightening a bit. She reached out to run a smooth hand gently over the ranger's firm visage. "Know that I'll be lookin' for yer return, son o' Bellerian."

"And know that I shall return," Belexus assured her.

Brielle's concern did not diminish. She knew the vendetta that the ranger carried with him, and knew that he could not defeat Hollis Mitchell. "Ye mean to find the wraith?" she asked bluntly.

Belexus looked away, unable to deny the question that rang out more as an accusation.

"Before, I have telled ye that the thing is beyond yer knowin' and yer power," Brielle said to him. "All me fears for ye are suren to come true if ye go against the likes o' the wraith o' Hollis Mitchell."

"Andovar will be avenged," Belexus said grimly.

"Not to doubt," Brielle agreed. "But not by yerself, not now. Ye have no' the weapons to strike the wraith. Not yet."

"Then when?" Belexus snapped, a sudden fire in his pale blue eyes. "Give me the weapons, Brielle. Grant me the power to avenge the death o' me friend!"

Brielle shook her head helplessly. "I know not o' them," she admitted. "Nor even if they exist at all." Belexus started to turn away, but she grabbed his elbow and forced him to look at her. "The wraith is but a tool o' the Black Warlock," she said. "Stop Morgan Thalasi. Crush his wretched army and drive him back to the west and ye'll find yer revenge."

Belexus had no choice but to agree—for now. He had fought the wraith, had seen the hopelessness of the battle all too clearly. "Find me the weapons," he pleaded to Brielle again, and he swung up in the saddle of his mount, ready to join the column.

"The day will come," Brielle promised. "But remember yer cause above yer vengeance, son o' Bellerian. More's at stake then the fire in yer blood."

"I know me duty," answered Belexus, "to the rangers, and to the good folk o' the world."

"And come home again," Brielle said softly. "To Avalon, where ye belong."

"And I'm knowin' me duty to Brielle," Belexus continued. "I shall return to walk by yer side in Avalon, me Lady, and suren 'tis that very thought that'll carry me through the trials o' battle."

He kicked his powerful steed into motion and bounded off across the southern field.

Brielle could only watch him go and hope—for Belexus and for all the world.

And then she had to go again, for another storm had risen from the wastelands beyond the western borders of Avalon. Morgan Thalasi had come calling upon her forest once again.

Chapter 20

Teamwork

RHIANNON HAD NO trouble at all as she continued to make her way through the seemingly endless talon lines, though she did not know whether her inconspicuous movement was a matter of the talons' inattentiveness or an unconscious effort on her own part, using her magic to disguise her flight. However she managed it, the young witch finally got beyond the southern fringes of the talon encampment and was cutting a southwesterly course toward the Baerendel Mountains before the night was halfway through.

She had a general idea of where to find Bryan, but the land seemed vast indeed and the mountains held innumerable hiding spots, and the witch's daughter grew concerned with the wisdom of her decision. She could take care of herself, she knew, with or without the young hero, but without Bryan's understanding of the landscape, Rhiannon believed that she would be of little help to any refugees wandering out alone in the Baerendels.

But Rhiannon found the answer to her dilemma early the next day. A bluebird fluttered down to her as she slept on a mossy bed, recognizing her as a friend. When Rhiannon opened her eyes, she saw the thing hopping along the length of her arm, its head cocked as it stared into her face.

"A good mornin' to ye," the young witch said with a sincere smile, glad to be greeted by so friendly a face.

The bird chattered a response and Rhiannon's eyes widened. She could understand it!

She had talked to birds, to all the animals, back in Avalon, but she had thought it a blessing of her mother's enchantment, not an ability of her own.

"So it's me own magic," she pondered, tapping a finger on her pursed lips. And then those lips spread into another smile as Rhiannon came to understand the implications of this particular ability. "Go get yer friends," she whispered to the bird. "I'm needin' to talk to ye all."

A short while later a dozen birds flitted all about the blueberry patch on the side of a mountain where Rhiannon had found her breakfast. She chatted a few "good mornings" with the avian creatures, then sent them off on a mission.

Before the sun had climbed very high in the eastern sky, the young witch had a growing network of spies soaring all about the land.

Bryan watched anxiously as two talons pulled their cart through a narrow gorge, two others flanking them. This would be a simple ambush, one of the easiest he had ever pulled, but the half-elf found himself jittery nonetheless. He gathered up a handful of arrows and crept down the rocky mountainside to the defensive bluff he had chosen earlier.

The talons came on unconcerned. Their standard marked them as a group from the south, from the Ballendul Mountains beyond the forest of Windy Willows, no doubt bringing supplies at the summons of the Black Warlock. Apparently they hadn't heard of the dangers to talons in this section of the Baerendels; Bryan's reputation wasn't as widespread as he had feared. He smiled at his continued good fortune and put an arrow to his bowstring as the cart neared the trip wire.

It was a simple trap: a loose stone along the rocky path holding down a length of cord, which in turn secured several boulders on the opposite cliff face. The cart bumped across the loose trip stone, bouncing it up and releasing the cord. A moment later the boulders came cascading down the cliff, leaping higher with each thunderous rebound.

Bryan didn't expect to actually get any of the talons with the boulders, but the diversionary effect was well worth his efforts in putting the trap together. As the four beasts screamed and scrambled to get out of harm's way, Bryan set his bow into action, firing off three shots before the terrified talons even knew he was there. Two of the arrows found their marks, killing one talon and dropping another in writhing agony on the stony ground.

And as the remaining two talons turned to consider their fallen comrades, Bryan sprang down upon them.

The closest beast turned and charged, spear leading the way, as Bryan came down to ground level. But the talon was confused and it overbalanced as it roared in. Bryan fell backward, his shield easily lifting the spear tip harmlessly high. Unable to break its momentum, the talon rolled right over the half-elf, and when Bryan completed his roll and came back to his feet, he had to pause and brace himself to pull out his sword, buried to the hilt in the unfortunate monster's gut.

The last talon launched its spear, but the heavy, unbalanced thing had little chance of connecting with the nimble half-elf. Bryan slipped right by it in its flight and charged out after the talon. It shrieked and fled back toward the wagon, where the small avalanche had ended.

"Too easy," Bryan muttered to himself as he closed the

gap, and his words rang out as a warning in his own ears. Before he could consider them more closely, however, he found the truth of them painfully clear.

A spear caught him in the side.

Reeling and grasping the weapon to keep its bounce from tearing him apart, Bryan glanced back up the gorge, where five more talons, ambushers for the ambusher, were now coming on, howling with glee.

He knew he had gotten careless, had overestimated himself and underestimated his enemies. The talon at the wagon was still unarmed, but Bryan had no strength for any battles. He limped and scrambled to the side, to the cliff face, and put his back against it for support.

The talons closed in cautiously, not understanding the extent of the half-elf's wounds. They had indeed heard of the "ghost fighter," and were not so eager to plunge in at him, however assured their victory seemed.

But Bryan, hardly conscious, could only inch his way along the rough wall, hoping against reality that he would find some way out. He put a small thicket of growth, barely more than a knee-high bush and a finger-thin sapling, between himself and the talons before he found that he could go no farther.

Still the six talons took their time, fanning out around the half-elf in a semicircle. One threw a spear in, but its aim was not so good and Bryan managed to block it weakly with his shield.

The largest of the talons, standing next to the spear thrower, slapped it on the head for wasting its weapon. Then the big beast, apparently the leader, took a bold step in, continuing slowly to within ten yards of Bryan, studying the sweat and anguish on his fair face.

Bryan could hardly see it. Tears glistened in his eyes. He had known all along that it would eventually end this way, but he never would have believed that he could feel such pain, or such terror. And the terror only heightened when he did finally focus on the big talon, its crude and wicked spear tip waving menacingly out in front.

Then the talon roared and charged, leaning over the spear. Bryan couldn't begin to get his shield back up, and even if he had managed it, he had no strength to deflect such a heavy blow.

At full speed and only two steps away, the talon roared a cry of victory.

But then, in his daze, Bryan saw the shaft of the spear snap as if the weapon had been plunged into stone, and he heard the talon thump face first into a solid object.

Where the sapling had been now stood a full-grown oak.

The talon bounced back a step, considering the tree with stunned incomprehension. As if in response, the oak sent a heavy branch swinging down that split the beast's skull and drove its head right down between its shoulders. The other talons, when they had recovered from their shock, turned to flee.

But the oak wasn't finished. Thick limbs pounded down on the closest of the monsters, while longer, more supple branches reached out to snatch those farthest away.

Bryan somehow knew the tree was an ally, and he was not afraid, just amazed and even a bit horrified as the slashing and pounding continued. One talon went up into the air, a branch firmly about its neck. It dangled and kicked for a few agonizing moments, then hung very still, turning slowly on the afternoon breeze.

It was over as quickly as it started, and not a talon, not even the one wounded by Bryan's initial arrow, remained alive.

A bit of his strength returned with the realization of his

salvation, Bryan slipped out tentatively from behind the enchanted oak.

And then he saw her.

Rhiannon stood on a small outcropping of rocks across the gorge, near the bluff where Bryan had begun the assault. Her gossamer gown caught the sunlight and held it, surrounding the witch in a preternatural glow that enhanced the spectacle of her power. Her eyes were closed, her expression one of grim satisfaction, and she stood perfectly still, one arm remaining upraised in its call to the powers of the heavens and the earth. Only Rhiannon's gown whipped about her in the breeze, that glowing, mysterious gown that seemed so much a part of the young witch.

She had come upon the gorge as Bryan's ambush began, remaining in the background to consider the work of the noted young hero and having no intention of interfering with the events at hand—on either side.

But when the talons forced Bryan against the wall, rage flooded through Rhiannon. It was Andovar she saw there, helpless and facing death, and when the power gathered within her limbs, she did not try to push it away.

And now it was over, and sooner or later, Rhiannon knew, she would have to look down upon the carnage she had wreaked. Grim satisfaction turned into a painful lament, another stain upon the innocence of the witch's daughter. The power, its task completed, flowed out of her, leaving her empty and weak, and only by great effort, and by continually reminding herself that Bryan had been sorely wounded, was she able to climb down the rocks to the floor of the gorge.

The half-elf was still conscious and standing when she reached him, though she suspected that he would fall to the ground if the stone wall was not holding him up.

"Who?" Bryan gasped. "How—"

"Me name's not important for now," Rhiannon said softly. She moved to examine the wound, and eased Bryan down to the ground. The spear had dug in deep, and no doubt its tip was barbed. But Rhiannon had been numbed to such sights over the past weeks, and she went about her task calmly and efficiently. She realized that she could not hope to remove the spear through any normal means, not here in the dust, with each movement of the shaft causing the young half-elf such incredible pain.

Instead she spoke the runes of a spell—none that she had learned, but simply words that now came to her in her time of need—and the spear shaft warmed to her touch. A moment later it came alive, a serpent writhing in Rhiannon's hands. At her call, it backed out of the wound, leaving the spear tip unattached and still inside the half-elf.

Bryan watched it all through the blur of his pain, hardly believing his eyes and unable to utter any of the dozen questions that flooded through his daze. Rhiannon eased her hand across the open gash, numbing the pain, and she watched as Bryan slipped down and closed his eyes. Then Rhiannon stood beside him, considering where she could take him to finish the healing.

But though her gaze began up over the steep rocky slopes of the gorge, it inevitably came back to the scene at hand, to the giant oak and its gruesome victims. She had killed again, had allowed the possessing power its outlet to devastation. She thought Bryan asleep and moved to the tree, stroking its bark and whispering apologies for the decades she had stolen from its life.

Bryan half opened one eye and watched the raven-haired woman, understanding her even less than he had when she first appeared. He understood her to be a friend beyond all doubt, and knew that he would be safe enough under her care. For the first time in so very long, Bryan put his faith in someone other than himself and let a comforting and necessary slumber overtake him.

"Oh, damn," Bryan whispered when he opened his eyes and found himself barely inches from the face of a gigantic brown bear. He was in a cave, and if he had taken a moment to consider anything other than the snuffling nose—and the white teeth beneath it—of the bear, he would have noticed that the pain was altogether gone from his side. Right then, though, the half-elf lay very still, looking for some way out of this unexpected predicament.

"So ye're awake, then?" came a voice from the other side of the shallow cave.

At first Bryan disregarded the question, concentrating on holding his breath and keeping his eyes lightly closed, feigning death. *Bears do not feast on dead meat,* he silently reminded himself, a lesson from his father that he had hoped he never would have to put to the test.

But gradually, as nothing happened, Bryan's curiosity got the better of him. He peeked out again. The bear had slumped back on its haunches, munching on some unknown treat, and its inquisitive stare had been replaced by one that Bryan found much more pleasant.

Rhiannon's thick black hair hung down, brushing his bare chest, and her dark eyes considered him for a long moment unblinkingly. "How do ye feel?" she asked.

Her question reminded the half-elf of his wound, and his hand reflexively went to his side. But neither blood nor bandages greeted him, just the smooth skin of a new scar.

"Who are you?" Bryan stammered, looking at his still clean hand in disbelief. It was all coming back to him: the spear, the charging talon, the intercepting tree, and it all seemed too preposterous to be true. But here was the perpetrator of the impossibilities, barely half a foot from his face.

"Me name's Rhiannon," the young witch replied. "And I'm knowing yerself as Bryan of Corning."

"How did you know?"

"Ye've made quite a name for yerself." Rhiannon smiled. "Many's the one coming across the river and giving ye credit for the escape."

Bryan accepted the compliment humbly, a bit embarrassed, but too caught up in the beautiful woman's name for any self-conscious feelings to take hold. "Rhiannon," he muttered under his breath, certain that he had heard that name before. Perhaps in one of his father's tales.

"Ye've slept through most o' the night," Rhiannon remarked, seeing the confusion on the half-elf's face.

"How many nights?" Bryan asked, giving up on trying to remember and more interested in going forward with this introduction.

"Just the one," said Rhiannon.

Bryan's jaw dropped open. "I took a spear," he gasped. He forced himself up and looked to the scar line on his side. "A wicked hit."

"So it was," said Rhiannon. "But you're a tough one."

Bryan had been unconscious during the healing, but even in that state he had felt the presence of Rhiannon. In the witch's healing sessions she and her victim became linked, two souls battling one wound, and now Bryan began to unravel some of that strange bonding. "You healed me," he said matter-of-factly, and looked up at her blankly.

" 'Tis a gift o' me mother," was all that Rhiannon could offer. "Fret not on it. The pain is past, and nothin' more is of any concern."

"When can I—we, leave?"

Rhiannon glanced over at the surly bear. "As soon as ye feel up to leavin'," she replied. "Me friend wants his cave back to himself, and I'm not for arguin' with that one!"

"You, you and he, carried me up here?"

"Couldn't be carrying ye by meself," Rhiannon answered. "He's friendly enough if ye don't cross him." She sent a wink Bryan's way. "And he'll work for a drop o' honey."

"But how can you talk to a bear?" Bryan had to ask.

Rhiannon accepted this next question, and the next, and the next after that, as inevitable, considering the surprises she had shown the half-elf. She answered him honestly each time, though she took care not to reveal too much about herself and she reminded Bryan in every other sentence that their bear friend wanted his cave back. All in all, it was a lighthearted conversation, almost a celebration, for these two who were seemingly destined to become close friends and allies. But then Bryan asked something that changed the entire tone of the discussion.

"That tree!" he exclaimed. "How did you make it grow so quickly?"

The half-elf did not miss the black cloud that crossed Rhiannon's fair face.

"I . . ." she began hesitantly. "Me powers . . . I could not let ye die!" Rhiannon exhaled a deep breath and looked away, her light eyes rimmed by tears.

Bryan was sensitive enough to let it go at that. He propped himself up on one elbow and draped an arm across Rhiannon's shoulders.

They said no more through the rest of the night, and when dawn came, they walked out of the bear's cave to the animal's grunting relief—and into the sunlight.

"I have a secret camp," Bryan said after discerning their location. "Not far from here." He pointed to a distant spur of the mountain.

"Let's be going, then," Rhiannon replied, and she started off along the rocky trail.

Bryan paused a moment to watch her go. She had freely

discussed her powers concerning the healing, even of talking to the birds to learn of his whereabouts. But when he had shifted the conversation to the darker side of Rhiannon's magic, to the killing wrath of the animated tree, she had choked up. Apparently the young woman wasn't comfortable with that facet of her existence. Bryan had to pity her, for he knew that if she meant to spend any length of time on this side of the River Ne'er Ending, she would have to use those destructive tactics quite often.

The notion intrigued Bryan. What was the extent, he wondered, of Rhiannon's strength? With her by his side, how much more could he do against the talons? Or even more important, what part might this magic-worker play in the overall outcome of the war?

Bryan took up his bow and started down the path after Rhiannon. He would have to let those questions hang unanswered for a while at least, for he had no intention of pressing Rhiannon about them. For all of his curiosity, he could not bear to see that dark cloud pass over her fair features again.

Chapter 21

Enter the Wraith

THE BLACK WARLOCK paced anxiously about the field, his eyes darting from talon to talon, and each of the beasts in turn fell to the ground in abject terror. They knew that their boss was nervous and angry, and they knew, too, that the Black Warlock often released his anger on the nearest living target, friend or foe.

But more than angry, Morgan Thalasi was afraid. He had returned several days before, eager for his next, most glorious assault across the bridges. Mitchell, with his ghost horse, should have returned the very next day, but the wraith had not yet made his appearance.

"I cannot do this alone," Thalasi growled at a nearby talon. He clenched his bony fist in rage, and the talon slumped to the ground, choking, as if a replica of the Black Warlock's fist had appeared within its skinny throat.

Thalasi stormed away without concern for the dying thing. He needed Mitchell. Every day, it was necessary to renew his attacks against Avalon and the White Tower to keep his archenemies on the defensive and prevent them from striking out hard against his army. That alone was draining enough, but with no sign of Mitchell, Thalasi also had to continue to manage the rabble forces of the talons, a task made even more difficult by the constant pressure applied by King Benador and his trained and talented army. Several times each day the Calvans charged across the bridges, cutting into the closest ranks of talons, and then retreated to the safety of their seemingly impregnable defenses.

To further the Black Warlock's troubles, reports from the Baerendels told of groups of heroes harassing the supply caravans and the lines of reinforcements.

Thalasi simply could not keep track of it all. He wondered how many more mistakes he would make, how many more opportunities he would lose for the lack of organization in his army. They should have swept through the western fields and right across the Four Bridges long before the King and his troops ever arrived on the field.

Yet here they sat, hopelessly stalemated.

The Black Warlock's greatest concern of all was his personal strength. Trying to do so many things prevented him from concentrating on the most important task: the defeat of the other wizards. Though the continuing tie of harmony between the two spirits of the Black Warlock should have added to his power, each day he grew more weary, his strength slipping from him. And Thalasi knew, to his horror, that if the fourth wizard, Ardaz, made his appearance on the field, he and his talons would surely be crushed.

His creation of the wraith was supposed to have changed all of that. With Mitchell handling the day-to-day affairs of the army, the Black Warlock would be free to pursue his magical growth. Only then could he hope to destroy his more powerful enemies, the other wizards and that infernal witch.

"So where are you?" Thalasi screamed to the empty black horizon of the northland.

* * *

He rested when the sun was at its brightest, unable to stand its shining glory. But his march in those darkest hours was tireless, calling on energies unlimited by the restrictions of a mortal body. Mitchell knew the need for haste; he could see the fires of the opposing camps far to the south. But Brielle had stolen the wraith's mount, and the distance from Avalon to the Four Bridges was a long walk indeed.

Finally, though, the wraith came upon the talon army. His first encounter with the troops he would lead came in the form of a thrown spear. Mitchell saw it coming and merely puffed out the apparition of his chest, accepting the blow from the meager weapon without the slightest flinch.

Three talons charging in behind the throw stopped in their tracks, the blood draining from their hideous faces when they recognized the wraith for what it was.

"Hold!" Mitchell commanded. One of the beasts fled anyway, but the other two could find no strength to move their legs.

"What is your name?" Mitchell demanded of the one who had thrown the spear.

The talon cowered and trembled, giving no indication that it would answer.

"Name?" Mitchell roared, moving right up to the pitiful thing.

The talon garbled something in its native guttural tongue, a language quite unknown to Mitchell. The wraith reached down and grabbed the beast by the front of its shabby jerkin and pulled it to its feet.

"A good throw," he said, handing the talon back its spear. "And a fine guard you all have set! It is promising to see my troops so alert!"

The talon exchanged a confused look with its companion.

"Who you?" it dared to ask.

Mitchell's grating laughter sent shivers through their spines.

"A friend of the master," he said. "I have come to lead you to victory over your enemies."

"What you?" the other asked.

Again the otherworldly laughter erupted from the wraith, a godless and eerie sound. "The general," was all Mitchell offered in reply. With a whisk of his hand he sent the two talons sprawling to the side, and he strode by them toward the center of the encampment.

The talons, chilled by the touch that promised a death of unspeakable horror, did not offer any further resistance, did not even rise from the ground until the wraith was far away.

Thalasi saw the entire northern perimeter of his encampment parting, talons running this way and that, and he heard the excited and horrified whispers erupting all about him. But more than anything else, the Black Warlock felt the presence of his child, this undead thing that numbered among his greatest achievements. For all the relief the Black Warlock felt at the entrance of Hollis Mitchell, though, his primary emotion remained his unending rage, and after his initial elation upon seeing the approach of the wraith, Thalasi went right to work scheming a suitable punishment for his tardy general.

If Mitchell realized that Thalasi would be angry, he showed no outward signs of it. He strode through the ranks of the talons and right up to the Black Warlock.

"Where have you been?" Thalasi demanded. "You should have arrived four days ago!"

"The road was not so empty," Mitchell replied casually.

Thalasi paused to weigh the implications of the answer and to survey the area around the wraith.

"Where is your steed?" he asked.

"Gone."

A flame of anger lighted in the deep sockets of Thalasi's eyes. "Gone?"

"Ashes to ashes," Mitchell replied sarcastically.

Now the Black Warlock was beginning to understand. He waved the curious talons away and led Mitchell to the privacy of his tent, not wanting to scold the talon commander in front of the creatures he would lead.

"Who have you battled?" Thalasi asked when he was certain they were alone. "Who was it that destroyed the horse I created for you?" Considering the route Mitchell had crossed, the Black Warlock already suspected the answer and was more than a little concerned.

"It was a witch," Mitchell answered. "A friend of yours?"

"Save your sarcasm," Thalasi hissed. "What brought you near Avalon? Are you that much of a fool?"

Mitchell laughed at him. "You fear her?"

"I respect her powers," Thalasi corrected. "As should you. Especially near the boughs of her domain. You are mighty, wraith, but do not overstep the limitation of that power. Consider yourself fortunate that Brielle did not reduce you to the nothingness you once were."

"Bah!" Mitchell spat. "Damn her and her wood! I had him! I had Belexus, that cursed ranger. But he got to Avalon and she appeared, the mothering witch."

"Belexus?" Thalasi stammered, knowing the name all too well from the disastrous assaults on the bridges and from the past encounters between the ranger and the being that had been Martin Reinheiser. "What . . . why did you meet with that one? You had your orders."

"I found him, and his friend—who is now deceased," Mitchell explained, his chuckle unnerving even the Black Warlock. "They had camped along the banks of the river, offering an opportunity for pleasure I could not bypass."

"So you crossed and attacked them."

"And I would have had both of them if that damned witch and her flying horse hadn't saved Belexus."

Thalasi slammed his palms together, releasing a jolt of black energy that blasted the wraith to the ground in a heap. Mitchell looked up at the master, fearful respect in his flaming eyes for the first time. He thought himself a doomed and damned thing at that moment, as surely as he had seen his doom when Reinheiser had revealed himself as the new Black Warlock at the bottom of the cliff in Blackamara those twenty years before.

"You revealed yourself to them," Thalasi scolded, but he was calm again, his outrage quickly dissipating as he tried to salvage his plans. "Brielle knows who you are, what you are, and now she will direct attacks against you. I had hoped to reveal you in the final battle over the river, to let King Benador and the others discover their doom even as it fell upon them."

Mitchell floated to his feet. "They won't stop us," he declared. "Maybe I should not have crossed, but the thought of catching Belexus, of stealing him so easily from the Calvan effort! I did not forget what that one did at the Battle of Mountaingate. With his strength and his leadership he can sway a battle as surely as an entire brigade of skilled warriors."

"True enough," the Black Warlock admitted. "The Four Bridges would surely have fallen on the first assault if it had not been for his efforts. The Calvans rally around him, throw themselves in the path of spears aimed for him."

"His friend, that other ranger, Andovar, is dead," Mitchell said, his evil smile returning. "And Belexus is wounded— perhaps he, too, is dead by now. I doubt that he will rejoin the battle anytime soon."

"Do not underestimate the healing powers of Brielle and her forest," Thalasi warned grimly, but he was also wearing an evil smile upon his face. The notion that his wraith had sent the mighty son of Bellerian running in fright amused him profoundly, so much so that he wasn't certain if the cost had been too high.

"I shall make you another steed," he said to the wraith. "But later, when I have the time. You are here now, and you must meet with the talon commanders at once and take immediate command of the army. Summer is slipping from us, and I mean to get to the walls of Pallendara before the first snow."

"We should cross the bridges this week," Mitchell agreed.

"Perhaps," replied Thalasi. "But we have many tasks before us."

"Boats," Mitchell said.

Thalasi considered the option and nodded, pleased that Mitchell was so quickly formulating the plans they would need. "I must leave the mechanics of crossing the river to your judgment," he explained. "It is my task to discern the best way to defeat the witch and Istaahl in Pallendara, or at least hold them at bay. And I must find you the tools to defeat Ardaz, for he has not yet shown himself, but I do not doubt that he shall."

"Then make me the tools," Mitchell replied, still grinning. "And worry about the wizard and the wretched witch. I will have the army ready to cross, and at their lead, I will see to the destruction of the Calvan forces."

"Among them, only Ardaz can stand against you," Thalasi declared with all confidence. "And together, we will take care of that one."

Andovar reached out to her, hopelessly begging her to save him. And Rhiannon reached back, stretched her arms out across the misty barrier to catch the doomed man.

But even as her fingers neared the ranger, the cold

*blackness of death fell over him in an opaque veil so final
that even Rhiannon's magic could not penetrate it. The young
witch screamed again and again, crying out in hopeless
denial.*

*And Andovar screamed back, a distant cry falling, ever
falling, away from Rhiannon.*

Away from the world of the living.

Her breath came in loud gasps; the streaked sweat on her
forehead loomed stark in the thin moonlight.

And Bryan was by her side. "A dream," he whispered into
her ear. "Only a dream."

Rhiannon looked at him for support, took comfort in his
touch as though it was some kind of material litany against
her inability to grasp the pleading hands of Andovar.

But even as the young witch began to separate the dream
from the reality about her, she realized that something was
wrong. "Evil," she said to Bryan's concerned look. "There
be great evil about this night."

Bryan glanced around, suddenly back on the alert. One
hand went to his sheathed sword.

"Not here," Rhiannon assured him. She let her sixth sense,
her witching sense, guide her eyes back to the east and the
north, to the talon encampment.

Bryan did not miss the direction of Rhiannon's gaze.

"What happened?" he asked.

Rhiannon shrugged. "An ally of the Black Warlock?" she
asked as much as answered. "Some great and powerful evil
has entered the battlefield." She groped for words to explain
her vague sensations. "Me heart sees a blackness."

Bryan considered her comments and their present position. They had moved deeper into the mountains, but the
half-elf knew paths that would get them back to the north-
easternmost slopes overlooking the battlefield in merely two
or three days. "Do you wish to go back there?" he asked.

Rhiannon wasn't certain how she might help against whatever was causing this insistent, frightening sensation, or what her role in such a large-scale battle might be. But she felt it her duty to go back to the field, as though somehow fate demanded that she be in attendance when the Black Warlock made his move.

"I must," she said to Bryan.

Bryan didn't try to argue. He, too, wondered what his final place in all of this might be. He had carved a fine niche thus far, but when all was over, his contribution to the overall effort would not be so dramatic, particularly if the Black Warlock proved victorious.

"We will set out in the morning," he agreed. "But for now, get some sleep. The trails ahead will not be easy marching."

Rhiannon squeezed his arm in thanks, then slipped back to her blanket bed. But she would find no more sleep that night, not with the vision of Andovar falling into darkness so clear in her thoughts.

And not with her suspicion that this evil she now sensed was somehow connected to Andovar's death.

The talons were no more comfortable around the wraith of Mitchell than they were around the Black Warlock himself. But like Thalasi, Mitchell incited more than enough terror in the beasts to persuade them to follow his every command. He met with the leaders that very night and laid the groundwork for the effort needed to get them across the river.

When the bright summer sun climbed into the sky the next morning, the wraith took shelter under the thick folds of a tent. But the 268talons went to work, organizing their troops into divisions and setting them about the tasks that General Mitchell had outlined.

* * *

Across the river, King Benador and his commanders watched with growing concern as all of the wood the talons could gather—deserted wagons, walls of buildings, even uprooted trees—was brought to the northern corner of the encampment.

"It seems that our enemies have found some direction to their meandering ways," the King remarked to an adviser at his side.

The other man scanned the entirety of the camp, his eyes falling on battle formations that several groups of talons were practicing. "The wedge," he remarked pointedly, surprised that the untrained things even knew of such advanced tactics. "We might find them better prepared the next time they decide to storm the bridges."

"A few days of practice." Benador shrugged. "It will not stand up against the lifelong dedication of the Warders of the White Walls. Alas for the talons, the result will be the same."

Benador's confidence did much to boost the spirits of those around him, but even the determined King had to pause in concern a short time later. For by the day's end, many boats had already been constructed.

Chapter 22

Bells and Horns

DAY AFTER DAY King Benador watched the activity across the river with growing concern. The talons seemed more of an army now, not just a collection of bloodthirsty killers. Someone or something was putting them in line and giving them the discipline they needed to strike out effectively against the Calvan army. And while the numbers of Benador's camp continued to grow daily as volunteers found their way in from all across eastern Calva, the talon army swelled even more. On a single day a troop of several thousand flowed in from the Baerendels, all eager to join the Black Warlock in his glorious conquest.

Benador and his troops kept the pressure on the talons constantly. Several times each day, brigades of cavalry rushed out over the bridges, trampling whatever defenses the talons had hastily erected and cutting down as many of the wretched beasts as they could before they were forced to retreat. Lately, though, the talons had found ways to counter the attacks, and the cost in soldiers for the excursions continued to escalate. And with Rhiannon gone, Siana had to work all the day through tending to the wounded.

But if the King's hopes had started to wane throughout

the remainder of that third week at the river, they were brought back tenfold one bright and shining morning.

"Let our ride be strong and proud," Arien said to Bellerian and Belexus at his side. "Let the shake of the earth and the winding of our horns announce our arrival this morn. And let the Calvans take heart and the talons pale in fright!"

Bellerian grasped the elven Eldar's outstretched hand as Belexus pulled out his great horn and winded the first call, and with that clear, strong note, the charge of the elves and the rangers was on.

The sudden blast of a hundred horns brought the Calvan camp awake, and sent Benador scrambling for the flap of his tent, thinking that the talons had launched their expected attack. But by the time the King got outside, he understood the truth of the disturbance, for the trumpeters of the Calvan camp took up a resoundingly joyful answer.

And then came the bellsong of the elven steeds, dancing in the joyful melody with the pounding of hooves. Benador clenched his fists, a determined grimace on his face, when he saw them break across the northern horizon, half a thousand elves and their escort of mighty rangers. Around the King, the Calvan camp erupted in cheers and shouts, and soldiers rushed out to greet the newcomers.

Once, under the rule of an unlawful king in Pallendara, these peoples, elf and human, had been mortal enemies, but now the Calvans recognized the arrival of Arien Silverleaf and his kin as their possible salvation. Many of the older Calvan soldiers had witnessed the elves in battle, and their prowess with horse, sword, and bow was nothing short of legendary.

Across the river the talons, too, watched the arrival of the children of Lochsilinilume, and under the shade of one tent, red dots of fire looked out to survey the scene. The wraith of Hollis Mitchell only smiled when he realized it was Arien Silverleaf who had come on the scene, another of his enemies from his previous journey through this world of Aielle.

Confident that the elves would not change the course of the coming battle, Mitchell viewed their arrival as a convenience, allowing him to defeat even more of his enemies in this single sweep.

The wraith's evil grin only widened when he learned that the rangers, Belexus included, accompanied the elves.

"It is good that you have come," Benador said to Arien and Bellerian a short time later, after the initial commotion had died away. He and the two leaders had retired to his tent to lay their plans. "There has been a change in the talon camp—more organization and purpose to their movements. I fear they might strike soon."

"The Black Warlock has raised a new commander," Bellerian explained. "And a monster that one is, a wraith from the netherworld come to lead the horde o' talons against us."

The King took the news stoically. "I had suspected as much," he said. "For no talon could have made such changes in the encampment so quickly, and the Black Warlock has not shown such understanding for battle tactics thus far."

"The wraith will be a formidable opponent," said Arien. "He was called Hollis Mitchell in his former life, one of the ancient ones who fell soon after the Battle of Mountaingate. Once, he was a commander in his own world and quite learned in the ways of warfare, beyond our experience. You will not find obvious mistakes in his tactics, I fear."

A grim expression passed over Benador's face, but it faded quickly. "But Mitchell will find few holes in our defenses," the King replied, his smile genuine above his firm-set jaw. "With the joining of the elves and rangers, we have the strength and skill to repel the talons. The defense of the bridges will not falter."

"Ayuh," agreed Bellerian, and he took the hand of this king who had been as a son to him for so very long. Then he turned his gaze, with Arien and Benador, toward the tent flap as his birth son entered, grim-faced.

"The witch's daughter is gone," Belexus said bluntly, and all eyes turned on Benador for an explanation.

"She is safe," Benador assured them, "though I fear that her heart will be long in mending."

"Andovar," Belexus reasoned. "She knew of Andovar."

"It is true, then," Benador remarked.

"It is," replied Belexus. "He fell to the wraith on our journey to the north."

"Then my fears are justified," the King said softly. "I knew that it would not be wise to doubt the guess of Rhiannon, but I had held out hope in my heart that she was mistaken."

"A great loss to us all," Bellerian put in. "But where is the daughter of Brielle, then? Her value to our cause canno' be undervalued."

"I knew not where she went," Benador admitted. "But I could not stop her going, and I know with all certainty that Rhiannon's role in this war is not yet through. She has trained another healer in her absence, a young lass who has performed admirably these last few days."

"Siana of Corning," said Belexus. "I have spoken with the girl and seen her at her work. But she would no' tell me o' the going of Rhiannon."

"Nor would Siana tell me," said Benador. "And I did not press her on the point; I claim no rank over the daughter of Brielle and would not hinder her choice, whatever it might be."

"A wise course," said Bellerian. "Me and me kin have lived for many years trustin' in the Emerald Witch, and I dare say that her daughter's also deservin' of that trust. Wherever Rhiannon's got herself to, not to be doubtin' that she'll help out in the best way she can."

That was all that could be said, but for Belexus, feeling almost like a father to the witch's daughter, mere words could not bring him any measure of comfort. He had seen first-hand the awesome power of Rhiannon, but he had seen, too, the young woman's vulnerability. The loss of Andovar would weigh heavily upon her innocent shoulders and might drive her to desperation.

But like the others, Belexus could only hope and trust in the decisions of the young witch.

They spent many hours in Benador's tent, laying out defensive strategies and playing through, with paper and ink, possible scenarios of a talon attack across the bridges. They all agreed that the next move belonged to Thalasi. With summer nearing its end, time was on their side, and they had no desire to risk defeat in their own offensive strike. They would continue their tactics of hit-and-run, but if a major battle was to be fought, the Black Warlock would have to initiate it.

Of the Black Warlock himself and his undead commander, the leaders could only put their hope in their own magic-users; in Brielle and Istaahl, and Ardaz, if that one could ever be found.

And in Rhiannon, Belexus reminded them all, if the young witch had truly come into her power.

The concern of the four battlefield commanders had to be the containment of the vast talon forces. If Morgan Thalasi managed to defeat their wizards, all of their horn blowing and sword wielding, however valiant, would be for naught.

But the mood of the council was not dark. Their armies were trained and fearless, and fighting under a combination of leaders—Benador, Belexus, Arien Silverleaf, and Bellerian—heretofore unrivaled in the history of Aielle. Each of these heroes held faith in the others, and they believed that together they could weather the tide of Thalasi, however dark.

"The elves have joined," Thalasi said to Mitchell when the wraith emerged just before sunset.

"I watched," Mitchell replied. "Are you afraid?"

Thalasi's hideous cackle scared away several nearby talons. "It only puts all of the pigeons in one pot," he answered. "I fear not mortals; they cannot defeat me."

"But talons feel the bite of sword," Mitchell reminded him. "You have erred, my master. You should have struck with a separate force to the north in the very beginning to keep Arien Silverleaf and his elven kin in their valley."

Thalasi's scowl showed that he didn't appreciate being reprimanded by his subordinate. "It will not matter in the end," he declared. "The world will be mine, wherever Arien and his kin might stand against us, wherever they might fall before us! In the end, they will prove insignificant."

"We will take them," Mitchell agreed. "But twice the pleasure to take them in their sheltered valley, to stain the silver trees and the enchanted mountainsides with elven blood. I think I might use Illuma when I am lord of all the land as a restful retreat from my duties in Pallendara."

For all of his arrogance, Thalasi liked the way Mitchell was thinking. "We will rule from the white city," he agreed. "And all the world shall be yours for the choosing. All except for one spot that I reserve as my own."

"And that is?"

"Avalon," the Black Warlock replied, a low feral growl escaping his lips at the mere mention of the forest. "Of all the places, of all the fortresses, in all the world, none can stand against me as mightily as the wood of Brielle. But it will all change, so very soon. I am growing stronger, my wraith. With you in command of the talons, I can focus my energies and seek greater depths of my magical power. Soon Brielle and Istaahl will be no match for my strength; my storms will ravage their homes and I will banish them from the world!"

"And the third wizard?" Mitchell asked, his fiery eyes simmering at the thought of dealing with that one.

"We will defeat Ardaz," Thalasi promised. "I will give to you darkness to match his light, to hold his power back from our assault. And when our talons have crossed the river, when the armies of Calva and Illuma are smashed and Brielle and Istaahl are no more, Ardaz will have to stand alone against us."

"I almost pity him," Mitchell snickered. But there was not a trace of pity in his grating voice.

Thalasi's cackle erupted again, chiming in with Mitchell's for several savored moments. "When will we be ready?" the Black Warlock asked, unconsciously rubbing his bony hands together.

"We are ready," Mitchell assured him. "And every day we grow more ready. We could go tomorrow to victory, but there remain two problems."

"Ardaz has not yet shown himself," Thalasi reasoned.

Mitchell nodded. "And I find my power diminished by the light of the sun. We could strike at them in the dark of night, but I do not know how the organization of the talons would hold up. The stupid things would probably get lost and land their boats miles to the south, leaving their comrades stranded on the bridges."

Thalasi considered the dilemma for a long while, then a

smile returned to his face. "A fitting solution," he explained. "I will deal with both our problems at once. I will send a calling card to Ardaz, and at the same time solve your discomfort with the light of day."

The sun started its climb above the eastern horizon the next morning, riding across the clear blue summer sky in all its glory.

But in the west, darkness rose to meet it, a gray gloom that seeped eerily upward over the western plain.

Noontime shone bright and clear, but when the sun started its inevitable descent, it fell behind the conjured veil of Morgan Thalasi, and a dimness as profound as twilight engulfed the land.

And still the gray shroud moved higher, rolling out endlessly from the west, from Talas-dun and the Kored-dul, the bastions of Thalasi's evil power.

From Avalon, Brielle watched in horror. Atop the White Tower in Pallendara, Istaahl put his head in his hands and moaned. And on the field by the Four Bridges, the leaders of elves and humans shared that concern.

"Has he grown strong enough to blot out the very light of the sun?" Benador demanded.

Belexus remembered the blackness of the wraith of Mitchell and he knew the answer. "So it would seem," he muttered in grim reply.

Far to the east, beyond the banks of the Elgarde River and the borders of the Great Forest, the wizard Ardaz climbed out of a tunnel he had been exploring, sensing some unnatural event in the world above. For some time he stared at the approaching line of dismal gray and the dull blur that was the sun behind it, instinctively knowing that it was more than a simple storm front.

"How very strange," the confused wizard muttered, scratching his bearded chin. "How very strange indeed."

Chapter 23

Arrows and Arrows
and Arrows

"WHAT DO YOU sense?" Bryan asked, recognizing Rhiannon's trancelike state. He had witnessed the witch's meditation several times over the past couple of days, as Rhiannon looked into the distance to report on talons flocking to Thalasi's side. "Another group?"

Rhiannon nodded and leaned on the half-elf for support. "Another big one," she replied softly. "Bearin' wagons and ridin' donkeys."

Bryan needed her support as well. How many talons had come to join the fight? he wondered. Ten thousand? Twenty? The call of the Black Warlock had spread wide indeed, for the columns of new troops flocking to join his army did not seem to have an end.

Rhiannon steeled herself against the despair that threatened to swallow her and moved away from Bryan. Earlier that day the young witch had witnessed Thalasi's greatest perversion: the gray that shrouded the sun. Now, as she felt the power of the earth once again tingling within her, she wanted with all of her heart to strike back.

"Not this time," she growled at the half-elf, and Bryan took a step back from the bared power in her voice. He watched from a cautious distance as the mysterious young woman moved to a nearby tree stump, hollowed and filled with rainwater.

"Come," Rhiannon bade him as she waved her hand and took up a chant over the still water. Gradually the darkness within the stump lessened, and where before the water had shown only the reflection of Rhiannon and Bryan, there appeared an image of a nearby trail.

"Hundreds," Bryan muttered, staring at the result of Rhiannon's divining. For along the trail moved a caravan of talons, some walking, some riding donkeys, and still more leading beasts hitched to dozens of wagons laden with supplies.

"They must be from Windy Willows," the half-elf reasoned, considering the donkeys. "The Black Warlock is reaching out to all the wide corners of his western domain."

"They're not far," Rhiannon remarked. "We can get to them."

"Why would we want to?" Bryan asked incredulously. "We can do little against so many. Unless . . ." His voice trailed off as he took a closer look at the young witch's grim face. "What tricks," he asked slyly, "might you have in store for this group?"

Rhiannon wouldn't let him in on her secret. "Come," was all she answered as she started off toward the trail. Bryan smiled widely as he fell into step beside her. He had seen the result of Rhiannon's wrath once before, and with her on his side, he was not afraid, no matter the odds. He slid his elven sword from its sheath, too eager to let it wait on his hip.

This was going to be fun.

* * *

Rhiannon chanted over each of the arrows individually, then handed the entire quiver back to Bryan. "Shoot for the biggest groups," she instructed.

Bryan took the gift reverently, not certain whether he wanted to ask the witch what enchantment she had put in the weapons or to just let them fly and watch the magic as it loosed its fury on the talons. Rhiannon offered no explanation, though, for something off to the side had caught her attention.

In the distance a tree shuddered to life and dropped a heavy branch on the head of a crouching talon.

"Talon scout," Rhiannon explained to Bryan matter-of-factly. She moved off through a thicket to take her position in front of the approaching caravan. Bryan followed a few steps behind, watching her every move.

Without a thought the young witch waved her hand, and another tree a bit farther in front of them rustled, catching a talon around the neck with a supple branch and hoisting it up off the ground, kicking and gasping for breath.

And Bryan found his own breath hard to catch. He had never seen Rhiannon so grim and callous, even when she had come to his rescue in the stony canyon. She moved on from the scene of her second kill, impassive and strong, a lioness at hunt.

The talon caravan rolled down the wide trail, unmindful of its impending doom. They came to answer the call of Morgan Thalasi, the father of their race, to join in his moment of triumph over the hated humans. They could not know the power that stood to block them.

Rhiannon sensed them before they came into sight. She remained in position behind the cover of a stony ridge and motioned for Bryan to ready his bow. Then the young witch moved away a bit and sat quietly, knowing that the magic she had let into her body would dictate its place in the confrontation.

Bryan drew his bowstring and waited as the caravan rolled into sight. He still did not know the extent of the power within his arrows, but he felt a tingle in the one he had notched, as if the arrow itself was eager for the coming flight.

"The biggest groups," Rhiannon said again, and so the half-elf took aim on the first cluster of talons, huddled around a wagon and fighting over the scraps of food they could pull from it as they went.

"Now," Rhiannon whispered, and Bryan let it fly. The arrow soared off into the night, leaving a glowing trail in its wake. And then Bryan had to blink to be certain that his eyes were not playing tricks on him, for the arrow split apart and became two, and those two split into four, and those became eight, and again and again until a score and twelve soared into the talon horde. Nearly two dozen talons dropped to the ground, mortally wounded, and all the caravan began hooting and howling to warn of the attack.

Bryan fired several more of the enchanted arrows off quickly, showering the confused monsters in a virtual rain of arrows before they could find cover. Even so, the half-elf's attacks barely dented the large force, and these talons had marched all the way from the Ballendul Mountains in search of battle. Ignoring the cries of their wounded, the group rallied and charged on against the onslaught.

But then the young witch started to sing.

Rhiannon's voice rang out strong and sweet in the night, filling Bryan with courage and draining the blood from the faces of the talons.

Trees along the edges of the trail danced to the witch's melody, swatting and strangling those talons that tried to move from the stony center of the path. Still the throng rushed on and Bryan cut them down. He fired off four shots that became six score and eight, evenly spaced across the breadth of the trail, and decimated the front ranks with a wall of killing darts.

Still the young witch sang, and now the donkeys heard her call. They bucked and spun, tossing their riders to the ground and trampling them before they understood what had happened. Those donkeys pulling wagons charged about wildly, overturning the carts and scattering lines of talons.

Rhiannon stepped out into the open, glowing with power. She thrust her hands out before her and sheets of flame sprang forth, reaching down the trail to engulf those talons brave enough, or stupid enough, to continue their charge.

"Rhiannon!" Bryan gasped, horrified and elated all at once. But the witch didn't hear him, too consumed by the power she loosed upon her enemies.

For the talons, the trees had been bad enough. But this open display of witchery was simply too much for them to accept. They scattered and fled, back down the trail and all the way through the pass toward their dark holes in the Ballenduls. This group would find no place of glory beside the Black Warlock.

Bryan meant to follow their retreat with a few showers of arrows, grim reminders of what awaited them should they return. But the half-elf could not. His eyes remained transfixed on Rhiannon, studying her expression as she completed her release of magic.

And while he had been in awe of her during the brief battle, he felt only pity when it ended. Rhiannon looked at him, tears streaking her face. So frail she seemed that Bryan could hardly believe she was the same being who had just wreaked such destruction.

"Help me," she whispered, and then she collapsed, thoroughly drained, into Bryan's arms.

* * *

If the Black Warlock had been paying attention, he most certainly would have sensed the display of magic in the Baerendel Mountains that night. But Thalasi was off on his own exercise of magic, creating the finishing touches to his army.

He strolled to a wide pit behind the vast talon encampment, an open grave for the many talons and humans who had fallen on the field in the previous days.

"Beigen kaimen dee," the Black Warlock chanted, waving his most powerful tool, the Staff of Death, over the pit. For a moment nothing happened.

"Beigen kaimen dee," Thalasi growled again, sensing the conception of the enchantment. There came a stirring in the pit and then several of the corpses rose up and crawled out to the summons of the Black Warlock. Thalasi chuckled as the wretched things, some missing an arm or a leg, one without a head, scrambled to his bidding, and all the while thinking it grand that he could so easily steal from the realm of death.

The Black Warlock repeated the spell several times until he sensed that the host of his zombie army had reached the limits of his control. These were not like Hollis Mitchell, not wraiths encompassing the spirit and consciousness of the beings they had once been. Rather, these were unthinking zombies, slow-moving and capable of following only rudimentary commands.

But Thalasi understood their value in the coming battle. How the humans would flee from the specter of his undead brigade!

"Rest, my pets," he bade them, and as one the zombie force dropped to the ground and lay still. Thalasi knew he would have to be very careful with them. Even his talons might flee the camp at the appearance of such horrifying comrades. The Black Warlock would give them over to Mitchell's command and let the wraith hold them in check until battle was fully joined.

"Then let all of Calva tremble," Thalasi muttered to the empty night. "Let them know the power of Morgan Thalasi. Let them know their doom."

Rhiannon shot up from the blankets Bryan had set out for her bed, her face stark with terror.

"What is it?" Bryan asked, rushing to her side.

Rhiannon just shook her head and buried her face in the front of the half-elf's tunic. Bryan rested a hand on her back to calm her trembling. "Yet another nightmare?" he asked.

Rhiannon looked up at him, unable to find the words to explain. But Bryan was sensitive to the young witch's dilemma; he had come to understand her quite well in their few days together, and he knew from the expression on her face that her release of power had nearly torn her apart.

"You did as you had to," he said to her. "You cannot accept any blame for your actions."

"Ye canno' understand," Rhiannon replied. "It takes me, steals me from meself."

"But it passes," Bryan reasoned.

"And leaves nothin' but destruction in its wake."

"Not true!" Bryan was quick to protest. "You saved my life! And many others, from what you have told me of your work on the field of Rivertown."

"Suren it is two-faced," Rhiannon admitted. "But the healin' side and the seein' side are at me biddin'. This other, this anger ye've seen, comes of its own and goes when it's through with me."

"Accept it for what it is," Bryan urged her. "How many lives did you save this night, dear Rhiannon? How many men would have died on the bridges fighting off the talons you dispatched?"

Somehow the answer seemed inadequate to the young witch. "I have scarred the earth," she said. "I have killed—talon and beast." The image of her black and white horse on the northern field, lying dead after it had split the earth with its enchanted run, assaulted her thoughts.

"You have done what you were forced to do," Bryan said stubbornly. "Thanks are owed to the daughter of Brielle. Yet to herself she gives only blame."

"Ye canno' understand," the young witch whispered again, and she dropped her face back into the security of the folds of Bryan's shirt.

Bryan did not reply; for all of his pretty words, he suspected that Rhiannon was right in her estimation. He had seen the coldness in her eyes as she executed the spells of destruction upon the talon caravan, a simmering wrath so foreign to the young woman's gentle character. Such emotions exacted a heavy toll, Bryan knew from his own grim experiences. He tried to remember the last time he had flashed a carefree smile, and he wondered if he would ever smile that way again.

"And it must be worse for you," he whispered, though his voice was so soft that the witch, finding comfort in slumber, did not stir. While his strength came from his skills, he could see that the power that Rhiannon used insinuated itself into her being, possessed her and controlled her.

That image of the young witch, standing coldly beside him as her fires burned away the stain of the talons, stayed with Bryan for the remainder of the night. He wanted to tell her that she would never have to use that destructive power again, that her world would be one of creation and healing. He wanted to help her fight off the insinuating power and be true to her gentle spirit.

But the thought of the armies on the fields beside the Four Bridges washed away Bryan's hopes. For all of his desire to shield Rhiannon, the awful reality told him the truth of his duties.

Rhiannon had a part to play in all of this, Bryan knew, a voice in the outcome of the war and the very future of Ynis Aielle. Her power was there whether she or he accepted it or not, and with the carnage of war so thick in the air, that power could not be denied.

"I will help you," Bryan promised when Rhiannon awoke the next morning—the first sunless morning.

Rhiannon considered the gray shroud of Thalasi's dark magic, now stretching from horizon to horizon, and knew she would need that help.

Chapter 24

Mortality

HAD HE LOOKED back to Kored-dul, to his black fortress of Talas-dun, Morgan Thalasi might have been concerned. In the weeks after he had found harmony of his twin spirits, before he set out with his talon army, he had reinforced the iron fortress to its previous state of power.

But now, with Thalasi out on the Calvan fields, pulling at the magical plane with all of his power-hungry desperation, some of those old cracks in Talas-dun had reappeared, and when the heavy sea breeze rolled in on the high cliff, the tallest of the black castle's towers swayed ominously, no longer able to fully defy the force.

The Black Warlock was consumed in the business at hand, with his eyes looking to conquest in the east, not back to those lands he already claimed as his own. He took no note of the strain his dominating will, and the responses of his magic-using adversaries, placed upon that shared magical plane.

Brielle walked slowly through Avalon, taking advantage of the unexpected lull in Thalasi's attacks to soothe her trees with comforting promises of a brighter time. But while the Emerald Witch held fast to the belief that Morgan Thalasi would once again be defeated and driven back to his black fortress, she honestly wondered whether Ynis Aielle would ever be as it had been.

Avalon, the shining light of all the world, had weakened in the weeks of Thalasi's assaults, and more than the border-lands of the forest had been affected. Even in the heart of the wood, in the fields and groves that Brielle held most dear, the colors of the flora seemed less vibrant and the permeating fragrance of the wildflowers could not hold up against the burning stench of decay and devastation. For Thalasi's assaults were more than physical manifestations of destructive power. The response demanded by the Black War-lock's attacks heavily taxed the defending witch, to the core of her magic itself. Brielle had aged more in the past weeks than she had in a dozen centuries, and her growing weari-ness, she feared, was merely a reflection of the exhaustion of her magical energy.

And it was that same magical energy, drawn upon by the Emerald Witch, that bound the forest of Avalon in its per-petual enchantment of beauty.

"What will we be when the last sounds o' battle echo o'er the fields?" she asked her forest. The cry of a loon sounded in the unseen distance, its mournful wail seeming a fitting eulogy to the ears of the witch. Brielle shared that lament fully. She reached out to lean on the trunk of a large tree, seeking solace in its enduring strength.

But the boughs of Avalon, wrapped in a silent sadness, could not grant her any measure of hope.

Istaahl also spent those hours of welcome calm surveying the damage and assessing how to effect some measure of repair to his home. The White Mage remained torn by his duties; he felt that he should be in contact with King Benador, his liege, preparing for the inevitable conflict that would erupt any day. But after a quick tour of the White Tower, Istaahl knew that he had no choice in his course of action.

Thalasi's assaults had both weakened him greatly and had struck devastating blows to his enchanted home. Great cracks lined the structure, running from the very tip of the tower all the way down to its foundations. Istaahl understood that if he did not take prompt action to reinforce the place with spells of strength and warding, it would crumble to dust with the Black Warlock's next attack.

And like his counterpart in Avalon, the White Mage of Pallendara was beginning to suspect that the scars of this war would be enduring.

"Alas for the wizards of Aielle," he muttered to himself that gray day. "Our time is passing; the race of mortal men may soon be left to their own resources."

All of the wizards had known from the beginning that this day would eventually come. But after centuries of serving as the guardians and advisers to the races of Aielle, the sudden apparent change had them perplexed indeed.

Brielle knelt over a pool of clear water. Its glassy surface showed only the dull pall of Thalasi's gloomy sky, but the witch ignored the dismay the sight brought to her. Waving her hand and casting a simple enchantment, she hoped that Istaahl was not too engaged in yet another battle against the Black Warlock to answer her call.

At that same moment, Istaahl was entertaining similar thoughts of contacting Brielle, and he was near his crystal ball when the Emerald Witch called upon him. He accepted the magical contact eagerly, needing the comfort of a friendly face in this dark hour.

"So the Black Warlock has granted you a period of rest as well?" he asked through a strained smile.

"Me thinkin's that he needs his own," Brielle replied. "Suren he's been putting his magics to their bounds these days—how much more has he got to throw?"

"I fear the answer to that question," said Istaahl.

"As with meself," Brielle agreed. "But I faced the dark one on me western borders a few nights hence. He's not Thalasi as we knew him. Joined with the ancient one, Martin Reinheiser, in spirit and thought."

"A dual being?" Istaahl asked, hardly able to believe the news. "Is that possible?"

"It would seem," Brielle replied grimly. "They've found harmony—"

"In hatred."

"Aye, focused in hatred," said Brielle. "And the result is mighty indeed, as ye've no doubt seen."

"The Black Warlock has wounded me deeply," Istaahl admitted. His wizened features twisted, searching for the right way to explain the pervasive sense of dread that hung over him. "Not physically, though. My tower has been savaged, indeed, but it was no more than uncut blocks when first I built it."

"But ye do no' know if ye can put it aright ever again?" Brielle asked, understanding the fears of the White Mage perfectly.

"Yes!" said Istaahl, relieved that she saw his meaning so clearly. Though when he took a moment to think about it, Istaahl realized that Brielle's understanding foretold a greater tragedy.

"Ye look tired," Brielle remarked.

"Weary is the better word," Istaahl replied. "I do not understand it, my dear friend." Again he struggled for the proper words. "I feel mortal. For the first time in my days as a wizard, I see my magic as a finite pool, not an unending source of power."

"Me heart tells me the same," said Brielle. "We've pushed on it too hard is me fear, bent the line o' power to where it will not come back to straight."

"Yes," Istaahl agreed. "No matter what the outcome of this war, I have come to the conclusion that Ynis Aielle will never be the same."

"The passing of an age," Brielle remarked.

"Perhaps not," Istaahl replied with a trace of hope. "Your brother has not yet entered the fray, nor has Brisen-ballas, his Silver Tower—" The words stuck in Istaahl's throat. With all that had been happening in Avalon and Pallendara, neither of them had given any thought to the fate of Ardaz's tower on the cliff wall above Illuma Vale. Had Thalasi struck out against the home of the Silver Mage in his absence? Istaahl wondered and Brielle read his thoughts from the expression of horror on his face.

"No!" the witch insisted. "He has not. The elves passed through me wood just a few days ago, and they spoke nothin' of any attacks. The power of Lochsilinilume is strong, me friend, and the Black Warlock has taken the absence o' me brother as a blessin'; he'd no' attack Brisen-ballas, for fear that his strike would alert Rudy to the war."

"But how much damage could Thalasi cause to Brisen-ballas in your brother's absence?" reasoned Istaahl. "Could he crush the Silver Tower and steal much of Ardaz's strength before he ever arrived to defend his home?"

"At what cost?" Brielle asked. "I've fought him meself, and I can tell ye with all o' me heart that he is strong, but not foolish. If Thalasi goes against me brother's home, I'll be layin' in wait. The Black Warlock'll know he's outdone himself when me magic catches him from behind, and when me brother hears the rumblin's in his tower and rushes back to defend it!"

"Then Thalasi will fight against three," said Istaahl, his spirits bolstered by the determination of the witch. "And what of your brother? Is there any word at all?"

"Not a one," Brielle replied, "Rudy's a one-minded sort, I fear. He's off to explorin' and not likely to turn his eyes back our way. I'd've looked for him meself, but I fear to leave me wood."

"As I fear to leave my tower," agreed Istaahl. "But surely he will return to us soon—even your one-minded brother will not miss the implications of Thalasi's darkened sky."

"That is me guess," agreed Brielle. "But also me fear. Thalasi understands the same; he would not've put out the sun without plans for dealing with Rudy's return. I fear that the moment of the battle is nearen upon us."

"Then fear not," Istaahl said, knowing it was his turn to lend some strength. "For when Thalasi moves, he will find three wizards standing against him."

Brielle nodded her agreement, leaving her hopes of her daughter's ascent into power unspoken.

"Farewell, then, my dear Brielle," Istaahl said. "And fight well. Glad am I that we have talked this night, though I fear that our shared belief in the passing of an age is well founded."

"And glad am I," Brielle replied. "And take heart, Istaahl of Pallendara. When the smoke has blown from the field and the screams o' the pained and dying are no more, we will remain."

The images faded from the crystal ball and the clear pool, and both wizard and witch slumped back, considering what they had learned this night. Both felt Brielle's parting words were the truth, but both questioned the implications. The godlike powers of the four wizards had dominated Aielle for centuries; what strength would rise to fill the gap when those powers waned?

Chapter 25

The Calm

"YOU GO SEE what it's all about," Ardaz purred to Desdemona, the black cat comfortably draped over his shoulders. Desdemona just rolled her back against the wizard's neck and pretended not to hear him.

But Ardaz, suspecting that the gloomy sky indicated something important, would not be so easily dismayed. "Enough of that, you silly puss!" he scolded, pulling the cat from her perch and shaking her before his eyes. "Wake up now, wake up! We've no time for your laziness; the catnaps will simply have to wait!"

Desdemona growled in protest.

"Now, I'll hear none of that," scolded Ardaz. "You go find out what you can find out. And be quick, you silly puss!" The cat let out a shriek a moment later when Ardaz threw her up into the sky. As she was falling, Desdemona transformed into a raven and stretched out her wings to catch the breeze. Then she was soaring up into the gray sky, reluctant but obedient to Ardaz.

"That's better," Ardaz muttered to himself as Desdemona faded to a black dot in the distance. "Sleep all day, silly puss. Pass her life away, she would, I do dare say!"

The agitated Ardaz, with typical focus, forgot all about Desdemona a moment later. "Oh, time to see, time to see!" he spouted, and he rubbed his eager hands together and turned back to the tunnel in the latest stretch of ruins he had uncovered. The darkened sky might be important; then again, it might not. But he honestly believed that this find, revealing a civilization in Ynis Aielle wholly unknown, could reshape the world. The wizard slipped back into the tunnel and paused, confused, for a few long minutes, scratching his beard and trying to remember in which direction he had been exploring.

Desdemona caught the updrafts and rode up high into the sky, almost glad now, with the whistle of the wind in her face, that Ardaz had disturbed her lazy slumber. She didn't really know what her wizard expected her to find up here, or where she would even begin her search to learn more of the unnatural gloom shrouding the world. But if there was information to be gained, Desdemona suspected that it would probably be found back in the populated world. Catching a wind current, the raven spread her wings wide and glided back toward the Elgarde River, just a silvery snake in the distance.

But then another form rose into the sky, much larger than Des and unmistakable in shape. Des swooped off toward her unexpected companion, thinking it grand that Calamus the Pegasus had come out to play.

Billy Shank noticed the approach of the large raven, and initially he reached for his sword hilt, thinking the bird to be perhaps a manifestation of Morgan Thalasi or one of his dark minions. Calamus recognized the familiar of Ardaz, though, and the obvious delight of the Pegasus as Des drew near reminded Billy of the creature's true identity.

"Desdemona!" he called, making room for the raven to alight on the Pegasus' back in front of him. As if in answer to his call, Desdemona became a cat again and rolled comfortably against Billy's belly.

"No, no," Billy scolded, remembering the cat's penchant for untimely naps. "You can't rest yet, kitten; you have to lead us to your master."

Desdemona's only answer was a steady purr as she rolled over onto her back, her paws stretched up into the sky and her eyes closed. Billy prodded her and called to her, but that only made her purr all the louder. He knew what Ardaz would do, though he held some reservations about that course of action. But as the cat continued to delay, the man found that he had no choice.

"It's for your own good," he explained, and he picked up the apparently boneless cat and tossed her off Calamus' back. Desdemona let out her second shriek of the morning, and Billy held his breath until the animal became a raven again, her wings catching the air and slowing her descent.

"Lead us, to Ardaz!" Billy called. "It is so very important!"

Desdemona, of course, couldn't fathom anything more important than her nap, but she wasn't going to get much sleep gliding around in midair. She cut back toward the east and soared off, landing a few minutes later beside the tunnel in the ruins.

"Finally," Billy breathed. He jumped from his mount's back and rushed to the hole in the ground, poking his head down into the darkness. "Ardaz!" he shouted. "Ardaz, are you in there?"

A few seconds later, just when Billy was preparing to drop into the tunnel and go off to find the wizard, the steady glow of a magical light appeared down one of the twisting passages and Billy heard the familiar voice.

"Oh how grand, how grand, how grand!" the wizard rambled, speeding along back to the exit. "Desdemona, my sweet, you have finally learned how to talk! How very grand! So many years—" Billy flinched when he heard a thud and saw the light drop as the wizard tripped and fell.

"Who put that—" Ardaz snapped angrily. "Oh yes, oh silly me," the wizard answered himself. "My own pack. Ha ha. Thought I'd lost it, too."

"Ardaz," Billy called again.

"Coming, Des," the wizard replied. He hopped and stumbled to the hole, his robes and face covered with dust, and stopped short at the unexpected sight of Billy Shank.

"Finally," Billy muttered again. "I have been—"

"Oh, Billy!" Ardaz interrupted. "Of course it wasn't Des," he scolded himself. "Glad to see you, my boy, I do dare say. Long way from home—what brings you all the way out here?—but I'll see that the trip is worth the trouble, I shall indeed!"

Billy held his palm out, trying to slow the wizard's frantic pace. "I did not—" he began again.

"Have you seen them?" Ardaz cried. "Of course you have. Ruins, my boy, ruins! Do you know what that means? Could you know? No, of course you couldn't. Ha ha!"

"But—"

"Other people, of course!" Ardaz cried. "There are, or were—oh, I hope it's not 'were,' I do so want to meet them, after all." He stopped, confused by his own banter. "But where was I?" he asked, though Billy knew that the wizard would not wait for an answer. "Oh yes, oh yes. Other people! An entire civilization existing right here on our back door."

Billy understood that he had to find some way to stop the wizard, or Ardaz's monologue could ramble on for an hour, and he knew of only one word carrying the shock value necessary to stop Ardaz in midramble.

"Thalasi," he said, with all the grimness that the name deserved.

"Of course, they are not—" Ardaz's eyes bulged and his tongue got all wrapped around itself. He lunged at Billy, attempting his usual hand-over-the-mouth technique whenever anyone uttered the name of the Black Warlock, but Billy expected the attack and pulled back out of the tunnel as the wizard came on.

Ardaz came leaping out of the hole in a shot. "Speak not that name!" he yelled, still coming after Billy with outstretched palms. By the time he finally caught up to the man, though, there seemed no need for his patented silencing technique.

"Speak not that name," Ardaz said again, his voice now a somber whisper. Ever did the name of Morgan Thalasi take the bubble out of Ardaz's voice. He glanced all around, as if he expected some demon to spring upon them where they stood, in punishment for Billy's foolishness. "You will bring the evil one upon us, I do dare say."

Billy's eyes led the wizard's gaze up to the dreary overcast sky, and Ardaz began to understand.

"But what brought you all the way . . ." the wizard began. "And with Calamus, indeed, why is he out of Avalon?" The wizard's eyes popped open wide. "You do not mean . . ."

Billy nodded. "I came in search of you. The Black Warlock has returned."

The blood drained from the wizard's face. "But he died! Got shot, he did—bang!—on the field."

"His talons stormed across the western fields and now

hold camp across the great river from the combined army of Calvans, elves, and rangers."

"Evil," Ardaz breathed.

"We do not know how many thousands have died already," Billy went on. "But we were certain that doom would overtake all of the known lands if Ardaz could not be found." He motioned toward Calamus. "The final battle might already be under way," he explained. "We have no time to tarry. I'll try to answer your questions as we fly."

"Of course," Ardaz agreed quietly. "If only I could remember the proper spell," he lamented, scratching his beard. "Could be there in a flash. But I don't like that way of travel—miss too many of the sights along the road, you know. Oh bother, well, it does not matter." He skipped over to the Pegasus and leaped onto its back. "I'll help Calamus speed along—are you coming? We have not the time to tarry, after all."

Billy didn't bother to respond—caught up in the news and trying to devise some plan of action, Ardaz wouldn't have heard him anyway.

And then they were soaring in the dullness that had become the Aiellian sky. Ardaz whispered some words of magical encouragement into the winged horse's ear and Calamus' flight grew doubly swift. Gradually, as the world rolled out below them, Ardaz calmed and settled silently into his seat. Billy recounted the events of the war to him, of the strange dual being that was now the Black Warlock, and of the wraith that had infected the land and had taken Andovar, the valiant ranger, from the realm of the living.

Ardaz, understanding the gravity of the tale, did not interrupt even once. He just sat very still and piped in with a "How very wicked!" or a "Terrible, just terrible!" every few minutes.

* * *

There were no skirmishes across the bridges that day, as both sides fell under the hush of anticipation. Tensions grew as thick as Thalasi's gray sky, and the King of Calva, with Arien, Belexus, and Bellerian at his side, walked his horse about the field, checking and rechecking the defenses and the morale of his troops.

"They will come on the morn," he predicted.

The others did not disagree. They could sense the pent-up excitement across the river, could see the talons pacing about, fingering their weapons in sweating hands.

"And we will be ready for them," Arien Silverleaf promised. The Eldar had fought against greater odds than he now faced, and if there was any fear at all behind his noble eyes, the others could not sense it. King Benador drew strength both from Arien and from the two rangers, who had long ago vowed that their principles were more important than their mortal bodies. A ranger did not fear death by the sword, and a ranger did not surrender his hopes no matter how dark the blackness.

"I have spoken with Istaahl this day," Benador announced, his tone more casual. "Thalasi has ceased his attacks upon the White Tower and upon Avalon, though it is not known if the cause is weariness or prudence."

"I suspect the latter," Arien said. "He gathers his strength, like his army."

"Then if the dawning o' the morrow harkens the dark day," said Belexus, "let us pray to the Colonnae for the strength we will surely need. Noble and just is our cause; the truth will bring us victory."

"And damn the Black Warlock to the hell he deserves," agreed a young woman behind them. They turned to see Siana, Jolsen Smithyson, and Lennard standing proudly, fully arrayed for battle.

"Your place is with the wounded," Benador said to her, though his tone was not scolding.

"They have been tended as well as they may," Siana assured her king. "And those who could travel are long down the road toward Pallendara."

"Go with them," Benador bade them, honest sympathy in his voice. "All three of you. You have done your part in this war, more than your part. No more sacrifices can we ask of you."

"Then take what is not asked for," Lennard replied determinedly. "We will stand beside the wounded who cannot be moved."

"And Thalasi will have to get across our lifeless bodies to strike at the helpless ones!" Jolsen agreed.

"Surely I did not heal them only to give them over," Siana reasoned. "You will see, my King, that I am of value with sword as well as with the healing powers Rhiannon imparted to me."

Benador could only smile at their defiant courage. "I do not doubt your words," he said. "But let us hope that you will not see battle. Let us hope that the talons do not get as far as the tents of healing."

The three young warriors nodded their agreement, but when Benador and his entourage moved away, their gazes drifted across the river to the swollen ranks of the talon camp, and they suspected that their leader's hopes were in vain.

And from across the river, other, darker eyes looked back.

"Has the stupid wizard answered your challenge?" Mitchell asked impatiently.

"Logic says that he is on the way," Thalasi replied. "Though I fear to rely on logic where Rudy Glendower is concerned."

"We must go soon," the wraith explained. "I have whipped

them into a frenzy, and any delay will only steal from their excitement."

"I want the missing wizard on the field," Thalasi replied. "I want him where we can watch his every move. Ever does that one have a trick to pull!"

Mitchell looked down at the Black Warlock's bony hands, clenched, as they always seemed to be, in fists of rage.

"But you are right," Thalasi went on, calming again. "And I commend your work with the talons."

"We will sweep the Calvans from the bridges," Mitchell promised. "And chase them all the way back to Pallendara."

"You understand the purpose of your undead legions?" Thalasi asked.

The wraith nodded, that evil smile spreading over his dark features. "I will hold them in reserve," he replied. "And when the battle reaches a critical moment, I will lead them in."

"The northernmost bridge," Thalasi said. "That is the one I enchanted in that past age. Its enchantment is strong; it will not be destroyed."

Mitchell nodded his assent. "And when—if—the wizard Ardaz appears to halt me? Have you prepared my weapon?"

Thalasi reached under the folds of his black robes and produced the wraith's skull-headed mace. Mitchell felt it vibrating with dark power when his master handed it to him.

"It feels different to my touch," he commented, a bit confused, for the instrument's heavy balance had changed, had lessened; it seemed less a striking weapon, and its mighty head, the mace that had split boulders, was now lined with tiny holes.

Thalasi laughed at Mitchell's hesitation. "Still you have not learned the true meaning of power," he remarked. "Think not of your weapon as a striking mace, my friend, but as your scepter. Strike with it if you choose—it has lost none of its battering strength."

Mitchell relaxed visibly.

"But the weapon has another feature now, a darker feature which should dim the light of Ardaz, or of any other fools who try to stand against you." Calling an unfortunate talon to come over and stand before him, he took the scepter from Mitchell.

The talon trembled and rubbed its hands together.

It understood, or thought it understood, the terrible implications of becoming a testing ground for the Black Warlock's powers, but the pitiful creature was simply too terrified to run away.

Still, for all its fears, the talon could not have been prepared for the ultimate doom that descended on it when Morgan Thalasi waved the scepter in its direction. Black flakes puffed out of the weapon's head, falling over the talon in a perverted snowfall. The talon's eyes widened in stark, disbelieving horror as it felt the coldness of doom engulf it, stealing its very soul. So terrible was its inner anguish that the talon did not even feel the physical burn of the flakes before it died. But burn they did, and in seconds the scepter's first victim had been reduced to a bubbling mass of smoldering, shapeless ooze.

A hiss of sheer elation escaped the wraith's mouth.

"You will come to understand power," Thalasi promised. "And you will enjoy your new toy. We will go in the morning, whether Ardaz has made his appearance or not. Let the Silver Mage come in late, if he will. Let him witness the rout of all the army of Calva." Thalasi's glare at the wraith seemed double-edged, promising ultimate glory if they succeeded and ultimate blame if they failed.

"The army is fully yours," Thalasi explained. "I must

prepare for my strikes on the witch and wizard. Tomorrow, Avalon burns to ash, and the White Tower crumbles to dust."

Mitchell brought the menacing scepter up before his fiery eyes. "And if Ardaz shows his face . . ." the wraith promised through his wicked grin.

Chapter 26

The Storm

A GLOBE OF darkness rested on the field behind the stirring talon army, a perverted black ball that scorched the grass as it moved. And in the center of this wicked sphere loomed a figure, tall and terrible. Morgan Thalasi called now upon the Staff of Death, tapping its lethal black heel against the soft earth and uttering arcane words of power. The staff responded to the commands of its master, its horrid magic drawing the life force from the ground beneath it and giving it to Thalasi.

"What is that?" Bryan gasped when he noticed the dark spectacle. He and Rhiannon had come over the northwesternmost slopes of the Baerendels just before the gray dawn and were still several miles from the talon encampment, but even from this distance, the globe of blackness shone clearly before their eyes.

"Morgan Thalasi," Rhiannon replied in a whisper, as if speaking that name would alert the Black Warlock to their presence.

"Angfagdul," Bryan muttered, using the name his father

had used for Thalasi when recounting the legendary Battle of Mountaingate.

"He's gathering his power" Rhiannon explained, though she had no idea of why she was so certain of her observation.

"Then we have arrived just in time," Bryan reasoned. "The battle is about to begin."

"Just in time?" Rhiannon balked. "To watch, then? What good'll we do against the likes o' that one?"

Bryan's expression turned angry. "Words of doom," he scolded. "You surrender before the first arrow is loosed!"

Rhiannon dropped her gaze and accepted his rebuke. Bryan was right: she knew that she would indeed play some vital role in the day's events. For all of her outward helplessness, the young witch could already feel the call of the power tingling within her body.

Thalasi's black globe sucked the very life and energy from the ground, killing the earth beneath its perverted darkness for eternity. More and more power swelled within the Black Warlock's body, wracking him with bulging pain. But he kept at his work, though he thought he would surely burst apart, and took in all that he could steal from the earth below him.

In Avalon and Pallendara, and high in the air on the back of a rushing Pegasus, the other three experienced wizards of Ynis Aielle felt the Black Warlock's pull against the fabric of their magic, bending the cord of the universal energies to his misguided commands.

"Too much," Ardaz gasped, feeling as if the very bonds of natural harmony would split apart, throwing all the world into chaos. In their distant seats of power, Brielle and Istaahl echoed the Silver Mage's grim words.

* * *

Thalasi cackled with delirious delight, literally drunk with the excess of energies pouring into him. "I am the god!" he proclaimed, his unearthly voice rolling out over the plain, across the river and across all Aielle, reverberating in every ear in the world.

Then the Black Warlock let loose.

He threw his arms upward, his fingers reaching for the sky, and out of his limbs came crackling bolts of black energy, hissing and sizzling as they rushed up to lend power to the gray clouds of the conjured overcast. Thunder rumbled to the Black Warlock's call, the clouds rolled in whipped fury, and a driving rain rushed out, bent by great western winds into the blank faces of the stunned Calvan army.

Still more black bolts exploded from the warlock's fingers into the sky, and two particularly dark clouds rushed off, one to the north and one to the east.

Brielle and Istaahl braced themselves, sensing the approach of the mighty storms, for they knew, as did all who witnessed the release of the storms, that the Black Warlock's targets once again were Avalon and the White Tower.

And this time he meant to have them.

The rain beat down on the soldiers defending the bridges, and the wind remained strong and urging at the backs of Mitchell and the talons. But the wraith knew that Thalasi had otherwise left the battlefield to his command.

"You have heard the master!" Mitchell roared at his lead talon forces. "Take the world for him! Let all the humans run from our fell blades!"

The charge of thirty thousand talons whipped into a killing frenzy by the spectacle of their god-figure and his dark general was on.

They hit the bridges running, heedless of the crossed stakes erected by the Calvans. Those in front willingly impaled

themselves that their ugly kin could run over their bodies
headlong into the next lines of defense.

The leaders of the defending forces could not have expected such unbridled fury, but King Benador took strength
from the aged wisdom of his commanders, from the calm
responses of Arien Silverleaf and Bellerian, and from the
unfaltering courage of Belexus. The mighty ranger prince
and his comrades from Avalon charged the length of the defensive line, rallying the soldiers with promises of victory.

And the value of their efforts could not be underestimated, for the terror on each Calvan soldier's face changed
to grim determination as the rangers passed, and when the
talons finally clawed their way through the defensive barri-
ers, they were met head-on by a Calvan charge that rivaled
their own in intensity. The Calvans fought for all of those
who had died, and for all of those helpless multitudes who
would surely die if they could not stop the black tide here
and now.

Then all the bridges were thrown into chaos, a clawing,
hacking swirl of talon and man. No quarter was asked and
none was given; to lose was to die. For the talons, to lose
was to face the fury of Morgan Thalasi. For the Calvans, to
lose was to realize the destruction of all the world.

Black bile wetted Rhiannon's throat, sheer horror and disgust at the sight of the conflict. The screams of agony and
rage rolled across the distance to her ears. Even Bryan, familiar with smaller-scale and more choreographed skirmishes,
felt his knees go weak at the sheer viciousness of the battle,
and he winced each time one death scream wailed above all
the others.

But Bryan soon steeled himself against his revulsion, reminding himself of the importance of the scene before him.

He turned to Rhiannon for counsel, but found the young witch fully entranced by the continuing spectacle of Morgan Thalasi, as if Rhiannon could better understand the deadly implications of his dark efforts.

Now the black bolts ripping upward into the sky from the arms of the Black Warlock came as one unending stream, one reaching north and the other east, fueling the frenzy of the storms as they raced to their destinations.

Bolt after bolt of lightning blasted into the defensive shell over Avalon, a bubble of energy that Brielle had created to protect her forest. The initial blasts were dispersed into showers of multicolored sparks. But each ensuing bolt jolted the Emerald Witch, strained her powers to their very limits, and she knew that soon her shell would collapse.

"Too much!" she yelled, echoing her brother's words and sending the thought through the connection of their magical energies to the mind of the Black Warlock. "Ye'll break it all, ye fool!"

Thalasi's answer came as another blast of lightning, a furious bolt that split the earth around the perimeter of Brielle's fortress forest.

Hurricane winds buffeted Istaahl's tower, swaying the tall structure far to the side and then back again. The desperate wizard evoked magical arms to engulf the structure, holding it together in its wild ride.

"Damn you, Thalasi!" Istaahl growled, for he, too, understood that the Black Warlock had broken all bounds of sensibility, had grabbed at the powers of the universe and pulled them to his evil will with such blatant ferocity that it all could unravel at his feet. All the world would feel the destruction.

But if the Black Warlock had any concern for such possibilities, he did not show it. The winds around the White

Tower slammed into the stone and swirled about it, and bolts of lightning scorched its sides and split the ground around its base.

And Istaahl, though he feared the consequences, could only respond by pushing his own magic further, by tugging back on the universal powers with an intensity that rivaled Thalasi's.

"I am the god!" Thalasi roared, his voice shaking the ground for miles around. "And all the world is mine! Behold Morgan Thalasi and know you are doomed!"

The power continued its twisted flow through the Staff of Death and through Thalasi's limbs, conductors that bent the natural strength of the world to suit the Black Warlock's foul purposes. Thalasi was drunk with it, fully enraptured in the ecstasy of unbelievable might. He had outdone his own expectation, had grabbed at the core of the world and pulled it to his hands. His black globe cracked and crumbled the ground below it into pockets of broken, barren rubble. And then Thalasi moved on to another spot, for the Staff of Death demanded more.

"I am the god!" Thalasi yelled again. One group of talons rushed by, spurred by the proclamations of their unholy leader.

Too close.

The black sphere of Thalasi sucked them into its vortex, and the unfortunate creatures came out as mere pulses in the black bolts the warlock aimed at the sky.

"What is it?" Bryan demanded. He shook Rhiannon violently, but the young witch showed no signs of consciousness. Her thoughts were fully turned inward as the evil spectacle of Thalasi continued its roar in her ears.

Still the magic grew in the young witch despite her efforts, born of sheer instinctual terror, to drive it out.

Bryan understood his companion's dilemma. He had seen her hesitation at calling forth the most destructive uses of her power, and he understood that the power now demanded more of her than ever before, more even than Rhiannon had used when she and he had routed the talon caravan back in the mountains two days before.

And that effort had nearly destroyed the young witch.

"Let it in!" Bryan implored Rhiannon. "Accept the power for the sake of all the world!"

Rhiannon did not blink, every instinct within her fighting against the awful possession, the complete surrender to a strength that might never let her go.

The lines on the bridges rolled back and forth, with each side gaining ground only to be hammered back to where they had started. A dozen men and a score of talons died each minute, and their blood mixed with the rainwater, washing from the sides and staining the great river itself in a garish crimson hue.

Arien still held his elven forces back. They had been assigned as the reserves of the army and would no doubt see more action than they cared to before all was finished. And with all that had gone on in the talon camp the past few days, the Eldar feared something else, a different line of attack. Surely this new general of Thalasi's army was skilled enough to know that he would not so easily breach the defenses of the bridges.

When Arien's daughter called out a short while later, the Eldar knew he had been wise to keep to the side.

"Boats on the river!" Sylvia yelled. A hundred craft, riding low under the weight of talon flesh, moved out from the western bank.

Arien put his archers to action and called for all the reserves that Benador could spare. The trip across the wide River Ne'er Ending would not be an easy one for Thalasi's wicked minions.

But a moment later the Eldar found his attention turned back to the bridges, or more particularly, to the northernmost bridge. The ranks of Calvan defenders split apart suddenly, the brave men fleeing in horror.

The wraith and his legions of undead had made their appearance.

Only the Rangers of Avalon, spurred by the unflinching courage of Belexus Backavar, came onto the bridge to fill the breach.

Mitchell stayed back and let his zombie minions pass him by. They fell by the dozen to the flashing blades of the rangers, but they outnumbered the brave warriors of Avalon by more than five to one, and gradually the press of rotting flesh made its inevitable way toward the eastern exit of the bridge.

Belexus held out in their midst, whacking away arms and heads with each mighty stroke, and soon he no longer even flinched when he beheaded a creature only to see it reach back toward him with its filthy, bone-clawed hands.

And then many zombies focused on the single rider, and they lashed at Belexus' horse, driving the thing down under their sheer weight.

Arien had to leave much of his force behind with Sylvia to contend with the closing line of boats, but the elves, with their deeper understanding of mortality and of experience beyond this life, did not fear the animated corpses as did the humans, and their charge caught the zombie horde at the eastern base of the northernmost bridge.

Arien spurred his stallion right through the zombie ranks, trampling the things to the stone in the singular path of his ride. He had seen Belexus fall and would not accept the death of the gallant ranger.

But Belexus was not finished. He found himself kneeling and then struggled against the press to his feet, brought his huge sword in a killing sweep that cut three of the monsters fully in half. Blood from a score of clawed wounds ran down the ranger's arms and chest, but he lashed out with sword and fist, smashing the zombies away.

Still, their sheer numbers would have buried him where he stood. But then, for some reason he could not understand, the zombies moved away from him, walked past without showing any concern for him at all.

Arien, finally halted in his attempt to get to the ranger, was glad when he saw the sea of corpses flow away from a still standing Belexus, but the Eldar's relief turned to dread when he, like the ranger, at last came to understand the meaning of the zombies' sudden disinterest.

For near the center of the arching bridge now stood only two figures, Belexus of Avalon and Hollis Mitchell, the wraith whose mere thoughts guided the zombie army.

"I could not let them kill you," Mitchell explained in his grating voice. "That task is for my pleasure alone!"

"Yer boasts are mere words," Belexus retorted, steadying himself and taking full measure of this newest adversary. Brielle had warned him about facing the wraith again, but the ranger could not control the rage within himself, which demanded he avenge the death of his dearest friend and banish this perverted creature and its horrid minions from the world of the living.

"Come and see for yourself, fool." Mitchell laughed at him, teasing him with an easy swing of the skull-headed scepter.

Belexus could not know the dark evil that was in that

weapon. He clutched his great sword in both hands and worked his way in.

The zombie army continued its push along the eastern range of the bridges, disrupting the defensive lines wherever they went. And on the great river, the line of boats steadily approached, heedless of the shower of arrows. Whatever his desires at that moment, Arien Silverleaf had an army to command, and he could not go to the ranger's side.

From the distant mountainside, Bryan surveyed the dismal scene. Only on the southern bridges, where King Benador and the Warders of the White Walls stood against mere talons, was the defense holding strong. On the northernmost bridge, and riding on a huge fleet on the river north of that, Thalasi's army was clearly winning through. And if they continued to pour across, all the efforts of King Benador and his men would surely be to no avail.

If Bryan's hopes were weakened when he took note of the course of the battle, they were blasted away altogether whenever he glanced at the unholy sphere of Morgan Thalasi. The evil warlock's fury did not relent; the black bolts of energy ripped up into the sky with continued power.

Clearly, some new variable had to enter the battle and claim it back for the forces of good. Bryan turned to Rhiannon, trembling and appearing so frail in her rain-soaked gown.

How could he lend her strength?

The flow of the power drenched the Black Warlock in ecstasy. "Still more!" he demanded, stamping the heel of the Staff of Death on a new patch of ground. A renewed surge exploded upward, nearly blasting the mortal body of the Black Warlock apart. But Thalasi contained it, and bent it, throwing it out to Avalon and Pallendara.

It came in the fury of a single bolt over the enchanted

forest. Brielle's weakened shield of defensive magics stood to block it, and the resulting blast dissipated the bolt to a mountain of sparks.

But gone, too, was the shield, and the next lightning bolt that descended on the witch's domain sundered a tree.

In seconds Avalon was burning.

It came in the fury of a wall of wind beside the White Tower of Istaahl, bending the structure far to the side. The civilian onlookers in Pallendara gasped in horror as Istaahl's gigantic conjured arms clutched at the tower like an imperiled mother holding her infant.

But the stones split apart around the enchanted limbs.

The White Tower crumbled to the ground.

Chapter 27

The Fabric Torn

"BY THE COLONNAE!" Brielle gasped as the flames ate at her forest. Thalasi's storm continued to flash and rumble, but that singular, massive bolt had taken the bite out of its thunderous bark as surely as it had shattered Brielle's shield.

Brielle reached down inside herself, called to the earth power that fueled her magic. Hers was the first school of magic, the guardian school wherein the energies used her as their guiding hand to fight back against that which went against the natural order of the universe.

"Ye've pulled it too far," the witch moaned when she at last contacted the fabric of her strength. Harmony was the norm for the universal powers, energy all working in accord toward the perfection of natural order. But Morgan Thalasi had grasped at that harmony with his perverted claws, had pulled the heartstrings of the powers beyond their limits.

Brielle had no time to stop and contemplate the grim consequences of the Black Warlock's actions. The battle was far from over, though neither would find the energy needed to continue to wage their destructive war across the leagues. Now the contest became more personal, a test of wills removed from the material world.

Brielle did not flinch when the specter of the Black Warlock entered the gray field surrounding her thoughts. She conjured a spectral manifestation of herself and strode calmly toward the evil one.

"All the world is mine," Thalasi cackled at her. "Witness how the magic bends to my control."

"Ye're a fool," Brielle hissed back. "What magic do ye leave in yer wake? 'Twas the Colonnae that blessed us with the powers of all the universe, but ye've ruined that blessing, Morgan Thalasi. Ye've torn the heart out o' our power to the ruin of us all."

"No!" Thalasi shouted back in angry denial. "I've stolen the harmony that gives you strength, wicked witch! And Istaahl in Pallendara is no more, buried in the ruins of his own tower. Who will stand against me when Brielle is gone? Your pitiful brother? The buffoon who plays with elves?"

Brielle offered no response. She had lived for centuries as the principal guardian of the natural world, and now that world was under siege more than it had been since the great holocaust that destroyed the original race of man. The Emerald Witch knew her duty.

"All yer grand words," she laughed at Thalasi. "First ye must beat me!" Her mental specter walked into battle, but as she reached the manifestation of the Black Warlock, the being split into two separate entities: Morgan Thalasi as he had been before the Battle of Mountaingate, and Martin Reinheiser. They moved out to flank the surprised witch, taunting her with laughter.

"Grand?" they asked together. "Minor claims against the truth of our being."

Then they rushed in on her. Brielle flailed at them valiantly, but within mere seconds icy hands grasped at her throat.

* * *

Istaahl climbed through the last layer of rubble, a garish sight of torn and tattered clothing and bruised and bleeding flesh. A thousand curious onlookers in Pallendara shook their heads almost as one, stunned again by the powers of their wizard. For no mortal man could possibly have survived the fall of the tower.

Istaahl started to walk the perimeter of the devastation, ignoring the curious and terrified gazes surrounding him and following his every move.

"You fool!" the White Mage scolded himself, suddenly guessing the logical continuation of the Black Warlock's magical campaign. How long had he tarried, wallowing in his own grief? Seconds? But even seconds could be too long in such a contest. Without further delay, Istaahl launched himself into the gray nothingness of the magical plane of existence, threw himself fully and bravely into the fight against the twin beings that were the Black Warlock.

"I have you—" Thalasi and Reinheiser started to proclaim in dual-voiced unison. But then the manifestation of the White Mage leaped onto the back of the spirit of Reinheiser, tearing his hands from the throat of Brielle.

The odds had suddenly changed.

"Did ye think one o' the Four so easily killed?" Brielle said to Thalasi. "But one of us has died indeed, Morgan Thalasi. Yerself. Centuries ago when ye forgot our purpose, when ye took it upon yerself to challenge all the goodness o' the Colonnae."

"Weakling," Thalasi retorted. "All the powers of the world at your fingertips and you play nursemaid to a copse of trees. Gods we could be! The world is ours to rule."

"Not ours!" Brielle retorted. "Never ours! Ye ignore yer place, and yer greed is suren to be the ruin o' all the world!"

To the side, the spirits of Reinheiser and Istaahl rolled

about in the fog in combat as vicious and desperate as any
that had been fought on the Four Bridges. And now Thalasi
sprang upon Brielle like a beast, his claws reaching out for
her fair neck. But Brielle's appearance, so innocent and beautiful, belied the strength of the woman. She accepted the
Black Warlock's attack and responded with her own, vicious
and mighty.

Venerable Bellerian had been assigned to the rear of the
army, directing wayward troops and relaying vital information to the battle commanders from his distant, more encompassing vantage point. But when the Ranger Lord saw
his son on the northernmost bridge, facing that horrid wraith,
he could not remain at his post. He was in his eighties now,
not old for a man raised under the beauty of Avalon, who, by
the words of Brielle, could expect to live a century and a
score of years beyond that. But Bellerian's fighting days had
ended abruptly many years before. He had been bent over
nearly double—he could hardly walk without the assistance
of a cane—by a wound he received in the foul swamp of
Blackamara, a wound so wicked that even the powers of Brielle could not fully heal it.

The Ranger Lord felt no pain now as he charged his mount
down to the bridges, leaping from the saddle when he got
there and rushing as fast as his crooked back would allow to
go to the side of his son.

"Ye should no' have come, me father," Belexus said to
him, truly concerned.

"Ye think I'd let ye fight the likes o' this one alone?" Bellerian replied, a smile on his lips.

"Yes," the wraith agreed. "Yes, old man, do join in our
play."

"Play, the thing calls it," Bellerian scoffed. "We'll see
the name the thing gives to it when we put it back where it

belongs!" And then the Ranger Lord struck out wickedly and cunningly, a swooping slash of his sword that forced Mitchell to stumble off balance. And by the time the wraith managed to straighten himself enough to return the blow, Bellerian was far out of reach.

Even Belexus looked upon his father with sincere surprise.

"Ye're not believin' that I had it left in me old bones," Bellerian chuckled at his stunned son. "I should've whipped ye in battle more often to keep yer thoughts in their proper place."

Belexus just shook his head and moved out a pace to the side, suddenly very glad to have Bellerian fighting beside him.

At Ardaz's bidding, Calamus soared over the eastern edge of the battlefield. In the west and visible from the wizard's high vantage point, the physical being of the Black Warlock remained firmly in place behind his charges, within his pool of perverted darkness and with those awful black bolts of energy still drawing on the fabric of the world, still shooting into the sky to fuel the unnatural gloom.

Ardaz understood the peril his sister and Istaahl faced at that moment, and he searched for a sanctuary where he could put down on the ground and join in the magical war against Thalasi.

But as the Pegasus neared the Four Bridges, another darkness beckoned to Ardaz, a call so doom-filled that the wizard could not ignore it.

"Yes, Ardaz," the wraith of Mitchell hissed. "Do come and join the fun!"

Belexus and Bellerian did not have to look over their shoulders to confirm that the Silver Mage had come. Shouts of hope echoed throughout the battlefield behind them.

The wraith, too, seemed preoccupied with the approach of the wizard, and both of the rangers were wise enough to grasp the opportunity. With a sudden ferocity that Mitchell had not anticipated, Belexus dove in at him, the ranger's huge sword cutting deep into his belly and striking at his very heart.

Black energy shot through the blade, a fire on Belexus' hands. The mighty ranger ignored the searing pain and held firm to his grasp, confident that he had struck a mortal blow. He closed his eyes and tightened his grip.

But then, unbelievably, the sword came loose from the wraith. Belexus looked down, mouth agape.

The blade had melted away.

From the distant sky, Ardaz watched in horror as the skull-headed mace chopped down at the ranger. Belexus' head would have certainly been crushed if not for the re-action of his father. Bellerian had started in for his own strike on Mitchell, but seeing the sudden disaster befalling Belexus, he reversed his sword for a defensive parry. Mitchell's weapon came down heavily, shattering Bellerian's sword to its hilt and numbing the Ranger Lord's arms with awful coldness.

But the sword deflected the strike enough so that Belexus only received a glancing blow. Still, the sheer power of the evil instrument jolted the ranger and sent him flying back down the length of the bridge, where he crumpled into darkness.

Blind rage contorted Bellerian's fair features. "Ye bastard!" he spat at Mitchell, and he threw his sword hilt viciously into Mitchell's face, smashing the wraith's contented grin.

* * *

Now Ardaz found himself truly torn. He felt that he must go into the magical plane to the aid of his peers, but he knew, too, that this critical battle on the bridges could not be won without his aid. Even if he and the other magic-users managed to defeat Thalasi, this horrid wraith would surely lead the dark forces to victory.

Ardaz, too, had his predetermined duty. He was a master of the second school of magic, a discipline that drew its energy from the universal powers to aid in the causes of the goodly races. The Silver Mage could not ignore that calling now. His sister and Istaahl would have to hold out; Ardaz could not forsake the needs of the Calvans and elves.

He brought Calamus down in a furious dive, landing in a wild gallop that took him right up to Bellerian, who was now steadily backing away from the wraith. The wizard jumped off, and Billy Shank swung the Pegasus around toward the still unmoving form of the younger ranger.

The wraith lost all interest in Bellerian at the sight of the wizard. "Come and play," Mitchell hissed at Ardaz, again waving that horrible scepter of darkness. Ardaz replied by summoning a ball of sunlike light atop his oaken staff.

"Go to your son," the wizard said to the Ranger Lord.

"Nay, I'll not leave ye in yer need," Bellerian replied, ever vigilant in spite of his feelings.

"You can do nothing here," Ardaz assured him. "This is a creature beyond our world and beyond your power. Go to your son, Bellerian, I beg you. You will only steal some of my concentration in this battle if you remain out here exposed."

Bellerian put a hand on the wizard's shoulder.

"Fight well, me friend," he whispered, and then rushed back to join Billy, working to comfort Belexus.

"This is our fight, wizard," the wraith agreed. "But when

I am through with you, your pitiful friends will have their turn."

Ardaz never even blinked in response. He held his staff out proudly and resolutely and strode in for the fight.

And they met on the middle of the bridge, darkness and light.

Bryan wept openly as he viewed the inner struggle of the young witch, repeating his plea to her, "Please!" over and over with all the voice he could muster.

Rhiannon, too consumed by the drama playing out within her soul, did not even hear him. Ecstasy and anguish flooded through her all at once, joyous tingles of magical energy that both thrilled and frightened her beyond anything she had ever known. She could not have imagined such pleasure and power being contained within her mortal form. Yet there was a darker side to it all, a possession that threatened Rhiannon's very identity.

Bryan hugged her close, fighting against her trembling horror.

Rhiannon, though, felt no comfort at the half-elf's touch, for she was no longer part of her physical being, was falling into a pit of darkness that had no bottom.

For the first time in his life, King Benador saw action in battle, and any of those close enough to witness the valor and strength of the man would hold no argument against his claim as their king. He had grown up among the Rangers of Avalon, had been trained in the ways of battle by Belexus himself, and it didn't take the talons long to realize that he was one to be avoided. With the Warders of the White Walls at his side, Benador swept back and forth across the two southern bridges, driving back the greater numbers of talons and securing the southern defense lines guarding Rivertown and the tents of healing.

Still, with the appearance of the wraith and Thalasi's undead brigades, the other two bridges had been fully breached. Thousands of talons poured across the bridge second from the north; none would cross the northernmost, where the wraith and the Silver Mage now faced off. Most of the Calvan defenders had been swept away in the dark tide, pushed back to the east beyond the protection of Benador and his elite corps.

Before long only Arien and his elven warriors stood to stem the flow. Their main concern had to be the undead brigade, and the zombies went down by the score to the slashing blades of the skilled elves. But so swift had been the zombies' initial rout that Arien could not hope to contain those talons who had already crossed. Instead the elf Eldar and his troops cut the talon forces in half, slicing back through the throng to the breached bridge and then trampling their way onto the structure. They were fully surrounded, fighting back to back, but they had quelled the terror of the undead monsters and halted the tide of talons.

"Our fate is in the hands of the Calvans," Arien remarked to Ryell, fighting by his side. "We have given them the opportunity to regroup and come back to the bridge, but if their charge is not swift enough, we will surely perish this day."

"If the fates decree it," Ryell said in stubborn determination. Arien looked at his friend with sincere admiration. Once Illuma's most notorious human-hater, Ryell had indeed amended his ways.

Surveying the situation, King Benador knew despair. He and his troops could hold the two bridges, and the Calvan forces who had been pushed back had already begun their answering charge back toward the second bridge. But too many talons had crossed for the Calvans to fully contain them. Even as the King ordered a contingent away to the south and east, he saw several bands of talons converging on the tents of the wounded.

"We wanted our fight," Jolsen remarked to Siana and Lennard. "Looks like we got it!" Almost on cue, a talon rushed through the flap at the burly lad. In his surprise, Jolsen never would have been able to block the attack, but Siana was not caught off her guard. A flip of her wrist put a dagger into the neck of the charging beast, and as it lurched over in pain, Lennard chopped it down.

"Teamwork!" Lennard cried.

But then a dozen more talons tore through the tent from every side, and the teamwork of the three, however complementary, however magnificent, hardly seemed adequate. Still, the young warriors could not complain, satisfied that they had more than avenged their dead kinfolk, had done more than their share in the efforts of this terrible but undeniably necessary war.

Most of their parents and kin had died in the fall of Corning and the subsequent retreat toward the river, they had learned, and they took faith now as the talons closed over them that those who had gone before them would be waiting to greet them on this, their last journey.

Farther to the north, beyond the bridges, the numbers seemed equally disturbing. Sylvia, the daughter of Arien Silverleaf, led a contingent of a hundred elven archers and twice that number of Calvan bowmen against the flotilla Mitchell's charges had constructed. The men and elves peppered the talon armada as it made its slow but purposeful trudge across the river.

As each boat landed, it was met by a charging force of whirling swords and spears, but each contingent of man and elf forced down to the banks to fight in the hand-to-hand melee weakened the rain of arrows on the approaching boats. And more and more boats were on their way, some just being launched off the opposite bank, a continuing, seemingly endless line.

Sylvia was battle-seasoned enough to realize that though she and her forces could hold out for many minutes, they could not hope to win unless help came down from the army at the bridges—an army, the elven maiden lamented when she looked that way, that was even more pressed than her own forces.

But Sylvia and the hundred elves had faced greater odds than this; to a soldier, they had fought in the Battle of Mountaingate, and their undying optimism lent strength to the fearful Calvans.

"The talons may win through at this position," Arien's daughter noted grimly. "But their victory will come at heavy cost." To accentuate her point, she let another arrow fly at an approaching boat. It whistled out over the water, true in its mark, and caught the craft's commander right between the eyes.

"Watch, wizard!" the wraith taunted. "Watch as all of the world is destroyed."

"Brave words, nonbeing," Ardaz shot back. He thrust his staff out, and rays of light slammed into Mitchell's dark form, burning holes where they struck.

Mitchell returned the effort, snapping his scepter above his head, showering Ardaz in black flakes.

Ardaz quickly pulled his light back to him, sensing the unearthly danger. He danced frantically, burning away as many of the flakes as he could with his staff. But many found their mark, and Mitchell struck again.

Ardaz stamped his staff to the ground, launching a blinding blue bolt that hurled the wraith to the ground.

But it was the wizard who was most dismayed, for when Ardaz had called upon that greater level of magical energy, he began to understand the depth of the breach that the Black Warlock had caused in the harmony.

"Thus ends an age," the wizard lamented. He hated the thought of taxing that magical plane any further.

But Mitchell was already on his way back in, that wicked scepter raised high.

No more tender words escaped Bryan's lips. Rhiannon fell limp in his arms, but he would not let her recline on the ground. "Stand against it!" he commanded, and he slapped the young witch across the face with enough force to raise a welt on her porcelain cheek.

Rhiannon tried to reach out and find a way to slow her descent, but the pit's walls were too far away. She called out to her mother, ever her source of strength and protection.

Then she realized the true depth of the horror.

Her call brought her mind into the magical plane, where she saw the mental battle in all its fury. Brielle and Istaahl fought bravely and savagely, but so, too, did the twin specters of the Black Warlock. And while Rhiannon's mother and the White Mage seemed weary, Thalasi and Reinheiser were only growing stronger, the Black Warlock feeding off the chaos he had created.

Rhiannon's stay was short-lived, for soon she found herself back in the hopeless pit, falling away. A single word escaped her lips, a word that may have saved all of Aielle.

"Bryan."

Spurred by her call, the half-elf doubled his efforts.

He pulled Rhiannon up straight, forced her to find her footing. "Beat it!" he yelled. "Do not surrender!" He had no idea of the true nature of the young witch's dilemma, but he understood well enough that the only thing he could do was help her to hold her bearing.

"Rhiannon!"

The call came from a great distance, but Rhiannon heard it clearly. She focused on the sound, sent her thoughts spiraling back toward it.

"Rhiannon!"

Nearer now, but still beyond her grasp. The witch forgot the pain, dismissed the despair. All that mattered was that she find the source of that call.

"Rhiannon!"

The jolt as the young witch regained consciousness sent Bryan flying through the air. He landed heavily on his back. His first reaction was to return to Rhiannon, but then he recognized that she did not need him anymore.

A glow of power emanated from her form, which no longer seemed tiny and frail. Her light eyes glittered as pale sapphires in a bright sun, and her face twisted into a visage of powerful satisfaction.

Rhiannon felt all the power that the world had left to give rushing to her call, its purity burning sweet in her veins. She waited a moment, letting the forces gather until she thought she would burst apart. Then she swept her arms up into the air, releasing a mighty line of energy, radiant green, at that spot of the overcast that hid the sun. It roared into Thalasi's cloud, sizzling and crackling.

Darkness rushed from every edge of the sky to gather against the bolt, but Rhiannon did not relent. Her mouth opened in a silent scream of stubborn rage, and she snapped her hands up higher, throwing every ounce of her strength into the battle.

Thunder rolled out, the rain crossing the path of the green bolt sizzled and steamed away, and as the black clouds rolled in, they were consumed. All the sky lightened, though the overcast remained unbroken.

But Thalasi's efforts were elsewhere, locked in mortal combat against Brielle and Istaahl, and his gloom could not be reinforced. Rhiannon thought that this effort would surely kill her, but she did not worry about that now.

"So be it," she muttered, throwing another pulse heavenward. Relentlessly, the green bolt burned away. The young witch, seeing into the very center of her energy bolt, squinted her eyes at the greater brightness as she cut through to the blue above the cloud.

Now the green beam widened the gap in the clouds, and Rhiannon called upon the sun to help her cause. A single ray came through, not angled back toward Rhiannon but shining through to the north, burning into the globe of darkness that surrounded the Black Warlock.

Brielle and Istaahl felt the weakening of their respective foes immediately, but before they could press further in and hold the twin spirits down, the Black Warlock's manifestations blended together into one and vanished from the scene of the mental battle.

Brielle took a moment to contemplate the change in events, then announced to Istaahl, " 'Tis me daughter!"

"We must go to her!" the White Mage replied, but then another call came to them, a call they could not ignore.

"All the world!" Ardaz cried.

"Me daughter!" gasped Brielle.

Ardaz could see the battle in the west clearly. The Black Warlock had regained his footing and responded to the sun ray with a bolt of midnight blackness. He had pushed the ray halfway back to the clouds, and the vile line of his blackness was still rising.

But the events at the river were even more desperate. Too many talons had come across, Arien and his troops would soon falter, and the defense along the northern banks was about to disintegrate altogether to the endless armada.

Brielle understood. Her every instinct told her to go to her daughter's aid, but Rhiannon would simply have to hold on for a while longer.

"It will never be the same," Istaahl lamented.

"But no choice is to us, then," said Brielle. "Call to yer sea, me friend. Pull with all yer strength." Then the witch went to her own work. She fell back into the magical plane, reached out with wide arms to gather all the power she could find.

And then she grabbed at the river.

Istaahl sent his summons out over the waves, calling to the ocean from the ruins of the White Tower. From far out, but rising swiftly and rushing in toward the mouth of the great river, came a wall of water.

Brielle pulled against the flow, drove the water back with an invisible wall of energy. In seconds the great river under the Four Bridges was an empty bank of mud. The talons in their boats, now sitting on soft ground, thought this a gift of their godlike master to speed their crossing. Whooping and shouting, they leaped from their craft and plodded out through the thick mud.

"See our power!" Mitchell hissed at Ardaz. "We rule even the river itself!"

But Ardaz recognized the truth of the event. He sent a magically enhanced shout ringing into the ears of all his comrades. "Get back from the river!"

At the end of the bridge, Billy and Bellerian finally got Belexus to his feet. Though wounded by the burning chill of Mitchell's scepter, the ranger would not retreat. Billy pushed him, trying to get him back from the river as Ardaz had instructed. But Bellerian understood the fire that drove his son.

"Leave him to his duty," the Ranger Lord instructed.

"Are ye coming with me?" Belexus asked. He knew the answer when he took a moment to consider his father, bent again under the pain of that old wound.

"No, me son," Bellerian said with a smile. "Me fightin's at its end."

Belexus kissed him on the forehead, then helped his father onto the winged horse's back as Billy turned Calamus toward the safety of the land.

Then Belexus strode out on the bridge to stand beside the brave wizard.

Benador and his troops needed no encouragement to heed the wizard's call. They pushed the talons on the southern two bridges back to the west one final time, then broke back toward the fields, where they could have run to safety. But the King and his elite corps would not let the valiant elves die for their cause, not while they had any strength left in their bodies. Benador spearheaded a small group, driving like a wedge through the talon ranks to get to Arien and his forces.

"Fly away!" Arien called to his warriors, while he and Ryell fought as a rear guard.

Up in the north, Sylvia and her forces wanted to heed Ardaz's call, but many talons had reached the eastern bank in the first moments after the river had emptied. The elven maiden rushed from group to group, freeing up men and elves and sending them on their retreat, but she remained on the muddy bank, refusing to leave until all the others had found safer ground.

"The weakling ranger returns," the wraith laughed. "I am glad that you live, Belexus. I would not want you to miss this spectacle of my master's glory."

Belexus cast a knowing smile at Ardaz. Only one being in all Aielle could make such a demand of the River Ne'er Ending: the Emerald Witch.

"Ye've ever been a fool, Mitchell," he spat at the wraith. "Ye think this yer master's doin'?"

"Who—" Mitchell began to respond, but the smug look on the ranger's face caused the wraith to glance back over his shoulder; then he saw the continuing struggle between the Black Warlock and the sun ray. The wraith spun back on Ardaz and the ranger, unbridled rage etched on its grotesque face.

"You'll not escape the doom!" Ardaz promised, and he slammed his staff on the stone with enough force to break the instrument, and that in turn exuded enough force to split apart the bridge itself.

The center of the structure crumbled down into the mud, and the wraith, Ardaz, and Belexus fell away.

Brielle and Istaahl could not know the particulars at the battle scene, nor reverse the tide of their actions in any case. When she sensed the approach of Istaahl's watery wall, the Emerald Witch let loose the gathered waters of the great river.

"No!" the Black Warlock screamed, turning back to the disastrous battle on the bridges for just an instant.

And Thalasi's despair only heightened in that moment, for Rhiannon and her sun ray did not let the moment pass.

A burst of light burned away the Black Warlock's sphere of darkness completely and slammed Thalasi to the ground.

And in a flash all of the Black Warlock's overcast was consumed, and the sky shone bright and blue once more.

Still Rhiannon continued her assault, determined, as was the magic that flowed through her, to rid Aielle of the Black Warlock once and for all.

The stupid talons rushing across the bridges and standing in the mud of the empty riverbank could only gape at the converging doom, and when the magics of Brielle and Istaahl came together, nearly half of the evil force was simply washed away. Another group remained trapped on the eastern side, helpless in the face of the wrath of the warrior King and his minions, who were already regrouping for another assault.

But oh so many heroes, human and elf alike, went away in that watery grave.

Indeed, the world would never be the same.

Chapter 28

Wizard's Lament

THE SKY SHONE a bright, crisp blue with sunshine general all across Aielle. But a more brilliant beam of the sun still held its course to the Black Warlock, pinning him to the ground mercilessly. Thalasi thought he would surely perish under its relentless heat; he could feel his insides bubbling and churning and could find no magical strength left within himself to battle back.

But up on the slopes of the Baerendels, a subtle shift in the flow of power was all the warning Rhiannon got. She felt vibrations within her form, discordant twanging that wracked her with electric shocks of pain.

Then it all broke apart.

With a vicious shudder that popped the muscles in her elbows and shoulders, Rhiannon swooned and fell.

Bryan, ever alert, was there to catch her.

Freed of the magical assault, the Black Warlock slithered to the west. His day was ended; all the talons on this side of the river were in full flight, and those across the way would soon be exterminated by the Calvan forces. There would be no more crossing of the river anytime soon; all four of the bridges had been washed away.

And now Thalasi had only one thought: get back to Talasdun, where he might lick his wounds. Little optimism remained in the Black Warlock, for even if he could manage the journey to his bastion of power, he understood that Brielle had been right in her scolding: he, and the other wizards in response, had ripped at the very heart of the magic energies that gave them their powers. And that heart, Thalasi now for the first time feared, would never mend.

Brielle leaned heavily against an ancient oak, her legs too weary to support her. "Ye stupid bastard, Morgan Thalasi," she panted, hardly able to speak the words. Weary as she was, the Emerald Witch understood that she had to regain her strength and her resolve very soon, for though Thalasi's storm clouds and her own enchantments had been blasted apart, the fires that now ravaged several sections of Avalon remained in full force.

Brielle would save a portion of the wood, and the rest would grow back in time. But the Emerald Witch's enchanted reign over Avalon had reached its pinnacle. Brielle was determined that she would stubbornly hold on to a portion of what had once been; she would keep a shining light burning in the heart of the forest for many centuries to come. But the rest of vast Avalon would survive only as an ordinary forest. What the witch already knew, and what the rest of the world would soon find out, was that Avalon had put its best days behind it.

Both it and the Emerald Witch were on the wane.

Even more disastrous was the scene in Pallendara, for Istaahl, just recently recovered from three decades as a prisoner of the Black Warlock, had fared badly in the conflict.

His tower was gone, and he knew he would never find the strength to rebuild it. Stone masons would flock to his aid, no doubt, but then the tower of Istaahl the White, like the greater part of the new Avalon that would eventually return, would be a normal work, not an enchanted one.

Istaahl showed no emotion to the many healers who tended his serious—mortal for a mortal man—wounds.

He sat silent and unblinking, his thoughts a lament for days gone by and a concern for the days ahead. For while the diminishing of the magics would also lessen the threat of the Black Warlock, the goodly people of Ynis Aielle, the men and elves, would have to stand on their own for the first time.

And with the tragedy of the battle across the bridges and the destruction of the western fields, they would begin their singular reign on a dark note indeed.

Benador and his troops soon had the bulk of the talons on the eastern side of the river fully contained. Smaller bands of the wretched things ran loose, fleeing every which way, and would have to be hunted down, but the determined King remained confident that the battle now neared its end. He focused his thoughts on the future of his kingdom, on the rebuilding that would have to be done, beginning with the construction of a new bridge across the great river.

He watched now as the swollen river subsided to its normal flow, wondering how many of his own warriors had been washed away in the deluge. Of the Four Bridges, only the eastern and western third of the northernmost remained, but they seemed so cracked that the whole of the structure would probably have to be scrapped.

Arien Silverleaf charged his mount up and down the northern edges of the battlefield, frantic in his search. Ryell, his dearest friend, rode beside him, but had already accepted the grim news as true. Sylvia, Arien's valiant daughter, had perished in the flood.

"Her death was not in vain," the human archer had told them. "Many are alive because of her valor in getting us from the edges of the river."

At the time, the archer's words had rung hollow in the ears of the elven Eldar, but in years to come, Arien would use them often as a litany against his unending grief.

He would have spent the entire day riding back and forth and all about the nearby encampments in search of his daughter, but a sight he could not ignore, no matter how deep his own grief, assailed him when he ventured near the broken bridges.

There, on the very lip of the blasted eastern spur of the northernmost bridge, hung two figures: the top with one hand locked on a jutting piece of stone, the other hand grasping the limply hanging form of his companion.

Arien and Ryell charged back up the bank and swung around toward the bridge. "Survivors on the bridge!" Ryell cried to the two men nearest the structure. Bellerian and Billy Shank.

Billy, supporting the Ranger Lord in his grief, was nearly knocked to the ground when Bellerian heard the call. They both had watched in horror only a moment before as the Silver Mage destroyed the bridge, and then as the floodwaters had surged through, apparently taking Belexus and the wizard with them.

And now Billy Shank had all he could do to hold the Ranger Lord back from the structure.

"It might not be safe!" Billy cried.

"Me son!" was all Bellerian replied.

"If you rush out there, you might cave in the whole

structure," Billy scolded. "Then there would remain no survivors!"

Bellerian calmed as he realized the truth of Billy's words.

King Benador noticed the commotion and charged to the base of the structure just as Arien and Ryell arrived. The two elves leaped from their saddles and tentatively started out onto the first stones of the spur, Billy and Bellerian right beside them.

"Beware the bridge!" the King warned.

Arien held out his arms to stop his companions. "I go alone," he insisted. "We know not how much weight the structure can support."

"Then I go," argued Ryell. "You are the Eldar of our people. Better that I should perish if the bridge falls away."

Arien turned a cold stare on Ryell. "I go," he said with bitter finality. "I have lost my daughter this day. I will not risk my closest friend as well." He turned and took a long stride out onto the bridge, and Ryell moved to stop him.

But Benador, understanding the grief on Arien's face, agreed that the Eldar must do this, and he grabbed Ryell's shoulder and held him back.

Arien got out to the end and dropped to his knees. Belexus—he had known all along that it could only be Belexus—hung below him, apparently unconscious. But even in that blackness the mighty ranger had not faltered. His left hand clutched the stone of the bridge with strength enough to defeat the pull of the flood. That feat alone would be the stuff of legends, but even more amazing, the ranger's right hand held with equal strength the thick folds of Ardaz's blue robes.

"It is your son, Ranger Lord!" Arien called back. "And the Silver Mage." With the confirmation, it now took Billy, Benador, and Ryell to hold Bellerian back.

Arien quickly pulled a length of rope from his pack and

crept down the facing of the broken bridge to a point where he could loop an end around the wizard. Ardaz opened one eye to watch and shot a hopeful smile at his rescuer. But the wizard did not dare move, aware that his robes had started to tear away in several places.

Arien winked his reassurance, then climbed back to the top, keeping one hand tightly on Belexus in case the ranger's grip should fail.

Bellerian, though sorely wounded and weary, scrambled out through the grasps of Billy and Ryell when he saw Arien come back up, dragging the rope.

"As I am your king," Benador said to Billy and Ryell, "I command you to remain here!" And then Benador, despite the horrified shrieks of his entourage, sprinted out onto the bridge.

"You should not be out here," Arien scolded Bellerian. As if to accentuate the Eldar's words, the spur creaked ominously under the added weight.

"He is my son," the Ranger Lord replied sternly.

Benador moved right past them both before they even realized he had come out. He dropped to his belly and immediately understood the problem at hand. "Get the wizard," he instructed Arien and Bellerian, then grabbed Belexus by the front of the ranger's tunic.

The other two had no choice by to comply, and when Benador was certain they had Ardaz safely in tow, he tugged with all of his considerable strength and raised Belexus to safety.

Arien nodded his approval. "Let us retire from this broken place," he advised, and he hoisted Ardaz over his shoulder. Benador did likewise with Belexus, and Bellerian led them off the bridge, to the cheers of the now fair-sized crowd that had gathered to watch it all.

The drama was only heightened a few moments later, when

the entire section of the bridge fell into the river with a thunderous splash.

"As though it waited for us," Benador said wistfully. "As though the bridge did not want us all to die this day."

"Doubt it," babbled Ardaz, spouting water with every word. "That was the northernmost bridge. Thalasi's bridge."

"Then thank our fortunes," laughed Ryell.

But Arien, staring out over the meandering flow of the great river, did not partake of the mirth. He found few fortunes to thank this day.

Rhiannon walked along in the dim fog, descending a twisting trail that led into a deeper blackness. The young witch was not alone, though—hundreds, perhaps thousands, now made the steady pilgrimage. Rhiannon continued on for many steps, but then stopped abruptly, feeling a certain kindred to another figure moving farther up the line.

"Siana!" she cried, though no sound emanated from her lips. The young girl, moving slowly and staring blankly ahead, did not even seem to see Rhiannon. Nor did Siana take any notice of Lennard and Jolsen Smithyson, walking in the line beside her.

Rhiannon was about to say something more, but an overpowering urge turned her back into the line and held her silent. She understood, then, the spectacle around her. These were the dead, walking to the nether realm, and though death somehow had a lesser hold upon her than the others, she could not but continue her descent.

There was nothing to grab on to, nothing to guide her out from the foggy land.

But once again a singular voice cut through the din of confusion and called to her.

* * *

"Rhiannon," Bryan whispered over and over into the pale woman's ear. He could not let her die. He would give his own life if it would only bring Rhiannon back. He didn't look at her now, so fragile. He just cradled her head close and kept calling to her, begging her not to die.

The voice rang like a clarion to the lost witch. She rushed toward it, focused all of her thoughts on it. And when she opened her blue eyes once more, the first sight that greeted her was the shining sun; the second was the smile of Bryan of Corning, brighter still.

Bryan knew at once that she would recover. She had no wounds, at least none that he could see, and the deathly pall that had fallen over her fair skin had already dissipated, gone away like the gloomy overcast of Morgan Thalasi.

"You could not die," he said to her. "Not now, not after what you did."

But the answering smile on Rhiannon's face was short-lived. "Yer friends," she said, and her grim tone sobered the half-elf's mirth. "Siana, Lennard, and Jolsen."

"Dead?" Bryan asked, not even questioning Rhiannon's source of information.

Rhiannon nodded. "I seen them meself, walking to the dark realm." Bryan looked away, and now it was Rhiannon's turn to provide comfort. She reached around his slender neck and pulled him close to her.

"Ye know they died bravely," she consoled him. She remembered the grim sight of the line of dead. "As have so many others. Ye know their death had meanin', for all the world is saved now."

"Then I must hope that my own death will be as valiant," Bryan replied softly, but the words, like those of the archer to Arien Silverleaf, rang hollow in his own ears; simple proclamations had no strength against the awful reality.

Together they looked back toward the northern fields, to

the mass of corpses and the destruction wreaked by the flood, the magics, and the trampling charges of thousands of soldiers.

Rhiannon considered Bryan's last words in the light of the scene before her. "Me hope's that ye'll not find the need," she said.

"A victory hard won," Benador remarked to Ardaz when they were alone later that day. The King had asked the wizard for some information regarding the fate of Istaahl, since the White Mage had made no effort to contact him in many hours.

"Harder won than you might imagine," the Silver Mage replied, his voice somber and controlled. "Indeed."

"Have you learned the fate of Istaahl?"

Arien Silverleaf entered the tent, saw the King in audience, and bowed and turned to leave.

"Pray remain, Eldar of Illuma," Benador bade him. "The wizard's news affects us all, unless I miss my guess."

"It does, oh it most certainly does," Ardaz agreed. "Arien's people more than your own, in the end."

"Illuma Vale, Lochsilinilume, remains as it was," Ardaz went on, seeing that he had their fullest attention. "But the age of wizards nears its end—might just be that it has ended already." He looked Benador straight in the eye.

"The White Tower is no more," he said, "though Istaahl has survived." Benador's sigh of relief was audible, and Ardaz offered him a hopeful wink. "We wizards are a tough lot, you know."

"We shall rebuild the tower as soon as I return to Pallendara," Benador decreed. "Sooner! I'll set men on the task at once. More glorious—"

"No," Ardaz interrupted, stopping him with the simple word. "You might rebuild a tower, but not the White Tower," the wizard explained. "It was created centuries ago by the magic of Istaahl. Masons, however skilled, will not replace what has been lost."

"Then Istaahl—" Benador started to reason.

Ardaz cut him short again. "No," the wizard repeated. "Istaahl will not find the strength for such a task. Nor can I or Brielle lend him the strength," he added quickly, guessing Benador's next inquiry before the King could voice it.

"But how do you know this?" Arien asked, concerned not only for the White Tower but for his own homeland, which was entirely the creation of magic.

"We draw upon the same sources of power," Ardaz tried to explain. "Our magics come not from within, but from a place removed, a store of energy that we can tap into and channel to our own needs and ways." The wizard's head drooped visibly as he muttered the possibilities aloud, lending even more despair to the two onlookers.

"But that place has also been a casualty, I do dare—"

His voice broke, and it took him a long moment to compose himself enough to continue. "We will find the resources for minor magics, and still we'll make our mark in the world. But the White Tower is gone, and Avalon has burned, though a part of it may remain."

"And Lochsilinilume?" Arien dared to ask.

"It has fared the best," Ardaz replied hopefully.

"But it, too, is on the wane," Arien reasoned. "For without the power of Ardaz, the enchantment will surely begin to falter."

"But faded, too, is the strength of the Black Warlock," Benador insisted, trying to inject some light into the darkness. "Even if the Black Warlock survived the attack on the field, never again will he pose so great a threat to Calva, and to all the world."

Ardaz nodded and looked away. "Witness the dawning of

the age of mortals," he said. "The time of the wizards has slipped away."

Arien and Benador looked at each other both hopefully and a bit afraid. They could complete the rout of the talons and eventually win back the western fields. And without the Black Warlock to regroup the talons and hold them in line, it seemed doubtful that the chaotic creatures would ever come back to war in such numbers. Certainly all the goodly peoples of the world would be more secure without the specter of Morgan Thalasi hanging over them.

But both the leaders thought then of wondrous Avalon, the forest of springtime; and of Lochsilinilume, the enchanted valley of the elves; and of the White Tower of Istaahl, the pinnacle of Pallendara's strength. And neither was sure at that moment that the cost had been worth the victory.

"Be strong," Ardaz pleaded to them, particularly to the Calvan king. "The world is yours now."

And so began in Ynis Aielle the Age of Man.

Epilogue

THE REMAINDER OF the scattered talon forces on the eastern side of the great river were found and destroyed within the course of the next two days. And as the planning for the construction of the new bridge began, the Eldar of Illuma and the Ranger Lord decided it was time for them to head home.

"You will be sorely missed," King Benador said to them one rainy morning. "I had feared this parting, yet I held out hope that you would continue to fight by my side when we crossed into the western fields."

"Would that we could, good King," replied Arien, the elf who had forgotten how to smile. "But my people have suffered greatly in this war. It is time, I think, that we go back to our valley and mourn our dead."

Benador could not disagree with the Eldar's assessment. With their efforts against the undead brigade and the sheer courage of their stand on the breached bridge, Arien and his people had played as vital a role as any in the victory at the river. But the cost had been staggering. The elves had charged down from the northland to the aid of Calva five hundred strong, yet only a handful more than two hundred had survived to make the trek back to Lochsilinilume.

"And we, too, must be going our way," Belexus added, standing by his father's side. "Yer fights in the west'll be won, I'm knowing, but we've another battle to attend."

"Avalon," the King reasoned. Ardaz had told Benador of the destruction to the wondrous forest and of Brielle's continuing efforts to restore some measure of its glory.

"Ayuh," replied Bellerian. "The witch's needing our aid. Suren we owe her that much."

"And more," agreed Benador. "And no one knows that better than I. Go then, my friends. Go back to your homes and be assured that Calva will prevail in the end, and that you have once more shown all my people the inestimable value of your friendship. My thanks."

And then Benador, the King of Calva, bowed low to them.

The solemn procession rolled out that same dreary morning, and somehow the jingle of the bells on the elven steeds did not seem so merry.

"Me head's hurtin'," Rhiannon grumbled. Bryan nearly jumped at the words, the first the young witch had spoken in the two days since the battle. She had lain in the soundest of slumbers—too sound, Bryan feared—and the half-elf wondered if she would ever awaken. He rushed to the side of the makeshift cot and kneeled, brushing her thick hair from her fair face.

"Good that you're back," he commented with a wide smile.

"Me head—" Rhiannon started to complain again, but Bryan hushed her by putting a finger over her soft lips.

But then the half-elf's contentment washed away in a flood of horror as he noted the spot Rhiannon was talking about, a pulsating lump in the middle of her forehead.

"What?" he gasped, and his stark terror frightened the

young witch. She put a hand up on the lump, her eyes widening as her skin began to tear apart.

But then the pain was gone, and when Rhiannon felt the cut-edged hardness, she understood and was no longer afraid.

"The wizard mark," Bryan realized with a sigh. He had heard enough of the tales of the four wizards of Ynis Aielle to recognize the significance of the gemstone that now adorned Rhiannon's forehead.

"The witchin' mark," Rhiannon corrected him. "Have ye a pool or a shinin' silver bowl?" she asked, a bit self-conscious. "Does it—"

"It is beautiful," Bryan assured her, and none could doubt the sincerity in his voice. For truly the gemstone of Rhiannon, a diamond glittering with the same inner sparkle that lit the young witch's eyes, outshone the marks of any of the other wizards: the black sapphire of Thalasi, the white pearl of Istaahl, the silvery moonstone of Ardaz, and even the emerald of her mother.

The blush in her cheeks only made Rhiannon seem even more beautiful to Bryan at that moment, and he hugged the witch's head close to his chest. "Rest now," he said to her. "You have saved the world, and now I will protect you in your need."

Rhiannon pushed Bryan out to arm's length to take a good measure of him, to better understand the implications of his tender tone.

"On my life," Bryan vowed, "I'll not let anything hurt you again."

Rhiannon did not question the jumble of confusing emotions that now churned within her. She just accepted the renewal of Bryan's comforting hug, closed her eyes and slipped away into the soft fog of a peaceful sleep.

* * *

A fifth wizard mark had found its place in the world, but that fact did nothing to diminish the damage done to that special place wherein the wizards garnered their power. Ynis Aielle's Age of Magic was quickly on the wane.

He could not know, then, that with the weakening of the wizards he was now the mightiest being in all of Aielle. All he knew was hate and an insatiable hunger for revenge.

The wraith of Hollis Mitchell pulled himself from the river.

Coming in hardcover
in October 1999!

/

STAR WARS®
The New Jedi Order
VECTOR PRIME

**by *New York Times*
bestselling author
R. A. Salvatore**

Published by Del Rey Books.

Now available in hardcover—
the stunning conclusion to the
DemonWars trilogy :

THE DEMON APOSTLE
by R. A. Salvatore

With *The Demon Awakens* and *The Demon Spirit*, R. A.
Salvatore set a new standard for fantasy adventure, creating the enchanted world of Corona—a world besieged
by the dark forces of an ancient, all-consuming evil. Now,
with *The Demon Apostle*, Salvatore brings his epic sym-
phony of good versus evil to its thrilling conclusion.

A fantasy of rare scope and accomplishment that seam-
lessly weaves unforgettable characters and events into a
brilliant tapestry of bravery and betrayal, sacrifice and
redemption, *The Demon Apostle* brings R. A. Salvatore's
sweeping masterwork to a triumphant close—and to a
new beginning.

THE DEMON APOSTLE
by R. A. Salvatore

Published by Del Rey Books.
Available in hardcover in bookstores everywhere.

Join us online and discover the thrilling
new world of *The DemonWars*!

THE DEMON AWAKENS
THE DEMON SPIRIT
THE DEMON APOSTLE
by R. A. Salvatore

Visit us at

www.randomhouse.com/delrey/promo/demonwars

**to find out more about the author, check out
the DemonWars map, see the list of key
characters, and much more!**

Don't miss Book One in
The Chronicles of Ynis Aielle:

ECHOES OF THE FOURTH MAGIC
by R. A. Salvatore

Jeff "Del" DelGuidice's mission had barely
begun when his submarine was sucked into a
mysterious undersea void. Propelled forward
through time itself, the crew surfaced in a
strange, magical world changed forever by
nuclear holocaust. But this new world, filled
with hope, had a flaw, a dark vein of evil. For
a sinister expert of the mystical arts had
embraced the forbidden third magic. And
only Del could defeat it—a hero sworn to
peace and fated to wield the dazzling power
of the fourth magic . . .

ECHOES OF THE FOURTH MAGIC
Book One in *The Chronicles of Ynis Aielle*
by R. A. Salvatore

Published by Del Rey Books.
Available at your local bookstore.

DEL REY® ONLINE!

The Del Rey Internet Newsletter...

A monthly electronic publication e-mailed to subscribers and posted on the rec.arts.sf.written Usenet newsgroup and on our Del Rey Books Web site (www.randomhouse.com/delrey/). It features hype-free descriptions of books that are new in the stores, a list of our upcoming books, special promotional programs and offers, announcements and news, a signing/reading/convention-attendance calendar for Del Rey authors and editors, "In Depth" essays in which professionals in the field (authors, artists, cover designers, salespeople, etc.) talk about their jobs in science fiction, a question-and-answer section, and more!

Subscribe to the DRIN: send a blank message to
join-drin-dist@list.randomhouse.com

The Del Rey Books Web Site!

We make a lot of information available on our Web site at
www.randomhouse.com/delrey/

- all back issues and the current issue of the Del Rey Internet Newsletter
- sample chapters of almost every new book
- detailed interactive features for some of our books
- special features on various authors and SF/F worlds
- reader reviews of some upcoming books
- news and announcements
- our Works in Progress report, detailing the doings of our most popular authors
- and more!

If You're Not on the Web...

You can subscribe to the DRIN via e-mail (send a blank message to join-drin-dist@list.randomhouse.com) or read it on the rec.arts.sf.written Usenet newsgroup the first few days of every month. We also have editors and other representatives who participate in America Online and CompuServe SF/F forums and rec.arts.sf.written, making contact and sharing information with SF/F readers.

Questions? E-mail us...

at delrey@randomhouse.com (though it sometimes takes us a little while to answer).